Hunting Shadows

ALSO BY CHARLES TODD

The Ian Rutledge Mysteries

A Test of Wills

Wings of Fire

Search the Dark

Legacy of the Dead

Watchers of Time

A Fearsome Doubt

A Cold Treachery

A Long Shadow

A False Mirror

A Pale Horse

A Matter of Justice

The Red Door

A Lonely Death

The Confession

Proof of Guilt

The Bess Crawford Mysteries

A Duty to the Dead

An Impartial Witness

A Bitter Truth

An Unmarked Grave

A Question of Honor

Other Fiction

The Murder Stone

The Walnut Tree

Hunting Shadows

An Inspector Ian Rutledge Mystery

Charles Todd

HARPER LUXE

An Imprint of HarperCollins*Publishers*

HUNTING SHADOWS. Copyright © 2014 by Charles Todd. All rights reserved. Printed in the United States of America. No part of this book may be used or reproduced in any manner whatsoever without written permission except in the case of brief quotations embodied in critical articles and reviews. For information address HarperCollins Publishers, 10 East 53rd Street, New York, NY 10022.

HarperCollins books may be purchased for educational, business, or sales promotional use. For information, please e-mail the Special Markets Department at SPsales@harpercollins.com.

FIRST HARPERLUXE EDITION

HarperLuxe™ is a trademark of HarperCollins Publishers

Library of Congress Cataloging-in-Publication Data is available upon request.

ISBN: 978-0-06-229854-6

14   ID/RRD   10 9 8 7 6 5 4 3 2 1

For Robin Hathaway, author of the Dr. Fenimore series, the Dr. Jo Banks series, and countless short stories.

Robin was a voracious reader, had an eclectic library that filled three houses, and possessed one of the most creative minds we've ever come across. She had plots and stories yet untold, and a love of the written word that was deep and abiding. And she was a good friend, something that was very precious to a great many people, including us. . . . What she didn't have was Time.

Here's to the Chrysler Building, Robin. And all that it stood for.

Hunting Shadows

Chapter 1

The Fen Country, Cambridgeshire, August 1920

He read the telegram with dismay, and a second time with a heavy sense of loss.

Major Clayton was dead. He'd been in hospital outside London since the closing days of the war, fighting a different battle. Sometimes winning. More often than not losing. They had kept in touch until three months before, when Clayton had been too ill to write, and his sister had been too distressed to write for him.

Dropping the telegram on the table, he gazed out his window. Clayton would be brought back to the Fen country for burial. Services would be held at two o'clock Friday next in the Church of St. Mary's, Burwell. Only a few miles away.

He intended to be there.

He'd tried hard to put the war behind him. Avoiding weddings and funerals alike, refusing even to deliver the eulogies for men he'd known well. It would bring back too many memories, and he wanted them to stay buried, along with the dead left behind in the torn earth of Flanders Fields. Unable to explain, he'd simply cited ill health as his reason for declining. Burying himself here, he had shut out as much of the rest of the world as he could. He had even stopped reading obituaries. They were too sharp a reminder of the fact that he had survived when so many had not. For the dying had not stopped with the Armistice.

The service for Major Clayton was different. Clayton had saved his life, and in doing so nearly lost his own. The leg had never healed correctly, and in the end it had become the source of the gangrene that overtook first his foot, then his knee, his leg, and finally his body. Dying by inches, he'd called it.

For Major Clayton, he would have to make an exception. He hadn't been asked by Clayton's sister to deliver the eulogy, even though he knew the man better than anyone living. And he was just as glad.

Instead the sister had invited a Colonel from London to do that honor. He wondered what Clayton would have made of that, given his feelings for HQ and the generals who had given orders they themselves would never have to carry out. Decisions that sent men to their deaths, maimed them, made them numbers on interminable lists, names and ranks and dates but never the faces or shortened lives that should have reminded the generals that they were dealing in flesh and blood.

Of course St. Mary's would be full for the service. He reminded himself that he would have to stay well back, where he wouldn't be noticed.

Only for Clayton, he thought on the Friday as he shaved and then dressed himself with more than his usual care. The Major had been a stickler for appearances; he'd said often enough that if a man respected his uniform, he would respect himself. It would not do to be less than parade perfect even in civilian clothes.

At half past one, he set out for Burwell, planning his journey to arrive shortly before the mourners went inside to take their places. He had no desire to greet anyone, exchange pleasantries or memories. Or to offer condolences to the sister. He barely knew her, and his brief words of sympathy would not lessen her grief.

As it was, by the time he'd reached Burwell and walked on to St. Mary's by a roundabout way, ending up on the street just above it, the hearse had arrived and only a handful of people were still standing by the west door. He slowed his pace, waiting until everyone else had gone inside ahead of him, and listened to the heavy bell above his head toll the brief years of Clayton's life. Thirty-five. It was a hell of a thing to die at thirty-five with so much to live for, leg or no leg.

He glanced up at the bell and then back at the church doorway. And there, to his utter astonishment, he saw a face he had never wanted to see again. Much less find one day here in this isolated corner of Cambridgeshire.

He brushed a hand across his eyes, certain that in the bright sunlight he'd been mistaken. That in his distress over the Major's death, other memories had forced themselves to the forefront of his mind. It would be too cruel—

But no. There he was, bold as brass, smiling and chatting with one of the men in uniform next to him. There could be no mistake.

Captain Hutchinson. *What the hell was he doing here?* He hadn't known Clayton, had he? Why was he among the mourners?

Quickly stepping back into the shadows cast by a large tree overhanging the street, he tried to think.

Hutchinson must have traveled up from London with the Colonel. That would explain his being here. Hutchinson was always quick to see an advantage. Or had he somehow discovered that Clayton's sister was inheriting everything and fixed his eye on her? There was a well-set-up estate in Gloucestershire, and the older property here in Burwell, presently occupied by a tenant. Both would bring in a tidy income.

It would be like Hutchinson, to curry favor before the will had been read, to prove he was no fortune hunter. But he was.

He felt ill, perspiring in the late summer heat like someone with a fever, his legs trembling.

The last of the mourners had stepped inside the church, the coffin had been lifted out of the hearse and shouldered to follow the Rector down the aisle of the nave. And still he stood where he was.

He couldn't—*in God's name he could not now walk inside.* He couldn't share a roof with Hutchinson. Not even for Major Clayton's sake. Not with the man who'd killed Mary.

He closed his eyes, trying to steady himself.

A woman's voice came from just behind him.

"Are you all right, sir?"

"Yes. Yes, I'm fine. Thank you," he said hoarsely, and in spite of himself, in spite of everything, he started moving toward the church door.

But that was as far as he could go.

Turning on his heel, he walked quickly back toward the shelter of the shadows under the tree. It was as good a vantage point as any from which to keep watch.

Standing there during the service only hardened his resolve. He would be absolutely certain before he left Burwell. It was imperative that he be sure his own emotional state hadn't made him mistake someone else for Hutchinson. But when the service was over and the mourners began to file out, preceded by the coffin, he saw Hutchinson quite clearly. He was *there,* a few feet from the Colonel, his hand on Miss Clayton's elbow as she walked with head bowed, her shoulders shaking with her sobs.

If he had had a weapon of any sort, he'd have used it then and killed the bastard. He could feel the rifle in his hands, the familiar smoothness of the wood, the heat of the barrel from long hours of use, the weight of it, so real to him that for an instant he could almost believe it was there. And with all his heart he wished it was true.

The procession was moving on toward the churchyard.

But just before the procession turned into it, something happened that held him pinned where he was.

Hutchinson lifted his head, like prey scenting the air, and for an instant he was sure that the Captain had stared directly at him.

It was impossible, of course. It was his imagination.

The moment passed, Hutchinson's back was to him now, and he almost went down on his knees, to vomit.

He stumbled away like a drunkard, away from the church and the churchyard, and somehow, he was never sure afterward just how, he made it to the sanctuary of his house. The first thing he did was to pour himself the stiffest whisky he'd had in five years. The second was to open the wardrobe door and reach far into the back where he knew the Lee-Enfield was hidden.

Drawing it out, he felt on top of the wardrobe for the cartridges. They were still there behind the carved pediment. He wasn't supposed to have brought either the weapon or the ammunition back. But he had, because the rifle had become a part of him. And no one searched his kit.

Thank God he had.

He was already loading the rifle, hurrying to reach Burwell and the churchyard in time.

And then he stopped, reason finally overcoming the strain and emotion that were driving him.

Foolish to do such a thing. First of all, it would mar Major Clayton's last rites. And that would never do. Secondly, he'd be taken up at once and tried and hanged. He would be *damned* if he'd hang for the likes of Hutchinson.

The man deserved to die. But not this way. Not sacrificing himself.

He removed the cartridges and put the rifle back into the wardrobe, shutting the door firmly.

There had to be a better way.

Look at it from a different perspective. God had brought this man to him once. He would do it again. All he had to do was wait. However long it took.

He began to read the newspapers, as many as he could find. Cambridge, Ely, Burwell, the *Times* from London. Even the racing news in nearby Newmarket. And he burned them in the grate as soon as he'd finished them, to be certain that once the deed was done, there was nothing lying about that would cause talk or arouse anyone's suspicion. He traveled as well, to Boston and King's Lynn, to Bury and Colchester, as far south as St. Albans, looking for anything that might be useful in carrying out his task. He studied people, the way they moved and talked and behaved. It became something of an obsession, the need to survive what he was about to do. There was no satisfaction in it otherwise.

His patience paid off.

Captain Hutchinson was to be a guest at a fashionable wedding to be held in Ely Cathedral in three weeks' time. His name was there, leaping off the page of the Ely newspaper, even though his was only one of a great many other names. Hutchinson was, it appeared, a cousin to the bridegroom.

The first of September.

He was ready. He'd already laid the groundwork. Now it was just a matter of fitting the plan to the place. Thinking through each step, finding flaws, looking for opportunities on the ground, and looking as well at possible escape routes. He covered the Fen country on his bicycle until he knew every lane and track, until he felt he could reach any point in the dark of night. And then he walked the length and breadth of it.

The Fens were dangerous for the unwary. Narrow flat fields stretched for miles, where a boot in the rich black soil would leave its mark for the hunter to find. Irrigation ditches, sometimes crossed by a road or a bridge over a pump, where a false step could mean falling in and drowning. And the roads themselves, running arrow straight, so that any movement could be seen, even at a great distance. No trees, no buildings to hide behind until the chase had passed. Indeed, nothing to offer cover at all, unless one had learned beforehand where to find it.

He'd thought he'd known the countryside well all his life. Now he knew it intimately.

He was ready.

And Hutchinson would come to *him* for the killing.

Chapter 2

The day of the wedding in Ely, a small crowd had gathered to watch the arrival of the wedding party.

A barricade had been set up so that only the bride, her father, and her attendants could drive directly to the Cathedral door. The bridegroom and the wedding guests would walk across the grassy Palace Green to the church, a parade of handsomely dressed gentlemen and their ladies, a sprinkling of men in uniform, and a dash of clergymen, for the bride's family included several deacons and a Bishop.

By the Cathedral clock, it was two hours before the ceremony. Last-minute preparations were under way, flowers and candles being carried in, a carpet being laid down the long aisle, the organist practicing for the following Sunday's service. But for the most part, the afternoon was quiet, an island of serenity before the excitement of the ceremony.

No one noticed the elderly man on an equally elderly bicycle who came up the street from the direction of the school and the Cathedral offices, his thin white hair blowing in the light wind as he pedaled. It wasn't unusual for pedestrians coming up the road to pass in front of the west door on their way to the busy streets on the far side of the church.

He paused by the wall enclosing the Cathedral precincts and wiped his brow, looking tired and thirsty. But he mounted the bicycle once more and got as far as the abutments that reached up to the tower. There was a narrow recess there where he could leave his bicycle out of sight.

The old man appeared to be a knife and scissors sharpener, his clothes threadbare and his canvas carryall dusty from the roads. He started to leave the carryall on his handlebars, walking away before thinking better of it. He went back, picked it up, and put it firmly under his arm, then stepped into the shadow of the Galilee Porch that led to the west doorway, leaning there, as if the shade was welcome, this warm afternoon.

No one challenged him. No one paid him any attention. Behind his back, the enormous Cathedral seemed to crouch, waiting.

After a while he turned and went inside, into the wide space beneath the towers. Beyond, in the nave, the choir was just finishing a last rehearsal, and someone was putting a final touch to the flowers, pinching off any wilted blossoms. No one turned to look up the long handsome aisle to see who had entered. The sound hardly reached the nave.

He stood there for a moment, then turned and made his way to the right, where there was a door to the tower. It was a long walk, fifteen feet or more, and he was at his most exposed.

No one came out of the nave to call to him, to ask his business or demand that he clear off.

The tower door was unlocked, as it had been the last three times he'd tested it. He looked back over his shoulder. No one was in sight.

The old man slipped inside the tower door, closing it quietly behind him, then began to make his way up the long flights of stairs, taking his time. It was dim and musty in the shaft, the bell ropes swaying a little, making him feel light-headed, and he dared not look down. The canvas carryall seemed to grow heavier with every step. He was winded when at last he reached the stone parapet just above the chamber where the bells were hung.

They wouldn't ring until the wedding party was leaving the sanctuary. He would be gone by then. One way or another.

Sitting down on the warm, sloping cone of the roof, he waited for a quarter of an hour, letting his heart rate settle again. Then he opened his carryall and began to assemble the rifle. It had served men like him well in France. It would serve him now. Better than the older versions.

A pigeon landed on the parapet, staring unwinking at him, and he stayed where he was. Finally satisfied that the carryall held nothing edible, the pigeon took off again.

He waited with infinite patience, as he'd been taught to do. There was no hurry. His quarry would come to him. Finally he heard the great organ begin to play once more, this time the first of the set pieces selected by the bride's family. There was a stir below as onlookers who had gathered behind the barricades to watch the guests arrive saw the first motorcar pull up. A ripple of applause quickly followed.

It was time.

Getting carefully to his feet, keeping low, he made his way to the outer wall, peering between the battlements. A motorcar moved away as several more behind it took its place. As the guests alighted, others moved up in line. Unseen from below, he took out the German scope and attached it to the rifle. They hadn't used scopes during his training. And the Germans in France had taken great care to prevent theirs from being captured and turned against them. The first time he'd looked through this one, he'd been surprised by the clarity it had added to his own keen eyesight.

He scanned the guests as they crossed the Palace Green toward the west door, but he didn't recognize any of them. Earlier in the week he'd paced the distance from where the motorcars stopped and where he himself would be waiting. He knew he was well within range of his target. He could take his time and wait for the perfect angle.

Not too soon. Not too late. He knew, almost to the blade of grass, where he wanted his victim to be. He could see the Russian gun clearly, at the opposite end of the Green from the West Tower, the long muzzle of the cannon pointing outward, as if its intent was to protect the Cathedral from the townspeople.

Kneeling there, his weapon beside him, he was fairly sure he was invisible from the ground, but to be safe, he pulled an old dark gray hood out of the scissor sharpener's blouse and draped it over his head and shoulders. It was, he knew, almost exactly the same color as the stone around him.

Once more, he settled down to wait.

It was ten minutes to the hour when he saw his quarry alight from a motorcar that had just pulled up.

Another man and a woman arrived with Hutchinson, chatting quietly as they turned toward the Cathedral. He could see the man's face clearly now, smug and satisfied with himself, a slight smile lifting his lips as he spoke to the woman beside him.

The angle was excellent. The target unsuspecting. He let the Captain come a little closer across the greensward, just clear of where the motorcars were stopping, steadied his breathing and emptied his mind of any emotion. Then he took careful aim, almost without thinking adjusting to the man's measured pace and the light wind. Old habits die hard.

And calmly, slowly, he squeezed the trigger.

The echoes against the stone were deafening, but he took no notice, his scope still trained on the quarry as Hutchinson's body reacted to the hit before he could even flinch from the sound of the shot. Without a word, he crumpled to the ground and did not move. Only the red stain spreading across his stiff white shirtfront showed that he had been struck.

The woman, her hands to her face, was screaming, and everyone at the barricade turned to stare in her direction, then looked wildly around for the source of the shot. The other man was kneeling, frantically trying to loosen Hutchinson's cravat and open his shirt. But it was useless. That had been a heart shot, there was nothing to be done. Still the man kept working, unable to believe that it was hopeless.

Satisfied, the scissor sharpener ejected the single cartridge casing and began to disassemble his rifle, taking his time, ignoring the screams and cries below. He knew what was happening, he didn't need to look. Some were running to the assistance of the fallen man, others fleeing toward the street behind them, toward The Lamb Inn, out of range for fear there would be a second shot. A few would be scanning the rooftops and windows of buildings on either side of the grass, looking in vain for the shooter. The greeters at the door had rushed into the sanctuary, crying havoc. He could hear the unnerved guests as they hurried out to see, and all the while, the organ music went on, as if in the loft the organist was unaware of what was happening below in the nave. Then the last notes trailed off as he must have realized something was wrong.

The scissors grinder made his way to the stairs and started down them, taking his time, careful not to lose his footing. When he reached the bottom step, he peered out a crack in the door, then opened it wider. No one. Either they were cowering in the nave or already outside. The bride's motorcar was just arriving, adding to the chaos.

He began that long walk again, taking his time, reaching the Galilee Porch and the open doorway. Appearing bewildered and afraid, he stared vacantly around. No one paid him any heed. He inched sideways, making his way to his left. His bicycle was where he'd put it, but he didn't mount it. Instead he walked it down the quiet street, back the way he'd come, toward the school. Several people from there were running toward the Cathedral, and one or two called out to him, asking what had happened.

He shook his head. "Terrible," he said, "terrible." His voice was shaking, he looked as if he might fall down from the shock, and they ran on. He continued his slow, painful way to the arch by the school. There just as the police were passing, he mounted his bicycle and pedaled sedately off, a graying scarecrow with a lined face and bony knees.

The police spent five hours searching the streets around the Cathedral, searching inside it despite the anxious wedding guests waiting to have their statements taken.

A constable reached the church tower, walking out into the narrow space around the battlements. He was an older man, staying on because the men who should have replaced him had long since rotted in the grave-yards of Flanders or had come home without a limb or with other injuries. He looked down from this height at the target area and felt his stomach lurch as a wave of dizziness overcame him. Swiftly concluding that it was impossible to make such a shot from this posi-tion without being seen, he hurried back to the stairs, staring anxiously into the dim abyss, and nearly lost his dinner. By the time he'd reached the last step his heart was jumping in his chest.

"Nothing up there but the bats," he told another constable on his way to climb to the Lantern tower over the crossing where the transepts met.

When it came time to take statements from those by the barricade, everyone's attention had been focused on the arriving guests. They had seen nothing. As one constable put it, "A herd of green pigs could have come by, and if they were dressed to the nines, no one would have taken a bit of notice."

In the end, the wedding went off at six o'clock, the bride red-eyed from hysterics, the bridegroom grim-faced. Captain Hutchinson had been in his family's party. It was generally accepted that only a madman could have done such a thing, with so many people to witness it.

Wherever the madman was, he had cast a pall over the day, and more than one guest leaving after the ceremony had felt his hackles rise as he skirted the place where Hutchinson had fallen, expecting to hear the report of a rifle once more.

Two weeks after the murder, the police had made no progress at all. It was then that they called in Scotland Yard.

But not before the killer had struck again.

Chapter 3

The by-election was scheduled for the next week. The popular Tory candidate, Herbert Swift, arranged a torch-lit parade down the High Street, to end with a speech at the market cross. It was Medieval, the cross, the last seven feet missing. But the base was still intact, and Swift was to stand on it so that he could be seen as well as heard.

All went according to plan. The parade began at the pub named for Hereward the Wake, the eleventh-century hero of the Fens, and some thirty supporters followed their candidate down to the cross, chanting his name, their torches smoking and leaving a reeking trail behind them. The constable, a man named McBride, walked along with them, with an eye to keeping the peace, but the marchers were orderly and in good spirits.

It was all very dramatic, Swift thought, enjoying the spectacle. His rival, the Liberal candidate, was a dour man with no sense of style in his dress, his voice rough and his language rougher, and his meetings in a hired hall were enlivened only by the occasional snore from one of his audience.

Swift reached the plinth of the cross and prepared to step up on the base. He looked at the gathering crowd, many of them villagers come for the show, and felt a sense of satisfaction. It was a better turnout than he'd expected.

The torchlight flickered in the darkness, casting lurid shadows up and down the street and across the eager faces waiting for the speech to begin. The shops on either side of the two village Commons had closed for the day, their windows unlit and blank. Above the shops most of the shopkeepers or their tenants had already drawn their curtains. And the trees by the pond were dark sentinels at the far end of the second Common. This had been an ideal setting to hold his rally, and broadsheets had announced it for three days.

Swift savored the moment as he took his place on the broad footing of the cross and turned toward his supporters, his back to the pond. He was a student of history, and he thought that the scene before him could have taken place a hundred—two hundred—years earlier. It added a sense of continuity to what he was doing: standing for a seat in the House of Commons. A long line of men stretching back in time who were prepared to serve King and Country to the best of their ability were in the shadows of those trees, he thought, watching this twentieth-century descendant, judging him, and with any luck at all, approving of him.

He raised a hand for silence.

"The war is over," he began, his voice carrying well, as it always did, giving his words added power. "And we are embarking on a peace that will last through our lifetime and that of the generations following us. *Their* children will not know what war is. Men have gathered at Versailles to hammer out the terms of that peace, and we here in England have paid a very high price for it. We are still paying. Even now our families don't have enough to eat, work is hard to come by, and what work there is doesn't bring a man enough in wages to keep his—"

His face vanished in a spray of blood and bone, and before anyone could move, he crumpled without a sound into the startled crowd just as the single shot rang out and seemed to fill the night with endless, mindless reverberations.

Chapter 4

Rutledge stepped into the office of the Acting Chief Superintendent with some trepidation.

He had had a loud and vituperative argument with Markham at the end of his last case, accused of following his own instincts rather than official direction. The fact that in the end Rutledge had been proved right had added to Markham's displeasure. He was a hardheaded, straightforward man who viewed intuition with suspicion and put his faith in the obvious. The dressing down had been personal as well as professional.

Keeping his own temper with an effort, Rutledge had drawn a deep breath, asking himself if every inquiry in Yorkshire, where Markham had come from when Chief Superintendent Bowles had had his heart attack, ended in a tidy packet tied with righteous ribbons. He had grimly withstood the storm, and then Markham had calmed down sufficiently to ask him if he was absolutely convinced of his facts.

He was. And said as much. Markham had thanked him and then dismissed him.

This morning Markham was finishing a report as Rutledge crossed the threshold, and looking up, he nodded in greeting.

"Cambridgeshire—the Fen country. Know it?"

"Around Ely? Yes, a little."

"Someone's walking around up there with a rifle, and so far he's killed two people. A Captain Hutchinson who was about to attend a wedding, and a man named Swift who was standing for Parliament—just as he was beginning a speech."

"A rifle?" Rutledge frowned. "They were turned in before we left France."

"Then someone failed to do as he was ordered."

"Are the two victims related in any way?"

"If Hutchinson was his intended target, no. If he got Hutchinson by mistake, we don't know. The wedding that afternoon was to be attended by prominent churchmen, members of the government, a number of the aristocracy, and military men. If his target was one of them, it will take weeks to interview them and find a connection."

"Was Swift a wedding guest as well?"

"He was not."

"Are we certain the killer was a soldier?"

"We're certain of nothing but the fact that we have two men dead, and too little to go on. Which is why the Yard has been asked to take over the inquiry." He paused, considering Rutledge. "It would not do to hear of a third murder by this madman."

In short, a swift conclusion to the inquiry was expected.

"I'll remember that," Rutledge said, not smiling.

Two hours later, he'd cleared his desk, packed his valise, and set out for Cambridge in his motorcar.

He spent the night there and the next morning headed north.

The sunny weather of yesterday had changed to damp, lowering clouds that obscured the unmade road, and the motorcar's powerful headlamps bounced back at him from the soft, impenetrable wall of mist. At the crossroads, the narrow boards giving the names of villages in each direction appeared and disappeared like wraiths, and sound was muffled, confusing. At one point he could hear a train's whistle in the distance but had no idea how far the tracks might be from where he was.

He drove with care, for the country could be treacherous. Lose one's sense of direction in this flat, featureless landscape and the motorcar could plunge into one of the many drainage ditches that ran arrow straight across the Fens. A missed turn could land him into a field of soft black earth, miles from the nearest house. For that matter, he hadn't seen a dwelling, much less another vehicle, for nearly half an hour.

The sounds of the train faded, then vanished altogether. It was, he thought, as if everything he knew, all that was familiar to him, even his senses, had been taken from him, leaving him to cope in a silent emptiness that had no yesterday or tomorrow, only the obscure present. Rather like death . . .

It was beginning to aggravate his claustrophobia.

Some time later, when he thought surely he must be nearing Ely, out of the mist came a strange sound, a clacking that he couldn't place. A hay wain? No, because he couldn't hear the jingle of harness or the familiar thud of hooves on the hard-packed roadbed.

Slowing, he peered through the windscreen, then stopped altogether. The last thing he wanted was to hit someone or something. Getting out, he walked forward a step at a time. He could see fewer than three paces ahead.

In the back of his mind, a voice was warning him to beware, but he had to know whether he was still on the road—or not.

Out of the gray mist, something stirred, then disappeared. He waited. In time it stirred again, creaking.
He frowned, listening before going forward. But now
there was silence.

What the hell was out there?

He moved on. Suddenly there was grass beneath his
boots, where there had been road before. He turned
and realized he couldn't see his motorcar.

In the same instant, the creaking seemed to come
from directly above him. His immediate reaction was
to duck.

A breath of air touched his face, and it pushed aside
the veil of the mist for a few seconds. Something loomed
just above his head, and he tensed.

He stood stock-still, waiting for whatever it was to
reveal itself. And again there was the faintest rift in
the white curtain, and he realized that he was standing
only a matter of feet from a windmill. Its sails, laden
with damp, were creaking as if complaining of the
weight.

A few more steps and he'd have collided with the
nearest sail.

But where the devil was he? Surely he'd already
passed Soham. Many of the windmills had been
replaced with steam pumps, ugly black fingers of chimneys reaching skyward. But Soham's still stood.

The sail above his head creaked again. Listening, he thought he could hear a pump somewhere in the distance.

A voice came through the mist.

"Who's there?"

"A visitor," Rutledge answered. He couldn't make out the accent. "I think I've lost my way."

"Do you need help?"

"Only to be told where I am. What is this mill?"

"Wriston Mill."

And how the hell had he got to Wriston? It lay south of Ely, and a little west. Where had he missed his turn?

The voice said, "Are you walking? On a bicycle?"

"I have a motorcar. I left it back there. I didn't know what the creaking sound was, and I got down to investigate."

"Yes, well, you'd be better with a horse out here. They know what they're about."

"I didn't have a choice in the matter. I'm—from Cambridge."

"Schoolmaster or don?" the voice said, and from the tone of it, either occupation was equally to be despised.

"Neither. I'm trying to reach Ely. On a matter of business."

"Well, you won't make it alive in this. Foolish to have tried."

"That may well be," Rutledge answered. "But here I am."

There was silence for a moment, and then Rutledge heard footsteps walking away.

Swearing to himself, he stood where he was, peering through the fog, trying to find something besides the windmill to serve as a landmark. This kind of mill stood by water, a pump, and he dared not choose the wrong way.

And then he heard the footsteps returning.

"Your motorcar is safe enough where it is. Follow me."

But Rutledge couldn't see him. All he could do was walk in the direction the footsteps were taking now, and that was a risk. His hearing had always been acute, not as sharp as Hamish MacLeod's had been in the trenches, but more than sufficient to serve him now.

He couldn't go wrong if he watched each stride, looking no more than one or two ahead. And so he followed the sound and soon was off the grassy sod, back to a road that seemed to be no better than a lane. They were walking along it now, he could hear the difference in the footsteps leading him. When he had gone some thirty paces, he knew he couldn't possibly have returned to his motorcar again. He stopped and said, "Where are you leading me?"

"Just along here. Another twenty or so feet. There's a house. You can shelter there until this passes."

The voice was odd in the mist. Distorted. He wasn't sure he could recognize it again in more ordinary circumstances. All he could do now was to trust it.

Eighteen. Nineteen. Twenty. He'd gone the twenty feet. He stopped.

The footsteps ahead of him stopped as well.

"To your left. There should be a gate."

Rutledge turned, reached out. His hands touched nothing. He put out a foot. Ah. There was indeed a fence here—iron, he thought. Leaning forward, his groping fingers found an iron picket, the top shaped like a flower. As he moved closer, he could just make out more of them. And there, just beyond, was the gate. His ghostly guide had been right on the mark.

Rutledge called, "Thank you."

But no one was there. That sixth sense so many people possessed told him so, and yet he hadn't heard the man leave.

He walked up what appeared to be a short path and found himself at a blue door. There was a knocker with a brass footplate. He lifted it and let it fall.

After a moment the door opened. A woman stood there, and even against the lamplight that made her appear to be no more than a silhouette, he could see her surprise.

He wondered fleetingly if his unseen rescuer had just come from her and she had expected—hoped—he'd returned. Or was she expecting another caller? The man in the mist had questioned him. Looking back, Rutledge wondered if he was waylaying someone.

"Sorry," he said, smiling. "I'm rather lost. Somehow in the fog, I made a wrong turn. I was on my way to Ely."

She blinked, as if his answer was unexpected. "Were you walking in this? I'm astonished you didn't fall into one of the ditches. Come in, then."

As she stood aside to allow him to pass, he said, "My motorcar is somewhere near Wriston Mill."

As if that explained everything, she said, "Just as well to leave it where it is. I was about to make a pot of tea. Would you care for some?"

In the lighted room he could see that she was quite pretty, dark haired and dark eyed. She was studying him as well. Behind her the front room contrived to look both smart and comfortable. A small fire burned on the hearth, and on a rug beside it a white cat lay curled up and asleep.

"That would be very kind. Yes."

He followed her through to the kitchen. It was a pleasant room, warm and friendly, but the windows showed only blankness beyond the panes. He felt suddenly anxious, claustrophobic because he couldn't see a world outside.

She was busying herself with the kettle and the tea. "You're a stranger, aren't you?"

"I drove up from Cambridge this morning."

"At the university, are you?"

He wouldn't have pegged himself as an academic and yet twice now he had been asked if he was. He was briefly amused. No Oxford man cared to be mistaken for a Cambridge man. "No, sorry. I have an engagement in Ely. This afternoon. I expect I shall miss it."

She glanced at the windows.

"It might clear," she said doubtfully. "But I shouldn't like to raise your hopes."

"Is there anywhere I could stay the night? If this doesn't lift, it would be foolish to press my luck."

"Indeed it would. We're hardly more than a village. But there's a small inn where hunters came in season. For the waterfowl. The hunters haven't been here since the war. I hope the shooting won't start up again. I don't like the sound of the guns. And it's cruel to hunt the birds. There's been some talk about protecting them. It's been done in other places."

The kettle was beginning to boil. From a shelf she took down two cups and saucers, two spoons, and the sugar bowl, setting them on the table. Then she went through a door next to the large dresser, returning with a small jug of milk. "There."

While the tea was steeping, she said, "I'll take you to the inn. Priscilla will be glad of the money."

"If you tell me how to go, I'll find it myself. You shouldn't be out in this mist alone."

"You'd find it very easy to be turned around. I'm used to it."

"You grew up here?" he asked as she lifted the teapot's lid, stirred the leaves, and let them settle again before pouring.

"I lived here as a child. My father was the village doctor. We moved away when I was seven or eight. My mother was insistent that we live in a place with better schooling. And so we went to Bury St. Edmunds."

"But you came back."

She frowned. "Yes, I suppose I did." It was an odd answer, but he didn't press.

They sat across the table from each other, and an awkward pause followed.

"I don't know your name, Mr. . . . ?"

"I'm sorry. Ian Rutledge." He smiled. "You really shouldn't invite strangers into your home. It isn't wise. But I'm grateful you did."

She nodded. "Marcella Trowbridge."

He inclined his head in acknowledgment. "Tell me about Wriston," he said. "I know where it is on a map of Cambridgeshire. Besides the inn, what else is there?"

"Shops and houses, of course. An old market cross. Cromwell took a dislike to it and destroyed the top. I'm told there's a very nice drawing in Christ Church in Cambridge showing how it once looked. One of the early abbots at Ely kept a journal, it seems, recording his travels. We owe him a great debt, because he described the village. It was hardly even that then. Our church was only a pilgrimage chapel in Saxon times, but as Wriston grew, so did it. There's a Green Man on one of the ceiling bosses. A very old one. As a child I used to stare up at it, certain that it was staring back at me, watching to see if I was behaving." She smiled whimsically, remembering. "The abbot must have been taken with it as well, because he mentioned it in his journal along with one of the gargoyles. The windmill, on the other hand, has been here since the reign of James the First, although it's been rebuilt many times. It's one of the few that haven't been replaced by steam, because it's really all but redundant. Drainage elsewhere stole Wriston's thunder, as it were. But in heavy storms, we're still grateful for it."

She realized all at once that she had given him more information than perhaps his question had intended. Shrugging a little, she added, "Otherwise it's rather a small, unprepossessing village."

He noticed that she had said nothing about Wriston's latest and less reputable claim to fame. The murder. He hadn't intended to come here until he'd spoken to the Ely police. But here he was and he should make the most of his opportunity.

"And that's the entire history of Wriston?"

She was still all at once. "I'm afraid I don't quite—I don't understand your question."

He let it go. She had taken him in and been kind. "I was wondering if Cromwell had done other damage to the town, perhaps in the church itself."

She visibly relaxed. "There's the usual story, that he stabled his horses in the nave. He was willing to run roughshod over the beliefs of others. In school I always found him a less than sympathetic character. That didn't sit well with my history mistress, who rather admired him." Making a face, she added, "It was whispered that the body in Westminster Abbey in London wasn't his. That it was hidden here in Cambridgeshire from the wrath of the Royalists."

Rutledge remembered the tale—that on his Restoration, Charles II had had Cromwell's body taken from its resting place in the Abbey and hanged, then beheaded, the head left to rot on a pike.

"Tell me. Was this the mill keeper's cottage?"

"That's on the far side of the mill. I'm not surprised you didn't see it. It burned down before the war and was never rebuilt. If you'd tripped over the foundations, you could have been seriously hurt. My father bought this cottage for my grandmother after she was widowed. She went away for a time, then decided not to return to Bury. Instead she lived here for many years, and then left it to me."

Finishing his tea, he looked up at the windows. There was a difference in the light now, although the fog hadn't thickened as far as he could tell. "It will be dark soon. Perhaps you should tell me how to find that inn."

"Yes. Of course."

She rose and led the way to the front of the house and the door. Rutledge had left his hat in the motorcar along with his valise. But it would be impossible to retrieve either of them until this weather broke.

Miss Trowbridge reached for a shawl on the back of a chair and spread it around her shoulders. "Stay close. Stray and I shan't be able to find you."

"Yes, all right."

As she came to the gate, she said over her shoulder, "This could go on for days. It has, sometimes."

"I'll say my prayers tonight."

She laughed. It was an odd sound in the mist, as if there were an echo.

They turned to their left and walked along the road. He could see her, but not very clearly. There was nothing but the soft cotton wool that touched his face with clammy fingers. If anything, he thought, it appeared to be getting chillier.

Miss Trowbridge stopped. "You'd better take my hand. The road bends just here."

He clasped her soft fingers in his, and they set off again. For all he knew, he thought wryly, she could have been leading him down the road to hell. And then she dropped his hand.

"Here. Do you see the steps?"

And he did. Just. He wondered if she'd been counting off strides, as the man earlier must have done, to bring him safely here.

"I'll wait until you've gone inside," she said. "But I should think Priscilla—Miss Bartram—will be at home."

He climbed the steps, but before he lifted the door knocker, he said, "Will you be all right?"

"Yes, of course."

He let the knocker fall.

A woman a few years older than Miss Trowbridge came to the door. "We're closed," she said.

Miss Trowbridge's disembodied voice said, "Priscilla? This is Mr. Rutledge. He's lost his way in the mist. Can you give him a room for the night?"

"Marcella?"

"Yes, I discovered him wandering about lost. I brought him to you." Nothing was said about offering Rutledge tea. He took note of that.

"A good thing. What brought *you* out in this?"

"I was looking for my cat," she said. "Clarissa. And found Mr. Rutledge instead."

"Well, then. Come inside, Mr. Rutledge. Marcella, are you coming too?"

"Thank you, no, Priscilla. Clarissa is probably waiting for me by the gate."

Rutledge was ushered inside, the door closed behind him.

"Will she be all right?" he asked, still concerned for Miss Trowbridge.

"Oh, yes. She'll find her way." She led him down a dimly lit passage to a sitting room. "Do you know Marcella well?"

"In fact, not at all." He took his lead from Miss Trowbridge's comments about the cat. "She rescued me. I nearly walked into Wriston Mill."

Miss Bartram crossed the room to turn up the lamp. He saw that she was wearing a man's trousers and shirt, but her short hair was becomingly cut, framing her face. He thought she must be in her early thirties.

She looked him up and down. "Where are you from, Mr. Rutledge?"

"I was on my way from Cambridge to Ely," he explained once more.

"Indeed. You're well off the right track." She gestured to the hearth and several comfortable chairs set in front of it. "You see the sitting room. Now, if you'll come with me?" Leading the way upstairs and down a short passage, she said, "This room has been aired. I'll put you here." Holding the door for him, she waited for him to enter.

The room was smaller than he'd hoped, seeming even smaller with the white world outside the windows. The bed boasted a blue coverlet that matched the curtains.

There were two chairs and a table that could serve as a desk, a washstand and basin, and an armoire, crowding together around the walls.

From the shelf above the bed, a pair of stuffed waterfowl in a glass case stared back at him as she stepped in and lit the lamp. Their glass eyes reflected the flare of her match and then the increasing light as the wick caught, giving them a haunted look. Rutledge found himself thinking that if he'd had his hat with him, he could have flung it over the mallards.

"No luggage, then?"

"It's in the motorcar."

"It will be there tomorrow. No one will touch it," she said complacently. "Now, will you be wanting a light supper?"

"Yes. That would be very kind."

"Then come along downstairs when you've settled in."

She left him then, and he went to wash his hands. He gave her five more minutes and then, not turning out the lamp, he took her at her word.

Looking into the sitting room once more, he realized she'd lit a second lamp and that other waterfowl were set here and there, some on shelves enclosed by glass, smaller ones in bell jars, and others in what appeared to be specially designed glass cases.

Each display had a small brass plate giving the name of the bird. COOT. BITTERN. SEDGEBIRD. A kite and a hawk. RUFF. SPOONBILL. AVOCET. REEVE. Even a snipe. There was also a rather unusual copper-colored butterfly perched on a bare twig. He gave up reading the labels. To his eye the specimens seemed tired, their feathers lackluster.

For her usual guests, they might be an advertisement of what to expect when they took their guns out. Or what had been there in the distant past, perhaps in her father's or grandfather's day. He remembered what Marcella Trowbridge had said about hunting. Seeing this display, he had to agree with her.

Down the passage he found the kitchen. Priscilla was just taking a meat pie from her oven. He wondered if she'd intended it for her own dinner, then realized that there was another just behind it. The table had already been set, and he could see that he would be dining here.

"I hope you don't mind," she said, looking up in time to see his glance at the table. "It's a lot of extra work, opening up the dining room. With only myself here, I have no need of it."

"This is fine," he assured her. "Thank you, Miss Bartram."

"Everyone calls me Priscilla. I haven't used Miss Bartram in ten years. Now. Sit down and I'll just dish up."

Rutledge took one of the chairs, saw that the tea was steeping, and was about to get up and move it to the table.

"No, just sit there, if you will. Better than getting underfoot."

Besides the pie there was cabbage and parsnips, with an excellent chutney.

"I made it myself," she said as he tasted it, and he told her it was very good.

She began to ask questions about his encounter with Miss Trowbridge, and he could see that she was a gossip by nature, reinforced by what must be a rather lonely life.

"If it hadn't been for her cat, I'd have still been lost in this mist. Or worse," he replied. "I don't know how she found her way here."

"We're used to it, I expect." Finding that topic a dead end, Priscilla asked if the news of their late disturbance here in Wriston had reached as far as Cambridge.

"The papers carried the account. A Mr. Swift killed as he was starting to address his constituents."

"Well, hardly an address," she said. "He's standing for office, and he was making his opening remarks when the shot rang out. But he was already falling, disappearing out of sight, and the cry went up that he'd been hit. Then Mrs. Percy exclaimed that she'd seen a monster. There was general pandemonium after that. The constable—we've only got the one—had run toward Mr. Swift, and by the time he looked around to where she was pointing, there was nothing to be seen. You'd have thought the shot fired itself. And try as he would, he couldn't discover anything more. This, mind you, following on the heels of that poor man killed in Ely not even a fortnight ago. They've made no headway in finding *his* killer, either."

"Were you in the square when Mr. Swift was shot?"

"I was. Most of us went for the entertainment, you see. There's not much else to do of an evening, and the torches were coming down the road from The Wake Inn. Like a parade, you might say. Then Mr. Swift was stepping up on the stump of the old market cross, and the crowd quieted down to hear him speak. He's—he was—a much better orator than the Liberal candidate. We expected to be well entertained. And just like that he was falling, cut off in the middle of a word. The noise seemed to come from everywhere at once, giving me the shock of my life. The butcher, Mr. Banner, was standing beside me, and he ducked, and so did the owner of the pub, as if expecting more shots. I don't think I could have moved if my life had depended on it. Mrs. Percy began screeching at the top of her lungs. I thought she'd gone into strong hysterics. After a bit she calmed down a little and I heard her claiming that it was a monster, up there at the ironmonger's window. What's more, the constable and afterward that Inspector from Ely, Warren is his name, tried but they couldn't shake her account. We don't run to hobgoblins here in the Fen country. I ask you!"

Rutledge smiled. Her vehemence told him otherwise. "Whatever she saw, it must have frightened her. Where was she standing, in relation to where Mr. Swift was speaking? Did you see her?"

"Not before she cried out. She was a little behind him, on the far side of the cross. She had her hands over her face. I thought she was shocked by his death—she was close enough to see what happened to him first-hand. Someone told me later his blood was on her apron."

Enough to shock anyone, he thought. It also meant that while looking up at the speaker, she must also have been looking almost directly at the killer. Had movement caught her eye just as the shot was fired? Most certainly not in time to warn Swift, but in time to absorb the fact that a monster had been there, looking down at his handiwork. While everyone else faced the speaker, watching him break off and begin to collapse, what had she actually seen?

The question was, who else had been in that same position and why hadn't he or she come forward? Were they afraid to be made a laughingstock? Apparently Mrs. Percy was not . . .

"How well does Mrs. Percy see?" he asked

"Well enough to be a gossip. She must wear spectacles for close work."

"Then what manner of monster?" Rutledge asked. "How did she describe what she believes she saw?"

"Now that goes to the heart of the matter. What she *believes*. All she would say was, there was a monster's face looking out at her from the ironmonger's dormer window. Bold as brass. Then it vanished. But by the time everything was sorted out, and Constable McBride went up the stairs to the dormer room, there was no sign anyone had ever been there."

"Did Mr. Swift have any enemies? Anyone who might want to see him dead?"

"There's the other candidate, of course, but I'm not convinced that any of that lot would have thought of shooting Mr. Swift. They're more likely to set upon him as he walked home afterward. Cowards, all of them."

When he'd finished the pie, Miss Bartram brought out a cake baked with sultanas and offered him a slice. She was an excellent cook, and he rather thought that her culinary skills, not the long-dead waterfowl, had brought her regulars back year after year.

"Was Swift married?" he asked, returning to the earlier subject.

"A widower. His wife and the babe died in childbirth. Late 1914, early 1915? That sounds about right." She sighed as she began to collect their dishes. "I don't remember the last murder here. I wish I hadn't seen this one."

Miss Bartram failed to hide her disappointment when Rutledge said good night after the meal ended, and went up to his room. A lonely woman, she would have enjoyed passing the rest of the evening in the sitting room with her guest. But it had been a long day, and the next would be even longer.

He worked at the table desk for a time, making notes on what he'd been told and adding questions that had come to him as he listened to Miss Bartram. Satisfied that he'd overlooked nothing, he went to bed. Later he would compare her remarks to the statement she'd made to the police.

But he couldn't fall asleep. The bed was comfortable enough, but the small room seemed close, and the mist wrapping the house beyond his windows was oppressive—a solid, impenetrable wall where even sound was trapped, for he could hear nothing out there. Not a dog's bravado bark or the hooves of a passing horse. He had the feeling that nothing existed beyond the wall of his room, and tried to laugh at such a fanciful notion.

Hamish didn't laugh. "That's what death is like. Nothing. Not sight nor sound nor friendship nor love."

And Hamish ought to know, Rutledge thought grimly. For he was lying buried in a grave in France, dead since the summer of 1916 and the Battle of the Somme. Rutledge shivered at the memory of that dawn. For as he had looked down at the still body of his corporal, he himself had nearly been killed by a shell landing too close to the trench and covering the living and the dead with unspeakable black earth that reeked of everything that had rotted in it. When he had finally been pulled out, more dead than alive, he had brought Hamish with him. Not just the man's body, taken up by the burial detail, but the young Scot's presence. Not the man's ghost—he could have understood a haunting—but an unwavering sense of guilt over the circumstances of Hamish's death. It had seemed easier at the time to accept the voice than to exorcise it by facing why Hamish had refused a direct order, and why he, Rutledge, had had to make an example of Corporal MacLeod, one of the best men who had ever served under him.

He had brought the voice back to England, an unbearable burden. He had toyed with the idea of killing himself to be rid of it. But to do so was to kill Hamish as well—a second time. And he couldn't bear to do that.

One night—one agonizing dawn—he might still find the courage or the strength to do what the Germans had failed to accomplish. If they'd killed him that week—the next month—even the next year, it would have been all right. He could have accepted that death. It would have been fitting, lifting from his soul the weight of guilt for taking his own life. Instead he'd come through four years in the trenches with little more than flesh wounds, seemingly invulnerable, and the bitter irony was, his men had thought him extraordinarily brave when, in fact, he was courting death.

Rutledge abruptly shut down the stream of memory. It wouldn't do to frighten Miss Bartram out of her wits by screaming the house down. She didn't deserve that.

And so he lay there, holding on to his wits by sheer will and refusing the dreams that would start whenever he shut his eyes.

When as last he did drift into sleep, his nightmares overtook him. He awoke with a start, his body cold with sweat, on the brink of shouting to his men to put on their masks as he clawed his way through the heavy ground-hugging fog of gas.

He was never sure afterward what had disturbed him. The dream or something more than a dream. The house was quiet, he'd heard nothing from downstairs, yet he felt a distinct sense of unease. He turned toward the window, and as he did, he saw that the moon had broken through and was shining across the floor of his room in bars of bright light. He got up and went to look out.

Between the two cottages across the way, he could see for what seemed like miles across the flat landscape. Except for the village itself there was no sign of habitation, no light in a farmhouse window, no headlamps as a motorcar made its way along the thin ribbon of road. And the street below was just as empty. He found himself thinking that even the companionship of the white cat—Clarissa?—would have been welcome. A living presence sharing the night with him.

Instead of what had walked in the fog.

Shaking off his mood, he went back to bed and slept quietly for a few hours.

After breakfast, he settled his account with Priscilla Bartram and thanked her for taking him in without any warning.

"I was glad of the company," she said. "There's no knowing what's abroad on such a night as we had. I haven't seen a mist that heavy in some time."

But someone else *had* been abroad last night. He was sure of it. Trained by four long terrible years in the trenches of France, he'd survived by knowing such things. By intuition and quick thinking, by experience and by the driving need to protect his men where he could.

Whoever it was, he must have stood outside the inn for a time, but Rutledge was nearly sure he hadn't come inside.

As Miss Bartram closed her door behind him, Rutledge turned to look up at the house where he'd spent the night. There was a sign above his head, made of iron. It bore a silhouette of geese in flight and beneath them, on what appeared to be water, was the name, THE DUTCHMAN INN. And he realized that unlike its neighbors, the inn looked more Dutch than English with its stepped gables. He'd seen paintings of Holland with just such fronts to the houses. He wished he'd thought to ask who had built the inn. But above the door there was a stone set into the facing of the lintel, and he could just make out the date, 1647, although he was fairly certain the inn as it stood now wasn't that old.

He'd intended to go directly to search for his motor-car. Instead he turned to walk down the street into the village proper.

Fen villages tended to be either new and without much character, thanks in part to the railway, or quite old. Wriston was one of the latter. Like Ely, it had been built on higher ground, an island of dry land rising above the once-waterlogged Fens. Some of them, like Ely or Ramsey, had begun with a church or abbey. Others were home to the fiercely independent men who eked out a fair living here and who had fought long and hard to stop the draining by the Dutch engineers hired for the purpose centuries ago. They had wanted no part of newcomers bringing in new ways. An independent and contrary lot they were, according to one historian he'd read, and content to be left alone.

In fact, long before the Dutchmen were brought in by an English king, Hereward the Outlaw had defied William the Conqueror's Normans in this watery landscape of the Fens. It wouldn't be the first or the last time that the inhabitants had gone their own way.

The question was, what had stirred them to murder in 1920? As far as he, Rutledge, knew, there were no new drainage plans, but it would be worth looking into. Was Swift contemplating changes that his future constituents would object to violently enough to turn to killing the man? And where did Hutchinson come into the picture?

Wriston spread out along the ridge of its high ground, a ridge too narrow to have been chosen for an abbey or even a small priory. What must once have been a small meandering stream had been forced into a channel on one side of the village, while fields encroached on the other, defining it for all time.

To Rutledge's surprise as he walked toward the stump of the market cross, he saw there were two elongated greens stretching to either side of it. The second one possessed a pond occupied at the moment by a dozen or so gleaming white ducks. Cottages and shops huddled together, facing the open space, many of them roofed with a distinctive thatch, very different in style from the beetling brows of the West Country. Here it was more like Cromwell's Puritan crop.

The small church appeared to have been added as an afterthought—he could see its tower beyond the second green at the far edge of the village—although Miss Bartram had indicated that it had Saxon roots. Ely and Peterborough cathedrals had been thriving houses long before the Normans took them over. At the far end of the village, where the road turned toward distant Ely, he could see the pub where the rally had begun.

He wondered which of the religious houses claiming Wriston had set up the market cross. What had been brought in for sale in those days? Eels for a certainty, fish and waterfowl, and whatever subsistence farming they'd been able to wrest from the wet land. It was, he thought, an ideal space in which to set up a market. Or a political gathering.

He stopped within a few feet of the cross, and turning in a circle, he began to study the nearest rooftops.

As Swift had begun speaking, all eyes would have been on him. And the shot therefore must have come from behind most of his audience. But which direction had he been facing? Surely toward the first green, his back toward the one with the pond. He had come from the pub, after all.

Very well, he asked himself, weighing each possibility in turn, if I were stalking that man with a rifle, where would I choose to wait? And from how far away could Mrs. Percy have seen me and called me a monster?

Hamish was on the point of answering him when a voice from just behind Rutledge said, "There's nothing to stare at. Move along, if you please."

He wheeled to find a constable standing there. He'd been so absorbed in his own thoughts he hadn't seen the man come up behind him.

This was not the time to introduce himself.

Rutledge said, "Thank you, Constable," and walked on. But he'd seen the dormer above the ironmonger's shop, and it offered both the clearest view and the best protection. Mrs. Percy had been right. But he'd wanted to see the setting for himself.

And it had brought home another truth.

Whoever he was, the killer was not suicidal. On the contrary, he'd planned his murders with an eye to disappearing as soon as possible after he'd dropped his man.

Rutledge walked on as far as the duck pond before turning around. The morning was fair and there were any number of people on the street now, going in and out of shops, stopping to chat with one another. Some of them cut their eyes to look at the stranger in their midst, and he caught the ripple of uncertainty, of wariness, as he passed.

Just beyond Miss Bartram's inn, on the other side of the road, he could see Miss Trowbridge's cottage ahead of him, the black iron pickets around the front garden distinctive. It was most certainly not as far away as it had seemed last night, and yet he'd have been lost a dozen times over if he'd attempted to find the inn himself.

The tiny space marked off by the fence was lavish with flowers, unlike its neighbors, whose seedy grass sometimes reached from the road to the door. Compared to Kent or the West Country, there was a noticeable lack of flowers, as if the rich black soil were too precious to be wasted on anything that didn't bring in pounds and pence.

A small sign on the gate—invisible in the mist last night—identified the cottage as THE BOWER HOUSE. Rutledge smiled. Miss Trowbridge had said that her father bought the cottage for his widowed mother. Who had named it, tongue in cheek, for a hideaway? Situated as it was at the bend of the main road?

Miss Trowbridge had been right about the mill. It was not very far away, and she must have grown up listening to the sails turn whenever she visited her grandmother. It was a squat mill, tall enough to allow the arms to sweep almost to the ground, clearing the high grass at its base by inches rather than feet.

The remains of the mill house were beyond as well, and Rutledge realized how perilously close to them he'd come in the mist. The blackened timbers were gone, of course, but the ragged foundations were a trap for unwary feet. Closer to he could see what appeared to be the traces of rooms, raised footings where the walls had once met the foundations. He winced at the thought of breaking a bone tripping over them in the fog. Even in the dark it would be far too easy to stray in their direction and take a nasty fall.

In the sunlight the mill was ordinary, its sails turned to catch the light wind. Painted black with white trim, it stood at a bend in the road. And behind it, as far as the eye could see, were those long flat fields, far lower than the ground on which he stood.

He remembered reading somewhere that as the Fens drained and the peat that made them so dark and fertile dried, the surface had sunk lower and lower with each passing year, until it reached a point where it stabilized. And the early practice of burning the peat to clear the land had enriched the soil but also left it vulnerable to east winds off the stormy North Sea. Indeed, some of the fields must be four and five feet lower than the road he'd been traveling. Only the embankments designed early on to hold back the water protected the unsuspecting traveler from stumbling into a field or, even worse, into a ditch.

He walked on and found to his chagrin that his motorcar had been as near to disaster as he himself had been. For the road he'd been traveling rose over an arched stone bridge across a pitch or waterway. And on the near side of the bridge, instead of continuing in the direction he'd expected, the road curved sharply to the right, skirting the strategically placed mill and the cottage where Miss Trowbridge lived, before running straight for the village, cutting it in half. He could easily have crashed into the ruins of the mill keeper's house, injuring himself and doing considerable damage to the motorcar.

To reach Wriston instead of Ely, somewhere he'd missed an important turning.

Looking out across the fields, he could see a stand of trees in the far distance, and rising above them was a church tower. Closer to but still some distance away, a line of pollarded willows marked another track. A third wandered off to his right.

Hamish said, in the back of his mind, "It was foolish to go on."

It was true, in hindsight. But he'd expected to run out of the mist eventually, or to find his way into Ely.

The motorcar seemed to be just as he'd left it, but then he noticed that his valise, which had been in the rear seat, was not precisely where he'd remembered setting it. If he hadn't been looking for it, he'd have never noticed the difference, but he'd suspected that the man who had rescued him had gone to have a look at the motorcar—and perhaps its contents.

He snapped the latches and scanned his possessions. Nothing appeared to have been disturbed, and everything seemed to be there—his gold cuff links were the only thing of real value that he'd packed, and they were under his shirts, where he'd put them. Still, someone had searched his belongings. He was fairly sure of it.

"Ye canna' be certain it was the man in the mist," Hamish pointed out. "It could ha' been anyone. The moon came oot in the night."

Hamish was right, of course, but someone had been curious about a strange motorcar abandoned in the middle of the road.

Still, there was nothing in the vehicle or the valise to indicate that he was from Scotland Yard. He carried his identification in his pocket.

Cranking the motor, he got in and reversed. Shortly thereafter, he found the turning he wanted, which must have been all but invisible last night, and was well on his way to Ely once more. The road ran true for some time, until it reached Soham, and there it headed north.

Now he could see the profile of the massive Cathedral across the flat landscape, rising above it like a great mirage floating on a flat green sea. It must have been, he thought, quite amazing in Medieval times to see it there, a wonder to behold in such a wet landscape. The Isle of Ely it truly was. And in the haze of sunlight, it was still quite magnificent. The town surrounding it seemed not to exist at all.

Inspector Warren looked up as Rutledge was ushered into his office.

"You're a day late," he said, rising to greet his visitor, noting the dark stubble of beard and the unpressed suit. "Did you sleep rough?"

"Near enough. I was caught in the weather yesterday. But that put me close enough to Wriston to have a look at the market cross this morning."

Warren raised his eyebrows. "Wriston? You *were* well and truly caught out, weren't you? All right. Sit down."

Rutledge took the empty chair by the desk. The other was piled high with paper. Statements, he realized, with a sinking feeling. Days' worth of work before any progress could be made. That was, unless Inspector Warren was prepared to sort them for him.

Warren wore a harried air. A tall man, stooped and fair, his hairline only just beginning to recede, he had a strong face, with laugh lines that crinkled at the corners of his eyes.

But the Inspector was not in the mood to laugh at the moment.

"Since you've been to Wriston, I'll start there. Did they tell you half the village had followed the victim to the market cross, where apparently they were met by the other half? We interviewed every one of them. Not all of them were constituents, mind you, but Swift usually gave good value at his rallies, and the curious had come to hear him as well. I expect there were a number of hecklers in the crowd, but he was dead before they could interrupt him. We searched the buildings nearest the cross, but of course by the time we reached the scene, there was nothing to find. We settled on two vantage points. The roof of the ironmonger's shop has a dormer. He and his wife live above the shop, but both of them were in the street." He gestured to another stack of papers. "A dozen people saw the ironmonger and his wife. They're in the clear. Nobody locks anything, worst luck, and the killer could have helped himself to half a dozen vantage points. Cheek by jowl to the ironmonger's, there's a fine pair of chimneys. The greengrocer's shop. But if he'd chosen *them*, he couldn't have got away unseen. My money is on the dormer window."

"Then the shooter could have easily come and gone through a rear door without being seen or disturbing anyone."

"Oh, yes. It was dark, all the light was in the square, torches smoking enough to blind a regiment. But Mrs. Percy, our only witness, claims she saw a face in the dormer window. That has to be where the man with a rifle was standing, not the chimney pots. I believe her. Not, mind you, a monster's face, which is what she initially described to Constable McBride and then to me. But something." Warren grimaced. "As if we didn't have our hands full enough with what happened here in Ely."

"I must agree with Mrs. Percy, from my own observations this morning. Especially if the wind was blowing the smoke away from that window. But what she saw wasn't a man with a rifle."

"Yes, well, there's that. But you won't convince me that there were two people in the dormer."

"How did she describe the face?" Rutledge asked.

"She wouldn't. She told me it was monstrous, the stuff of nightmares. My words, there, but close enough. She was badly frightened then and later when I came to speak to her. What's more, she is a little hard of hearing. She couldn't get any closer through the crowd of people, and being rather short, she moved around behind Herbert Swift. Lucky for us."

"There are several possibilities. Someone wearing a gas mask from the war—although that would make firing his rifle more difficult. Someone badly burned. Or even someone who wrapped his head, to be certain he wasn't recognized."

"That last would mean someone local."

"Very likely." Rutledge paused. "There's been no trouble in Wriston before this? You said no one locked his door at night?"

"They do now," Warren replied grimly. "But no, nothing major. Petty crimes, quarrels, that sort of thing. The last murder in Wriston was back in the 1890s."

Rutledge remembered what Miss Bartram had said about being glad of someone else, even a stranger, in the house last night when it was impossible to see who—or what—was outside the windows.

"Did Swift have enemies? Had he stepped on any toes in announcing he was standing for office?"

"Not that we can discover. The general view was, he was well liked, and likely to win. The other camp had only put up a token candidate to oppose him. Mind you, he wasn't here during the war. Any friends—or enemies—he made while he was away are another matter."

"That's when he could have met Hutchinson."

"Possibly. Yes. But proving it will be difficult."

They moved on to the first shooting, in Ely.

Warren stood up and said, "Come with me, you'll want to see this for yourself."

They walked from the police station to the Cathedral. Warren was saying as they went, "We've enough statements to fill the nave. And they come down to a single fact. We have damned little to go on. I'd hoped, when word reached us about what had happened in Wriston, that he'd made a mistake we could use, but he hasn't."

Ely's Cathedral Church of the Holy and Undivided Trinity came into view then. It was unique among English Cathedrals with that elegant octagonal tower, called the Lantern, set above the crossing of the transepts and the nave. Now, as the two men approached, the massive, battlemented West Front loomed before them. There was a small double-arched west door, and few of the embellishments or niches for saints to decorate the opening. Compared to Salisbury, for one, or Lincoln, it was more or less plain. And yet it was both elegant and powerful.

Warren said, pointing, "Here is where the motorcars pulled up. At the top of the Green. Arriving guests descended and walked toward that west door. Captain Hutchinson was among the last to arrive, in the motorcar belonging to the Honorable Reginald Sedley and his wife."

"Why was he with them? Any particular reason?"

"He was staying with them. I gather they hadn't met before. The bridegroom's family had arranged accommodations for many of the out-of-town guests, and Hutchinson was up from London."

"Go on."

"According to the statements from the Sedleys, they were talking about the wedding as they moved toward the west door. And behind them, another motorcar had followed their own, stopping to set down its passengers. That was the bridegroom and his best man, as we were to discover. The chauffeur of that motorcar was already moving on, making room for the one behind it. This meant that the bridegroom was only a little way behind Captain Hutchinson, and perhaps about five feet to his right. And then everything seemed to happen at once."

Warren moved forward, then stopped again.

"Hutchinson went down just here. The reverberations of the shot shocked everyone for an instant, and then Mrs. Sedley began screaming for a doctor as her husband knelt to try and help the victim. When we were finally able to speak to her, it was clear she hadn't seen anything but the Captain collapsing at her feet. Nor did Sedley, for that matter. He was intent on doing what he could to save Hutchinson. But of course that was hopeless."

Now Warren pointed toward the Cathedral. "There was general pandemonium. Guests who hadn't yet entered the west door and local people who were stand-ing behind a barrier set up just there, to keep them out of the way of the wedding party"—Warren pointed to the spot—"while watching the show, ran in every direction, expecting more shots to be fired."

"It must have been difficult to account for everyone who was a potential witness."

"Believe me, it has been a nightmare."

"Better you than me."

"Yes, well, I hope they give you more than they have given us. There was an artillery Major, man by the name of Lowell, who more or less took charge. He sent someone for the police, another man to find a doctor who was amongst the wedding guests, and ordered everyone within hearing to stay where they were. Unfortunately, he himself had been standing just inside the church doorway and couldn't tell us where the shot had come from. But he informed us at once that it had been a rifle. And of course that was borne out by the distance. Still, it saved an inordinate amount of time trying to sort out the various accounts."

"Very convenient. Could he have fired that shot, then hidden the weapon?"

"I don't see how. He arrived just before Hutchinson and was speaking to one of the canons by the door. In plain sight. There were other former officers attending the wedding, but they had taken their places in the nave with their wives. Lowell is unmarried and was in no hurry to go inside."

They were walking now toward the West Front and the door to the Galilee Porch. Warren was saying, "Those buildings to your right belong to the Cathedral. We searched them as well as the Cathedral itself. Top to bottom. The Gallery—that's the wall there, still to your right—encloses the church grounds, offices, and the homes of various churchmen. We discovered a ladder placed up against the wall on the inside, out of sight from where we are, of course. See there, where that woman with the small child is passing? We left it where it is. I refused to allow them to move it because no one would admit to putting it there, not a churchman, not a gardener, no one. It's possible our man used it as a fallback position. Climbing it and resting his rifle on the top as he fired, then ducking out of sight. The problem is, he'd have been visible to anyone in the grounds who looked that way. Still, it offered the best means of escape. The artillery Major told us the angle was wrong, unless the killer was going for a head shot."

Rutledge looked toward the wall and then turned to the spot where Hutchinson had fallen. "Yes, Major Lowell is right."

"Our next possibility was to the left of the Cathedral door. There, see that makeshift wall? It runs out from the Lady Chapel and then turns down by the lane." Warren began to walk in that direction. "And there's a door in it. It's closed now, but it was standing ajar that day. We found a single cartridge casing on the ground, just about where you'd step through and then step back. It had rolled into a clump of grass by the wall, half hidden by the door. He didn't have time to look for it." He stopped, waving in that direction. "The doctor and the Major disagreed over that one."

Rutledge looked at where Hutchinson had fallen and then turned back toward the gate. "It would be a fairly easy shot," he replied. "It wouldn't take a marksman to do it. As long as the people at the barrier were out of his line of fire. Why did they disagree? The doctor and the Major."

"Lowell felt that the gate was a possible shot, just as you said. But when the doctor examined the body, he claimed the shot had come from above. Up there."

Warren pointed up at the west tower. "A constable climbed all the way up there and told me the slope of the roof would have prevented a decent shot. People were walking toward the door, and anyone standing up there with a rifle was bound to be noticed."

Rutledge shielded his eyes from the sun as he stared upward. "Surely there was room to kneel."

"He says not. And no one has brought it up save for the doctor. Of course, Dr. Bradley has had no military experience, but later during the postmortem, he showed me the course of the bullet. It would seem he was right, although the only evidence, the casing, was here."

"What did Lowell have to say about that?"

"At the time, he never turned Hutchinson over. There was no reason to." Walking on toward the Cathedral, Warren added, "By the time we arrived, there were at least two hundred people milling about. Wedding guests, bystanders, those drawn from the school down there to your right. Ordinary people who heard the shouting and screams and came to see what had happened. My men began to sort them and take down names to collect statements. And I began to realize that no one had seen anything useful. By this time, the bride's father was pressing us to allow the wedding to go on, late as it was, and as soon as the body was removed, we really saw no reason to prevent it."

"Are there any statements in particular I should pursue?"

"There are several it wouldn't hurt to look at. Oddly enough, the bridegroom was convinced he was the target, while the bride, arriving in the middle of the chaos, thought he was the victim and was hysterical. It would probably have been wiser to postpone the affair."

By this time, they had reached the west door and Warren pulled it open.

"Is it usually closed? This door?"

"As a rule it's open during services and for occasions such as the wedding."

They walked inside. It had been some time since Rutledge had been in this Cathedral. Beyond the porch, to his right the lobby spread out toward the shorter twin towers overlooking the wall where the ladder had been left. Ahead, through another set of doors, he could see the unusual painted vault of the nave. It was quite long, leading down to the crossing, which supported the Octagon, which in turn supported the Lantern overhead. Thence to the choir. Ely was, in a way, a glimpse of what churches and Cathedrals must have looked like before the Reformation, when there were frescoes and painted statues and ceilings. The Victorians had reveled in adding color too, but not always successfully.

As he made his way down the aisle, he looked to his left and saw a rose petal, dried now, the color faded, that had escaped the cleaning women. It was caught under the edge of one of the kneelers, a sad reminder of the wedding's chaos.

Silence surrounded them in the nave, their footsteps echoing to the stone walls. It was cool and dimly lit after the warm sunny afternoon outside. Warren's voice was subdued as he said, "We had people out in the Lady Chapel, up on the roof, up in the Lantern, searching all the buildings in the Cathedral precincts, the Bishop's quarters, everywhere we could think of. This place is a rabbit warren, did you know that?"

"Most Medieval buildings are. Do you suppose the killer was dressed as a priest or the like, someone who wouldn't be noticed because he appeared to belong in a church?"

"Carrying a rifle?" Warren went on toward the choir. "But then he could have hidden it in a valise, a musical instrument case. Still, he'd have to open it, wouldn't he, and assemble the rifle. A grave risk."

"Was there a published schedule for the guests to arrive?"

"No, none. He couldn't have known when to be prepared."

"And so he must remain invisible until he was sure."

"The organist brought a large portfolio with him. His music. But he was playing when the shot was fired. There are dozens of witnesses to that. The florists brought in long boxes full of flowers for the arrangements. Some of the flowers were quite tall at the back of the baskets. We searched the lot. Even the van they came in. Under the seats. The organ loft. Behind the organ pipes—have you ever looked behind those pipes? I had the altar cloth and the misericords in the choir searched. Everywhere we could think of, in the event he'd hidden his rifle and planned to retrieve it later. But he hadn't. Or else he'd extracted it before we got to him."

There was nothing to see, Rutledge thought, but the beauty around him.

He started back toward the West Front. "Without the rifle, there's no way to learn where he got it. The Army, most likely. But when? At the Armistice? Was he still in France then? A few must have been smuggled into the country without the Army's knowledge. Still, they were damned thorough." Then over his shoulder, he added, "Why did Captain Hutchinson have to die? And on that day? Was there a particular order in the two deaths? Was it opportunity or was there a pattern behind the order?"

"I can tell you why that day. Hutchinson had come up from London for the wedding. It was very likely that he'd return to London on Sunday evening at the latest. There were a number of parties and dinners before the nuptials, of course. But they were private and by invitation only. That means that his arrival here at the Cathedral would be his only public appearance, so to speak. The local newspaper carried several accounts of the wedding festivities, mostly after the fact. My wife had read them, and so I looked them up. Hutchinson was mentioned several times. And the wedding in general created quite a stir."

"Which means our man—the shooter—could be local."

"Yes, very likely," Warren said harshly. "More's the pity."

"Why was Swift running in the by-election?"

"That I can answer. Swift had been a solicitor before the war. There was no one to take over for him during the war, and his chambers were closed. When he came home again, the view is his heart wasn't in it. He must have seen standing for the seat of his late MP as offering a way out."

"What happened to him?"

"Mr. Davidson died of cancer in the early summer."

"If Hutchinson was related in some way to the bridegroom, was Swift connected to the man as well? However distantly? Grandmothers, wives, great-aunts? Any questionable inheritances?"

"I asked the bridegroom that question. He's not related to Swift in any way. But whether Swift and Hutchinson are related is another matter." Warren took a deep breath as they left the Cathedral and stepped out into the late afternoon sunlight. "I can't walk in there without thinking of that Saturday. Where was I? Oh. For what it's worth, I think they're random, these killings. Targets chosen for no other reason than that they are *there*, wherever the shooter wants to try his luck again. I don't envy you having to get to the bottom of this one. I'll help you in any way I can." He began to walk briskly back toward the police station. Over his shoulder he said, as Rutledge followed him, "But the truth of the matter is, with all due respect, I don't believe you'll have any better luck than I've had. You can see for yourself, it's hunting shadows."

Chapter 5

Rutledge took the man's comments as they were intended, a measure of his frustration. Warren had had nearly ten days to solve the first murder and four to tackle the second. That in itself was trying; add to it the necessity of calling in the Yard, and the man had every reason to feel he had failed in the eyes of his own Chief Constable.

"Do you think the killer is satisfied? Or will he find a new target?" Rutledge asked after a moment. "Now that he's twice successfully evaded the police?"

"Who knows what's in his mind?" Warren sounded tired. "The question is, is he moving west, looking for victims? Or is he choosing a village or town and then picking someone? Mind you, these aren't ordinary folk—the butcher's boy, an elderly seamstress, the dairyman.

Hutchinson had something of a reputation, I'm told—he moved in the best London circles, and all that. Swift was a solicitor, standing for public office for the first time. God knows who might be in this killer's sights next."

Rutledge had already considered that possibility. If there was no personal connection between these men, then it had to be something else. And fame, however minor, might draw someone's attention if he was searching for another target.

They carried on in silence, and when they reached the station, Rutledge stopped by his motorcar. "Anything else I should know?"

"We've covered every possibility. Everything but a hot air balloon. But I'm at your disposal if you think of anything. There's an inn close by the Cathedral. The Deacon. I've booked a room for you there."

"Thank you."

Warren put a hand on the bonnet of the motorcar, brushing at an invisible speck. "I like tidy murders, if I must have one. Something I can follow through to a reasonable conclusion. Most of them are like that. If I don't know what's going on, my constables will, and in the end we'll find our killer. The wife, the brother, the lover, the husband. Or the jealous neighbor, the child-hood friend, the man who owes money he can't repay." He stopped.

"This inquiry could turn out to be as simple."

"Yes, well, pigs fly." Warren hesitated. "I was never in the front lines. They put me in charge of transport. We ran the gauntlet of submarines, but no one was shooting at us. You said you could have made that shot. Were you serious?"

Rutledge bent to turn the crank. "A good marksman could have done it easily. At any one time I had ten men in my command who could have made either the shot here or the one in Wriston. Hutchinson must have been moving at a walking pace, conversing with friends, and in no hurry." He nodded. "A woman could have made it as well, if she'd been trained. It's not necessarily a man we're looking for."

Warren smiled, dusting his hands. "You've just doubled the number of your possible suspects."

"Was Hutchinson married?"

"His wife is dead. Has been for a number of years. Early in the war. So I'm told." Warren hesitated. "You can't believe we're looking for a woman."

"If we can teach shopkeepers and the sons of farmers to shoot straight when they're being shot at, why can't a woman learn to do it as well?"

"If I brought a rifle into my house, my wife would run screaming out the door. She doesn't care for weapons of any kind."

"Then we should hope our killer has a wife who feels the same way."

"When you're ready, I've got the names of witnesses you might wish to speak to. A list I've drawn up."

"Now is as good a time as any."

Leaving the motorcar quietly ticking over, Rutledge went inside the police station. The list was on the blotter of the desk, and Warren handed it to him.

"Tell me what you think after you've spoken to them."

"What about the artillery Major who was so helpful? Lowell, wasn't it?"

"Nothing there. He didn't know Hutchinson at all."

"But he was with the police at every turn. I'd like to speak to him."

Warren quickly added that name to the list. "Anything else?"

"Just tell me how to find The Deacon. That will do for now."

He was unpacking his valise, putting his clothes into the armoire, when Hamish spoke into the silence. "Ye ken, he's washed his hands o' these murders."

"At least he's been helpful."

He crossed to the window and realized that it looked out toward the Cathedral.

"Ye ken, if a woman knows her husband has a rifle, she's too afraid to report it, for fear of losing him to the hangman."

"There's that," Rutledge agreed. Over the rooftops, the Cathedral's Lantern gleamed in the late afternoon sun, its windows holding the light. It dominated the town, although Ely was building out from its center, as many prosperous towns were beginning to do before the war and would surely continue to do. Did the killer live here? Or was he a Wriston man? Or had he come from the half-dozen other villages scattered over the Fens where the ground was high enough for habitation.

Where then to begin? He took a deep breath.

The bride and bridegroom. Their marriage had set the wheels of murder turning. Or at least it appeared to have done so.

He shaved and changed his clothes, leaving the wrinkled suit to be pressed while he was out. After asking directions from the clerk behind the desk he decided it was too far to walk and went to his motorcar.

The Fallowfields had returned from a brief wedding trip and were staying with the bride's family before traveling on to London. The house was in a fashionable part of the town, and when he'd been admitted and asked to wait in the drawing room, he could see that there was old money here.

The furnishings were elegant and the carpet was new, replaced, he thought, for the wedding. The walls were a lovely shade of blue, set off by white trim, and the hearth was white Italian marble. A dark blue vase filled with white roses graced the small table beneath the windows.

Fallowfield had done well for himself, Rutledge found himself thinking as he waited. Was that why the man had expected to be the victim rather than Captain Hutchinson? That his good fortune was too good to last?

After several minutes, the door opened and a young, fair-haired man came into the room.

"Inspector? Jason Fallowfield. I'm sorry to keep you waiting. My wife asks to be excused. She's tried to put the events that day out of her mind, and it hasn't been very easy for her." He gestured to one of the chairs and took another just across from it. "She arrived after the event, there's nothing she can add."

"I can understand her distress. A wedding should be memorable for its joy."

"Yes, thank you. I don't know how I can help you. But I'm at your service."

"How long have you known Captain Hutchinson?"

"I saw him from time to time when we were children, and to tell the truth never really took to him.

Then we served together in France. At Passchendaele. Sort of thing you don't forget, surviving that. We kept in touch afterward. Both of us live—lived—in London, and there was the occasional dinner or a weekend where we were houseguests at the same party. Tennis. Golf. The usual sort of thing when you move in the same circles."

"Tell me a little about his background. We're looking for anything that could point toward his killer."

"When I stop to think about it, I realize I didn't know him very well. And yet I thought I had. He was a private person, you see. He told me his father left him enough to be comfortable, and then before the war he married a rather wealthy woman. I never met her. She died while we were in France. There was some gossip at the time—I'm not precisely sure what it was about, but I gathered it had to do with her possible suicide. At any rate, Gordon should have gone home on compassionate leave, but there was a push on and I heard he was moved to another sector instead. By the time we met again, we were in Paris, of all places, on leave. And when I offered my condolences, he said something that I interpreted as a reference to a stillborn child. That would certainly explain why people believed she'd taken her own life, if she'd died soon after. I had the feeling he'd been hurt by the rumors of suicide.

Although I must say, he appeared to be handling it well by that time. God knows, childbearing is a common enough cause of death. As a married man, I've begun to worry about it myself. But what can you do?"

"Who were his friends? His enemies?"

"I have no idea. I mean to say, he appeared to be well enough liked. He never lacked for invitations, at any rate. If there was any trouble, it never reached my ears." He hesitated, then added, "He *collected* people. That was my impression of him. He seemed to know everyone who was important. It was sometimes a matter for amusement, the way he could make friends. Like a chameleon, changing himself to match his surroundings, as it were. It sounds like an unpleasant quality, but in reality he could be great fun and a very good friend."

"Does he leave any family?"

"Only a sister. I've been on the telephone, speaking to her. She's in London. She couldn't face coming north alone to accompany the body home. I can't say that I blame her."

"How were you and Hutchinson related?"

"Our mothers were distantly connected. To tell the truth, most of my friends never came home from France. I daresay it was true of Gordon as well. Kinship matters then. Sometimes that's enough to stave off loneliness."

Rutledge understood what he was saying. Many of his own friends were dead or had gone on with their own lives while he was struggling to rebuild what was left of his.

"Why did you invite him to attend your wedding?"

Fallowfield was surprised. "It never occurred to me not to. I mean to say, we were talking about it one day, and I simply told him I wanted him to come. We were cousins, after all. We'd served together."

There it was again, that bond between men who had served together. Rutledge understood it well.

"Had your wife met him before the wedding?"

"Yes, on several occasions when she was in London and I escorted her to parties."

"Did she like him?"

His face flushed. "What are you suggesting?"

"Only that women are often more intuitive about people. They will dislike someone for no reason at all, and only later understand why they felt that way."

"I don't think she ever expressed an opinion one way or the other. Certainly when I added his name to the list of wedding guests I gave to her mother, she made no objection."

"I'm trying to discover any reason why someone should dislike this man enough that when he came to Ely for your wedding, he was killed. Even at the cost of nearly stopping the ceremony altogether. I understand it was several hours before the police would agree to the marriage going forward."

Fallowfield got up and walked to the window, his back to Rutledge. After a moment he said, "To tell you the truth, I thought at first I myself must be the intended target."

"Why?"

Fallowfield cast a glance over his shoulder. "Egoism, I expect. I was the center of attention, so to speak, the bridegroom. It never occurred to me that one of my guests might be shot. It's unheard of."

"There must have been a better reason than that."

Fallowfield turned and crossed the room to stop in front of Rutledge. "I was *there*. Not five paces from Hutchinson. With my best man." His face was intense, his voice tight. "I was expecting to hear a second shot—intended for me. I even turned toward Harry to warn him to move away. And then I realized there *wasn't* a second shot. It was—harrowing. I came through the war somehow. It flashed through my mind that it would be unthinkable to die on my wedding day."

"I still don't understand why you were so certain Hutchinson was not the target."

He paced away again, too agitated to sit down. "I suppose I never quite believed my luck. I survived

France. Barbara was waiting. She waited for *me*." He turned back, his expression deprecating. "You see, Barbara could have had her pick of suitors. I've never quite understood why she accepted me."

"Is she—I'm sorry, but I must ask—is she wealthier than you?"

"Oh, not at all. I'd say we were about even. But her family goes back to the Domesday Book, and mine made its money in the previous century. In South Africa, with Cecil Rhodes. Hardly an aristocratic background, is it?"

"And you saw nothing, there by the Cathedral?"

"I saw Hutchinson start to fall, just as I heard the shot. I was nervous, for God's sake—I daresay anyone is, under the circumstances. Will everything go off well, will I muddle what I'm to say, will Barbara's little goddaughter be sick halfway down the aisle? It's a very long nave, you know. Especially for an anxious child. What if I drop the ring? What if it rolls under someone's feet and I'm down on all fours, scrambling after it? I wasn't thinking about murder. If anything I was feeling grateful that it hadn't *rained* all day."

"Your best man?"

"Harry saw Gordon fall. He thought he must have tripped, and then the report followed almost at once." Fallowfield smiled wryly. "Harry went down flat on his face. He's done that before, when a motorcar back-fired. He's more than a little ashamed of that. I can't fault him. I'd have done the same, if I'd had my wits about me."

Rutledge smiled. His first Guy Fawkes Day after the war had been a nightmare, with fireworks going off right and left. "What can you tell me about the artillery Major—Lowell, his name is—who was so helpful when the police arrived?"

"I hardly know him. He's older, you see. His father and Barbara's father went to Eton together. Nice enough chap, career officer. He spent most of his time talking to Barbara's parents. His father isn't well, he must be into his late seventies now. I expect he was asked in place of the elder Lowell for the sake of an old friendship."

"What did he say to you after the shooting?"

Fallowfield frowned. "He hustled me into the build-ing next to where I was standing, and I didn't see him again until the reception. The usual congratulations then, rather subdued, of course. Harry told me I mustn't go to Barbara. She'd just arrived, I could hear her crying. He told me I must stay where I was. Bad luck, you know, to see the bride before the wedding. It seemed so silly, in light of what had just happened, but I was terrified the police or the Bishop might not let the wedding go on. Even so, it was a near run thing. If the police had had their way, everyone would have been sent home. Barbara's father persuaded them that it was unfair to the guests who would be leaving on Sunday." His voice was wry as he went on. "They remembered to fetch me when Inspector Warren allowed the ceremony to continue. I did hear Barbara's father say that he was grateful Lowell was there, he'd been a sane voice in the chaos. To tell the truth, I think that my father-in-law would have been glad to see Barbara marry the man, if Lowell had been closer to her age. For the sake of the friendship."

It was an interesting comment.

And interesting too that the groom hadn't taken charge in Lowell's place. If only to impress his future father-in-law.

Fallowfield said into the silence that followed, "Is there nothing you can tell me about who did this murder?"

Rutledge gave him the usual answer: "I've only just arrived. It's too early to know where the inquiry will take us."

"But Inspector Warren has had nearly a fortnight."

"He hasn't been idle, I assure you." Rutledge rose. "You've been very helpful, Mr. Fallowfield. And I appreciate your assistance. It can't have been easy to relive that afternoon."

"God, I can hardly put it out of my mind. I try for Barbara's sake." Fallowfield saw him to the door and closed it after him, Rutledge thought, with sheer relief.

But there was nothing here to be going on with. In some respects it had been a wasted hour. Fallowfield had been absorbed in the wedding, and rightly so. Rutledge doubted, in all fairness, that the man would have noticed much of anything until his vows had been said and he could walk up the aisle with his bride.

He went next to call on the Sedleys, hoping for more useful information.

They lived one street over from the bride's family, and both came into the drawing room to speak to him. They were a handsome couple. Sedley had an air of the successful man about him, and he looked the part: of good height, distinguished, with the first threads of gray showing in his dark hair. His wife was still an attractive woman, and the dark green scarf she wore in the neckline of her paler green dress was just the color of her eyes.

Rutledge asked more or less the same questions as he had before, and got much the same answers. Neither of them had seen anything except Hutchinson crumpling at their feet. And neither of them could suggest any reason why the Captain should have been a target.

In fact, Sedley's view was that his death was related to something in London. "I can't quite believe that someone followed him all the way to Ely to kill him. I mean to say, whoever it was took a dreadful risk. Still, there you are. The other possibility is that someone in the town had it in for the Captain, but he mentioned at some point that he'd never been to Ely before."

Mrs. Sedley added, "We ran him by the Cathedral after we met him at the railway station. He was interested to see it."

Both Mr. and Mrs. Sedley answered freely, with as far as he could tell nothing to hide. The shock of death arriving so close to them still had not quite worn off, and they appeared to be glad to help in any way they could.

"What can you tell me about Major Lowell?"

"Surely, you can't believe—" Sedley began in some consternation.

Rutledge smiled. "Not at all. He offered his assistance to the police, and Inspector Warren was grateful. I wondered what his background might be."

"Artillery, of course. Career officer. I didn't have much opportunity to speak to him, but he was quiet, competent, a good man in an emergency. You must remember that Eugenia and I were there with the Captain. Within touching distance when he was shot. Fallowfield and the best man were just behind us and as stunned as we were. Lowell had been standing by the entrance to the Galilee Porch, and so he was not immediately involved in what happened to Hutchinson. He ran to help me, saw that it was hopeless, and then he got the groom out of there as quickly as possible. There hadn't been other shots, but of course who knew? We were all targets in that moment, and I was worried for my wife. I couldn't leave the Captain, not lying there dead, and Eugenia refused to leave me. Lowell simply dealt with everything quietly and efficiently."

"No one challenged his right to take charge?"

"One of the other guests, Colonel Rollins, spoke briefly to him, and then left him to it. I did see that exchange. When it was perfectly clear that there was no further danger, people were converging on the Cathedral. The Colonel got all the wedding guests back inside and shut the doors to the nave. I didn't know where the bride and her father were taken, but I learned later that the chauffeur had had the presence of mind to drive on as fast as he could until they were certain it was clear. Very sensible of him."

Eugenia Sedley added, "It didn't take the police very long to arrive, but not in sufficient numbers in the beginning to make a dent in the confusion. It was fortunate that Major Lowell was there."

Rutledge had been watching her. From the start she had answered without apparent reservations. And yet there was a niggling feeling that she was holding something back. He wasn't sure what was behind that feeling, except for the fact that Hamish had noticed it too. Eugenia Sedley was too well-bred to speak ill of the dead. Was that it?

Rutledge acknowledged her comment and then, keeping his voice pleasant, more inquisitive than pressing, he said to her, "Often a hostess notices more about a houseguest than anyone else. I wonder if you saw anything that would be useful?"

Mrs. Sedley glanced at her husband, then answered Rutledge. "As a houseguest, he was charming and agreeable and no trouble at all. The servants were shocked that he'd been killed." Hesitating for only a moment, she added, "But Barbara's family has a long history, and over the centuries there have been quite a few distinguished members. Among the wedding guests was the Bishop, of course, and Colonel Rollins, and then someone from the Foreign Office, a man named Tuttle. I began to think that Captain Hutchinson was—seeking to make powerful new friends."

Her husband said impatiently, "We should not speak ill of a man who died while he was a guest in this house. I can't think your remarks have any bearing on what happened."

She sighed impatiently. "No, of course not, I can't imagine that they would have done. But, my dear, it's precisely *because* he's dead I must tell Inspector Rutledge what I think. He must be the judge of whether it's helpful or not. We want the Captain's murderer found, don't we? It will do no good to pretend he was perfect."

"Did anyone seem to take offense at his attempt to impress the more important guests?"

"I don't know that anyone realized precisely what was happening. It was a very busy few days. And he was quite good at it, you see. But as I was his hostess, I was sometimes anxious that he might be becoming a little obvious, ingratiating himself. Just happening to find himself next to the Bishop or the Colonel or Barbara's rather influential father a trifle more frequently than was usual in a guest who was not of the immediate wedding party. I must say, he was interesting. They seemed to enjoy his company, but I witnessed the maneuvers that made it possible for him to stand or sit next to one of them. And I wondered if someone else might have noticed. Barbara's mother, for one. She doesn't suffer fools lightly. And she wouldn't care to be used in that way."

Sedley said, "That's a little harsh."

"Yes, I suppose it is," his wife responded. "But if the Captain was behaving like this in Ely, perhaps he had behaved in the same way in London."

"I appreciate your honesty," Rutledge cut in, before Sedley could say more. "It's something to bear in mind.

Jealousy is a powerful emotion." He hesitated, then added, "I know it will be very painful, but could you tell me what happened as you walked across the grass toward the Cathedral?"

She turned slightly to look toward the drawing room window, and at first he didn't think she intended to answer him. Then she said, bringing the moment back in her mind, "I had just turned to Captain Hutchinson—I can't even tell you what I was about to say. Something trivial, it's completely gone from my mind now—when his face changed. I've never seen anything like it. Shock? I don't think it was pain. Just—surprise that something was happening to him. And suddenly noise was everywhere, and the front of the Captain's white shirt was turning red. All this before he began to fall. As if time had stopped, somehow. To my surprise, I was screaming for help, and my husband was on his knees, trying to stem the flow of blood. But there wasn't much of it after all." She shuddered, and her husband put his hand over hers.

"That's enough," he said. "You've upset her enough, Rutledge. We've told you we saw nothing. How could we, we didn't even know where to look."

But Rutledge had got what he came for—a first insight into the dead man. And from that he would have to build a case.

There was time for two other interviews in what was left of the afternoon. First was a young man who had been behind the barricades. One of the several dozen people who had collected to watch the spectacle of a fashionable wedding.

The reason this witness had been of interest to Inspector Warren was because he was deaf. He hadn't heard the shot, he hadn't been distracted by the screams.

His name was Teddy Mathews. He had come to the barricade wondering why people were gathered there, to see what had drawn them—what was happening.

Rutledge found him at the house where he lived with his sister. It wasn't far from the Cathedral, and it was Mathews's custom to walk there on the grounds every day for exercise.

When Rutledge arrived, it was the sister, Sadie, who admitted him. He asked to speak to her brother and added, "I'm not sure how to manage the interview."

"I'll translate for you, of course. And he can read lips as well." She led him through to a sitting room where Mathews was reading by the window, and made the introductions as her brother rose to greet their visitor.

He was slim, with dark hair and very bright blue eyes, and his handshake was firm.

As they were seated again, Rutledge explained why he was there, and the young man nodded.

"I'll help in any way I can," he replied as his sister translated his signs. "But first I must ask. Do you know who it was who did this thing? I've found it hard to sleep, thinking about it."

"We're hoping to make an arrest soon," Rutledge answered. "Anything you tell us will be useful."

"Yes, I can see that being deaf might have its uses here." He smiled, but his sister couldn't quite bring herself to answer it with one of her own.

"I saw people at a barrier, and wondered what was happening. There was obviously going to be a wedding, judging from the guests who were arriving on the other side of the Green, and I stood there for a moment or two, enjoying watching like everyone else. I had no idea who the bride or groom was, mind you. It was just a way to pass the time. There was a lull in arrivals, and I was about to turn away when another motorcar pulled up and three people got out. A very beautifully dressed woman and two men. I was staring at her when two other men arrived just behind them and started toward the Cathedral as well. I couldn't ask anyone, but I rather thought one of the two men with the woman must be the bridegroom. The tall one, perhaps thirty or so, fairly handsome. It was something in the way he carried himself. As if he knew his worth. I was looking directly at him when he was hit." He broke off, then went on more slowly. "I didn't know what was wrong. He just stopped short for the briefest moment, and then fell backward. I wondered for an instant if his heart had given out."

"You couldn't hear the shot at all."

"No, not at all. I'm totally deaf. But I could very quickly see from the faces around me that something was badly wrong."

"What happened then?"

"I turned to the man beside me, asking for an explanation. But he was very upset, and I couldn't read his lips."

"You were turned to face the Lady Chapel at that moment?"

"I was."

"Did you see anyone near the wall or the gate into the Cathedral grounds?"

"I don't think so. I was struggling to understand what the man was saying, why people were jostling us now, pushing to get away as fast as they could. I couldn't tell why they were so frightened. Still, if something had been going on in that direction, something unusual, I think I'd have noticed. Inspector Warren has already asked me the same question, and I keep trying to remember anything that might help."

"Have you remembered anything?"

He shook his head, unhappy. "Sorry. No."

"Go on."

"When I turned back, I realized that the man was hurt, was even possibly dead, and people were rushing out of the Cathedral just as the bride's motorcar was turning into the street and starting in our direction. An Army officer and another man were bending over the fallen man, and then the officer stood up and began to look at the buildings on either side and then up at the Cathedral, as if searching for something. I realized then that nothing more could be done for the man on the ground. It was shocking. I couldn't begin to imagine what the bride must think, seeing all this turmoil. I left shortly afterward, because it was distressing not to know what was going on. It wasn't until later, when the police came to our door, that I realized the man had been shot and that I'd been mistaken in thinking he was the groom."

"How did the police know to find you?"

"I believe someone there at the barrier recognized me. I hadn't stayed long enough to see the police arrive. They wanted to know why I'd left, but my sister explained about my deafness. I think they understood."

Mathews was, Rutledge saw, a very good witness, clear about what he'd seen, even though he'd only partially understood it at the time. It explained why Warren had suggested that Rutledge speak to him.

"When you left, how did you make your way home?"

"I turned away from the barricade, walked straight to the next street, and made my way home from there. On foot."

"Did you see anyone or anything unexpected as you turned away from the Cathedral? Workmen with their tools, a priest carrying anything unusual, a person with a large bundle or package?"

Mathews watched his sister's busy hands, then nodded. "By that time, other people were hurrying toward the Cathedral. There was a sweep, I remember, his tools over his shoulder, and a priest, and then there was the man with a barrow. He'd been going in my direction, but he turned and hurried back toward the Cathedral, leaving his barrow standing in the road. A number of people stopped me to ask questions. I couldn't tell them what I'd seen. By the time I reached my house, I was shaken, I admit it. I wouldn't go out at all the next day. I don't like to feel—different. But this brought it home to me very clearly that I was."

There was anguish in his face as he finished. He had, Rutledge thought, managed to come to terms with his deafness. And then, caught in the midst of chaos, he'd kept his head until he'd reached the safety of his house. Only then had he given in to the shock.

"The man with the barrow. Could you see what he was carrying in it?"

"I seem to remember it was covered with a ragged cloth. I didn't think about it again until the constable came to interview me."

It had been the last thing on Mathews's mind, that was clear.

"Are you sure he'd been leaving the Cathedral area?"

"I don't know. He was ahead of me on the street, but he could have come from the pub just there or one of the shops. I expect I assumed he was going about his business when the excitement began." His brows twitched together as he tried to remember. "People do cut across in front of the Cathedral. Every day. But I was at the barrier, and I hadn't seen him there. He could have come from that lane running down beside the Lady Chapel."

A man with a barrow. Anything could have been under that cloth.

It was a place to start.

Rutledge thanked him, and Mathews's sister showed him to the door.

She said, as he stepped out into the late afternoon sunlight, "My brother is a good man. He manages quite well, actually. But he was very upset when he reached the house. I hope this is the last time you will need to interview him. It's difficult to relive what happened."

"We'll try to spare him, Miss Mathews. But we're searching for a killer."

"Ask someone else, then. There were dozens of people there. Perhaps if they *heard* the shot they can tell you where it came from." She closed the door, leaving him there.

His last interview was with a Mrs. Boggs, who was going to market, noticed the cluster of people by the Cathedral barrier, and stopped to see what had brought them there. Someone told her it was a wedding, and she'd stayed in the hope of seeing the bride arrive.

She lived in one of the poorer sections of Ely. She walked home daily from her work as a washerwoman for one of the large homes not far from the Sedleys'.

She was surprised and more than a little flattered to find Scotland Yard at her door.

As he asked his questions, he realized that she was more astute than he'd realized. Her red face, strawlike fair hair, and rough hands were a badge of her occupation, not her mind.

"What I know about guns," she said, "you could put in a thimble. But I was watching that Captain Hutchinson coming across the grass. He was a well-set-up gentleman, and I saw him step out of his motorcar and offer the lady with him his hand."

It had been Sedley's motorcar and Sedley's wife.

"Tell me about him," Rutledge asked.

She cocked her head. "Nearly as tall as you are, a man to take notice of. Now the gentleman with him was quite handsome, but a little old to be the bridegroom. Still, you never know, do you? The Captain—they told me his name when they took my statement—was smartly dressed, as if his valet had taken special care. I do know something about valets. They like their gentleman to be well turned out."

"What did you see just before he was struck by the bullet?"

"The lady was speaking to him, but he looked up, as if he knew something was about to happen, and then he was shocked, as if he couldn't believe what it was. At first I thought the lady had said something unpleasant, but we heard the shot in the same breath, only I didn't know what it was, I couldn't think for the sudden noise. And he was falling over, and everyone was screaming." She shook her head. "I never saw anything like it."

"What do you mean, he looked up?"

"The way you do sometimes when you hear something you don't believe."

And Mrs. Sedley couldn't remember what it was she was saying to Hutchinson just as he was shot.

"Did you see anyone by the gate that led into the precincts of the Cathedral, the one close by the Lady

Chapel? Or anyone at all who seemed to be out of place? Either the way he looked or because of what he was carrying."

"There was no one by that gate. Not that I saw. Why should there be? You couldn't very well watch all the finery from there. As to anything out of place, I do remember something that struck me as a little odd. But for the life of me I can't bring it back. Just something ordinary, you know, but I was in a state by that time, and it clear went out of my head."

Try as he would, Rutledge couldn't coax whatever it was from her memory. In the end he had to thank her and ask her to notify the police if she brought it to mind.

Back in the center of Ely once more, he found a telephone and put in a call to Sergeant Gibson in London.

Gibson's voice as he came to the telephone had a cautious note in it.

Rutledge said, "Two of the people involved in these murders in the Cambridgeshire Fens came from London. I shall need whatever you can find about one Captain Gordon Hutchinson. He's the victim in Ely. The other man is the bridegroom here, Jason Fallowfield. He was walking very close to the victim and might well have been the intended target. They're distantly related, although they called themselves cousins. Most particularly I need to know if the second victim, the one in Wriston, had any connection with either of the other two men. Herbert Swift is the name. There's no link we can find here—it must lie in London. Finally, there's an artillery Major, one Lowell, first name Alexander. Does he have a connection with Hutchinson or Swift? He couldn't have been the shooter. But he may have been involved in some way."

Gibson said only, "That's a tall order. Sir."

Rutledge smiled grimly. Whatever was happening in London must be requiring a good deal of manpower, and Gibson was alerting him to the possibility of delays before he received any information.

So much for Markham's dictum. Unless there was a break here in Cambridgeshire, there was no possibility of an early arrest.

He thanked Gibson, adding, "Give it your best try. That's all that matters."

Gibson was silent for a moment—Rutledge could hear voices, as though several men were walking past where the sergeant was standing. Finally in a rush the sergeant said something that was nearly unintelligible coming down the line, then added "Sir" before ringing off.

Rutledge would have sworn that what he'd heard was *new broom*.

An ominous sign.

Chapter 6

Shutting the door behind him as he walked into his room under the eaves, Rutledge sat down in the only chair and gave the problem facing him some thought.

He'd seen the mountain of interviews that Inspector Warren had painstakingly collected. It would take days to sort through the rest of them, in the hope of finding something, anything to be going on with. His time was better spent elsewhere.

But there was still the question of the man with the barrow.

Rutledge made a note to deal with it tomorrow, and went out to find himself some dinner before going to bed.

But the room felt still, airless, when he came in again, and a little after two in the morning he could stand it no longer. He got up, dressed. The streets were empty and quiet when he let himself out of the inn door and walked as far as the Cathedral.

In the nearly full moon, it was at once imposing and mysterious. The silvery light shone through the Lantern, giving it a ghostly glow that seemed to emanate from inside. Where it could be seen from his vantage point, the roof gleamed like dull pewter, while below it the stone walls seemed to squat in darkness with very little definition, the occasional spire rising into the night sky, like fingers pointing to God.

The Palace Green stretched before him, full of shadows, the Russian cannon that Queen Victoria had dedicated on a visit to Ely black and ugly. Looking at it, he thought it had been an odd welcome for the wedding guests, but then it had stood there so long it was likely that no one noticed it.

He began where the motorcars had drawn up, at the top of the Green, then took the route that Warren had pointed out to him. There was no one else about, although he thought he heard an owl in the distance. He walked across the grass, now damp with dew, and stopped where Hutchinson had fallen. Standing there, he did what Major Lowell had done, turning slowly in a half circle, his gaze taking in every possible vantage point and then discarding them one by one.

There was no clear line of sight from the Diocesan buildings. It would have had to have been a head shot. But the killer had gone instead for the heart. Why?

The high stone wall, which began next to the Cathedral's own walls, stretched down the road toward an arch that led into the school grounds. The same wall where a ladder had been placed. Neither Inspector Warren nor his constables had discovered who had put the ladder there. But again the angle was wrong. A bullet from there would have had to traverse the chest, exiting below the left arm after striking the heart. The head would have been a more certain target.

Hamish spoke into the silence. His voice seemed to echo ominously through the darkness. "Yon battlement."

Looking up at the dark mass of the great west tower, Rutledge was inclined to agree with him. But a constable had climbed up there and found nothing. And it was very exposed, more so than the gate on the far side by the Lady Chapel. Any of the arriving guests might have looked up at the wrong time, attracted by movement—even a pigeon flying up—and spotted the killer. He would have been well and truly trapped, no way out but through that single tower door inside the Cathedral itself. He couldn't have hidden, unless he was dressed as a guest and could mingle easily. But that meant abandoning the rifle until it was safe to go back for it. Where in hell's name could he have hidden it? The killer must surely have known that someone would climb up there to have a look. But he couldn't have come through the tower door with it, hoping to secret it somewhere else. Even broken down, it would have been difficult to conceal. Inspector Warren had even searched the organ pipes.

And yet, if he'd been the killer, Rutledge knew he would have taken his chances there because it was the most certain platform from which to make his shot.

While the gate on the north side was exposed as well, at least there were choices of direction for the man's escape. And that's where the cartridge casing had been found.

But a cartridge casing could be dropped anywhere, far from where it had been ejected. The killer could have come down from the tower, left the Cathedral by a different door, and then as he came around the apse and the Lady Chapel to that gate, lost the casing without knowing it.

Misdirection? Both the ladder against the wall and the dropped casing?

"Ye ken," Hamish said after a moment, "it isna' sae important to know how it was done. He's sae verra' clever, he's killed twice withoot being seen, save for the auld woman who swore she saw a monster."

"Not much to go on, that monster," Rutledge answered aloud with a wry smile.

"Aye, it's verra' similar to the problem here."

"Yes," Rutledge answered slowly. "Misdirection again. But tomorrow I'll climb to that tower."

And shortly after breakfast, when the sun was bright and a mist clung to the lower-lying villages, hiding them from sight, Rutledge came back to Ely Cathedral, and without much notice being taken of him, he wandered about for a time. Much to the horror of Hamish's Covenanter soul, who had a distaste for ornamentation and splendor that smacked of Popery.

He'd walked down to the choir and thence to the Lady Chapel, exploring as a policeman rather than a worshipper, made his way back to the Galilee Porch, and from there went unchallenged to the tower door. It was a climb. Two hundred eighty-eight steps, unless he'd missed his count. But in the end he came out onto the battlemented top of the tower.

It was a dizzying height. Two hundred feet or more, with splendid views over Ely and across the surrounding Fens.

The constable had been right, the slope of the roof made it difficult to walk around, offering little or no space for footing.

Instead of walking, he got down on all fours and crept around to the position he was looking for. When he came to a spot where he could look down, he saw that he had a perfect view of his field of fire.

He could see where Hutchinson had fallen so clearly that he himself could have taken that shot.

He knelt there, thinking it through, ignoring Hamish in the back of his mind.

There was still the problem of getting the rifle safely away. But the man couldn't have made the shot with any other weapon. It was too far for a revolver, and by the time Captain Hutchinson had come that close, the man would have had to stand to aim.

There was no proof he was right, of course. But it had been a daring plan, if this had been the place the killer had chosen.

And that was a measure of what the man had felt toward Hutchinson. A savage hate, to take such a risk. Or a cold one?

Which meant, Rutledge realized, that of the two victims, it was Hutchinson who had been the more important one. Herbert Swift could have waited. Days. Weeks. Hutchinson would only be within reach for a stated length of time. And as Inspector Warren had pointed out, the wedding ceremony was the only public appearance the Captain had made. The private parties and dinners hadn't been announced, there was no way to plan for any one of them. But here—here at the Cathedral, Hutchinson would be certain to appear, and *that* fact had been known for some time.

Rutledge couldn't blame Inspector Warren for not working it out the way he himself had. Warren had been the man on the scene, he'd had to deal with the bride's irate father, the Bishop and the Colonel and all the other important men connected to the family. He'd had to depend on his constables to do much of the legwork. Those endless statements had taken time, and the pressure to find the killer had built with each passing day. But Warren had only had a handful of days. Swift was killed then, and a second inquiry had been set in motion, stretching his resources to the limit.

Damned on every side, he'd at least had the courage to ask the Yard to send someone. And he had cooperated fully when Rutledge arrived, knowing he was acknowledging his own failure.

Rutledge could respect that.

He made to rise and move away from the space between two blocks of stone where he'd been crouching, when he realized what it was Hamish was saying to him.

Caught on a bit of rough stone was a single gray strand of cloth, so nearly the same color that it was all but invisible.

He gently tugged at it and brought it free. Worn cloth, he thought, and easily snagged. But how had it got here? More important, *when*? That was the question. And unfortunately there were any number of answers. All the same, if he'd been a betting man, Rutledge would have wagered that it had been the cloth with which the killer had wrapped himself and his rifle, shielding both from view. It made sense. The color alone was not likely to have come from a casual visitor's clothing. It matched too perfectly.

Taking out a clean handkerchief, Rutledge laid the tiny strand of cotton there and folded it again.

Satisfied, he left the tower and climbed down the multitude of steps once more, carefully opening the door and finding it a simple matter to slip out of it unnoticed. But then there was no wedding today. He had just reached the west door when a man in clerical dress came out of the sanctuary. Rutledge turned.

"Beautiful building, isn't it?" the man said, his accent strong Scots.

"It is indeed," Rutledge answered.

The man nodded and went on his way.

Rutledge watched him as he strode out of sight, his mind elsewhere.

After a moment he said, "I'm going back to Wriston. There are too many people involved in what happened in Ely. If I find anything there, I can backtrack to this place."

Hamish said, "Aye, but will you tell yon Inspector what you found?"

Rutledge shook his head. "Not yet. Not until I can be sure."

Inspector Warren was not best pleased to hear that Rutledge was already leaving Ely.

"Giving up, are you?"

Rutledge said, "Early days for that. No, I've spoken to those witnesses, and I've looked at the ground. I don't know that we can learn any more here at this stage. What I hope to discover in Wriston is whether or not someone else saw Mrs. Percy's monster. Surely someone did, and hasn't had the courage yet to come forward. Would you willingly admit you'd seen something that you couldn't explain?"

"I probably would, if asked by a policeman," Warren answered stiffly.

"Yes, perhaps you'd speak to him. But not to your local constable, who would be sniffing your breath or wondering if you'd fallen down and hit your head. You would know full well the constable would file away your vision along with Mrs. Percy's and remind you of it later, when next he saw you staggering down the High at closing."

Warren grudgingly agreed, striving to keep amusement out of his gaze.

"Our quarry was faultless here. He'd planned meticulously for this kill. He couldn't have got away with it if he hadn't. And then he tried again. He might have been careless." Rutledge paused. "And if he wasn't, he could well be searching for a new target, because he knows we can't touch him. Yet."

"I hope to God you're wrong." Warren took a deep breath. "The Chief Constable is already demanding answers, and he'll be in *your* face if there's another murder. The wedding was bad enough, given who was attending, and then Swift on top of that."

But there was very likely to be a third, Rutledge thought. He could almost feel it.

He was halfway to the street when he remembered the barrow. Turning, he went back to Warren's office, poked his head around the door, and said, "The deaf fellow. Mathews. He saw a man with a barrow walking away from the scene. After any number of people had rushed past him toward the Cathedral, he left the barrow and went to see for himself what the excitement was about. He's not likely to be our man, but if we don't follow up on him, we'll never know for certain."

"Any idea what was in that barrow?"

"According to Mathews it was covered by a cloth." He thought about the strand of gray cotton in his handkerchief. Had it come from that barrow? It would be luck indeed if it had. But where was the barrow's owner now? Much less that cloth—long since tossed into a tip?

Inspector Warren was nodding. "Very well, I'll see to it. Do you think Mathews can identify him? There must be twenty or more men with barrows in Ely."

"We'll have to trust that he can." Rutledge thanked him, went back to The Deacon, thought about it, and walked on to Teddy Mathews's house.

He was in and alone. Rutledge apologized for coming in unannounced, when the man's sister was away.

Mathews shrugged. Rutledge said, speaking clearly, "The barrow the man abandoned to run back toward the Cathedral. You said there was a cloth thrown over the contents."

He handed his notebook to Mathews, who took up the pen and wrote on the first empty page he came to, *I expect I ought to have said sacking. It was so filthy you could hardly tell that once it had been yellow.*

Yellow, then. Not gray.

He'd probably sent Warren's men on a wild-goose chase. Still, he was reluctant to rescind the request. And who knew what lay under the sacking? Whatever color it had been.

He thanked Mathews, who scribbled something more on the page, then passed the notebook back to Rutledge.

I'm sorry I couldn't be more help.

"You're a good witness," Rutledge assured him, then took his leave.

At The Deacon Inn, Rutledge asked Reception to hold his room but took his valise with him and set out for Wriston, stopping briefly for petrol.

It was a village, not a town. Fewer people were involved. Ely was the proverbial haystack, and for all anyone knew, the needle was already back home in Soham or Burwell, even London. Wherever he'd come from.

Hamish said as Rutledge threaded his way through Ely to the Cambridge Road, "For a' anyone knew, he was walking the mist in Wriston."

Chapter 7

Now that he was in the village in his official capacity, Rutledge's first duty was to call on the constable.

He'd arrived at Wriston by a roundabout way, crisscrossing the Fens to explore several nearby villages, and there was not much to choose between them save for size. Isleham was smaller, Soham a little larger, and Burwell, the largest, a bustling town with a fine church. And the fields that ran for acre after acre in their long narrow beds for the most part held the same variety of market crops—oats, peas, and barley.

It was late in the afternoon when he walked into the police station, across from the duck pond. Constable McBride was at his desk, reading an Ely newspaper.

He was a burly man with thinning brown hair, and he looked up at Rutledge with some surprise, recognizing him at once as the stranger he'd chivvied along only yesterday for excessive curiosity about the site of Swift's murder.

"Back again, are you, sir? Anything I can help you with, then?"

But there was a guardedness in the offer.

Rutledge handed him his identification, and McBride studied it for longer than necessary, and then, getting to his feet, he said in a slightly aggrieved voice, "I'm sorry, sir, but you didn't tell me who you were."

"I hadn't yet reported to Inspector Warren in Ely. I'd been caught out in that mist the previous night, got thoroughly lost, and when I realized that I was in Wriston, I wanted to take a preliminary look at that cross."

"Yes, I see." But it was clear he didn't. "Is there anything new, sir? From Ely?" He held up the newspaper still in his hand, then set it aside. "There's nothing in here. And the last report I'd had from Inspector Warren was three days ago. Even that was not what you might call informative."

"What does the Ely paper have to say about the murders?"

"Precious little. A nine days' wonder, as it were. It's no longer on the first page." Gesturing to the chair on the other side of the desk, he sat down. "How can I help you, sir?"

"Tell me what happened here in Wriston."

"Surely Inspector Warren has already done that."

"I'd like your point of view. You live here."

McBride gave him a concise report. It differed very little from what Rutledge already knew. "We searched and we found nothing. Not even a cartridge casing. The shot must have been a difficult one. Night, flickering torchlight. I'd not have tried it, I can tell you that. I mean to say, what if he'd missed?"

But whoever it was had had no problem making his shot count.

"The question is, what ties these two deaths together? There has to be a very good reason. For one thing, they were killed within days of each other, and only a matter of miles apart. For another, they were fairly prominent men. This wasn't a grudge killing between neighbors, because they weren't in any sense neighbors."

McBride shook his head. "I've spent hours thinking about that, sir. I can't see how they could have known each other. Perhaps someone only believed they did."

Which, Rutledge thought, was a very perceptive comment.

"The war. Is there a connection there?"

"I can't think how that could be. The Swifts have been farmers here for generations. Our Mr. Swift spent most of his war in Glasgow, serving with the Navy as a civilian. Still, he liked Scotland, it seems. He wrote the Rector to say that when he could, he'd take long walks. He thought it cleared his head. He was still mourning his wife."

"Did Swift have enemies?"

"We haven't found any. If you want my opinion, whoever did this isn't a Wriston man, and that means the quarrel, if there was one, didn't have its roots here. Mr. Swift wasn't one to visit Ely or Soham or Burwell often, but he went there if it was a matter of business. I'd say look at his clients or *their* enemies. A quiet man, and well liked. He'd have won, you know. Hands down. I daresay his killing could even have been political, although that's a stretch, in my view."

"What about his opponent?"

"I doubt he could be bothered. What he liked best, if truth be told, were the free beers his supporters bought for him down at The Wake."

"What was Mr. Swift talking about the night he was killed?"

"He was hardly into what he'd planned to say. It had to do with the war ending, but the legacy of the war was still with us. I doubt anyone would argue with that."

"His private life, then."

McBride smiled. "As to that, his wife ruled the roost until she died in childbirth. It nearly killed him as well. I don't believe he'd have gone on, if the war hadn't changed things. Scotland was good for him, taking him away from here."

"Someone wanted him dead."

"It's true, but try as I will, I can find nothing in his life to explain that. Unless . . ." McBride's gaze stared into the past, somewhere behind Rutledge's left shoulder.

Rutledge felt an instant burst of panic, then caught himself. No one could see Hamish where he kept watch at Rutledge's back, as he had done so often in the trenches.

"There was something before the war. Mr. Swift was serving as a witness in a trial in Ely. There was a man sent to prison for putting another man in hospital with a skull fracture and broken ribs. It was claimed the victim was thrown down a flight of stairs. The man swore it wasn't true, that the victim, after an argument, turned to have the last word, lost his balance, and fell. But the jury thought otherwise." McBride lifted a shoulder in a shrug. "That man might've held a grudge against Swift, because he gave evidence against him, but I can't see how Captain Hutchinson fits into it."

"Do you remember the man's name?"

"That I don't. The only reason I remember the trial at all is that my wife's brother was bailiff at the time."

"Then I'll ask him if he recalls the trial."

"Dead on Passchendaele Ridge," McBride answered somberly. "More's the pity. A good man."

"Turn it another way. Who has such a rifle?"

"There's the catch," McBride agreed. "They aren't lying beneath every bush, are they? The question is, did he keep it back when he left France, or was it one used to train troops?"

It was time to mention Mrs. Percy.

"I've been told that at least one of the onlookers described our man."

McBride pushed aside his newspaper. "Mrs. Percy. I don't know who spoke to you about her. But I'd discount what she said, if I were you, sir."

"Why? She saw *something*. It wasn't what you expected from a witness, perhaps. But it was information we have to investigate."

"Sir, I can't see how we can explore what she described. She's an elderly woman whose eyesight is not the best. I mean to say—a monster."

"The question is, was she the only one who looked up just as the shot was fired? There may be other witnesses who don't want to come forward. We need to find them."

"There's nothing in the statements we collected that show information has been withheld."

"I'd like to question her, all the same."

"She's still that upset, sir, I doubt she'll make any sense."

"Then I'll go alone. She might speak more freely. Tell me where to find her."

Mrs. Percy lived in the last cottage on the lane called Windmill Row.

There was no windmill now. Instead the fields began not twenty feet beyond her door, and a bulwark of earth separated them from the end of her lane. He could just see the darker green of late season crops growing several feet below the level of the higher ground on which her house sat.

She was snapping beans in the kitchen when Rutledge tapped at her open door. "Come," she called, and he stepped inside, following the sound of her voice. She was a small woman, gray hair pinned up on her head, blue-veined hands working with the beans in a large earthenware bowl. He didn't think she even looked down at them, her fingers busy on their own.

"Who are you?" she demanded, peering at the tall stranger who'd just appeared in her kitchen. "I was expecting the butcher's boy."

"My name is Rutledge, Mrs. Percy. London has sent me to Wriston to find out what I can about the death of Mr. Swift. I understand you were by the market cross that evening, when he was shot."

"I was. It was a warm evening, no clouds, and I felt like walking up to the cross to see what the shouting and those torches were all about. When I got there, the smoke made my eyes water. I pushed my way around behind Mr. Swift, where it was a little better, and just then he started to speak. I'd hardly got settled when he dropped like a stone." She shuddered, her hands pausing in their work. "I wish I'd never gone up. I wish I'd decided to do my mending instead." Her fingers found their rhythm again.

"Had anyone else moved around behind Mr. Swift, to get away from the smoke?"

"Paul Ruskin was there—he's the cooper from Soham. I knew his father. But most everyone wanted to be out in front, of course."

Another name. So much for McBride's pessimism.

"Anyone else?" Across from where he was sitting, a pair of worn wooden stilts were standing in the corner, and on a shelf just above them, a pair of wooden skates for use on ice. A hundred years or more ago, men had walked the fields on stilts, and they'd been quite good at it, striding out boldly and swinging across ditches, fording streams.

Mrs. Percy considered his question, then shook her head. "No, I think it was just Paul and me. Mr. Ruskin and me."

It was time to ask the question that had brought him here. There was no way to soften it, to draw her out. But he tried.

"Scotland Yard was very pleased to learn there was a witness to the shooting, someone who could describe Mr. Swift's killer."

Mrs. Percy lips thinned to a tight line. "Well, they're wrong," she said after a moment, when he didn't press.

He listened to her fingers snapping the crisp flesh of the beans.

"Have they made light of what you told them? The constable and then Inspector Warren?" he asked gently.

"I didn't see anything. I told you. The smoke was making my eyes water. All I saw was smoke."

The damage was done. Rutledge couldn't shift her. And that he laid at the door of those who had questioned her in the beginning. A monster was not evidence. And in their own desperation, they had hounded her to make sense of the senseless. Now she was refusing to acknowledge her own statement, denying she had seen anything after all.

She rose, the beans half filling the bowl, the sack that had held them empty now.

"I have to cook my dinner," she said, dismissing him. "There's the door."

Rutledge swore to himself. He needed her testimony, he needed to watch her face as she described the monster she'd seen. But he would have to come back—as often as necessary until she relented.

Meanwhile, there was still the man in Soham.

Thanking her, he turned and found his way back to the door where he'd come in.

The question, he thought as he made his way back to the market cross to stare up at the dormer window once more, was how much he could discount the monster as part of her shock or as part of her eyes watering. He squinted, distorting the window as much as he could, but the circumstances were very different here on this sunny day.

And it was possible that someone else besides Ruskin had had a similar vantage point, but what had been done to Mrs. Percy would have been a warning that the truth would be rejected out of hand. And so any hope of locating those witnesses—if they actually existed—was small.

He drove on to Soham, finding the High Street and the square, then asked a man crossing it toward the shops how to find the cooper.

The man nodded. "Out that way to Fox Lane. You can't miss it."

And he didn't. The front of the shop was open, and the scent of fresh-cut wood filled the air. He found Ruskin in the yard, gathering staves together one by one in a raising hoop, frowning as he worked. Perhaps in his late thirties, he had graying hair and a strong face. He looked up, nodded to Rutledge, and without stopping what he was doing, he asked, "Help you, sir?"

"I'm looking for Paul Ruskin."

He straightened. Behind him in the shed was a shelf with the tools of his trade, and beyond them against the far wall was a row of his finished goods. Butter churns, coal scuttles, a firkin and a bucket, dwarfed by a pair of hogsheads.

"You've found him, then."

"I've come from Ely. My name is Rutledge. Scotland Yard sent me to help Inspector Warren find the man who killed Captain Hutchinson and Mr. Swift. I understand you were in Wriston the evening Swift was shot."

Ruskin set the staves aside and considered Rutledge. "Who told you I was there?"

And Rutledge realized that this man hadn't been questioned by the police. That somehow in the chaos, he'd left Wriston before McBride could collect all his witnesses. If Mrs. Percy hadn't recognized him, he'd have been in the clear.

Rutledge sat down on a finished barrelhead. "Someone saw you and reported it to me. Why? Did you have anything to hide?"

"No." But there was a wariness in the man's voice. When Rutledge said nothing, he added, "I saw no purpose in hanging about. The man was dead, and I'd had aught to do with it."

"Sensible of you," Rutledge said affably. "What brought you to Wriston?"

"I'd delivered a half-dozen barrels for one of the farmers. Burrows, his name is. I stopped off at The Wake after delivering them. There was talk that Swift was planning to speak. He came in just after that, walking around, having a word with everyone. And I decided to hear what he had to say. It'ud been a long day for me, but I wasn't ready to go home. My wife and I'd had words that morning, and I didn't want to open up the quarrel again."

"So you followed the torchbearers and the others to the market cross?"

"I did. But I'm not a Wriston man. I didn't care to draw attention to myself, like. Not that I didn't have every right to be there, you understand, more a question of not wishing to push in."

It was something Rutledge had heard many times before. A village only five miles away could be as foreign to its neighbors as if it were fifty or five hundred miles distant. This was a Wriston rally.

And so Ruskin had moved away from the main body of Swift's followers and found himself next to Mrs. Percy, behind the market cross.

"Did you see Swift fall?"

"I couldn't help but see it. One minute speaking, the next pitching over, and half his head missing." Something changed in Ruskin's face. "It brought back the war. I can tell you that. I thought I was done with the dead falling at my feet and the sound of gunfire. I'd put it behind me, and it all came rushing back. So I left. I saw no need to stay. There must have been forty some people who could talk to the police. They didn't need me."

That explained his leaving. It was something Rutledge could understand. And Hamish as well, stirring in the back of his mind.

"What did you see?" Rutledge asked quietly. "Up there in the dormer window?"

"God knows. It happened so fast, I thought it was a flashback to the war."

"Describe it for me."

Ruskin shook his head. "No. I don't want to remember. It made my blood run cold. I told myself I was wrong, and that I'd imagined it. And so I set it aside."

"Did you see the rifle?"

"No. No, not that."

"Then what?"

He shook his head.

"You must tell me. I can't find this killer if I don't know what I'm searching for." He waited. "Ruskin, I can have you arrested for refusing to cooperate with the police. Don't make me take that step."

The man looked directly at Rutledge then, his eyes haunted. After a moment he said, "Will you go away and leave me alone? I don't want the police here, hounding me. I don't want to dredge it up again and again."

"I won't tell Inspector Warren. Or your own constable. No one knows I'm here anyway. I came on my own."

Barely satisfied, Ruskin searched Rutledge's face. And then, against his will, Ruskin stood up.

"A helmet," he said. "I saw a German helmet. I know, it's impossible. But that's what I saw. "

And with that he walked away, disappearing into the back of his shop.

Rutledge sat where he was for a moment.

Hamish was saying, "He saw what he feared to see. Only that."

Taking a deep breath, Rutledge got up and walked back to his motorcar. Across the rooftops facing him, he could see the elegant tower of the village church. He bent to turn the crank and got into the motorcar.

Had Ruskin imagined the helmet? He must have done, Hamish was right. Shocked by the rifle's report and the dead man almost at his feet, he'd reverted to what he knew, the war and the trenches. Who else would be shooting at him but his German foes?

Still, the fact remained. He *had* seen something.

"Will ye tell the ithers?" Hamish demanded. "Ye gave your word."

"Warren and McBride? The constable here? No. We'll see what comes of it."

Reversing the motorcar, he added, only realizing too late that he'd spoken aloud. "Who's behind this business? Who is using the war to exact his revenge?"

If he was to remain in Wriston for several days, he needed somewhere to stay. Rutledge wasn't certain that Priscilla Bartram would accommodate him. It was one thing to take in a stranger lost in the mist. Quite another to go to all the trouble of opening her inn to someone who might spend only a night or two there. Still, he hadn't seen any other lodgings in the village. The Wake Inn was small, more pub than hostelry.

Then he remembered something Miss Trowbridge had said. *She needs the money.*

Leaving the motorcar by the police station, he walked down the High Street to The Dutchman Inn.

Hamish said, "She willna' be pleased ye didna' tell her who you were."

There was that. But he rather thought Miss Bartram would choose company in the evening over turning him down out of pique.

Whether she would talk as freely once she knew he was Scotland Yard was another matter.

When she came to the door, it was clear she was happy to see him again, telling him almost in the same breath that his room was still available.

"Have you finished your business in Ely?" she asked, urging him toward the sitting room. "Well, then, you've earned a bit of time to yourself. Not that spending it here in the Fen country is anything special, when the waterfowl aren't coming in."

Her face, however, changed when he told her who he was. She wasn't best pleased.

"Scotland Yard, then. You could have told me when you were here. I'd have said nothing, you know, not even to Constable McBride, if you'd asked me not to. As it was, I may have said too much. About the people here. Mr. Swift."

"I had yet to report to Inspector Warren in Ely. It was proper to do that first. In fact, it was happenstance that I came here first at all. It wasn't where I intended to be."

"You told me you'd come from Cambridge. Not London." There was an accusing note in her voice now.

"And so I had come from there. I thought at the time you might prefer someone from Cambridge to a stranger from London."

"Did Miss Trowbridge know? What brought you here?"

"She never asked," he said carefully. "After all, if it hadn't been for her cat, I'd have likely stumbled over the ruins of the mill keeper's house and broken my neck."

That mollified her, but she said stiffly, "What brings you back here now?"

He told her the truth. "I came to confer with Constable McBride. And to speak to Mrs. Percy. Although she appears to have withdrawn her remarks about a monster. She now claims she saw nothing at all."

"Yes, well, who can blame her?" Finally satisfied, Priscilla Bartram relented and invited him to join her in the kitchen. "I was just about to put the kettle on."

Rutledge followed her and sat down where he'd had his dinner the night of the fog. It had been a very different evening. Now the sun came through the windowpanes in golden shafts of light that fell across the well-polished floor, and the door to the yard was standing open. The light breeze carried in a sweet scent from the cut-flower garden just outside.

"Well now. Scotland Yard. My heavens. I never thought I'd be speaking to Scotland Yard," Miss Bartram went on, the kettle filled and beginning to boil, the tea things set out.

"I remember looking at the waterfowl in the glass cabinets. Which reminded me of the reason this inn is here. Was there any hunting with a rifle?"

"My grandfather and his father owned a flat-bottomed boat, with a screen made of reeds raised above the bow. The hurdle maker made a new one each season. There was a duck gun hidden in it, only the barrel visible. A great noisy thing. One shot from that could bring down a dozen or more birds, and their dogs were hard-pressed to bring them in. But that was for market, you understand. In my father's day, he'd take out guests in his boat and they'd wait for the birds to come in of an evening. A shotgun was all they required. There was nothing in the Fens of a size to warrant a rifle."

"Perhaps someone used to do a little deer stalking in Scotland? Or shooting in Africa? Bringing his gun along to show the other guests."

She smiled as she turned to the teakettle. "None of our guests had such lofty ambitions. They were shooting for pleasure and for the table. Mostly they'd come up from the south. London, some of them, and the Home Counties. One man was writing a book on migrating waterfowl. He drew the birds he brought back, then used watercolors to fill in the outlines. Quite lovely, the drawings were. Very clever. He'd pin the birds up into position against a painted backdrop, then start to work. Every feather in its proper place. When he'd finished with them, his wife plucked and cooked them."

Not a very fitting end for the man's models, Rutledge found himself thinking.

"How well did you know Mr. Swift?"

She went to the pantry and brought back slices of meat and bread, and the chutney he'd liked before. "Of course I never had any need of his advice. My father's solicitor was in Burwell. Still, I'd met him here and there, but more a nodding acquaintance than *knowing* him. When he returned from Scotland and reopened his law business after the war, he kept to himself."

"What was his background? Was his father a solicitor as well?"

"His father was a farmer, and he married more acres. There was money enough to send the two sons to university, but Swift chose the law, while his brother wanted the farm. They had words when the father died over what to do with the land. Swift wanted his share of the inheritance."

"Trouble?" He took the sandwich she'd made up, and realized how hungry he was.

"In fact they came to an amicable agreement. I'll tell you where there might be jealousy, though. There was a third boy. Wild oats, before the elder Mr. Swift was married. Still, he acknowledged the lad, paid for his education and the like, but he wasn't legitimate and there was nothing for him in the will. He was apprenticed to Ned Miles. The barber. And the day the father died, Anson left Wriston and has never came back."

"Was he in the war? This Anson Swift?"

"If he was, nobody knew of it. He didn't join with the local men, if that's what you mean."

She brought the pot to the table and poured Rutledge's cup.

He thanked her and then said, "No one seems to think that the Swifts were acquainted with the first victim, Captain Hutchinson."

"Well, you never know," she said, considering it. "Stranger things have happened. But on the whole, I'd say it's not likely. Did you know that the Captain was here in the Fen country some months ago?"

Rutledge nearly choked on his tea. "What? Are you sure?"

"Well, not in Wriston, of course. But he came to a funeral in Burwell. The only reason I know of it is that later I recognized his photograph in the Ely newspaper."

"Tell me."

"I went to the service myself. The dead man, Major Clayton, was from Burwell, although he lived in London. His father was a military man before him, but their roots were here in Cambridgeshire. My father had known the family, you see, and I felt I ought to go. At any rate, there was a Colonel to give the eulogy and this Captain Hutchinson came north with him."

"Have you told Constable McBride about this? Or Inspector Warren?"

"I thought surely they must already know."

But Inspector Warren had been concentrating on Ely, and by extension, on Wriston. He'd said nothing about Burwell.

Rutledge sat there, trying to think. Was this the only time that Hutchinson had come north, before the wedding? Or had he had connections here that no one knew about?

Hamish, stirring in the back of Rutledge's mind, said, "Ye ken, it changes everything."

It bloody well did.

"Was anyone else from Wriston at Major Clayton's funeral?"

Priscilla Bartram frowned. "I don't believe so. No, I don't remember seeing anyone I knew from Wriston. But that's not surprising. I told you, Major Clayton lived in London. I never met him myself."

The question now was, why hadn't the murderer taken that opportunity, if he'd been intent on killing Hutchinson? Why wait for the far more public venue of Ely Cathedral and the wedding?

And the answer, Rutledge thought, was that Ely offered the killer a better chance of escape.

"Did Captain Hutchinson travel to Burwell with anyone in particular?"

"I have no idea. When I saw him, he was generally with the Colonel or the Major's sister. There was no reason to pay particular attention to him, it was just that he was a rather handsome man, and you tend to notice such people."

What had Mrs. Sedley told him? That the Captain had managed to find himself in the company of the prominent guests more often than was usual? A man who courted the wealthy or the powerful . . .

It was the first break he'd had. And he was going to make the most of it.

"What sort of man was Hutchinson?" he asked Miss Bartram.

"Well, of course I didn't speak to him. I was just one of the mourners. But he was very pleasant to everyone. It seemed to me that the Major's sister was grateful for his support when we went to the graveside. But then he left with the Colonel after the luncheon, while Miss Clayton was staying over with friends, unable to face the journey south that same day. At least that's what I heard someone say. I really didn't know anyone there, you see. I expect that's why I noticed what was happening."

Which must have been unpleasant for Miss Bartram, but very useful for the police.

Rutledge asked, "Was Herbert Swift at that same funeral?"

"I don't believe he was. I never saw him if he was there."

"How did you learn about the funeral in the first place?"

"There was an obituary notice in the Ely newspaper."

Rutledge finished his tea and thanked her. She reminded him to leave his valise in the sitting room, and he saw to that before going out.

Ten minutes later, he was back at his motorcar and reversing to drive to Burwell.

It was necessary to pass Wriston Mill on his way, and at that moment Miss Trowbridge was opening her gate and stepping out into the road.

She was surprised to see him again and stopped by the gate.

Rutledge slowed. "Thank you for rescuing me. I spent a comfortable night at Miss Bartram's inn," he said, smiling.

"I thought your business was in Ely. Are you returning to Cambridge, or have you misplaced the road again?"

He was amused, but there was another side of the coin that had to be addressed, and laughter was not the best way to handle it. "Neither, as it happens. I'm afraid my business in Ely is only a part of what I'm here to see to. Miss Trowbridge, I'm an Inspector, Scotland Yard, here to investigate the murders of Captain Hutchinson and Mr. Swift."

Her expression had been friendly, surprised, and a little pleased to see him again. But at his words it changed. "Indeed," she said coldly.

"I have fences to mend," he replied wryly. "But the fact is, I hadn't reported to Inspector Warren in Ely. I was still—en route."

"Are you not still an Inspector, 'en route'?"

"Yes. In truth. But it's not always pleasant to be reminded of duty."

She had nothing to say to that.

"You and I didn't discuss the murders. It was not official, that encounter."

"Indeed," she said again. "I shall remember that when we meet again."

There was nothing for it but to touch the brim of his hat in acknowledgment and drive on.

It was a straight run across the built-up embankment that comprised the narrow road to Burwell. He could see trees in the distance, and the church tower reaching above their green tops long before he could pick out the village itself.

Larger than Wriston, and more of a town than a line of cottages strung along a ridge, Burwell was still a village. Trees shaded the streets and filled the churchyard, unlike Wriston, which had perhaps only a dozen trees to its name, and those mostly by the church on the far side of the second green.

He found the church of St. Mary's easily enough, and began to look for the Rectory. But when he knocked at the door, he was told by the middle-aged housekeeper that Rector was in the church. There had been a death to register.

Rutledge went back to St. Mary's. There he found Mr. Hurley just coming out the west door.

Greeting the Rector, Rutledge introduced himself.

"Scotland Yard?" Hurley peered over his glasses. "Is anything amiss? What brings you here?"

"Is there somewhere we could speak privately?"

"Yes, of course, my study." They turned to walk toward the Rectory, and Hurley went on mildly, "You make this sound very mysterious."

"Not intentionally. No. I'm looking into a death. I'm told that you conducted a funeral some time in the summer for a Major Clayton."

"Ah. Yes, I remember that one well. A number of the men who'd served under him came. They spoke highly of him."

"Why did he choose to come back to Cambridgeshire to be buried?"

"He'd wanted to rest next to his parents, even though he hadn't lived in Burwell for some time. When he made the request several weeks before the end, he wrote that his only ties in London were military. His sister lives there, at least for the moment. But she's engaged, and when she marries she'll be living in Norfolk. I expect he thought she might find it easier to visit his grave from time to time if he was laid to rest here." They had reached the Rectory steps. Hurley turned to look up at

Rutledge. "Does this have to do with the Major? Is that why you're here?"

"No. Not at all. But there were several guests from London, I believe. Not including the men who'd served under him or who knew his sister. Do you remember a Captain Hutchinson?"

"Yes, indeed, he arrived with Colonel Nelson, who was to speak at the service. And quite a nice eulogy it was, I must say. I gathered he'd known the Major personally."

They went inside, stepping into the dimly lit hall after the bright sunlight outside. Hurley led the way to his study, down a passage from the door, and gestured to the chairs arranged around his desk.

"Please. Hutchinson is the man whose death you're investigating? Yes, I should have realized. A terrible tragedy, that and Herbert Swift's murder. I hope you find whoever is responsible," Hurley continued as he took his own chair behind the desk.

"Do you know if the Captain had visited Burwell before the funeral?"

"I don't believe so. He asked me about the terrible fire we'd had here some years ago. It too was a tragedy, one most of us would rather forget, as it killed a great many people, all of them family members or friends. No one was spared grief. And of course he was curious about the Fens. Most people are. The Colonel was asking when steam had replaced the windmills."

"What was your impression of the Captain?"

"I can't say I formed one. There were half a hundred people here. I managed to speak to most of them, but there wasn't time for more than the niceties and words of sympathy. I was concerned for Miss Clayton. She was in some distress. But I did suggest that the Colonel speak to Mr. Harvey, who loves nothing better than to discuss our windmills." He hesitated. "I will add this. The Captain was a pleasant man, and he had a knack for putting people at their ease. Once or twice I had the oddest impression that it was an—an act. Wrong of me to speak ill of the dead, but I must be frank with the police. I'm sure I was quite wrong in my judgment."

Rutledge understood what Hurley was getting at. That while the pleasantness, the openness were accepted at face value by most people on casual acquaintance, it did not come naturally to Hutchinson.

"He wasna' born with a silver spoon," Hamish said quietly in the back of Rutledge's mind. "He had to make his ain way."

And yet Jason Fallowfield had suggested that Hutchinson's father had left him in comfortable circumstances. Was it that Hutchinson had had to learn early in life that to succeed, he must cultivate his bet-ters? And leave the impression he'd come from money? That would have allowed him to move more freely in some circles.

Hutchinson wouldn't be the first man to learn such a lesson. Not quite ingratiating, not a hanger-on, but making every effort to be likable, accepted. Even when it went against his own nature.

It would be interesting now to hear what Sergeant Gibson had to tell him about Hutchinson's past. Rutledge made a note to find a telephone as soon as possible.

Hurley could add very little more to what he'd already said about Hutchinson. Shrugging, he smiled wryly. "I never dreamed—none of us did—that it would matter months down the road. Or that the man would be dead before the summer was out."

"Still, no one thought to tell Inspector Warren about this visit?"

Surprised, Hurley said, "But nothing happened here. It didn't seem to be important. After all, it was an Ely matter."

The old way of life, of isolation from one village to the next, here in the Fen country, where water had separated everyone and made foreigners of people ten miles distant. Even draining the land had pitted the old

villages making their living from the marshy waterways against the new ones springing up to tend the vast
fields and keep the land dry.

As if he'd heard what Rutledge was thinking, Hurley
said, "My great-grandfather hated the changes to this
part of Cambridgeshire. He told his children that nothing good would come of it, that the land would feed a
few generations and then be worn out. He was wrong,
of course, but there was nothing to show at the time
that he wouldn't be proven right."

Rutledge said, "Did you notice any other strangers
at the service?"

"One or two. A Miss Bartram spoke to me. Her
father and Clayton's father had known each other years
ago. It was kind of her, and Miss Clayton remembered
Miss Bartram's grandfather as well. He had brought
a doctor from Ely when the elder Clayton had appen-
dicitis. Then there were the people up from London,
strangers to me, but they all seemed to know each
other from the Army or they were friends of Miss
Clayton's, here to support her through her ordeal. I
don't recall anything that was said or done that would
give even a hint of what was to come. More to the
point, Captain Hutchinson was here for only a matter
of hours. What harm could be done in such a short
period of time?"

Rutledge asked the name of the family with whom Miss Clayton had stayed while in Burwell, and he found Mrs. FitzPatrick at home. She agreed to see him—more, he thought, out of curiosity than to impart any information—and the young maid showed him to a sunny room where Mrs. FitzPatrick had been writing letters.

She was a small woman, perhaps thirty-five, with fair hair and brown eyes. Greeting him, she said, "I can't think why Scotland Yard should wish to see my husband or me, but of course we'll be happy to help in any way we can."

"The Rector gave me your name. I'm looking into the funeral service for Major Clayton, and he tells me that Miss Clayton, the dead man's sister, stayed with you while she was here in Burwell?"

Frowning, she said, "Yes, of course, but is anything amiss with the service? I can't think what it could be."

"There was an Army officer who came up from London with Colonel Nelson. A Captain Hutchinson. Do you remember him?"

"Yes, of course," she said again, "he'd served with Major Clayton, he said, and he was very kind to Vera—Miss Clayton—on the journey up from London." Then the frown deepened. "Are you telling me—is this the man who was shot in Ely a fortnight or so ago? I couldn't imagine it was. My husband agreed that Hutchinson wasn't an unusual name. I went to school with a Gracie Hutchinson in Kent."

"I'm afraid it was the same man."

"Oh, dear. I'm quite shocked. But are you investigating that—that murder?"

"I've been sent here by the Yard to look into the Captain's death as well as Mr. Swift's," he said.

"Mr. Swift. We knew *him*, you see. Socially. I was never so shocked as when I heard of *his* death. Who on earth would wish to do him any harm? He was encouraged to stand for the vacant seat, but I don't think he was very enthusiastic about it. Still, he had a sense of history, and he thought perhaps he might do some good. My husband felt that Herbert—Mr. Swift—found himself surrounded by too many memories when he came back to Wriston after the war, and that that had played a part in deciding to stand. He'd never really recovered from the death of his wife."

"Did he have enemies? Either personal or through his work?" When she looked confused, Rutledge added, "Not everyone is happy when a will is read."

"Yes, but you don't blame the solicitor, do you? And he wasn't the sort of man to attract trouble, if you know what I mean. Even his opponent had little to say against him. He was a good man."

"And Captain Hutchinson?"

"He was considerate, charming—very solicitous for Miss Clayton's welfare. It was very hard for her, you know. Her brother had been in hospital since before the end of the war. In December 1918 gangrene set in, and although they took the foot, it moved slowly upward. The stump never healed properly, according to Vera. In the end, they went up to the knee, and then almost to the hip. After that, it was only a matter of time. He couldn't leave hospital, but she visited him nearly every day. I'm very pleased that she's marrying soon. It will be good for her to put the past away."

"Was her fiancé here for the service?"

"No, he's been in Canada. His grandfather died just before Major Clayton. But he's expected back any day now."

"What was your impression of Captain Hutchinson?"

"My husband didn't care for him. He thought the Captain was paying too much attention to Vera. He was a widower, after all. But of course, without her fiancé, she was alone through this ordeal. Friends were with her, yes, but I think because the Captain had known her brother, it was a comfort to her. The Colonel was an older man, while the Captain was more her brother's age. And of course he didn't stay—he went back to London that evening, which was quite proper."

"Where did he serve with Clayton?"

The frown returned. "To tell you the truth, I was never really clear about that. It was just—accepted. I did hear the Captain say that one felt the need to support the family of a fellow officer. 'I would hope someone would do as much for my sister.' Those were his words. I thought them very respectful."

"Did Miss Clayton indicate how long she'd known the Captain? Did he come often to visit her brother in hospital?"

"That was months ago. I've hardly given the man any thought since then. I did ask Vera if she had met him during her visits to her brother, but apparently he came most often at night, because he was busy during the day with his duties."

Mrs. FitzPatrick approved of the Captain. Her husband hadn't. But he, according to his wife, was presently out in the fields having a look at one of the ditches, and he wasn't expected home before dinner at the earliest.

"Sometimes voles burrow into the earthworks that protect the fields. It's very trying, because they can do so much damage. He took Bob with him—the terrier—in the event that was the problem. But I don't think my husband can add much more. We spent only a matter of hours in the Captain's company, after all."

Rutledge thanked Mrs. FitzPatrick and took his leave. Walking through the town for a time, he listened to Hamish in the back of his mind, but it was the Rector's words that seemed to follow him.

What harm could be done in such a short period of time?

There had been no quarrels, there had been no unsettling remarks that would lead to murder months later, Hutchinson had stepped on no toes, and perhaps more important he hadn't encountered an old friend or an old enemy here in Burwell. He had simply escorted a grieving sister of a fellow officer to her brother's funeral, and then left, his duty done.

Perhaps it was the Colonel whose company Hutchinson had really sought, and escorting Vera Clayton had been a way of putting himself in the presence of the Colonel and made it possible for him to travel back to London on the same train.

Mrs. Sedley had indicated that Hutchinson had been busy cultivating the bride's relatives during the events before the wedding. And yet neither in Ely or here in Burwell had the man put anyone's back up. He seemed to know just how far to go in his push for attention, surely indicating he'd had a great deal of experience over the years.

That brought him back to Hamish's comment.

It was time to speak to Sergeant Gibson, at the Yard.

Rutledge inquired of a passerby if there was a telephone in Burwell that he could use to put in a call to London, but there was no public telephone, and he hesitated to carry on a conversation about Hutchinson or Swift within hearing of interested ears in a private household like the FitzPatricks.

In the end, he walked again to the church and then went inside. He tried to picture the funeral in his imagination, searching for anything that might help him explain Ely and then Wriston. But that led nowhere. As far as Rutledge could judge, it was nothing more than happenstance that Hutchinson had come to Burwell some months before he traveled to Ely.

He drove back to Wriston in the late afternoon, watching the shadows shift across the long lines of green fields. He stopped halfway there, got out of the motorcar, and walked along the road for some distance. It was a strange land, if you were used to the rolling countryside of Somerset or the Downs of Kent. And yet very different from the marshy coast of Norfolk or the long stretches of reeds and tidal rivers along the Essex coast. No one in sight for miles. Just the heat of the sun, the smell of the damp, rich earth, and a sense of isolation that was in its way claustrophobic.

No trees, no grazing horses or cattle, no sheep, no birds hopping along the rows in the fields, not even the distant sound of a dog barking.

Just—emptiness.

Rutledge was nearly to Wriston when he met someone coming the other way. An elderly man on a bicycle, a knife and scissor sharpener, pedaling slowly home after a day of making his rounds.

Chapter 8

Rutledge had nearly reached Wriston when he saw a signpost on a rutted lane that led in an irregular fashion to a farmhouse in the distance. He'd passed it on his way to Burwell but had missed the significance of the small bird painted on the sign.

A swift . . . Swift?

On impulse he turned down the lane, disregarding the warning from Hamish that he would rue his decision. But before very long he had to abandon the motorcar where it was and continue on foot when the lane dwindled to little more than a track. How anything but a horse, he thought, could manage this, he didn't know.

Ahead he could see the farmhouse. Like so many others here, it was built on one of the tiny bits of dry earth rising like islands in the peaty marshes of the Fens. It had been rebuilt at some point, possibly around 1900, Rutledge thought, for now it was two stories, brick and substantial.

This track led not to the door of the house but to the farmyard, where farm equipment and a pony cart, a small carriage and a stable, were fitted into the space like a puzzle, using every inch of high ground. To one side was a small kitchen garden, cut out of the surrounding fields and protected by banks. One of the rows held flowers for cutting—zinnias, marigolds, stalks of what must have been foxglove.

Walking around the house he could hear voices in the kitchen, but he proceeded to the front door, smiling when he saw the newer lane that led up to it. He had come in the back way, probably the original approach.

He knocked, and after a moment a woman in an apron came to ask his business.

"I'm looking for Mr. Swift. Brother to the man who was killed in Wriston."

She stared at him, uncertain what to do.

"I'm from Scotland Yard, I've taken over the inquiry into what happened to Mr. Swift and Captain Hutchinson."

Her frown disappeared in an uncertain smile.

"Do you have anything to prove who you are?"

Rutledge took out his identification, and she looked at it carefully.

"I'm sorry," she said when he had put it back in his pocket. "But we've been worried, you see. We saw you coming down the track, and we didn't know . . ."

He understood her alarm. Nodding, he said, "I didn't know there were two ways into the property. I'm sorry if I disturbed you."

She led him to the sunny kitchen where her husband was standing, clearly listening to what had transpired at the door. Rutledge saw that there was a shotgun leaning against the wall behind him.

"Mr. Swift? I'm from Scotland Yard. My name is Rutledge. As you may have heard, I'm here to look into the death of your brother."

"I'm Swift," the man said, his accent definitely Fen country, his face browned by the sun, and his hands rough from working the land. His hair was rather long and bleached almost to whiteness, it was so fair, and thinning. Rutledge thought he must be older than his wife by several years. But that might also have been put down to the life he led. "I'll trouble you for that identification, if you don't mind."

He studied it as his wife had done, then passed it back to Rutledge.

"Sit down, then," he said, nodding to the chair nearest Rutledge. "The two men who work for me are in the fields today. I didn't see a weapon, but then I don't think my brother did either."

"Were you in Wriston that night?"

"No, I wasn't, thank God. Summer work on the land goes on to dark, and then you're up at four to start again. I don't see Wriston from week to week."

"I understand your brother chose the law and you chose the farm."

"There was some trouble over that in the beginning. He wanted his share of the land to pay for setting up his chambers. But we settled it to suit us, in the end. If you're asking if I still carried a grudge, the answer is no. I expect I've done better than he did. In many ways." He glanced at his wife.

"You work harder for your living than he did."

"If I'd shot him twelve times over, what good was his law to me?"

"Surely you inherit?"

"After burying him, there's the wait for the will to be settled. And then I'll have to find someone to buy the house where he had his chambers. I'll see nothing for a while. Besides, if there was a bad year on the land, I could borrow from him. I always paid it back, and he knew I would. So he helped when I asked. That's finished. And I don't think his death will bring me any new way of finding the money."

"I should think the farm pays well."

"It does. But it's not selling the crops that matters. It's the buying of the seed and sowing and waiting to learn what sort of spring we're to have, then seeing that the crop is watered enough and not too much, looking out for it in the storms and watching for breaks in the banks that guard the ditches. We have ten milk cows on another part of the farm, it came with my wife, and we have a man to take care of them. I make a living, a good one in good years. I also pay the wages of the men who work for me."

Rutledge couldn't decide whether the man was listing his troubles to impress Scotland Yard with his very different life from his brother's or to prove he had no reason to kill him. And Hamish was silent on the subject.

"Did your brother have enemies?"

"I doubt it. He wasn't the sort of man who would make trouble or look for it."

"He was a widower, I understand."

"Yes. He worked in Glasgow for the Admiralty during the war, couldn't stand to be alone in that empty house. He studied charts, checked them for accuracy, that sort of thing. He was a civilian, all the same, and perhaps that's why he came back calmer than he'd been when he left. I think he stayed too busy to think. It was what he needed."

"His wife died in childbirth? With the child?"

"Yes. A fever took her, and the child didn't thrive. I thought he'd run mad with grief. He shut himself up in the house and wouldn't see anyone or talk to anyone. He gave Susan good references and told her he didn't need her anymore. It took Ruth, here, three days to put my brother's house to rights after he'd left for Scotland. You'd have thought it had been lived in by Travelers. We were glad he came to his senses and found a new housekeeper to keep him in good order up there."

"Who is Susan?"

"She works at the Rectory now. A good woman, steady and dependable. Rector says she's a blessing. But she nursed my brother's wife during those last months before the child was born. Eileen should never have got pregnant in the first place, and it was trouble from the start. The doctor told my wife he didn't think it would end well. And it didn't. But they were over the moon with joy about the child, it was what they both wanted. Or thought they did. I wondered sometimes if he regretted it when she died. If he blamed himself."

Rutledge remembered what Jason Fallowfield had told him about Hutchinson's wife, that there had been whispers of suicide when she lost her child. The hazards of childbearing were many, from complications to fevers to stillbirths. That grief Swift and Hutchinson had shared.

"Did your brother often go to London? On behalf of a client, perhaps? Or for a holiday with his wife?"

Swift laughed. "I doubt he'd been farther south than Cambridge, where he read law. He dreamed of Greece and Rome but never strayed far from the Fens until he went to Glasgow."

"So everyone says. But he might have gone farther, without telling you."

"There's that. But I'd not like to take a wager on it."

"There's no reason you can think of for your brother to be killed?"

"None. And it's what keeps me anxious."

"But if he had no connection to the Captain who was killed at Ely, why did his murder follow hard upon the first death? And why should yours follow hard upon your brother's?"

"The only man who can answer that shot them both. If I had to answer to God tomorrow, I can tell you I had nothing to do with it."

"Were you in the war?"

"Six months in 1915. I lost three toes to frostbite and was invalided out."

"Did you bring a rifle back with you as a souvenir?"

He laughed without humor. "I spent two of those months in hospital. How was I to bring home my rifle? They took it from me when I was carried by stretcher to the aid station."

Rutledge believed him. He'd seen the alarm in Mrs. Swift's eyes and the wariness in her husband's when he'd arrived unannounced. Born of fear, not guilt.

"I understand there was a third brother. Anson."

"He left Wriston as soon as my father died and the will was read. There's been no word of him or from him since then. And if it was Anson, why would he shoot that Captain? It would make more sense to come for the two of us."

Rutledge thanked them and left. It was one hell of a struggle to turn the motorcar and retrace his steps to the main road.

So much, he thought, for exploring out here on his own.

Wriston was not on the telephone, Rutledge was told when he arrived at the inn and went up to his room to wash his hands. It would be necessary to travel to Ely to find one.

He thanked Miss Bartram and avoided a question about how he'd spent his day.

He wasn't ready to talk about Hutchinson and Burwell, although he knew very well that Priscilla Bartram was eager to hear more. She would have no trouble guessing where he'd gone. He could pass it off lightly, and make no mention of his visit to the Swifts.

And so when he came down later to join her for dinner, he was prepared.

She had roasted a hen, and with it there were potatoes and a dish of stewed apples. Serving him, she asked, "Did you find your way to Burwell, then?"

"Larger than Wriston, isn't it? Interesting church, as well. But a wasted journey, all the same."

Miss Bartram had clearly hoped her information would prove to be more useful.

"Did you speak to the Rector there?"

"I did, and he recalled meeting you. Apparently Vera Clayton, the sister of the dead man, remembered your grandfather."

She smiled, pleased. "Yes, I did tell her of the connection. I wasn't sure she was old enough to have any memories of her own grandfather. He was interested in collecting stories about the old days in the Fens. There's a family that claims descent from Hereward the Wake, who fought the Normans when they tried to bully their way north. Did you know? They called him an outlaw. He interviewed the family to see if they could tell him more about Hereward, if there were family documents or legends or the like. Hereward's something of a hero to Fen people. And there's no proof he was executed or exiled. Perhaps he made his peace with the Normans in the end."

Rutledge encouraged her to tell him more about the elder Clayton, and she was soon confiding in him that the inn had once been the home of one of the Dutch engineers who had drained the land and set up the first windmills.

"The village is named for him. Wriston. Although of course that wasn't his name, it was as close as anyone could come to it."

The conversation moved on to the fishing that was once a popular sport in the Fens, and he wondered if somewhere in this house there might be displays of pike and roach and bream, with whatever else her father or grandfather had caught.

It was still early, and he decided after his dinner to drive back to Ely to find a telephone. He reached the Yard without difficulty but was told that Sergeant Gibson wasn't there. The gruff Inspector who had answered the call added that Gibson was away on official business and there was no certainty when he'd be back.

Rutledge hadn't given his name, he'd simply asked for Gibson. He was glad afterward that he'd been circumspect.

It was late when he reached Wriston. It would have made better sense to stop at The Deacon Inn. But his valise was at The Dutchman, and he knew Miss Bartram would be watching for him, for he had given her the impression he intended to return.

He left the motorcar in front of the inn and decided to stretch his legs. There was no mist tonight—the wind had picked up a little and small clouds were scudding across the sky, promising a change in the fair weather.

Turning in the direction of the mill, away from the village greens, he saw the ghostly shape of a white cat walking toward him down the road.

Kneeling, he called to her by name, and she came trotting to him, wrapping herself around him. But when he tried to lift her, to carry her back to the house, she turned and scampered away.

He followed her, and after a moment or two, he saw Miss Trowbridge, not at her gate or even in her doorway as he'd have expected, but standing in front of the mill, looking up at the arms moving above her head, the creak of their wooden parts almost soothing in its regularity. Like a rocking cradle, he thought, for no reason at all.

Afraid of startling her, he called, "I was out for a walk and encountered Clarissa."

Miss Trowbridge turned quickly, as if he'd interrupted something he shouldn't have seen.

"Mr.—Rutledge." She was pretending to have difficulty recalling his name, but he knew very well she remembered it.

"Looking up at the stars? When I was in France, on clear nights I watched for Orion as we moved toward autumn. He was familiar. Comfortable."

"Yes. The hunter."

He realized that she was referring to him obliquely.

And then she surprised him. "I was just going to put on the kettle. Would you care for a cup of tea before you go back?"

He thought she assumed he was staying in Ely. He answered only, "Yes, I'd like that. If it isn't too late."

She said nothing, just walked to the gate, opened it, and preceded him up the path. The cat was there, a white streak in the darkness, leaping through the door almost before there was room for her to pass.

When he entered the cottage, Clarissa had already claimed her chair, as if to warn him off.

He followed Miss Trowbridge to the kitchen, as he had before, and watched as she put the kettle on.

Hamish, in the back of his mind, was asking why this young woman had invited him into her home at such an hour—it must be going on ten o'clock. But the answer could be that she had no near neighbors to gossip.

Did she also want to know how the inquiry was going?

That suspicion brought with it the question: was it curiosity or was there some other motive?

Not that he suspected her of firing the shots. But was she fearful that she might know who had? Or thought she might know?

She turned, reaching for the cups and saucers in the dresser, carrying them to the table.

"Do sit down," she said, as if his standing there made her nervous. "Or we could carry our cups into the front room."

"I would feel awkward sitting there, carrying on a one-sided conversation with Clarissa," he said lightly, and that brought a smile.

"For heaven's sake, you sat in the kitchen before."

"I did." He pulled out a chair. "I'm staying at Miss Bartram's again. There's not much I can learn in Ely—" He broke off as she almost dropped the bowl of sugar.

Flushing a little, she set it down on the table and disappeared into the pantry for the jug of milk.

"Why is Ely a—a dead end?"

"Too many people, Miss Trowbridge. They witnessed the—er—murder, but they saw nothing useful. Looking in the wrong direction at the moment the shot was fired. Inspector Warren has interviewed most of them, I've interviewed a handful myself, and we've got almost nothing to be going on with. But here in Wriston, someone saw the killer."

"Mrs. Percy," she said flatly, setting the small jug next to the bowl of sugar. "But what did she see?"

He was intrigued. When he'd first met her, the night of the fog, she had avoided any mention of the murder here in Wriston. Now she appeared to want to talk about it.

"That's the question."

"No, I mean, she saw something, a monster. I've heard the gossip. But of course there's no monster running about with a rifle in his hands. What did she really see?"

"I wish I knew."

The kettle came to a boil. She went to it, her back to him again, and began to make the tea. He wondered if Miss Trowbridge had been waiting for him, the kettle filled and ready to set on the heavy black range in her kitchen. But she couldn't have known he would walk that way.

Was it someone else she'd expected? He remembered the man in the mist. Where had he been going? Or coming from?

"It makes no sense anyway," Miss Trowbridge was saying as she brought the teapot to the table. "Killing Mr. Swift, much less that man in Ely."

"Did you know Swift?"

"Everyone *knew* him. He was the solicitor. But I don't suppose anyone really knew him well. He'd been away, for one thing, and he wasn't a gregarious sort. I think he had grown used to his own company and his books."

"Did he handle your grandmother's will? Leaving you this cottage?"

"No, that was a man in Bury. She lived here in the cottage, of course, but she was a very private woman and she felt that her business was her business."

"What do you think was in that dormer window?" he asked.

It caught her off guard. They had left that question behind.

"I don't know. Someone who wished for a better view of the speech? Everyone leaves his door unlocked—or did. Someone could have gone up to that dormer window and looked out."

"Were you there, that evening?"

She took a sip of her tea after stirring in the sugar. "No. I really had no interest in the by-election or hearing Mr. Swift speak."

"But you'd have voted?"

"Yes, of course, one does."

"Then you'd already decided which candidate you supported?"

"I'd already decided which man would represent us best in London."

A very different way of putting it.

"If the shot didn't come from that dormer window, where was the killer?"

"I know nothing about firearms. I expect Constable McBride and the other men present that evening would have a better idea about the direction." She was toying with her teaspoon. "But does direction really matter? Wherever he fired from, Mr. Swift's murderer got away."

"The problem is, we have so little to go on. Anything Mrs. Percy tells us could be useful in tracking him down."

Miss Trowbridge rose, collecting their cups. "I'm afraid I'm no use at all."

"It depends. On whether anyone passed your door directly after the shot was fired. It isn't that far from this house to the market cross. You'd have heard the report, surely, and wondered what it was. You know a few people still come here in autumn and winter to hunt. But this isn't the season for shooting. Did you go to your door and listen to see what was happening? Or stay here, the door shut tight, because you were afraid to know?"

Color flared in her face. "What are you accusing me of? I will tell you straight out that I had no reason to want anyone dead."

"But you did hear the shot?" Rutledge persisted. "I can't believe you didn't."

She was standing there with their cups and saucers in her hands. "Yes, all right, I heard the shot. Clarissa was in and safe. I didn't want to go rushing out to see what it was."

"Still, you heard someone pass your door. Who was it?" His voice was cold now.

"I was here in the kitchen, putting away the dishes from my dinner. You can't hear someone passing, unless he's on horseback or in a motorcar. And not always then." She crossed to the sink to set down the cups. "I think you should go now. I shouldn't have suggested tea in the first place. But you were a stranger here, and I know what loneliness is."

Turning her back to him, she stared out the windows that overlooked her small back garden.

And so he left, walking briskly to the door and closing it behind him.

Chapter 9

When Rutledge reached Miss Bartram's house, she was waiting for him, calling his name as he came through the door.

"Mr. Rutledge? I thought perhaps you'd like a cup of tea after your long drive from Ely. Or perhaps a small whisky. We always kept a little here for the hunters, coming in cold and wet of an evening."

"Thank you, Miss Bartram, but I have a long day tomorrow and I think I'll go directly up."

"Yes, of course," she said, disappointment in her voice. And then, as if she couldn't stop the words, she said, "I noticed half an hour ago that your motorcar had returned." Unspoken was the follow-up: *Where have you been?*

"I was tired, and I thought if I walked for a bit, I'd be ready to sleep."

"Oh. Then I'll bid you good night. Breakfast at seven-thirty?"

"Yes, thank you very much." With a smile, he turned and went up the stairs.

The next morning he paid an early visit to the police station and found Constable McBride just opening the door.

"You're still here, Mr. Rutledge," he said as Rutledge walked up.

"I've a question about the night that Swift was killed. You've told me that most of the village was present. What about those who weren't, someone living on the outskirts of Wriston. Did anyone there notice someone leaving the village while most people were rushing to see what could be done for Mr. Swift? Did they hear a motorcar passing, or a horse?"

"No one saw or heard anything unusual. Or if they did, they aren't speaking up."

"But surely the sound of the shot reached every house in Wriston. Did no one hurry to a window or a door to see what the matter was?"

"The only way the killer could have gone was toward the mill. He'd have been seen if he'd chosen to go past the church instead. It's too open. We did question everyone in Wriston. Those present for the speech, and those who stayed at home."

"Even the person who lives out by the mill? The cottage with the gate?"

"Miss Trowbridge? She couldn't help us. No one came that way as far as she could tell."

"The killer couldn't have vanished. Or had he disappeared across those fields?" Rutledge asked impatiently.

"If he knew what he was doing, he could follow the narrow path along the top of the hummock that separates the edge of Wriston from the fields."

Rutledge had seen such a mound at the end of the lane beyond Mrs. Percy's house.

"You're saying that a stranger couldn't depend on the path taking him to safety."

"I should think if he came here to shoot Mr. Swift, he would have reconnoitered an escape route. He must have done, to decide he could use that dormer."

"And yet no one saw a stranger walking about, looking out for such places."

"He could have done six months ago. No one would remember him now."

Or he could have come at night, Hamish suggested. When he could be sure he wasn't seen . . .

"What about Anson Swift? He wouldn't need to explore. He knew Wriston well enough."

"How did you hear about Anson?"

"The question is, what became of him?"

"He left here and never came back, to my knowledge. I did hear a rumor that he went to Australia. I expect it was just that. A rumor. And if it was Anson, why would he kill the Captain in Ely? Just to frighten his brothers?"

Rutledge could sense how defensive McBride was. The man had done everything he could—everything he could think of doing, and here the stranger from London was questioning him as if he had somehow failed in his duty.

"I was hoping we'd missed something, that's all." Rutledge smiled. "This killer manages to appear and disappear like a magician. I thought perhaps he'd disguised himself as a priest in Ely, where he wouldn't be noticed coming in and out of the Cathedral grounds. The question is, what disguise would work here?"

"That seems to point to someone local," McBride said, not at all mollified.

"It could. But more likely it's someone whose presence wouldn't draw comment. Take myself, for instance. Scotland Yard, every right to be here asking questions. No one would take issue if I went into the church or called on the constable or sat by the duck pond to eat my lunch."

"We've had no weddings this past six months. Only one funeral. Three christenings. Are you saying that someone came here to look around Wriston and find out what he needed, all the while pretending to be a mourner at the funeral or one of the family at the christening?"

"I know, it's far-fetched. On the other hand, if I were a quarter of an hour early for something like a christening, I could wander freely around Wriston, passing the time, and no one would look at me twice—or remember me after I'd gone."

"Six months ago no one knew Mr. Swift would be standing for Parliament or for that matter, that Captain Hutchinson would be attending a wedding in Ely."

McBride was taking his suggestion literally. Rutledge let it go for the moment.

"Well, it was worth pursuing. Anything might trigger a memory that could help us."

McBride nodded. "I haven't had to deal with murder these past five years. And then it was straightforward. A drunken brawl that ended in a killing. I don't like the feeling that we're vulnerable. I don't like to think of someone planning murder on my patch and then getting away with it."

"No, I'm sure you don't. Inspector Warren feels the same."

"I'd say the connection starts in London, not here. Only Mr. Swift hadn't been to London. He hadn't been elected."

"If it wasn't London, it was somewhere else. The problem now is to find out just where the paths of these two men crossed that of their murderer."

Rutledge left the police station and walked toward the church, Hamish busy in his mind. It was the frustration of dead ends, he knew that, but Rutledge felt the past creeping into the present, and he knew that the safest thing to do was find a place where he could let it happen, out of the public eye.

The inn wouldn't do. Not with Miss Bartram hovering . . .

Reaching the churchyard, he scanned the tombs, the trees, anything that would offer shelter, privacy. There was nothing, only the tombstones and one mausoleum with an iron gate in front of the iron door. He could just make out the name carved over the gate, but it would not help him now.

Pressed for time, he opened the church door and stepped into the dimness, cool and quiet. Above his head was a wooden ceiling similar to many in this part of England, beautifully carved, dark wood, barrel-vaulted.

He quickly searched the small church, but it was empty. Sitting down on the stone steps of the pulpit, worn smooth by centuries of feet climbing up them to deliver homilies and eulogies and sermons, he pressed against the stone so that it was a bar across his back. It was the nearest he could come to hiding himself.

He waited.

Just as the darkness came down, he looked up and saw the face.

The Green Man. The carving that Miss Trowbridge had watched on Sundays, a child sitting through the long service. It was the decorative knob where the ribs of the ceiling crossed each other.

It was still there some twenty minutes later as the darkness and the sounds of battle slowly receded. He was trembling, his mouth dry, his heart beating rapidly.

He concentrated on the carving until his heart rate and his breathing steadied. The guns faded, the shouts and screams, the firing that had seemed to reach a crescendo in his head.

And then it was over. He took a deep breath and, badly shaken, buried his face in his hands.

This had been one of the worst daylight relapses into darkness that he could remember in some time.

Getting to his feet at last, he was about to turn and walk back up the center aisle when a voice said, "My son, are you all right?"

Rutledge froze. He'd been alone, he was sure of it. Where had this man come from? And what—*in God's name, what had he heard?*

Realizing in that same instant that he must be facing the Rector of the little church, he said, fighting to keep his voice steady, "I'm all right. A—a touch of sun."

The elderly man came toward him. "Does it happen often, this return to the war? For surely that must be what it was."

The man couldn't have heard the guns or the screams or the shouted orders . . .

But he was saying, "I've seen it before, you see. And you needn't worry, I have no intention of giving you away. You're the man from London, aren't you? The Inspector from Scotland Yard. My name is March. Andrew March."

Rutledge didn't give his own name. Instead he replied, "I'm all right."

"You are now. Yes. Come with me, we'll find a place to sit."

He led the way to the nearest pews, not looking over his shoulder to see if Rutledge was following. Sitting down, he patted the wooden bench, as if inviting a child to sit with him. Rutledge leaned against the nearest pillar, watching him.

"Have you lost your faith? Is that it? Or is it just the unbearable past that haunts you?"

"A little of both, I think," Rutledge answered against his better judgment. Part of him was urging flight, getting out of this church as quickly as he could, his secret intact. Another part of him wanted the peace of confessing. And that was denied him. He moved inadvertently, still rattled by what he'd just been through.

The Rector nodded, misinterpreting it as a need to go. "Yes, it happens. Well, they say that time is the healer. But it isn't, always. If you want to come to the Rectory and talk, you can generally find me there."

And he turned and walked toward the altar, leaving the way clear for Rutledge to reach the west door unhindered.

He walked out into the sunlight, blinking a little, and then went to where he'd left the motorcar.

For the rest of the morning he drove through the Fen country, stopping in each village and walking, as he had done in Burwell, learning the landscape.

Soham, with its larger mill and handsomer church and quiet streets. Tiny Isleham with its beautiful church set apart in its churchyard like a grande dame presiding over her charges. And then back to Wriston, and dead ends.

The journey hadn't done much to sweep away any lingering cobwebs, but he was hungry now. He found a small shop that served sandwiches and ordered the first item on the pretty hand-printed menu.

The middle-aged woman who served him said as she brought his meal, "You're the man from London. Scotland Yard."

"That's right. Were you standing by the market cross when Mr. Swift was shot?"

"I was. I shut my eyes almost at once. It was the most horrible thing I'd ever seen. One minute he was speaking and the next his head had just—fallen open." She shivered at the memory. "I couldn't sleep that night, or the next either."

"And so you didn't see anything—who was shooting or from where."

"No, I didn't even know what had happened at first. I didn't recognize the sound of the shot because it was so sudden, just everywhere all at once. Deafening. Echoing."

Shaking her head, she added, "He was dead. Just like that. People were screaming."

"Do you think anyone else besides Mrs. Percy saw the man with the rifle?"

"No," she said quickly. "No, I'm sure they hadn't."

But it was too fast, almost as if she wished to shut off speculation or questions. Confirming his suspicions, she turned to move away to greet an older woman who had just come into the tea shop.

Rutledge touched her arm, stopping her.

"There wasn't a monster," he told her. "The flickering torchlight, the movement of the smoke, and the sudden shock produced him. Even the most ordinary person looks different in such circumstances. Remember that."

She stared at him for a moment, then almost tripped over a chair at the next table in her haste to go.

Hamish said, "It will be all o'er the village by sunset."

Yes, Rutledge silently answered him. That was the point.

When he'd finished and paid his bill, a younger woman came to the counter to help him. The middle-aged woman was studiously wiping down a table by the window.

It was time to call on the ironmonger. He should have done it earlier, but when the darkness came down, he had had to accommodate it.

Walking through the shop door, Rutledge was met with that familiar, slightly metallic scent that seemed to be a part of such places.

The shop was empty, except for a portly man with black hair liberally streaked with gray and the shadow of a heavy beard. When he looked up and saw that it was Rutledge, he came hurrying toward him.

"Mr. Rutledge, is it?" he asked, a slight echo of Wales in his voice. "My name is Ross. Martin Ross."

"I'd like to have a look at your dormer window, if you have the time to take me upstairs."

"I'd thought you might come to speak to me first thing—Constable McBride told me you were in Wriston."

"I came as soon as I could. I understand that you weren't at home that night, that you'd gone out to hear Mr. Swift speak."

"Yes, yes, my wife and I and our grown son. The shop was closed, but the house was open. I mean to say, we hadn't thought to lock the doors, back or front. I feel responsible, somehow."

"You couldn't have foreseen that someone would use your house in such a way. He could easily have broken in."

"That's true enough. But people seem to be avoiding the shop. It's worrying. Both Constable McBride and the Inspector from Ely, Warren his name is, both of them went through the house inch by inch. There was nothing. No spent cartridge casing, not even a mark on the sill of the window. He hadn't tracked in mud or stopped to help himself to the biscuits in a box on the kitchen table. And yet he was *here*. At *my* window. Where else could that shot have come from, I ask you?" His words spilled over each other with barely suppressed anxiety, a man caught in a situation he didn't know how to cope with.

"He left no traces of himself in Ely," Rutledge reminded him. "I wouldn't have expected him to betray himself here." He said nothing about the gray thread still folded into his handkerchief.

"Yes, but don't you see? He was *outside* in Ely. Everyone says so. He was in *my* house. My wife hasn't been able to sleep, knowing he was here. And when people come into the shop, they look around uneasily, as if he's hiding amongst the hammers or under the table where the nails are set out. Someone dropped a spanner the other morning, and I saw two people start, as if they thought it was a gunshot."

"The man who came into your house cared nothing for you, Mr. Ross. He chose your window because it was convenient. He won't be returning."

"Still, I have the strongest feeling my neighbors blame me." He led the way down a passage that opened into a small room. The rear door stood open, and beyond it was an empty space where there must have been outbuildings at one time.

Noticing his glance, Ross said, "We had a shed and a small barn—for the horse, of course. They blew down in a windstorm the third year of the war, and I never replaced them. Well, the Army took our horse, of course, and never brought him back."

There were only two houses on the lane that ran behind the shop, and beyond them was the embankment that bordered the fields. Just as he'd seen it at Mrs. Percy's cottage. He leaned out for a better look. It went as far, he thought, as the raised bridge where he'd stopped his motorcar the night of the fog.

That was how the killer had come, then. Unseen, because everyone was drawn to the torch-lit parade down the street.

He turned and followed Ross up two flights of stairs to the second-floor room where the dormer let in light and warmth. What had once been a small bedroom for servants or a nursery was now given over to a collection of boxes and barrels, a few outworn chairs, a woman's dress model, and other oddments accumulated over the years.

He threaded his way through to the window. The sash was raised, a warm breeze drifting in.

"Do you leave this window open?"

"Yes, in the heat of the day. Someone generally comes to close it each evening. It allows a little circulation of the air, you see. It was warm that night, there was no expectation of rain, and I was in a hurry to shut up the shop before the crowd moved down the street. I didn't think it mattered. I could easily have come up the stairs and shut it. But it seemed unimportant. Still, he could have opened it, couldn't he? It wouldn't have mattered if the window had been shut."

So that, Rutledge thought, was the source of the man's anxiety, that he'd made it easy for a killer to do his work. One small oversight . . .

And yet—if the killer had had to open the window, he might have been seen by someone as he rose to raise the sash. Mrs. Percy might have seen more than a monstrous face.

"You didn't look this way when you heard the shot?"

"I don't know that I've ever heard a rifle being fired before this. The report seemed to come from everywhere at once. I don't think I even registered the fact that it was a shot, I was too shocked by what I was seeing. And then people were pushing back, away from where the body had fallen, and there was general panic. Only afterward, when Constable McBride was looking for a source of the shot, did we consider my window. It was the butcher who was first to Mr. Swift's body. I closed my eyes, feeling a little sick, trying not to think about what had happened."

Rutledge looked down, saw the market cross clearly. "Swift was standing on the base of the cross?" He made a point of leaning out the window.

"Yes, it raised him above the crowd just enough that we could see and hear him. I'd have said the ideal place for a speech. That's why we all saw him die."

And panic had taken over, giving the killer a chance to escape.

Rutledge noted the sill, but Warren's reports had already confirmed that there was no mark where the rifle had rested, and not enough dust for a footprint to be found.

"Thank you, Mr. Ross, you've been very helpful. I wish I could say that there was something here to help us catch our man, but he's been very clever."

Ross was nodding, drinking in every word. "Yes, yes, that's true. I'll tell everyone who comes in. Thank you."

They went down the stairs again, and as they turned at the first-floor landing, Ross said, "I wonder if you know. There was an ex-soldier passing through here not three weeks ago, looking for work. He'd been a cobbler, he wanted to set up by the market cross, but Constable McBride wasn't having it. He said that we'd soon have every mendicant in Cambridgeshire wanting to do the same. But Rector took pity on him and let him set up by the church. I don't know how many shoes he mended, but he was gone the next morning. I was told the butcher's lorry gave him a lift to Ely."

It was clear to Rutledge that Ross had been racking his brain for any memory that might divert attention from his shortcomings and the now-notorious dormer window. Still, it would have to be pursued.

Thanking him, Rutledge went directly to the police station to speak to Constable McBride.

"For one thing," McBride told him, "this ex-soldier came through nearly six weeks ago. Not three, as Mr. Ross led you to believe." He sorted through a handful of papers from the side drawer of his desk and passed a sheet to Rutledge. "For another I spoke to him myself. His name is Peter Jenkins, he comes from Warwick, and he was a corporal in the Buffs. He'd been a cobbler in Warwick before the war and until the shop closed last spring—the owner had died and the widow couldn't carry on. Nor did Jenkins have the money to buy the shop from her. He had no choice but to take to the roads. But we can't have every Tom, Dick, and Harry setting up at the market cross on days when there's no market. And so I told him. When he'd moved on, I sent a query to Warwick, and his story was confirmed by a Constable Godwin."

"Well done," Rutledge told him, glancing through the information on the sheet.

"I can't think he'd give me his right name if he was here bent on mischief. But we've had no trouble in this village, and the next peddler might be a Traveler, out for what he can find. Still, when the Rector took pity on him, I let it go."

"There's no one else who came through?"

"No, it's been a quiet summer. And we're a little out of the way, you see, not on a direct road anywhere. Did you have a look out that window while you were calling on the ironmonger?"

"I did. You couldn't ask for a better position for a shot."

"No," the constable said morosely. "It's too bad Swift didn't find another site for his speech. He might still be with us."

"I wonder," Rutledge said, "if the killer came late at night, when the village was asleep. He could have stayed in the shadows, learned whatever it was he wanted to know, and then gone away again without arousing suspicion."

"How did he know what Swift was planning?"

"That shouldn't have been too difficult. Surely it was no secret, that rally."

"True enough," McBride said.

"I'd like a list of every man in the village who served in France during the war. And if you will, send a request to your opposite numbers in the surrounding villages asking them to draw up one as well and send it to me here in Wriston."

"Here, you're saying that one of *ours* is this killer."

"No. But once we know the names of men who can handle a rifle, then we can find out if any of them knew Hutchinson."

Rutledge was just about to take his leave when some-one came galloping down the High Street on a lathered horse. He was a tall man, lean and weathered.

"There's been another shooting," he called as soon as Constable McBride and Rutledge appeared in the police station doorway.

"Where?" the two men replied almost in unison.

"Over by the Burrows farm. It's all right, Mr. Burrows wasn't badly hurt. But he like to had a heart attack afterward. It was that close run a thing."

Rutledge was already sprinting for his motorcar, McBride at his heels.

"Where is the farm?" he asked the constable.

"It's over toward Burwell. You'll see a line of trees going into the farm. Not a large place, there's not enough land for more than a house and a few outbuild-ings. He keeps some of his larger pieces of equipment in Burwell."

Rutledge reversed the motorcar and headed for the Wriston windmill, letting McBride show him the way from there.

They came to a long straight road—not the one Rutledge had taken on his way to Burwell, but half a mile distant. As they turned into it, he could see the line of trees that McBride had described. When they reached the track, he realized that the farm must have been there for a very long time. The track was rutted and uneven, and the house was low, rambling, as if it had been designed to fit into the flat profile of the land around it, then added to as necessity or money dictated.

But the steps to the door were swept, there was a fresh coat of paint on the outbuildings, and a small bed of marigolds where the path widened added a dash of color.

Someone had heard the motorcar arrive, and a tall, thin woman held the door open for them.

"Do come in," she said in a voice thick with unshed tears. "My father is in the front room."

They followed her through to where an older man was sitting in a chair, hands on the arms, his face flushed. There was a red streak across one cheek, and someone had tried to wash away the worst of the blood. It still stained his shirt and coat.

Looking up, he nodded to McBride and said to Rutledge, "And who might you be?"

"My name is Rutledge. I've been sent by Scotland Yard to look into these shootings."

"Well, it wasn't soon enough," Burrows said, glaring up at him. "It's a wonder I'm alive. I can't think how he came to miss." He added, "Do sit down, it hurts to twist around like this."

"I think you should start at the beginning, Papa," the woman said as Rutledge took the chair offered and McBride went to stand by the window.

"I was on my way home, on horseback. I'd gone into Burwell after a part for the pump in my kitchen. The road was empty. I'd swear to that. Nothing to be seen anywhere, midday and quiet. And then a face appeared over the edge of the bridge across the ditch. He'd been hiding there like—like some sort of water creature. I'd hardly taken it in when something stung my face and the report of the rifle frightened the hell out of my horse. It took off at a great pace, and by the time I'd got it under control again, I wasn't about to go back the way I'd come. And so I took a round-about way home, my face bleeding all over my coat. I couldn't stop it."

He put up a hand, touched the crease gingerly. "It's still wet," he finished.

"Leave it alone, Papa, you'll only make it worse," Miss Burrows told him.

"Don't fuss, Meg," he warned her sharply.

"Describe what you saw," Rutledge asked after a moment.

"I told you, it was like something out of a tale, this wormlike thing with a face you didn't want to look into twice. Cold and hard. Eyes that had nothing human about them. He must have kept the weapon under him until he was ready to fire. I tell you, I should be out there on the road, dead, a bullet through my skull. All I can think of is that he couldn't bring the rifle up properly, lying on it like that. There's no sense to it, else."

"But why should he wish to kill you?" Constable McBride demanded. "Did you know Mr. Swift, or that Captain in Ely?"

"Of course I knew Swift. Everybody did," Burrows answered testily. "As for that Captain, I doubt I've ever clapped eyes on him. I was too old for the war. And I've never been any farther south than Cambridge. Rumor has it he was a London man."

"He was," Rutledge replied. "But he was in Burwell recently. For the funeral of a Major Clayton."

Burrows started to shake his head and stopped abruptly. "I knew a Clayton years ago. He bred horses. He died in '05 or '06, I think it was."

"Inspector Warren never told me that Hutchinson was in Burwell," McBride cut in to ask. "When exactly was this?"

"Earlier in the summer," Rutledge answered. He'd been watching Burrows's face, and he thought it likely that the man was telling the truth. He didn't know Major Clayton or Hutchinson. "Tell me, Mr. Burrows, do you own any weapons?"

"I've a shotgun. I expect everyone in the Fens must have one. But this wasn't a shotgun, I tell you, else he'd have taken my head off, not cut my face."

"Yes, I understand. But Constable McBride here has been making a list of men who'd served in France. It's possible that someone who worked for you was a soldier and brought back a souvenir."

"Two of my men died in France. The other came home without his arm. The only souvenir he brought back was one of those helmets the Hun wore. With the spike on top. Bloody silly thing to wear in the trenches, if you ask me."

But these were parade helmets. In the trenches they were covered, the spike removed.

Rutledge was suddenly reminded of what Ruskin had told him, that he'd seen a German helmet.

"Where is this helmet now?"

"His wife made him get rid of it."

"Could that be what the man was wearing?"

Burrows glared at him. "I know the difference between a helmet like that and the face I saw."

"It would be best if you went to a doctor. I'll drive you there, if you like," Rutledge suggested, watching a thin beading of blood reappear along the line of the cut every time Burrows impatiently dabbed at it.

"Meg is better than a doctor when it comes to taking care of me. What I want to know is when are you going to bring in this fool? Before someone else is killed. And the next question is, will he come looking for me and mine, now he's missed his chance? I don't relish walking around with eyes in the back of my head or looking over my shoulder. And there's Meg here. What if in the dark she's mistaken for me?"

"To tell you the truth, I don't know if you're still in danger—or if he's satisfied that he marked you. But I'd stay close to the house for a day or two."

"I can't stay close to the house. I've a farm to run, and I'm short two men as it is. Three if I had my way. Who is going to see to things if I don't?"

"A few days, Papa," Miss Burrows interjected. "It's not time for the harvest. Surely you could spare a few days?"

"I won't be kept prisoner in my own home. By God, I won't."

But it was half bluster, Rutledge thought. Burrows had been thoroughly frightened, and there was no mistaking the stiffness in his body as he sat in the chair. Or his uncertainty about the future. Having looked Death in the eye, so to speak, he was not likely to do something foolish.

And then Burrows said, "I'll keep the shotgun to hand, and if he comes nosing around this house, I'll shoot first and ask later."

"Just be sure," Rutledge warned, "that you're firing at the right man. You don't want to make any mistakes.

Or you'll be up for murder yourself." He rose. "I need to report what happened to Inspector Warren in Ely. Will you describe that man again?"

"I never really saw him. Just that wormlike body and a face as cold as death. As if he could look down at my corpse without feeling anything except—satisfaction."

Miss Burrows turned away, biting her lip to hold back tears.

"Which of your enemies will feel satisfaction at your death?" Rutledge asked.

"Good God, I don't know any who would shoot me down in the road. There's competition in this business. A better yield, finding a stronger seed. That sort of thing, but not murder. I'd done nothing a man might want to kill me for."

When they had left and Rutledge was driving with care through the ruts and holes of the road leading up to the farmhouse, McBride said, "What do you make of Burrows, then?"

"He couldn't have shot himself. And I don't think the daughter could have shot him. Besides, she was frightened for him."

"He knew Swift."

"Yes," Rutledge said slowly, trying to ignore Hamish in the back of his mind. "But so did everyone in Wriston. Still, it's worth keeping in mind. Show me where this ambush happened."

McBride gave him directions, so that they came up on the bridge just as Burrows had done. Rutledge stopped the motorcar well short of the spot and got out. He could see droppings on the road some fifty yards back. Testing the light wind, he realized that it was blowing toward the bridge, which meant that the horse probably hadn't caught the scent of the man who was waiting. Farther along, the turf on the right side of the road was torn, where the horse was startled, and started dancing, fighting the bit, before taking off in fright.

Rutledge stood there, looking down toward the bridge.

It was a clear shot, the man's head well above his mount's, and the distance was good, the wind hardly a factor, the pace steady as the horse trotted home.

He asked McBride to stand in his place while he walked down and over the hump of the bridge.

The late season grass was matted where someone had been lying there waiting. In some places it was already beginning to spring back. He couldn't judge the height or the shape of whoever had lain there. But there was enough evidence to verify what Burrows had claimed.

Rutledge scanned the area, looking for anything the killer had left behind—a cigarette stub, a cartridge casing, anything that would be useful. But the man had left no trace other than the bent blades in a patch of grass.

He stretched out full length, to see what the killer had seen.

From this position, it would have been easy to watch Burrows coming from at least a mile away, even if the sound of hooves hadn't alerted the killer to his approach. And yet the height of the old bridge concealed the waiting man until he had lifted himself long enough to aim and fire.

Rutledge rose slightly, raising an imaginary rifle, then bringing it to bear on McBride.

It was an easy shot. Easier than peering over the edge of the parapet at Ely Cathedral, easier than shooting at Swift through the wavering torchlight and wafting smoke. Why then had the killer missed?

Hamish said, "The horse. As soon as he moved, yon horse would see him."

It was very likely. Even a slight shift by the horse could have made the difference between life and death. The other two victims had either been standing or walking slowly.

And that was a miscalculation on the part of the killer, if he'd known nothing about horses.

The question now was, had Burrows been the target? If so, how had the killer tracked him to this particular place? Had he seen him in Burwell earlier?

Or had the man with the rifle missed at the last minute when he realized that Burrows was not the rider he was expecting?

Finally, would any target have done? Was this a third attempt to murder? Or just a tactic to muddle the issue?

Rutledge got to his feet and walked back to McBride, who jogged forward in his turn to have a look at the far side of the bridge.

Driving on to Wriston, Rutledge said, "I'm intrigued with Burrows's description of what he'd seen. I want to go back and speak to Mrs. Percy. And then I'll continue on to Ely. Get me that list of men who were in France. I'll need that when I get back."

But **Mrs. Percy** wasn't moved by Burrows's close call or his description of the killer.

"I never saw anything," she told Rutledge a second time. "When I gave my statement to Constable McBride, I'd been blinded by the torches and all that smoke. And there's an end to it."

"It isn't the end. You signed your statement. By doing so, you were swearing to the truth of it. Is the memory of what was in that window too frightening to think about now?"

"How can I be afraid of something I didn't see?" she countered.

"If you won't describe it, will you try to draw it?" Rutledge took out his notebook and held it out to her. "I'd like to show it to Mr. Burrows."

But she refused to take it, and finally he withdrew the notebook.

"I didn't see anything to draw. There was only a man with a rifle in his hands."

He didn't think she'd seen a rifle. He wasn't sure she would even have recognized the difference between it and a shotgun. Not in the few seconds she'd had to take in what she was looking at. According to McBride, there had been no mention of a weapon in her original statement.

But she'd been questioned. Not only by the police but just as surely by her neighbors, curious about her monster.

And in the end, she had recanted. *A man with a rifle in his hands.*

What was acceptable to the world. What would never again make her a laughingstock.

"A pity. We might have confirmed what you'd seen, on the basis of what Mr. Burrows has reported. It would have vindicated you."

Something flickered in her eyes. "That's as may be. It was daylight when *he* saw what he saw. There's a difference."

He thanked her and left. He was just bending down to the crank when he noticed that in the house next to hers a curtain twitched.

Mrs. Percy's neighbor would be over as soon as he had turned out of the lane, out of sight, to find out what the police had wanted. And the news of Burrows's wounding would spread like wildfire.

It couldn't be helped. He'd had no choice but to tell Mrs. Percy she wasn't alone in seeing something incomprehensible, hoping that the fact that the killer had struck again would encourage her to talk to him. Putting together her evidence with Ruskin's and Burrows's, he might just have something more definitive than *monster*.

Rutledge stopped to tell McBride that he'd got nowhere and would be driving on to Ely.

McBride shook his head. "Stubborn woman. But the main question now has to be where does this man go when he's not using that rifle? Cambridge? Peterborough? King's Lynn? Even Inspector Warren doesn't have enough men to look everywhere."

"Nor can we take a chance that there's another target out there who might not be as lucky as Burrows."

"Do you think he'll try to come back for Mr. Burrows? Just wounding him might not be enough."

"God knows. But I think Burrows will stay close to his house for a while. Which is probably his best protection just now."

"But not in the long haul."

Rutledge took a deep breath. "True. He could bide his time, whoever he is, and try when we've given up. Or brought him in."

"A soldier. A solicitor. A farmer. It makes no sense."

When Rutledge reached Ely and reported to Inspector Warren, he heard the same comment. *It makes no sense.*

"If he's satisfied," Rutledge pointed out, "he can disappear as easily as he appeared. If he isn't, Burrows won't be his last target. We don't have time to worry about motive or connections. We've got to find him."

"Will he come back for Burrows, do you think?" It was the same question that McBride had asked, but this time it was from a different perspective. "Do you think we could use that possibility to trap him?"

"God knows. It depends on why he shot at him. How deep his feelings went. What worries me is that he missed. It was a clear shot, an easy shot. Was it the shifting of the horse? Or was he having qualms of conscience?"

"My money is on the horse. He's shown no signs of a conscience so far, interrupting that wedding and then killing Swift in front of women and children."

"I've asked McBride to send out word that I'd like a list of all the ex-soldiers in each village. Can you draw up one for Ely?"

"It will take time, we'll have to go door to door. It's the only way to be sure we have all the names. Do you think it's one of them?"

"If they didn't do the shooting, they could have brought back a rifle as a souvenir for themselves or someone else. Or know who did. Meanwhile, I've spoken to Swift's brother. He seems to think he's a likely target as well. I must say, isolated as the farm is, he could easily be picked off from a distance. The question is, how to protect a population as scattered as it is here in the Fen country. You can't watch them all. On another matter: What do you know about Hutchinson's sister? Did you inform her of her brother's death, or did Fallowfield?"

"Fallowfield asked if he could tell her. I thought it best. He also identified the body and saw to it that the remains were taken to London as soon as they were released, accompanied by a man of the cloth, someone related to the new Mrs. Fallowfield. He felt responsible. After all the man had come to Ely for his wedding."

"Burrows swears he had no connection with the other two men. That could mean that whatever links them is in the mind of the killer. Not something we can easily track down." Hamish was saying something. Hearing him, Rutledge asked, "Do you have ghosts, phantoms, or other specters in the Fens here?"

Surprised by the question, Warren laughed. "Do you think our killer is a phantom?"

"No. But if he can appear and disappear at will, perhaps he keeps himself out of sight in some place people are afraid—or unlikely—to go."

"We have a great hound—Black Shuck—who is a sign that something is about to happen. A harbinger, so to speak. I don't know anyone who has seen him in the last few years, but I was told that he was spotted near Isleham the day before we declared war on Germany. It was never confirmed. Excitement was running high then, and people were ready to believe in any omen."

"Is this Black Shuck like Conan Doyle's Hound of the Baskervilles?"

"Oh, yes, the story. Our black dog hasn't been known to harm anyone. On the contrary, he's a warning. Then there's the black mill at Wriston. People have always thought it was haunted. A man was killed there a century or more ago, hung up on one of the arms. An accident most likely—no one was ever taken up for the crime. Several of the old mills have stories attached to them. And one of the old lagoons had a legend about something that lived in the water. That's gone, along with the lagoon. Not much help, I'm afraid."

It wasn't.

Rutledge went back to the telephone he'd used before—in the passage to Reception at a hotel—and this time he found Sergeant Gibson at the Yard.

"There's not much to tell," Gibson said. "I spoke to the Captain's sister. She was upset, said no one could possibly hate her brother, and told me that it must have been a madman that shot him."

"What's their background?"

"Hutchinson and his sister were orphaned young and shifted from relative to relative until he went to Sandhurst. He was a young Lieutenant when he met and married a woman who had money of her own and a house in London, where they went to live. There was some story she'd been engaged to another man, but I couldn't confirm that. Hutchinson had his first taste of war with the Expeditionary Force that went over in those early days, trying to stop the German advance. He was wounded at Mons but not sent home. His wife lost the child she was carrying, and her death was put down to despair. The short of it was, she didn't want to live. The sister—she lived with him and his wife—says it was a very happy marriage, but another source claims the wife was unhappy." "No foul play suspected in the wife's death? If he married her for her money, he could have killed her for it as well."

"It appears he was in France at the time."

"What about the jilted lover?"

"Never heard of again. I'd guess he decided he was well out of a bad bargain. The sister couldn't even remember his name. She said it was never official, their engagement, just something understood from childhood."

"Did Hutchinson's wife have any relatives who might have felt she was married for her money and then neglected?"

"None the sister knew of. There was an uncle who was her guardian, but he's long since dead. I did speak to the Rector at Mrs. Hutchinson's church. St. Timothy's, in Warwick, where she's buried. He was inclined to agree with the official cause of death. I did learn that a maid disappeared from the London house not long ago, but she wasn't there when Mrs. Hutchinson was alive."

"What became of her? Did you ask Miss Hutchinson about her?"

"I was told there was probably a man involved. The girl had come highly recommended, and she did her work well, they had no complaints of her. But she was young, unused to the city. Then one day she seemed very unhappy and just walked out. Miss Hutchinson called in the police after she failed to return by the end of the week, but they had no luck finding her. She wouldn't be the first to wind up in the river. Miss Hutchinson says she was young enough to believe promises made to her by a man, only to find herself deceived."

It was not uncommon.

"She wasn't pregnant, was she?"

"There's no way of knowing the answer to that. But she hadn't confided in anyone at the house."

"What about Hutchinson?"

"The sister says he was away more often than not, and she was indignant that we should think her brother had interfered with the maids. Besides, there's no evidence of that anywhere. The staff said he left the management of the house to his sister and treated the staff with indifference."

Digesting what Gibson had said, Rutledge could see that Hutchinson had probably married for money, using that charm several people had spoken of to find himself a rich wife, then ignored her. He'd been kind to Major Clayton's sister, but more or less as his opportunity to spend time with Colonel Nelson. It was a pattern of sorts. A housemaid would hold little interest for him.

"Turning to Fallowfield. What did you learn?"

"Well liked, no skeletons that I could discover. The same with the Sedleys. Above reproach, I was told at Mr. Sedley's London club. A good man, according to his solicitor."

"That leaves Swift."

"He's never been to London. At least if he came, he kept himself to himself and left no trace. He was to come down the week after the election to look for a flat that would serve when he was in Commons. He'd written to ask if there were any likely places close by Westminster. He was told there was no such list, he'd have to find something for himself before the House sat. I had that from an acquaintance at Westminster. He said Mr. Swift would wait until he was elected before making living arrangements. But it appeared that with his lackluster opposition, he was the most likely to win the by-election, and the general view was, he'd be a happy backbencher."

That corroborated all he'd learned in Ely and Wriston about Mr. Swift, the solicitor.

"There are two new names for you to look at. Anson Swift, the illegitimate brother of the dead man. And a farmer named Burrows. Any luck with Lowell, the artillery Major?"

"Good officer, careful of his men. A bachelor. Steady. No vices."

"Good." Lowell, it seemed, was not a suspect.

"There've been changes here, the new broom and all that. Constables reassigned. And speaking of that, the Acting Chief Superintendent was wanting to know if there was any news from Ely. Sir."

"Yes, well, it's more complicated that we had anticipated."

"That may be, but Himself is looking for an arrest sooner rather than later."

"I'll keep it in mind," Rutledge said dryly and broke the connection.

He sat there in the little enclosure for the telephone, thinking over what he'd learned.

Nothing useful. Nothing that would lead to Hutchinson's death in Ely in the summer of 1920.

Somewhere there had to be a strand of information that would help in the inquiry. A list of ex-soldiers was not likely to produce a killer in time to make Markham happy. But there would have to be a report in a day or two, and Rutledge accepted that with a sigh. Even if it offered no motive, no suspects, and no evidence to be going on with.

Leaving the telephone closet, he went back to the police station, but Inspector Warren, he was told, had already gone home for the evening. He scribbled a note to leave on the man's desk. It said simply, *Nothing useful from London.*

On his way back to Wriston, Hamish was busy in the back of his mind.

Trying to ignore the probing, the querulous demands for answers, the unsettling reminders of France, he looked up at the western sky. Clouds were streaked across the horizon, a blaze of color, and visible wherever the road took him, because of the flatness of the land and the lack of woods or towns or hills to break the view.

A fiery gold in the last bank of clouds, a blazing red above that, and then, as the red faded to rose and the rose to lavender, the earth seemed to reflect the light.

Not a night to be looking for a murderer, he thought. But he had the feeling that he should not linger on the road, he should be in Wriston by nightfall. It was an odd feeling, very like the one he'd had when he woke to find the fog lifted, as if someone had been there, looking up at his window.

And yet the sky held him in thrall, for the light seemed to fill the motorcar, to warm his face, and as he drove he watched it slowly fade until there was nothing but the afterglow.

When at last he could shut out Hamish no longer, he heard what the voice in his head was telling him.

"He can see ye as clearly as he saw yon farmer. Ye're a target. Ye're Scotland Yard, and he knows ye're after him. This land is no' as empty as it seems. Ye'll be dead before ye hear the shot."

Was it a reflection of his own mood, or was Hamish warning him?

By that time he was less than two miles from Wriston. Beside him in the ditches and the fields, insects and frogs set up an invisible chorus. Over the quiet running of the motor, it was unexpectedly loud. And as he drove into the village, his headlamps picking out the road ahead now, that sense of vulnerability seemed to increase.

Death could be lurking anywhere. Behind the buildings, among the trees, in the shadows by the church . . .

In this inquiry, McBride and Inspector Warren, with the best will in the world, had come up empty-handed. Scotland Yard was expected to find those elusive answers.

And right now the killer had no way of knowing that Rutledge too was getting nowhere, had so far learned nothing useful.

Chapter 10

The list of ex-soldiers arrived the next morning by a special messenger who came roaring into Wriston on his motorcycle, his goggles and cuffed gloves a souvenir of France.

Leafing through it, Rutledge could guess how many men had set out from this handful of villages to fight the Kaiser. Perhaps less than half had returned. He remembered the small corner of Isleham churchyard where a memorial had been set up, and the long rows of names on the plinth of the cross. He had not paused there. It had seemed too much of a burden to carry with him just then.

The constables in the various villages had been thorough, giving him ranks and sometimes other brief notations by some of the names.

Lost his leg.
Lost his arm.
Blind.
Gassed.
Troubled.

Rutledge needed no explanation of that last. Men who had brought the war home with them, physically or mentally.

He could mark off the severely wounded, those who couldn't manage a rifle, much less the stairs in the ironmonger's house or those up into Ely's tower. They might hate as much as the next man, but they weren't the killer he was after.

Still, he'd have to interview the troubled men. He could feel his stomach clenching at the thought.

McBride, who'd heard the roar of the Indian coming down the road, had hailed Rutledge and was trotting toward him.

"Inspector Warren has been thorough," he said, looking up from the sheaf of papers in his hand.

"I can't see that it will help all that much," McBride commented. "They're not likely to confess when you walk in the door."

"If someone has a rifle hidden in the thatch of his roof, he'll find it hard to deny it to my face. And that just might give him away."

"I doubt you'll find him in Wriston."

"Possibly not. On the other hand, if he does live here, he knew the risk he was running, and he's found a way to keep you in the dark."

It was clear McBride disagreed, and Rutledge let it go.

They crossed to the police station. Rutledge sat down at McBride's desk to make notes on the sheets while the constable paced restlessly, then left on his rounds.

Finally satisfied that he'd narrowed down the numbers, Rutledge sat back, waiting for McBride to return.

Hamish was saying, "It's likely he lives alone, this man. Else, how has he kept the truth from his wife or his bairns?"

"He could have a cowshed or some other—"

He could hear McBride returning, and broke off, aware he'd answered Hamish aloud.

"There's a problem," the constable said almost before he was through the door.

"Another shooting?" Rutledge asked, quickly getting to his feet.

"No. Monster fever," was the sour reply.

"What brought it on?"

"Sam Turner was walking back from the pub last night. He swears he saw something moving out in the fields. Lights, he said. And it wasn't a man with a lantern. It didn't stand on two legs, it was up in the air. Leaping and turning, without rhyme or reason."

"How drunk was he?"

"Fairly. He admits to it. His wife is a termagant, and he spends most of his evenings at the pub. Still, he swears it was real. He's telling half the village to lock their doors."

"Someone searching for something?" Rutledge asked with interest. "Or merely stirring up trouble?"

"Turner says spirits. A lost soul, looking for peace. He's fairly clear about that. He claims it's Burrows. That he's dead."

Rutledge came around the desk, folding the papers in his hand in half. "No one has come in from the farm, bringing the news. We'll have to drive out there and see for ourselves."

"It could be, no one's found him yet," McBride agreed.

They hurried to the inn, where Rutledge had left the motorcar, and on the way McBride asked, "What do you think the chances are that something—or some-one—was out there? That it wasn't just the drink that made Turner see the lights?"

"Fairly poor. But if they were real, I'll wager who-ever it was used stilts. Like those I saw in Mrs. Percy's kitchen. There must be other old pairs lying about. If not, it would be easy enough to make new ones. It's the most likely explanation. We could search for prints, but even if we found them, they wouldn't tell us much more than we know already."

McBride whistled as he bent to turn the crank. "I never thought of stilts. My father had a pair when he was a lad. I could never get the hang of them."

Remembering the man in the mist, Rutledge asked as he drove over the bridge by the windmill, "There's another possibility. What was he wandering about in the dark looking for? Or perhaps that ought to be *who*? Surely not Sam Turner."

"It won't matter to Turner or to half of those he's told. There are old tales about lights out in the Fens. Fox fire. Someone will remember them."

They fell silent then, and it wasn't until they were turning in on the long track that led to the Burrows house that McBride brought up something that clearly had been worrying him for some time.

"There will have to be another by-election. With Mr. Swift dead, the seat in Parliament won't go by default to Mr. Johns, the other candidate. There's been some talk. Most people think Johns won't stand now, for fear of being shot in his turn. But if you ask me, he wasn't all that eager to begin with. The party needed a name, and he was persuaded. Nor did he exert himself overly."

"Knowing that Swift was likely to win."

"I'd say that was his thinking. But who will stand in Swift's place? I'm hearing whispers that no one appears to be that eager to fill *his* boots."

Inspector Warren had raised that question as well.

"Who would be likely to come forward? Surely not Swift's brother? Or Burrows?"

"I doubt you could pry either man off his land. Certainly not for London."

"Then we'd better unravel this puzzle quickly."

They had reached the house now, and Miss Burrows must have seen them coming, for she was at the door, calling to them, "Has there been any more trouble?"

"We've come to look in on your father. How is he?" McBride asked.

"Well enough. Last night he was planning what had to be done in the fields. Today his face is hurting, and he's using the wound as his excuse not to go outside. How long will that excuse hold up?"

"There was a—rumor in Wriston today that he was dead. Your father," Constable McBride said.

"Started by whom?" she asked anxiously. As they joined her in the doorway she led the way to a sitting room. It was comfortable and well kept, but the furnishings were late Victorian, the wallpaper dark.

"A man walking home from the pub said he saw lights out in the fields. He claimed they were the souls of the dead." McBride was wishing he'd said nothing about Burrows having died. Shrugging uneasily, he added, "A silly business, but we can't ignore the story."

"No. But who was out there in the field? Was it someone coming in this direction?"

"He said the lights were just—there. Not that they were moving in a particular direction."

Rutledge added, "On the other hand, we felt it was a good idea to look in on you."

"I don't like it," she told them flatly. "It's strange, all of this business. The monsters, the faces, the lights. I don't believe in such things. But there's got to be some truth to it. Some explanation that makes sense."

"Or—he was drunk. This man was walking from the pub to his house. McBride tells me he'd stayed until closing, as he sometimes does, and had to be turned out. Everyone else had already left. He was in the street alone. His imagination could have played tricks on him."

"And there's a pair of owls that live in the church tower," McBride put in. "Some people don't care for them."

McBride was trying to ease Miss Burrows's anxiety. But the best view of the fields was looking down Windmill Lane, past where Mrs. Percy lived, well before the churchyard. The power of suggestion?

Rutledge wondered again. Or had the man actually seen something?

They could hear someone moving about on the floor above, and after a moment footsteps on the stairs.

"My father," Miss Burrows said, adding quickly. "Please, say nothing about the lights. At least not until you *know*—" She broke off as her father came through the door.

It appeared he'd been sleeping, his hair mussed and his face slightly flushed. The mark on his cheek was still inflamed, and Rutledge suggested again that a doctor should have a look at it.

"I don't want a fuss made," Burrows said testily. "What brings you here? Is there fresh news?"

"Nothing to report," Rutledge said easily. "We thought it best to see how you were faring. You had a narrow escape."

"I don't think I slept a wink last night," Burrows said morosely. "The face burned like fire, and I woke with a start at every noise. But he didn't come. I sent my daughter to a neighbor's for the night. I didn't want her here. And I didn't want her coming in every half hour to ask me if I was all right and getting the shotgun in her face for her trouble."

And so he must have sat up, guarding the house, possibly from an upstairs window where he had a full sweep of the approaches. Rutledge knew that he should have sent McBride out to keep the man company, but he wasn't convinced that the killer would return. And McBride was needed in Wriston. The danger—if danger there still was—would come later, when Burrows's guard was down.

Burrows had been the third choice on the killer's list. Was that significant? Where was the pattern? Or was there a pattern?

"Where are the two men who work for you?" Rutledge asked.

"I sent them away home. I trust them, of course I do. But last night I didn't want them lurking about."

But Rutledge wondered if it was a matter of trust after all. Burrows hadn't seen the face of the man firing at him.

"You could come into town for a few days," Rutledge suggested. "Miss Bartram has extra rooms, she can put you up. It might be more comfortable for you and your daughter."

To his surprise, Miss Burrows added her own arguments to Rutledge's.

"It might be as well, Papa. What do you think?"

"I won't be run out of my home," he said tightly. "Go if you like. I can fend for myself. I managed well enough for both of us after your mother died."

"I don't want to leave you."

"I'll take Miss Burrows back with me if you like," Rutledge offered.

"It will be all right after tonight," her father answered. "Bill Waters is bringing me one of his dogs. A big brute, bark like a railway locomotive. No one can slip up on me if the dog is here. He'll see him or smell him before I do."

But a man with a rifle could stay downwind and kill from a distance. It was a fragile line of defense.

"I'll come back tonight, shall I?" Rutledge asked. "To spell you. We can watch turn about."

Burrows hesitated, then shook his head. "If I'm alone, I know who's out there. And I'll shoot first, ask his business later."

"Not a good idea," McBride began.

But Burrows said stubbornly, "You've lived here all your life. Do people walk about out there in the dark? Not God-fearing souls. Only someone bent on trouble, and you know that to be true as well as I do."

Rutledge was reminded again of the man who had helped him in the mist. He'd appeared and disappeared like a wraith.

McBride was saying unwillingly, "I'd have to agree with that. After midnight, the frogs have the ditches and the fields to themselves. But I don't wish to come out here in the morning to find you with a body on your hands and a story that you thought it was someone else you were firing at."

"Never fear," Burrows told him grimly. "If I fire that shotgun, I won't miss. And I'll have the right man."

Miss Burrows wouldn't accept their offer to take her into Wriston. She was closer by at a neighbor's house, could come in the morning to prepare breakfast for her father and the men who helped him in the fields.

"I'll be all right, it will be daylight and he'll hear me walking up the track."

But the truth was, Rutledge thought, she wanted to be near enough to hear the shotgun go off in the night. Or the rifle . . .

Rutledge and McBride left them to it and turned back toward Wriston.

"Stubborn old fool," McBride said under his breath.

Rutledge was of the same mind.

"What about the men who work for him? Were they in the war, are they on our list?"

"The older one, Bill, was in the Navy. He's not likely to be our man. Steady and quiet and never a trouble-maker. I don't see him shooting anyone. Besides, how was he to get to Ely to kill Captain Hutchinson? It's quite a way."

"By bicycle?"

"Possible, if he had all day to do the journey. No, my money would be on the younger one. I say young, he's thirty-five if he's a day. He's a good worker, and to be trusted. But he's a moody bastard, and about once every six months, he takes a day off and drinks himself blind. The next morning he's back at work as if nothing happened."

"I doubt the killer did his work in a drunken stupor."

"No, there's the rub. Besides, the two men share a cottage over by the cattle byre, and there would be no hiding a rifle in there. You'd stumble over it sooner or later."

"On the farm there must be a dozen safe hiding places."

"Still, it would come to light. And someone would ask whose it was. Bound to. No, I don't think Burrows has anything to fear from his help."

Back in Wriston, Rutledge went to the little café for his lunch, the menu running to sandwiches, and then he set about interviewing the names on his abbreviated list of Wriston's ex-soldiers.

Seven of them had been in the square the night Swift was killed, and witnesses had verified their presence. That was made clear in the statements Constable McBride and Inspector Warren had collected. Two men had stayed home with their wives because they didn't intend to vote for Swift. Three others had remained in the pub, not interested in what the candidate had to say. Another had a sick calf to watch over, and one had a teething child, walking the floor with it by turns with his wife.

The last two on his list had no alibi and no apparent reason to do murder. Still, he put a question mark by their names.

Conferring with McBride later, he learned that one of them was "too shiftless" to be troubled by revenge, and the other was courting a girl at one of the farms.

The next day Rutledge set out for Soham and spent the morning looking up the ex-soldiers that Constable Peckham had included in his list.

The cooper was on there, but Rutledge had already spoken to him. One by one he tracked down the others, and one by one he cleared them.

Until he came to the rat catcher.

The man lived down by one of the small streams that still crisscrossed the area. His house, if it could be called that, was hardly more than a hut, a single room that served for sleeping and eating. A narrow cot in one corner was his bed, a table in the middle of the room must be where he ate his meals, and he cooked over a small open fire just outside the door where boards had been nailed together to form a rough lean-to that kept out the rain. A tan and white terrier lay sleeping by the door, his muzzle on his paws.

The man was tall and rangy, with long fair hair and a scruffy beard. His eyes were a light gray and never wavered from Rutledge's face as he gave his name and why he had come.

"A policeman," Jeremiah Brenner said, looking him up and down. Then he added, "I haven't been to Ely since the war."

"Then you've nothing to hide," Rutledge said. "What did you do during the war?"

"I don't remember." His gaze turned to the wall, and Rutledge realized that there was a large rat in the cage sitting on a shelf. "He's tame. I call him Isaac. I found him when he was no larger than my thumb, pink and blind. So I kept him. He doesn't judge me, I don't judge him."

There was something about the man that put Rutledge off. He wasn't sure whether it was the light eyes that seemed as cold as icy water, or if it was the rat.

"Do you make a good living as rat catcher?"

"Does it look like it? But my father was rat catcher before me. And it's all I'm fit for now. I drink too much."

And yet Rutledge was sure the man was cold sober just now.

"I drink to forget," Brenner went on, as if he'd heard the next question in Rutledge's mind. The cool eyes came back to Rutledge's face.

"What do you want to forget?"

"Ah, that would be telling. Is there anything else?"

"Did you know Herbert Swift?"

"I know who he is—was."

"And Mr. Burrows?"

"I've caught rats in one of his barns. Twice the size of the barn cat, they were."

"Did you know the man who was shot in Ely?"

Brenner smiled. "I knew of him. Only I wasn't the one who shot him."

"Then who do you think did?"

"Even if I knew I wouldn't tell you. Whoever it was, he must have had his reasons. Some of us didn't like our officers."

And that was all he could learn from Jeremiah Brenner. He put a question mark by the name. But if there was a rifle in the bare hut, Rutledge wasn't sure where it could have been concealed. Still, the rat catcher answered to no one, and he could have found half a hundred places to keep the rifle safe.

Rutledge drove next to Isleham. The day was hot now, the air heavy. He left his motorcar in the shade cast by the trees in St. Andrew's churchyard, and walked to each of the addresses on his list.

The first three names were easily eliminated. One had actually come to Wriston to hear Swift, "to make up my mind, once and for all," he'd added. What's more he had been seen to give Swift a hand when the man stepped up on the base of the market cross, just before he'd begun his speech.

The other two had perfectly good alibis, one working behind the bar at the local pub, and the other playing cards with the brother of the Isleham constable. They had been together most of the evening.

Numbers four and five had no alibi, but one had served in Egypt, well away from France where Captain Hutchinson had spent his war, and the other had been a conscientious objector and had served as an orderly in a hospital in Devon.

Their names received a question mark, but after the interview he was inclined to think they were in the clear. And Hamish agreed.

The sixth name lived just below the church in a house set back from the road. Rutledge's first impression was that Lieutenant Thornton must be one of the more prosperous denizens of Isleham. There was a garden on either side of the steps, and the path leading up to them branched there to go toward a small folly, like a round Greek temple that must serve as a garden house. It reminded him vaguely of the Temple of the

Winds he'd seen in a book on Athens. And one of the two small wings on either side of the house was mainly glass, a conservatory, he thought.

The middle-aged woman who answered his knock wore the uniform of a housekeeper. He gave her only his name, asking to see Lieutenant Thornton.

"I'll see if he's receiving visitors, sir. A moment, please."

He waited several minutes for her to return.

"Mr. Thornton will see you now," she said. "This way, if you please."

He followed her into a central hall and down a passage that led to a very masculine sitting room, framed maps on the wall and a large globe on a stand in one corner.

Thornton was standing by the cold hearth. A tall slender man with fair hair and blue eyes, he greeted Rutledge pleasantly and offered him a chair.

"Is this about the Memorial Fund?" he asked. "I've been intending to send in my contribution. I'm sorry someone had to come all this way on my account."

"I'm from Scotland Yard, sir. I'm here in connection with the murders of two men, Captain Hutchinson in Ely and Mr. Swift in Wriston."

Thornton frowned. "Yes, a tragic business. I'll help in any way I can, but I don't precisely know how I can be of service."

"Had you ever met the Captain? While you were serving with the Army during the war? Or perhaps afterward, in London."

"I may have met him somewhere in France. If I did, I don't recall it. But I never served under him, if that's what you're asking. I don't often go to regimental functions and the like." He smiled grimly. "My rank is a battlefield commission. I joined as a private soldier and was promoted more or less against my will."

Rutledge gestured to the room they were in, indicating the house in general. "You could have trained as an officer."

"I didn't want the responsibility for the lives of others. Rather selfish of me, perhaps. I killed Germans when I had to, but sending other men out to die on my orders was something I couldn't face. Were you in the war? Yes. Then you'll know what I mean."

Rutledge did. All too well.

With Hamish rumbling in the back of his mind, he answered, "No one did that by choice. Only by necessity."

"Very true. Still, I was happy to serve under someone else."

"I understand Captain Hutchinson was in Burwell for a funeral several months before traveling to Ely for a wedding. A Major Clayton's services."

"I knew the Major, of course. I served under him. But I make it a point not to attend funerals. There have been too many. Men are still dying, although the war is nearly two years over. I didn't know the Major's sister very well—I'm sure my absence wasn't noticed."

"And Mr. Swift?"

"I've heard him speak, of course. But I'm not interested in politics. I do my duty, I vote. I don't mean that. Still, I haven't seen this better world we were told we were fighting for. If you want the truth, it's something I try to avoid thinking about. The future." It was his turn to gesture to the room at large. "I stay in the past, where it's safely, unemotionally over." A wry smile accompanied the remark. "I can do nothing to change the past and I have no responsibility for it."

"If you were in the ranks, you were given a rifle. What became of it?"

"*My* rifle? I daresay I had more than one whilst in France. The last one I turned in with the greatest relief when I was given my commission. That was in the last days of the war. I don't think I shot anyone after that. I tried not to. There were rumors of Armistice. It was all about to end, and I couldn't see any reason to kill another man whose only hope was to live a little longer and then possibly go home." He shrugged. "Not that they didn't do their best to kill us."

"Do you have any idea who might have wanted to see these two men dead? Or who shot at Mr. Burrows the day before yesterday, narrowly missing him?"

"Burrows? The farmer? My God," Thornton said blankly. "As for the other two, I don't know enough about the matter to do more than hazard a guess. And that would be someone who hasn't finished his war. For whatever reason. Rather frightening to think about. I have my own nightmares, God knows." His eyes were suddenly different, his features twisting with pain. "Mostly about the machine guns. I can't hide from them, and I know I'm going to die. The doctors told me this might pass. So far . . ." He shook his head, unable to finish. Getting up, he walked to the window and stared out at nothing until he could turn to face Rutledge again.

"Is there anything else?" he asked. "I'd rather not talk about the war any longer."

"Are you married? Do you have a family?"

"Sadly no. I thought I was engaged once. And then the war came along. I don't think there's anyone now who would wish to share this life. How do you explain to a woman who hasn't been to war what it was like, and why you have changed so much?"

Rutledge had no answer to give him. He'd carried his love for Jean throughout the war as a promise of happiness when it was finished. And instead he'd had to find the courage to set her free, rather than tie her to the shambles he had become. To add to his pain, he could see how relieved she had been, how happy to walk away and not have to deal with what she didn't understand and didn't want to face. Very soon thereafter, she'd married someone else.

And there was Meredith Channing, who had also left him to find the man she was married to, and whom by her own admission, she hadn't loved.

The room around him seemed to close in, and he made his escape before he could say or do anything that Thornton could recognize. *Shell shock.* Disgrace and cowardice and lack of moral fiber . . .

Outside he walked on to the churchyard, tree-shaded and quiet, avoiding the memorial to the war dead. It struck him that this island of tranquility was only a matter of miles from the hustle and bustle of Newmarket, the center of horse racing.

Someone was coming in through the lych-gate, carrying a pot of flowering plants and a small trowel, walking toward a fresh grave he could just see near the apse. Avoiding the woman, he turned and went into the church.

It was lit by the small but elegant clerestory illuminating the dark framework of the magnificent hammer-beam roof. He stood there and stared up at it, letting the conversation with Thornton fade. The emotions the man had roused were always too near the surface, like exposed nerves, sensitive to the touch, even to the air. No matter how many times he might tell himself he had begun to heal, he could see that Thornton had not, and it was a reflection of his own guilt.

And then, concerned that the woman planting the flowers might well come into the church to say a prayer for the dead—remembering how the Rector in Wriston had come upon him unexpectedly—he hastily turned to leave.

Taking with him, unwittingly, the thought that there had been no Green Man here, only angels decorating the ceiling above his head.

It was tempting to go to the rambling old Red Lion pub for a drink, but Rutledge had other calls to make.

Finishing those, he walked around the village a little, looked at the old priory that had become a barn, and then made his way back to the motorcar. And still Hamish was there in his mind, refusing to go, reminding him again and again of his encounter with Thornton.

Giving up, he drove back to Wriston. Had it been a mistake to interview the ex-soldiers? But where else

was he to turn for answers, if not to men who had handled rifles, knew them intimately, and could probably
still shoot as well with them as they had in the trenches.

Priscilla Bartram was on the lookout for him, and
met him at the door, for all the world like a wife awaiting her husband's return from the fields or the shops.
Her life was a lonely one, and he could understand that
his presence was at once comforting and comfortable.
But there was nowhere else in the village to stay.

She offered him a drink, but he was no longer interested in a whisky. Instead he told her he would work
in his room, writing up the day's report for Inspector
Warren in Ely.

"You'll be down later for dinner? I found a nice bit
of beef at the butcher's."

"In an hour, then." He smiled and went up the stairs.

But not to work. He stood by the window for a time,
then sat down at the desk to take out the stationery
there, imprinted with the same scene that was on the
iron sign outside.

He wrote a note to his sister, Frances, telling her
where he was—she had not been in London when he
left—and adding that it would probably be a longer
inquiry than he'd expected. He asked her to collect his
mail and then could think of nothing else to say.

In the end, he balled the note up and tossed it aside.

Thinking better of leaving it for Miss Bartram to find, he collected it from the floor and put it in his luggage instead.

It was while he was putting his valise back in the armoire that he had the thought.

And Miss Trowbridge had unwittingly given it to him.

The Green Man.

A face, often smiling without real humor, in a circlet of leaves, as if the man were poking his head out of them to see what was happening around him. Sometimes the leaves grew from his head or his face, half concealing it, like a man's hair and beard. A pagan symbol, yet popular in churches or in the names of pubs in a few places he'd been. Something so commonplace and conventional that he'd missed the significance.

And now, suddenly, it had triggered what must have been in the back of his mind from the start, but locked away in his other memories of the war.

Chapter 11

How many times had he and Hamish worked with a sharpshooter, turning him from a British soldier into a tree or a mound of straw or a ragged edge on the trench wall, creating their own Green Man, so to speak, but with deadly intent? Changing his face, disguising his body, wrapping his rifle so that it was invisible to the enemy?

It had taken patience and ingenuity, and the Germans were quick to see through whatever scheme they'd come up with. It was an ever-changing battle of wits.

But then the Germans had had snipers—sharpshooters—from the very start of the war. Trained men who were very good with a rifle and equally good at concealing themselves. Some would lie in wait for days, or from the middle of the night to midday, invisible in bits of straw or sacking, using whatever came to hand. Shell-blasted trees or stumps, the ruins of a building, or even the rim of a shell hole. Their targets were any head that popped up above the top of the trench—in the beginning the British soldiers had worn soft caps, not helmets—to see what was happening on the opposite side. Making the British and the French keep their heads down also left them blind.

In fact, the German telescopes were so good that sharpshooters were ordered not to let them fall into enemy hands.

It was an old concept, sharpshooters, not new to the Great War, but the British had been reluctant to employ such tactics. Sharpshooters had been used in the Second Boer War, but the British had had to begin all over again when they finally saw the necessity of fighting fire with fire in 1914. Even so, it was thought to be not quite the thing. Not sporting to take out a chap who didn't even know anyone was there, who didn't have an equal chance to kill as well as be killed.

And the men who did this work were often shunned, generally considered beyond the pale. They seldom boasted about their skill, passing themselves off outside their own companies as regular foot soldiers. But sometimes when the truth did leak out, they were pariahs. Even back in England they told no stories, never

bragged about their best kills, and often kept to themselves . . .

"Like Thornton?" Hamish asked.

That jarred Rutledge. He hadn't considered the possibility. Yes, Thornton was reclusive, but he was also a very
different sort of man from the sharpshooters Rutledge
had dealt with. Scots, most of them, and often retain-
ers on an estate where deer stalking was popular in the
autumn, and for the rest of the year, they were more than
a little feared by poachers. They possessed the eye of an
eagle, one Highlander had told him, and steel nerves. It
was all that was needed to take such a skill to war.

But now someone had brought that skill home with
him, and for some reason had begun to shoot again.

It wouldn't be the first time Rutledge had dealt with
a sniper. Then he himself had been the target.

The question now was, had the war returned to *this*
man, or had he found his former skill useful when he
decided to commit murder?

Hamish said, "It doesna' matter which came first."

And Hamish was right. It didn't. But to know might
make it easier to find a killer.

Those lists of ex-soldiers he'd asked Inspector Warren
to draw up were useless now, Rutledge could see that.
Finding out who among them had served as a sniper
would mean searching the War Office records. What's

more, he himself had often enlisted the help of the best marksman in his company, unofficially putting him to work when faced with a German sharpshooter who was pinning his men down. That had seldom gone into any records, a tacit agreement when the request was made. But they had got their man, and he'd been grateful.

Still, it hadn't hurt to let these village men know that they were under scrutiny by the Yard, whether one was the killer he was after or not. Somewhere on the lists was the name he was looking for, and if he was getting close—whether he knew it or not—it might force his quarry to keep a low profile for a while.

"Ye ken," Hamish went on, "that he's verra' guid. He didna' copy what he'd seen in the trenches."

That was true. This killer could think for himself. He could plan, he was patient, and he was willing to risk everything when he saw his opportunity.

And that made him all the more dangerous.

Rutledge considered whether or not to speak to Inspector Warren or possibly even Constable McBride. It was information that could be valuable.

And yet, if what Rutledge suspected ever became common knowledge, his advantage would be lost.

But he had his explanation now for the monster Mrs. Percy had seen. And it had been real enough. Only she hadn't known how to interpret it . . .

He wondered if the cooper in Soham had suspected the truth. It could explain why Ruskin had quietly left Wriston without giving McBride a statement.

Better to hunt the shadows alone, as long as he could.

Downstairs, he waited until his dinner was nearly finished. And then he said, "Tell me about the housemaid Herbert Swift dismissed after his wife died. Susan, her name was."

"Well, he was leaving for Scotland, of course, and Susan's roots are here in the Fens. She didn't want to go north. Nor did he want to take her. She'd been his wife's maid, she reminded him every day of his loss. I can't think she felt ill done by. And she's been such a help to the Rector."

"Perhaps she'll remember something that might be useful."

"It was so long ago, of course. Water under the bridge since then. But then Mrs. Swift came from Ely, didn't she? As I remember, she was a Phillips before she married."

That name hadn't come up in connection with the wedding guest list, not as far as he knew. He made a mental note of it.

"I was just a girl when she came to Wriston, and I thought her the most fashionable person imaginable."

Miss Bartram smiled at the memory. "I looked forward to seeing her Sunday morning, and I tried sometimes to copy her hats." The smile turned wry. "But of course it wasn't very successful. She was one of those women who could wear pretty hats, and I'm not. Still, it was a pleasure for me. And I expect for my mother as well. But it had an unhappy ending, didn't it? I don't think Mr. Swift ever looked at another woman after his wife died. Mrs. Prescott asked him how he expected to entertain in London, if he didn't take a wife. She's Teddy Prescott's widow, you see, and hopeful. But he told her he was intending to serve his constituents, not set himself up as a Londoner."

"Then after dinner I think I'll walk to the Rectory and have a word with Susan."

It was a quiet evening, and Rutledge stood for a moment, watching the ducks floating on the pond, gliding above their reflections and finally climbing out to waddle toward wherever it was they roosted at night. One of the dogs outside a house on the far side of the Green gazed after them with bored interest, then rested his head on his paws again with a drowsy sigh.

He had put it off long enough. It was time to face the Rector.

But March gave no indication that he mistook this call as a cry for help. He listened with courtesy to

Rutledge's request, called to Susan to come down and speak to the Inspector, and then left them alone in the small Rectory parlor.

She was older than he'd expected, her reddish hair threaded with gray, but her face was still smooth and her eyes were a bright blue.

"I'm trying to find something in Mr. Swift's life that may have led to his death," Rutledge began easily. "You worked for him for some time, and I wouldn't be surprised if you'd kept up a kindly interest in his well-being in the years that followed."

Susan Tompkins smiled. "He was a good man, you know. He had a love of history, and he was concerned about his clients, always looking out for those who needed his help but couldn't pay his fees. Once he took a pig in place of what he was owed, then he never had the heart to butcher it after it'ud grown to a good size. He said he couldn't bear to touch the meat."

"By history, do you mean the history of the Fens, the background of the people who lived here?" It was always possible that Swift had stumbled onto something that could mean trouble for a family or its holdings. Even if he kept it to himself.

"I can't count the times I dusted his bookshelves. There were books on Rome, six or seven, and weighty ones, you'd not dare drop one on a foot. And then there was Egypt. He bought all he could find. He told me once he'd have liked to go there. But of course there was no money for such a journey. Not for a country solicitor. I don't recall any books about the Fens."

But then as a solicitor he might have learned more than he should about his clients. He might not have needed a book.

"He had financial problems?"

"No, sir, he was comfortable enough, but it came from what he earned. And of course his wife's money. Not that that was excessive, but it was what he called a nice cushion. That's why he decided he might stand for Parliament now."

An interesting point.

"Why did he go to Scotland?"

"His wife had just died, sir, and he was at his wit's end. He wanted to close up the house, walk away from it. And then he was asked to go to Glasgow, for the Admiralty. Something to do with the ships on the River Clyde. Mr. Swift showed me where it was on the map. He'd always liked the sea, he even wrote to the Admiralty offering his services. And they took him on. It was, he told me, as far away as he could get from his memories. 'There'll be nothing there to remind me,' he said. 'I can step out my door of a morning and even the air will be different, and the weather, and the look of the land. I can shut out the pain and bury myself in my work.' And that's what he must have done because when he came back to Wriston, he was a different man."

"How different?"

Susan considered the question. "Settled in himself? I don't think the law was ever his calling. It was just a better way of making his living than farming. And in Scotland he'd done different things. It seemed to me that this made it possible for him to say yes when he was asked to stand for the vacant seat. He hadn't gone to Rome or Egypt, but he was no longer really here in Wriston, if you know what I mean. He'd tried to take up the law again, but his heart wasn't in it. I think perhaps it must have palled."

She was a perceptive woman, Rutledge thought. "Tell me about Mrs. Swift."

"Ah, she was the loveliest thing. Slim and fair and pretty as a picture. Her father spoiled her, but she had a sweet nature that made everyone love her. I was promoted to lady's maid when she was sixteen, and I came here to Wriston with her. My own father was from here, and I still had two aunties here. They're dead now, of course, but on my days off I'd go and visit them. So I wanted to stay here, after Mrs. Swift went. There was nothing left for me in Ely, you see, my parents being dead by then. Rector was happy to take me on."

"Swift must have taken a flat in Glasgow. Who looked after him there?"

"He wrote soon after he got there, to say he'd found a flat not far from the Cathedral, and there was a girl he'd found to come in twice a week. 'Nothing like you, Susan, which I must say is cheering for me. I don't care to look back. Not even to the happy times. But I hope you are content where you are. I want you to know I'll be all right, in a bit.'"

It was clear Susan had treasured her conversations with Swift, and that first letter. Rutledge could hear a slight change in the tone of her voice as she quoted her former employer. A softness too, that told him she'd been fond of the man.

But nothing in her memories helped him, as far as he could tell.

"After his return from Scotland, were there many visitors to Swift's house? Someone he'd known in Scotland or served with there?"

"I have no idea, but I think I'd have heard sooner or later, if there had been. Someone was bound to tell me if he'd had anyone in particular come to call. I could still serve at table if he had guests. Rector wouldn't have minded." There was the smallest touch of wistfulness in her voice. She wouldn't have left the Rector, perhaps, but the past still held her heart. She'd have gone to help Swift if he'd asked it of her.

"I believe Mrs. Swift was a Phillips before her marriage, and from Ely." He listed the names of Barbara Fallowfield's family and the Sedleys and several other people closely connected to the wedding, and asked if the Phillips family had known any of them.

But Mrs. Swift hadn't moved in such exalted circles, although her father had been a prominent barrister. Which meant that her marriage to a solicitor in Wriston hadn't been quite the step down he'd thought it might have been.

"Although pretty as she was," Susan said, defending her mistress's choice of husband, "she could have aimed higher. But she'd fallen in love, you see, and Society as such didn't matter to her. Still, I think her mother might have been pleased if she'd married better. She was more ambitious than Mr. Phillips."

A dead end, Rutledge told himself. Nothing here to lead him to a murderer. For all he could see, Swift had led a quiet and exemplary life.

Thanking Susan, he rose to leave, and then she said something that stopped him in his tracks.

"I remember one thing. It's probably not important. But perhaps I ought to mention it all the same. I'd like to see whoever shot Mr. Swift brought in and tried for it. Mr. Burrows's wife—she's dead now, she died of the influenza—told me once that Ben Montgomery and Mr. Swift had courted the same girl before Mr. Swift went to Ely for a trial and met Miss Phillips. She didn't marry either man, as it happens. But before she looked elsewhere, they'd come to blows over her. Out there on the Green, mind you, in front of half the world. I don't think they spoke again for years and years, Ben Montgomery and Mr. Swift."

"Who was this girl?"

"You'd have no way of knowing, of course, being a stranger here, but she was Miss Trowbridge's mother. Up from Bury to spend a summer here with the Montgomery girls."

The Montgomery family, it seemed, had owned one of the larger holdings, and it lay hard by the Swift farm in the direction of Soham. It was run now by the husband of one of the daughters of the house, Randolph Abbot.

The next morning, following Constable McBride's directions, Rutledge found the drive leading up to the farm and was met there by a large Irish wolfhound who sniffed his boots and followed him up the broad pair of steps.

The house was a little grander than that of the Swifts or the Burrowses, and there was a large bed of flowers where the drive looped in front of the door. Although as Hamish was pointing out, *drive* was more or less a courtesy term for the hard-packed clay that made up the roads, tracks, and lanes in the Fen country.

A young woman answered his knock and told him that her mother was in. He was led to a sunny room in the back of the house where a new sewing machine had just been set up and was being tested.

Mrs. Abbot was plump, there was no other word for it, and as her daughter brought a stranger through the door, she looked up, her face flushed from attempting to thread the machine's needle.

"Mama, this is Mr. Rutledge, here to see you. He's from Scotland Yard," the younger woman informed her mother.

"Indeed," she said, straightening up. "Do have a try, Charlotte, your eyes are better than mine. Now then, Mr. Rutledge, how can I help you?"

"I understand Miss Trowbridge's mother used to come to Wriston in the summer and was a houseguest of yours?"

The pinkness was fading from her face as she gestured to a chair, and she said, "My goodness, that was years ago. However did you discover she'd been here? Did Marcella tell you?"

"It was someone in the village."

"I wonder who. Well, then, what can Miss Trowbridge's mother have to do with Scotland Yard?"

"I understand that Mr. Swift and your brother vied for her attention one summer, and it resulted in a quarrel between the two men."

Mrs. Abbot laughed. "Hardly men. I think they must have been all of seventeen. I was ten, and my sister was nineteen. She had gone to school with Helena in Bury, and in the summer holidays she invited Helena to stay with us for a few weeks. Of course with a new and pretty face about, all the lads were falling over themselves to attract her attention. When Herbert and Ben fell to, it was more a scramble than a fight, and Helena was dying of embarrassment. As I remember, it began with a promise Helena had made to Herbert Swift to come and see the new foal at his father's farm. The lads didn't speak for a fortnight or so, and then Helena was gone, back to Bury."

"But would your brother have told you if that resentment had lasted?"

"They were far too young to be thinking of marriage. It was a summer's infatuation, nothing more. Two years later, Helena was engaged to James Trowbridge."

"Who was the village doctor in Wriston, as I understand it. Until his wife persuaded him to live in Bury."

"Well—yes, that's true. But you must understand that Helena had been brought up in Bury, her father had friends in Cambridge, and she was often taken to concerts and plays and the like. She enjoyed her summer fling on a farm, it was not her life."

He was listening to something Hamish was saying—that Herbert Swift had not been happy as a farmer's son.

Rutledge said, "Was it the visit of this girl from Bury that made Swift decide to become a solicitor rather than farm with his brother?"

Mrs. Abbot's eyebrows flew up in surprise. "I'd never thought about that, to tell you the truth. Perhaps it was. But of course he married a girl from Ely. Not Helena."

Still, Helena's visit must have sown the seeds of discontent. Even a gentleman farmer's lot was not going to satisfy a young man who had glimpsed another world, one where he had seen himself lacking the polish and sophistication to enter.

The question now was, how had that visit changed Ben Montgomery?

"And your brother? What has become of him?"

A cloud passed over her face. "Ben chose the Army. He went to Sandhurst, over his father's objections. We'd had a military band come to Ely that summer, and we all went to hear them play on Palace Green. Ben talked of nothing else after that. It broke my mother's heart. She was never the same afterward."

"Where is he now?"

"Ben? He lives in London. We don't see him very often. The Army changed him. He was such a sweet boy, kind to Shirley and me, always helping Papa and the men on the farm, and of course was the heir to it. But when I married he asked my husband to take it on." She looked around the room. "I was born in this house, you know. I still live here."

"And your older sister?"

"She married a trainer down in Newmarket. She loved horses, I wasn't surprised when she brought Ted home."

"How did the Army change your brother?"

"He was always such a skinny lad. You wouldn't know him now, his shoulders as wide as a door, and three more inches in height. But that was all right, you know. It was the grimness about him that made him a stranger to us. When I said something about that, he told me that he killed men for a living, and it was expected of him to live with it. I asked him why he didn't walk away, and he said he liked the Army, most of his friends were soldiers, and he didn't know what else he might like to do." She glanced toward her daughters, then turned back toward Rutledge. "I shouldn't have told you that. I can't think why I did. I doubt I've mentioned Ben to anyone in a long time."

"He survived the war, then?"

"Oh, yes. He was wounded several times and has the scars to prove it, so he says. But he's still a serving officer."

He asked for Montgomery's regiment and she told him.

It had seen heavy fighting in the first days of the war.

"Is he married?"

"He was courting someone, but nothing came of it. The Burrows girl. But her father wasn't keen on their marriage. And she's never found anyone else."

A tangle of lives, he thought, and it would be up to him to sort out whether or not Marcella Trowbridge's mother had set in motion something that had seen two men killed and one wounded.

"Did your brother know a Major Clayton? Or Captain Hutchinson?"

"I have no idea," she said, shaking her head. "It's not something he'd mention in his letters. They're usually no more than a few words to tell us he's well and to ask after us. As if he doesn't know what else to say."

"Mama," the younger daughter interrupted diffidently. "Charlotte has the needle threaded at last."

"Wonderful, my dear. Thank you. Is there anything else, Mr. Rutledge? I don't think I've been very much help."

But she had. He thanked her and left.

What he'd learned from Mrs. Abbot warranted traveling to London, but he was reluctant to leave the Fen country just now. He drove back to Wriston, intending to go on to Ely, but as an afterthought he stopped at Miss Trowbridge's door and asked if he could speak to her.

She greeted him coolly but allowed him to come inside.

For once Clarissa was awake, and she examined him with interest, picking up the scent, he thought, of the Irish wolfhound.

"I've just called on Mrs. Abbot," Rutledge began, taking the seat he was offered. "I understand your mother came one summer to visit the Montgomery sisters."

"She did. It was her first visit to the Fens. I don't think she'd have come again if she hadn't met my father. She liked Society, and there's very little of that in Wriston." Echoing what Mrs. Abbot had said, Marcella Trowbridge added, "Farmers and their wives work from first light to last. There isn't time for visiting art galleries or attending the theater or musical evenings. It was the way my mother had been brought up."

"And yet you—and your grandmother, who had this cottage before you—have been happy enough in Wriston."

"You don't know if I'm happy or not," she retorted sharply.

"Yes, that's true. Sorry. I was also told that Herbert Swift and Ben Montgomery quarreled over your mother."

She smiled suddenly, lighting her face with brightness. "I've heard that story. They were only boys. The fight was broken up by the man who kept the windmill. Angus."

"Angus?"

"He was a Scot. At a guess he left the Highlands to seek his fortune, and very likely he got no farther than Cambridgeshire before his money ran out. I do know he was more or less adopted by the old man who kept the mill at that time. Mr. Sherborne had no son, and Angus had no father. They hit it off, and Angus took over the mill when Mr. Sherborne was too ill to work it any longer."

"Where is this man Angus now?"

"I should think he's dead. He left Wriston years ago, but I remember him from my childhood. A quiet, lonely man. He liked my grandmother. But at the end of each December he got terribly drunk—some sort of Scottish holiday—and then was completely sober for the rest of the year."

"Hogmanay," Hamish said, in the back of Rutledge's mind, and before he could stop himself, he repeated the word aloud.

"I'm sorry?" Miss Trowbridge said, uncertain.

"It's the Scots' new year," Rutledge replied. "Celebrated with food and whisky."

"I don't think Angus was very much interested in the food. But he did enjoy his drink."

"You call him Angus. What was his full name?"

"I don't think I ever heard it. He was always just—Angus."

Another false lead.

"Why did the mill house burn?" he asked, curious.

"I don't really know. There are any number of stories. It was a windy, stormy night, and I expect a lamp blew over. Our roof was damaged as well, and two of the blades of the mill were broken. There was more trouble in the village. Slates from the church roof, a few trees down, a chimney, and even a few flowerpots dislodged from steps and doorways." She gestured toward the world outside. "It's so flat, you see. There's nothing to stop the wind for miles, and then suddenly there's a village in its path. Without the mill we feared there would be extensive flooding. But the rain passed with the wind. That was all that saved us."

He had a feeling she hadn't told him the truth. But why would she lie?

He thanked her and rose.

"The mill house is said to be haunted. Or was," she went on as she followed him to the door. "I don't know if fire destroys ghosts as well as buildings."

"How was it haunted?"

"Angus claimed it was haunted by his wife. I hadn't known he'd been married, and I asked if she had died. He told me that not all ghosts are dead. I thought it an odd thing to say. But Mr. Sherborne claimed it was haunted too. I never knew him, but apparently he often told the story that two of the Dutchmen brought over to drain the Fens had played cards there one night. There were two versions of the story. One version held that it was on a Sunday that they were playing, and the Devil came and took their souls, leaving only their bodies with nowhere to go. The other version claims that they fought and one killed the other, but not before he'd been gravely wounded himself. And he died later of his wounds. He goes back to the house, looking for his friend, to make certain he's dead."

She lived here alone, out by the mill, Rutledge thought, but the stories seemed not to trouble her. If ghosts walked, she didn't see or fear them.

But he thought she must be haunted in some way. He remembered finding her staring up at the mill, as if searching for something. Or waiting for someone?

"Who looks after the mill now?" Rutledge asked. "It's still a working mill, is it not?"

"Yes, it is. Currently it's the ironmonger who sees to it. It's a hobby, I think, that he's grown tired of, but no one else has come forward. The Rector offered, but then when it comes to machinery, he's rather at sixes and sevens."

In the afternoon Rutledge drove to Ely, to try again to reach Sergeant Gibson.

Clouds were building on the horizon now, and the air had that oddly heavy feeling that presaged a storm.

Rutledge paid a courtesy call on Inspector Warren before going on to the telephone, to report what he'd learned—but not what he suspected about the killer.

Warren smiled wryly. "You've not made much progress."

"I've brought that list of ex-soldiers." He took it out and spread the sheets across Warren's desk so they could study it at the same time. "This is what I've discovered thus far. What do you know about the sort of war these men had? The ones with the question mark by their names. I've spoken to them, but I wasn't satisfied when I left that they were in the clear." He stepped back and waited.

"A little. But I'm not sure what you're after," Warren said, parrying the question.

"Have they been troublesome in the past?"

"The only trouble has been occasional public drunkenness and assault. It's not unusual for a man who served in the war to find himself in an altercation with someone who wasn't. I've told you, we don't run to murders, here. Although you'd think, given the isolation of the Fens, that we'd regularly find a body or two in the ditches or under one of the bridges. There are people in Newmarket who might wish to be rid of a troublesome debtor or the like. But the thing is, people down there don't know the Fens; they couldn't hide a body as well as I could, for one. And since you can see for great distances, someone stopping a motorcar to toss a corpse into a ditch is more likely to be spotted than someone around, say, Norfolk, with its low hills."

Whoever his man was, Rutledge thought, he hadn't hurried into murder. He'd waited, and rid himself of his target in such a way that he wasn't a suspect.

"Thornton. Ruskin. Brenner. What do you know about them?"

"Nothing professionally. Thornton's family goes back a long way in the Fens—to the fifteen hundreds, I expect. There are memorials in the churchyard at Isleham to many of them. I'd be surprised if he turned out to be our man. Quiet, respectable, and no history of violence. Ruskin and Brenner haven't been quite the same since the war. But they've done nothing out of character that I got wind of. Brenner was drunk once or twice, but as a rule he's sober, and even if he's drunk he stays in his house. Ruskin keeps to himself, is surly sometimes with his custom, but no better nor worse than the others."

"It doesn't mean they don't have another life."

"If they do, then they've managed to keep it quiet. There's been no gossip."

"What about Ben Montgomery?"

"I don't think he's been home again more than three or four times in ten years. You're out of luck, Rutledge." He smiled to take any sting out of the words.

"Brenner knew Hutchinson. I'd swear to it."

"Did he, by God?" Inspector Warren said, rapidly rethinking his rather cavalier dismissal of Brenner and the others.

It was Rutledge's turn to smile. "And Montgomery is in the Army in London. What are the odds that he hasn't at least encountered Hutchinson? He most certainly knew the Swift brothers and Burrows."

"What else haven't we uncovered?"

"That's the question." Rutledge began to collect the lists.

"Are you going to London, then?"

"Not yet. But I shall have to if I'm to question Miss Clayton and Montgomery. And find out how Brenner knew Hutchinson."

"Miss Clayton? Captain Clayton's sister? I knew him before the war."

"Hutchinson came to his funeral. In Burwell."

"I'll be damned." Warren stared. "Are you sure of that?"

"It helps," Rutledge said, "to remember that even people we think we know well can kill."

The call to London yielded no fresh information. Sergeant Gibson had found little to pass on. "There's not been much time," he explained.

Still, Rutledge gave him the three names he'd mentioned to Inspector Warren. "I don't think you'll find skeletons in these closets, not unless we're very lucky. But I have to be sure."

He had intended to stop at The Lamb for his dinner. It was close by the Cathedral and even older than The Deacon, where he'd stayed earlier. But wind was already tossing the trees as he went back to his motorcar, and the sky in the east was black. He had no wish to be crossing the Fens in a driving rainstorm, and it appeared that that was what was coming.

He could hear the thunder behind him as he drove out of Ely, and it rode his coattails out across the Fens. There was the faintest line of sunset on the western horizon, and it seemed to intensify the darkness behind him. The storm loomed like a great black beast, shot with lightning and roiled by the wind.

Halfway to Wriston, he heard a motorcycle coming up behind him, throttle open, racing the storm. It passed him with a roar, but he could see it long after the sound had faded into the distance. Then it was over one of the humpback bridges and lost to sight.

Not five minutes later, great drops of rain, driven by heavy gusts, hit with the force of hail, and Rutledge picked up speed, putting the large motorcar through its paces on the straightaway. The duck pond was empty as he reached the second green, and the trees near the church were thrashing like tormented souls. He came to a skidding halt in front of The Dutchman Inn, and made it through the door just as a crash of thunder followed a blue flash of lightning.

"Mr. Rutledge?" Miss Bartram's voice came from the sitting room, sharp and anxious.

"Yes, I just missed the storm," he called, his words almost lost as the rain came down in wild sheets, pounding the roof and making the windows rattle.

She came to meet him, her face anxious.

"Something's happened," she said. "Constable McBride was just here, asking for you."

Chapter 12

Rutledge looked out at the High Street, almost invisible in the blowing sheets of rain. Lightning flashed, thunder crackling almost on its heels, and Miss Bartram cried out.

He slammed the door against the still-rising wind.

"Has anything happened to Mr. Burrows?"

"I-I don't know. I don't—Constable McBride didn't say—just that it was urgent."

He could hear the wind rising as the thunder moved toward them, and he debated trying to reach the police station. Almost at once he thought better of it.

Whatever had happened, it would have to wait. There was nothing either he or McBride could do just now.

Miss Bartram said, "I was intending to put the kettle on. I—" She broke off as thunder seemed to shake the house. The glass drops on the tall lamp behind her tinkled discordantly, and in the kitchen something fell with a crash. "I do hate these late storms so!" Turning, she hurried into the sitting room and sat down. "It will be over soon, that's the one saving grace. Meanwhile—" The lightning was blue, reflected in the glass of the displays, seeming to surround them. The next clap was deafening.

Standing in the doorway between the sitting room and the short hall, Rutledge said, "I think that struck something. But not here. It should be moving on now."

And he was right. They could follow the storm as it swept westward. In a few minutes the worst had passed, leaving behind a hard rain. Lifting the curtain to look out at the street, he could see that it was awash with puddles, and that surely meant that the ditches were full, nearing capacity. It was a sobering thought.

With a word to Miss Bartram, Rutledge opened the inn door. Turning to step outside, he encountered Miss Trowbridge, umbrella in hand, hurrying toward them. Her skirts were wet and heavy with mud.

"The lightning struck one of the arms of the mill. We need to repair it as soon as possible."

"Who do you need?"

"Mr. Ross. He'll know what to do."

"Come inside. I'll find him."

"My shoes are muddy—"

"Never mind, come inside."

He waited until she was safely indoors, took her umbrella with him, and got the motorcar started. Reversing in a spray of muddy water, he drove down to the ironmonger's shop. Ross was inside, tidying up the table with the boxes of nails.

As soon as he saw Rutledge striding through the doorway, he said, "Was it the mill?"

"Yes. I'm afraid so. One arm, according to Miss Trowbridge."

"Right. I'll get what I need and collect the others."

He turned toward the back of his shop as Rutledge said, "Can I help?"

"We've repaired it before. We'll manage."

Following him, Rutledge could see the fields beyond the shop, glistening with water as the sun tried to break through the heavy clouds in the east, a single ray lighting up the sky for a moment and then vanishing just as quickly.

Ross was right, he seemed to have everything in hand. Rutledge turned, went out through the High Street door, and made his way through the rain to the police station.

McBride was at his desk, and he rose as Rutledge came in.

"You're soaked, man," he said. "Were you on the road when this hit?"

"I made it as far as the inn in time. But there's an arm of the mill that's down. Lightning. Ross is collecting his people to see to it."

"I'm needed, then. This came for you. An hour ago." He passed an envelope to Rutledge. "Special messenger."

The motorcycle.

Rutledge tore open the envelope and pulled out a sheet of paper.

The message was from Jason Fallowfield, forwarded by Inspector Warren.

I've spoken to Mr. Lowell, the father of the artillery officer, Major Lowell, who offered his help to Inspector Warren. His son will be in Ely this evening, passing through from Lincoln. I thought you'd want to know. If you could call around seven, I'll be happy to arrange for a meeting.

Rutledge took out his watch. There was barely enough time to reach Ely.

"I must go. Miss Trowbridge is at the inn. Give her the umbrella. And tell Miss Bartram that I'll probably be staying over in Ely."

And he was out the door, back in his motorcar, and setting out for Ely. He could watch the clouds lift, and the Cathedral appear like a mirage again, floating above the steaming fields. The road under his tires, slick clay, with puddles concealing the pits and ruts, was treacherous and took all his concentration. He was aware of Hamish in the rear seat, just behind his right shoulder, but had no time for him. The bottoms of his trousers, one sleeve, and across his back where the rain had soaked his clothing felt the cool wind of his passage, but there was nothing to be done about them.

The Cathedral clock was showing five minutes after seven o'clock as he caught sight of it passing Palace Green. And it was nearly ten after the hour when he pulled up in front of the house belonging to the bride's family.

It was still raining as he walked up the path, and he could feel the wet soaking through his coat, damp against his flesh now.

The same maid opened the door to him. "Mr. Rutledge?"

"Yes, that's right."

"Mr. Fallowfield and Mr. Hale are waiting for you in the library. If you'll come this way?"

He followed her down the passage, where he was shown into a large library, shelves ranging around the

room, and long windows looking out on a garden drip-
ping and windblown.

Jason Fallowfield and his father-in-law rose to greet
him, and Fallowfield made the introductions.

"Major Lowell is just changing for dinner. He was
held up by the storm. Are you all right?"

"I'm afraid I was caught in it as well," Rutledge said.
"It's kind of you to arrange this meeting."

"Not at all. I'm glad to have been of some use."

Hale, who was tall, slender, and graying, said, "I
really don't see what can be gained by this meeting,
but Jason here tells me you were very anxious to meet
Alex."

"He was there," Rutledge said. "He may have
noticed something that the rest of us have missed."

"I am astonished that no progress has been made—"
He broke off as the library door opened again and the
Major walked in.

Fallowfield introduced Rutledge and then said, "I'm
sure you'd like to speak to Alex alone. Mr. Hale and I
will join the ladies in the drawing room."

It was clear that Hale would have preferred to
stay. And Rutledge could understand why—after all,
it was the wedding of his daughter that had nearly
been ruined by the shooting. But Fallowfield showed
unusual resolve in ushering him out of his own library.

Rutledge had used the moment to judge Lowell.

He was of medium height, his carriage that of a career military man, his fair hair already graying at the temples. He came forward, took one of the chairs, and said, "I have only a few minutes. I've given my statement to Inspector Warren, but I understand that you have several questions about that day."

"You seemed to take charge very efficiently."

"There were no policemen. Hale hadn't hired any to handle the traffic, as the motorcars were to stop at the top of the Green. I myself sent someone to bring the police to the Cathedral. Young Fallowfield seemed to be thunderstruck, and I got him out of the way as quickly as possible. My first thought, God knows why, was that the man with the rifle had meant to kill *him*. Hutchinson wasn't even in the wedding party, a guest only, and certainly Fallowfield thought it likely as well that he must have been the intended target."

"I'm afraid I don't understand the logic of that. Why should someone wish to kill the groom on his wedding day? Surely the man with the rifle knew what he was doing?"

"Who else would anyone be shooting at?" Lowell countered. "We most certainly had no idea why Hutchinson should be killed. Hale was arriving with his daughter; the other important guests had already been seated. The groom was there, a matter of feet away. I heard the shot, of course, and I looked at every possible vantage point. I saw no one. No one at all. Whoever it was hadn't stood there gloating, he'd vanished. But that didn't mean he wasn't going to take a second shot from another position. With the groom safely away, I waited for the police, who came promptly, I must say. And with all due respect, Inspector Warren hadn't been in France. He was doing his best, but he was as shocked as the rest."

"Where was the killer?"

Lowell frowned. "I would have said that the shot came from above my head, but the doorway confused the sound, it echoed and changed it. I don't know Ely very well and wasn't aware until later that one can go up into the tower. Still, the most likely source was by that gate into the Cathedral grounds. It was most certainly his best chance of getting away unobserved."

"You don't think he took a greater risk, using the tower?"

"I was there in the doorway. He'd have had to pass me."

"But you weren't. You ran forward to make sure Fallowfield was moved to safety, and the doorway was unguarded. I've climbed up there. It takes time to make your way down."

Staring at him, Lowell considered the matter. "Yes, of course. You're right. I should have remained where I was. But I didn't. And I don't know that anyone else stayed there."

"Did you see a man with a barrow?"

"A barrow. No. I don't believe so. Or I should say I never saw the barrow. But come to think of it, as I was motioning Hale and his daughter to leave the scene as quickly as possible, I did see a frightened old man with a bicycle. I don't know where he came from, but after I'd shut Fallowfield in the Bishop's quarters, I noticed him being buffeted by people running up the street from the school."

"Was he carrying anything?"

"No, both hands were on the handlebars, as I remember."

"Did you mention him to Inspector Warren when you gave your statement?"

"I don't believe I did. Until you asked about the barrow, I'd quite forgot him. Besides, he was hardly a threat."

There was a tap at the door. It opened on the heels of that and Jason Fallowfield said apologetically, "Sorry. But they're going in to dinner."

"I've kept you too long, Major. Thank you for your help."

Fallowfield politely accompanied Rutledge to the outer door, saying, "I must apologize for my father-in-law. He's still rather bitter about what happened that day. And I can't fault him for that. But we were there, and if we can help the police in any way, so much the better."

"I'm grateful," Rutledge said. "We'll have our man in the end. It's just a matter of time."

But as he walked back to his motorcar in the light rain that was falling now, Hamish was reminding him that he had been rash to promise.

He drove not to The Deacon Inn but to the house Teddy Mathews shared with his sister.

They too had just sat down to their evening meal, and Miss Mathews was reluctant to interrupt it.

"We have guests. It would be more convenient if you could return tomorrow."

"I won't be in Ely tomorrow," Rutledge told her. "And it's rather urgent."

She went to fetch her brother, and apparently he'd seen her displeasure, for he asked almost at once, "Has something happened?"

"I need to clarify one point in your statement," Rutledge said carefully. "Did you see an elderly man with a bicycle standing with you behind the barricade?"

"I don't believe I did," he answered slowly. "Should I have?"

"I can't be sure until we find this man. But thank you—and you as well, Miss Mathews—for taking the time to assist the police."

From there he went to the house of Mrs. Boggs, the washerwoman.

She had just finished her tea, and affably asked him if he'd had his.

"Yes, thank you, Mrs. Boggs," he told her. "There's just one question I'd like to ask. Did you notice anyone with a bicycle walking past the Cathedral doors just after the shot was fired?"

"A bicycle? I can't say that I did." She cocked her head to one side, as if listening to an inner voice. "But now you mention it, I did see an elderly man coming out of the church. I don't know where he went. I expect he'd been in one of the chapels, praying. Certainly not one of the wedding party."

"Did he have anything in his hands?"

"I don't believe he did. Just an old man looking as if he were ill."

He thanked her and left.

Inspector Warren had gone home for his own dinner when Rutledge called in at the police station. He was directed instead to a young constable who worked with Warren.

Constable Nash said, "Do we have a statement from the elderly man seen coming out of the church? I'll look, sir, but I don't recall that statement in particular. Was he one of the wedding guests?"

"I understand that he was not."

Constable Nash led him to Inspector Warren's office and went around the desk to open the center drawer. Taking out a list, he scanned it. "I don't think he's here. Unless he's that one." He pointed to a name on the second page. "He was with his daughter, as I remember."

"It's likely he was riding a bicycle."

"A bicycle, sir?" Nash scanned the list again. "Are you sure he was coming out of the church?"

"One source says he was on a bicycle. The other that he was coming out of the church."

Nash shook his head. "I must say, he's not on our list. But people had come from the direction of The Lamb, you know—that is, from the street behind the barricade—and simply kept going. They hadn't been present when Captain Hutchinson was killed, they'd just been attracted by the sound of the rifle and then hurried on after they saw a man lying on the Green." He smiled deprecatingly. "It was a Saturday, sir, and a fair day. Everyone was out and about, doing a little marketing, taking their children or their dog for a walk. We have well over a hundred statements here."

"Yes, I understand. It's probably of no importance, then. Thank you, Constable. I shan't disturb Inspector

Warren tonight. Will you leave a message for him? That I spoke to Major Lowell, and I think he can be removed from the list of suspects."

"I'll do that, sir. Thank you, sir."

It was close on nine now, and the rain had finally stopped. Rutledge had lost his appetite and decided to drive back to Wriston after all.

Clouds were still scudding across the sky, and the frogs had begun a chorus in the flooded fields and the ditches. In one place the embankment had been breached, and water covered the road. He tested the depth and changed his mind about driving through it in the dark. Reversing, he went back to the last cross-roads, and found the turning for Isleham.

He was nearly there when close by the priory barn he saw a man out walking, keeping to the shadows.

Rutledge slowed, and watched for a moment. There was something furtive about the man's movements, and he was carrying something in his left hand.

Hamish said, "He doesna' move like a man full of the drink."

Rutledge had been thinking the same thing. After a moment, he left the motorcar where it was and, walking across the wet grass toward the priory barn, followed the shadowy figure. It had disappeared around the corner of the building, and Rutledge went after him.

He'd just reached the corner and was about to turn it, when someone came around from the far side and nearly blundered into him.

"Who the hell are you and what are you doing here?"

Rutledge said, "I could ask you the same thing. I'm Scotland Yard."

The man moved back. "Indeed. Rutledge, is it? I'm Thornton. You interviewed me."

"What are you doing out here?"

"I saw someone lurking about in the churchyard. I was just coming home—I'd got caught in the rain over in Soham. I watched for a minute or two, couldn't decide what he was doing, and started after him to ask his business. But he went out through the lych-gate, doubled back, and disappeared in this direction. I'd like very much to know who he was."

"Where did he go?"

"That's just it. I lost him on the far side of the barn. He simply disappeared."

"Did you go inside?"

"The door is locked. To keep the young people out, and to prevent the Travelers from using it to sleep rough."

"What did he look like?"

"I've no idea. I never got a good look at him." Thornton raised his left hand. "I brought a stick with me. Just in case. There's seldom trouble here in Isleham, but after the shootings, it puts the wind up when you see someone hanging about like that. At this hour of the evening."

"Was he carrying anything?"

"I don't know. It looked like it. A satchel or something. Or it could have been his dinner and his bedroll. It was too dark to be sure."

Then which man had attracted Rutledge's attention? Thornton with his stick? Or the interloper with his bedroll? It was impossible to tell. And yet there was no reason for Thornton to be sneaking around in his own village unless he *was* following someone else.

"Let's have another look."

Together they walked around the barn, but there was no one to be seen.

"He could have gone through the fields, but I doubt it," Thornton was saying. "The thing is, they're wet, and the pitches are running high. What brings you to Isleham? Still interviewing ex-soldiers?"

"The road from Ely to Wriston is flooded."

"Not surprising. There are low places along there. And sometimes the banks are weakened and the water comes through. I'll report it."

"Can I give you a lift?"

"Yes, that's kind of you." They walked together toward Rutledge's motorcar. "What brings you out at this hour?"

"I was in Ely. Police business."

Thornton smiled, a flash of white teeth in the darkness as he turned toward Rutledge. "Successful, I hope."

"Early days," Rutledge answered.

It was not far to Thornton's house. Rutledge stopped and his passenger got down.

"Thanks. If I discover who it was, I'll let you know." He turned and walked up to his door, setting the stick to one side before going inside.

Rutledge watched him go.

And then he went back to the priory barn and searched a second time. But no one was there. Where had the man gone?

He stopped at the barn door and tested it, even though Thornton had told him it was kept locked. It swung open, a greater darkness inside.

"Anyone there?" he called, his voice echoing around the walls.

There was no answer. He stood there, testing the darkness. He'd left his torch in his motorcar. After a moment, he moved forward, working his way around the walls. But when he'd made a circuit of the interior, he found no one there. And no one had slipped out the door, he was nearly sure of that.

He went back to the motorcar and took out his torch. When he shone the light on the door, he saw that the lock had been broken. Someone then had forced his way inside while Thornton was moving around the walls outside.

He turned on the torch and cast the light about. Except for a few wet footprints on the dry, dusty floor, there was no other sign of whoever had come inside.

He must have escaped while Rutledge and Thornton were driving away. And where he was now was anyone's guess.

Rutledge went back to his motorcar and slowly drove up and down the streets of Isleham, but the only thing he saw was a dog trotting homeward. Rain had kept most people close.

So who had been out in the wet, lurking, as Thornton had put it, in the churchyard? Or had the man been a figment of Thornton's imagination?

Dissatisfied, he headed for Wriston, coming in from the direction of Burwell rather than the flooded Ely road and over the bridge past the mill.

In the flare of his headlamps, he could see the bald new repairs where the arm had broken. There was very little standing water, but Ross and his men had been quick, thanks to Miss Trowbridge's warning. Even so, he could hear the rush of water beneath the bridge, and there was the glitter of pooling in the ruins of the mill house.

A light glowed in the windows of Miss Trowbridge's cottage, and the door opened a little to let the white cat in. If she saw Rutledge she gave no sign of it, shutting the door as soon as Clarissa darted inside.

He continued to The Dutchman Inn and pulled up near the steps.

There was water on the street, puddles everywhere he looked as he splashed around the motorcar to the door. Miss Bartram had been watching for him. He walked in to find her just coming into the hall.

"I've put some dinner aside for you," she said cheerfully. "I thought perhaps there wouldn't be time to find anything in Ely."

It was kind of her, and he ate the food she warmed for him. But he couldn't satisfy her curiosity about what had taken him so long in Ely.

He wasn't sure he knew the answer to that himself.

Fog followed the rain. When Rutledge woke in the middle of the night, he could see the thick white mist outside his windows, wrapping the house in the eerie silence of three o'clock in the morning.

He went to the window to look out, but he could barely make out his motorcar.

Listening, using his ears rather than his eyes, he could have sworn he heard a bicycle being pedaled along the High. Was it his imagination, that half-asleep, half-awake moment when one is roused in the middle of the night? He couldn't be sure, and then the sound vanished, lost in the darkness.

What he heard next, he recognized instantly: the sound of a horse being ridden fast, coming from the direction of the mill.

He found his clothes without turning on the lamp, and slipping downstairs, he let himself out as quickly as he could.

The horse had gone past, he couldn't tell where, but he could no longer hear hoofbeats.

He began walking, using the High Street to guide him, staying in the middle of it. It wasn't long before he could hear voices in the distance, and using those as his goal, he walked on. The mist, mercifully, wasn't as thick as it had been that first night.

At length he could make out what sounded like McBride's voice, and then someone responding, urgent and frightened. A woman's voice? Miss Trowbridge, as far as he knew, didn't keep a horse. Who then? Miss Burrows?

"McBride?" he called, suddenly galvanized into action.

"Rutledge?" McBride answered. "I didn't know you were back. You'd better come."

He followed the voice, and there in front of a house door, not the police station, was McBride, his uniform donned over his nightshirt while Miss Burrows was holding the reins of her horse, peering anxiously into the mist.

Seeing him finally, she said, "I heard the shotgun. I was afraid to go to the house—in this. And so I came for help."

"You can't drive in this," McBride said to Rutledge. "You don't know the roads."

"I can try," Rutledge said. "But I think Miss Burrows ought to stay here."

"No. No, it's my father, I want to go." She hastily secured the horse while McBride was trying to persuade her to wait.

"We're wasting time," Rutledge said. "Are you coming, McBride?" He turned, hoping he could find his way back to the inn. The mist seemed to thin, thicken, and thin again. He recognized the dormer window of the ironmonger's shop and knew he'd passed the market cross without seeing it. And then the motorcar came into view. He bent to turn the crank as McBride hurried to open the rear door for Miss Burrows. Rutledge spared a fleeting thought for Hamish as she slid into the seat, then he was behind the wheel, reversing to drive back toward the mill.

It was difficult. He saw the gate to Miss Trowbridge's house and then nearly missed the turning over the bridge. Soon Miss Burrows, reaching over from the rear seat, pointed.

"There—the road you're after."

It was a straight run then, until the last of the trees lining the lane into the Burrows farm loomed to his left, and he made the turn with ease.

The problem was how to approach the house. He drove with care, missing the ruts he could see, slipping and sliding in the wet clay. Then the lights of the house glowed through the mist.

Out of the darkness came the most ferocious noise that Rutledge had ever heard. He stopped, and even as he pulled up the brake he realized it must be the dog that Burrows had been planning to borrow.

McBride was saying, "Good God, it's Black Shuck."

Miss Burrows countered with, "It's the dog. Something's wrong."

"We don't know that," Rutledge argued and blew the horn several times.

"Burrows?" he shouted. "It's Rutledge. And Constable McBride. We're here with your daughter. I'm coming in."

The shotgun fired, and even over the dog's barking, Rutledge could hear the pellets raining down in the trees on either side, ten feet ahead of his bonnet.

"Damn it, man, have you run mad?" Rutledge bellowed, angry now.

"Papa?" Miss Burrows cried, her voice breaking. "Please. Are you all right? What has happened? Please—I want to come in."

She was opening the door, getting out. Rutledge reached over the back of his seat and caught her arm.

"No. Stay where you are. He's going to shoot as soon as you come into range."

Miss Burrows fought him, crying and calling to her father.

Rutledge, keeping his eyes away from where Hamish should be sitting, pulled her back inside the motorcar.

And then through the mist Burrows shouted, "Is it you, Betty?"

Suddenly still, Miss Burrows said in a husky voice, "That's my mother's name. Betty."

"We'll have to wait for sunrise," McBride said. "But what if he's hit someone, and he's out there, wounded?"

"There's nothing we can do," Rutledge said quietly. "Walking up there is suicide."

"Betty?" Burrows called again. "Where are you?"

"Something's wrong," Miss Burrows was saying, "His heart—"

But Rutledge didn't think it was the man's heart. "Answer him. Let him think you're his wife."

"I can't."

"You must, if you expect us to help your father."

"Dear, is that you?" she responded, her voice trembling. "Why have you got out your shotgun? I want to come in. Will you let me?"

They sat there, waiting.

And then Burrows called, "McBride? Is that you, Constable?" The barking stopped. "What are you doing out here in the middle of the night?"

"I got word you'd seen something. I've come with the Inspector to see if you were all right."

"You aren't walking, are you?"

"No, we're in Mr. Rutledge's motorcar."

Rutledge turned the headlamps off and then back on again.

"Come in. Hurry. There's someone out there, and I don't think I missed him."

"All right. We're coming in," McBride called. "Don't shoot. We'll stop in front of the house."

And Rutledge eased in the clutch, moving slowly forward, prepared to reach for the brake if Burrows fired again.

This time he let them come as far as the steps of the house. Miss Burrows was out of the motorcar almost before Rutledge had stopped.

"Papa?" She ran into the house, calling her father. They could hear the dog's deep, throaty growl.

McBride was out and racing after her, calling to her to wait. Rutledge was at their heels.

They found Burrows sitting by the window of the front room. At his feet, its hackles rising, lay the largest brown dog Rutledge had seen in some time.

"Be quiet, Hector," Burrows said, then noticed his daughter. "I thought you were over with Ed and his wife."

"I was. I heard you fire. I didn't know what to do." She reached out to touch his shoulder and drew her hand back almost in the same movement.

"He's burning up with fever," she told the two men in a low voice.

Rutledge moved the lamp in order to see him better. One side of Burrows's face was swollen twice its size, red and inflamed where the bullet had grazed him.

"Hello," Burrows said now, as if they had come to call. He set the shotgun down by the chair, and added to his daughter, "I don't feel particularly well. Perhaps I ought to go lie down, now that you're here."

She turned quickly to Rutledge. "What are we to do?"

"He needs a doctor. As soon as possible," Rutledge said, moving around Burrows to put the shotgun out of reach, then leaning down to look at his face. The dog growled again, getting to its feet. "It's infected. The wound. I thought you'd taken care of it."

"He wouldn't let me. Not after that first day. He said it was healing."

But it hadn't.

Straightening up, Rutledge said, "Where is the nearest doctor?"

"Burwell."

"Then let's get him into the motorcar. The sooner he's there, the better."

But Burrows was rising to his feet, and the dog stood by him as if daring anyone to touch him. "I'm thirsty. I think I'll have a little water before I go up."

"Papa, we need to go to Burwell. To the doctor. Come with me, won't you?"

"I don't need a doctor," he said testily. "I'm all right. Just tired. What time is it?"

Rutledge stepped forward. "Mr. Burrows. Your daughter isn't feeling well either. I think we ought to take her to see a doctor. Will you come with us? I think she would be more comfortable if you did."

Burrows frowned as he looked at Rutledge. "Who are you?"

"I've come from London, Mr. Burrows. We need to hurry. Will you go with us?"

"All right," he said docilely. "If McBride thinks it best. Stay, Hector." The dog subsided, although it seemed uncertain.

"I do, I most certainly do," the constable said quickly.

Between them, Miss Burrows and McBride got her father outside and down to the motorcar. The dog followed as far as the door, then stopped.

Burrows, turning to look at it, exclaimed, "Here. Where's my shotgun?"

Rutledge answered him quickly. "It's in the boot."

"Well, then." He got into the motorcar, and Rutledge could hear Hamish in the back of his mind.

It was difficult reversing, but soon they were on their way down the dark drive, the headlamps trying to pierce the fog and getting nowhere. Behind them they could hear Hector howl once, and then he was quiet.

Burrows turned to his daughter, and said, "There's a mist coming in."

They managed to reach Burwell without mishap, but twice McBride had to get down and find the road ahead. All the while Burrows was complaining querulously that he was tired and wanted to go home. Passing the churchyard and then the Church of St. Mary's, where Major Clayton's services had been held, Rutledge said quietly, "McBride?"

"Down that street—to your left. Yes, that's right. Turn left again at the next corner." After a moment, he added, "There. The house just there. Dr. Harris."

"Go to the door. He'll know you, I think. Miss Burrows and I will bring her father as soon as the doctor answers."

It was nearly two minutes before a light came on, and then a figure appeared in the doorway.

"What is it? What's the emergency?" a man's voice asked.

"We've a sick man here, Doctor." McBride turned as Rutledge coaxed Burrows up the walk and to the door. Harris opened it wider to allow them to pass, and they stepped inside. In the lamplight, he stared at Burrows's swollen face.

"What happened?"

"He was shot," Rutledge said. "And neglected the wound. He's delirious." He quickly explained the situation.

"This way." Harris led them down a passage to the door that opened into his surgery. "Let me light the other lamp."

As the light flared, Harris said, "All right, Mr. Burrows. Let me have a look at your face."

But in the end, Rutledge and McBride had to hold the man in his chair while Harris examined the wound. Miss Burrows, stifling sobs, stood in a corner out of the way.

"The wound's badly infected," Harris said. "I need to clean it, and then we'll see what's to be done."

He worked steadily while Burrows assured him that all was well, he didn't need a doctor. Fifteen minutes later, he said, "I think he ought to stay here for what's left of the night. I can't take his temperature, as agitated he is, but it's high enough. I'll give him something for that, and also to help him sleep." He took out two powders, put them into a glass of water, and said, "Are you thirsty, Burrows? Drink this, if you will." When the glass was empty he added quietly, "Wait here."

He came back shortly and said, "The room's ready. I've prepared a bed for Miss Burrows as well. It will help her father if she stays."

By this time the sedative was beginning to take effect. They got a drowsy Burrows to the narrow room made up for him and put him to bed. Leaving Miss Burrows to sit with him until he was fully asleep, the doctor led the way back to his examining room.

"When was he shot? Tell me the details."

Rutledge gave him an abbreviated version of events, and Harris nodded. "It's going to be touch and go. I dressed the wound with a septic powder, but we'll know by tomorrow if it will work. Are you staying in Burwell?"

Rutledge said, "No, there's something we must attend to. We'll be back tomorrow."

"Very well. I'm glad you brought him in when you did."

He saw them to the door, and when McBride had turned the crank and joined Rutledge in the motorcar, he said, "Where now?"

"Back to the house. First of all to take care of the dog. As soon as it's light, we'll see if there's a body there. Or if Burrows was just firing at shadows."

McBride took a deep breath. "Think he'll be all right?"

"It's anyone's guess. Harris was worried."

By the time they had reached the Burrows house the mist was beginning to lift, helped by a light predawn breeze.

Hector was reluctant to let them in, but Rutledge finally managed to calm him.

They sat in the front room, McBride dozing in his chair, until the dawn had brightened, no more than a dull glow in the shredding mist, and then they went out to search.

It didn't take long. Hector, allowed outside, ran nose to the ground around the perimeter of the house and outbuildings, then trotted back to Rutledge and McBride.

"No body, then," McBride said. "It was all his fever, wasn't it?"

"I'm not sure," Rutledge said. "Look there." He pointed to where Hector was sniffing with particular interest in the thicker grass that grew around the tree nearest the house. He knelt for a better look. "Is that blood?" Reaching out, he touched one of the drops Hector had found. His fingers when he turned them over were a rusty red. "He hit something. Or someone. I wonder who . . ."

Burrows was no better in the morning. Rutledge had waited until full daylight to leave the farm because he wanted to look for more signs that Burrows had actually shot someone. But if there was anything to find, it had been so diluted by the damp ground that it was all but invisible. The first spots had survived only because they were by the trunk of one of the trees and well enough protected.

He and McBride took Hector back to his owner, watching the huge dog nearly twist himself in knots with joy at the reunion. Then Rutledge drove Constable McBride to Wriston, before turning back to Burwell.

Dr. Harris couldn't tell him with any certainty what the outcome of the infection would be.

"It could spread. Once in the soft tissue, it's harder to kill. I had one man come in with a small scratch, the infection got into his bloodstream, and there was nothing we could do. But Burrows is healthy, he has a chance. My wife is looking after Miss Burrows. She's been too upset to eat, but I'll give her something a little later to help her sleep. She won't do Burrows any good collapsing over his bed."

"I think when Burrows fired his shotgun last night, he hit someone. You haven't seen any wounds of that sort, have you?"

"Not so far. No. I'll report it if I do." He paused for a moment. "You know, I'm sure, that Captain Hutchinson was here for the funeral of Major Clayton. Earlier in the summer, that was."

"Yes, I've been told he was in Burwell. Only for the day."

"I don't like to spread gossip. But the man was murdered. You're here to conduct the inquiry. All the same, I wouldn't have sought you out. But now you're here . . ."

"Is there something you know about Hutchinson?"

"Not really. No, not about Hutchinson. My wife's cousin lives in London. Apparently she knew Mary Hutchinson rather well. They grew up in the same village."

"Mary Hutchinson? His sister?"

"His wife."

"I believe she's dead," Rutledge said, not sure where the conversation was heading.

"Yes. I wonder—I wonder if you've looked into that."

There had been no reason to look into Mary Hutchinson's life. Or her death. She had been a part of the background of the victim.

"What can you tell me about her?"

"That's just it. I can't. It's my wife who told me. When her cousin Alice learned about Hutchinson's death, she wrote to my wife. She'd said nothing for all these years, but with Hutchinson dead, she felt free to speak. It seems she'd been very worried about Mary for some time. There was a letter that Mary wrote to Alice shortly before she died. Alice sent it to my wife to read." He coughed in embarrassment. "This is awkward. Perhaps you should speak to my wife."

"Perhaps I should," Rutledge said, "if she can shed any light at all on these murders."

"I doubt she can do that. Just go through the passage there, turn left, and knock at the first door you come to."

Rutledge thanked him and followed his directions.

When he tapped lightly on the closed door, a woman's voice called, "Come."

He entered a small sitting room where a woman was working at a desk. She turned. Mrs. Harris was small, trim, and pretty, with the calm demeanor of a woman who knew her own worth. She said, "Mr. Rutledge," and rose to cross the room.

"Your husband tells me you know something about the late Captain Hutchinson."

Her mouth tightened as she gestured to the chairs by the hearth. "My cousin Alice is nobody's fool," she said after a moment. "I'll tell you that in the beginning. I'll also tell you that I met Captain Hutchinson when he was here for Major Clayton's funeral. I wanted to meet him, you see. To discover for myself what sort of man he was."

"What did you learn?" Rutledge asked.

"That my cousin was probably right about him. Charming and manipulative. He neglected his wife— Alice's friend—terribly. Mary was quite wealthy, you see. And her death was under questionable circumstances."

"What sort of circumstances?"

"To put it bluntly, suicide. It was decided that she had been grieving for her child, who was stillborn. But Alice believed that she regretted her marriage and couldn't go on with it. The charming man she thought she was marrying didn't exist. Mary was—how shall I put it?—Mary wasn't a very pretty woman. And the Captain was a very attractive man. She wouldn't be the first to be captivated by such attentions."

"Go on."

"I wrote to Alice to tell her I'd met the Captain, but it wasn't until he was killed that she sent me a letter she'd received from Mary only a few weeks before her death. I think you ought to read it."

She went to the desk, found the letter, and held it out to Rutledge.

"Are you sure your cousin wouldn't object to my seeing it?"

"Not at all."

Lifting the flap of the envelope, he took out the folded sheet inside.

It was very brief.

Darling Alice, I'm so sorry I haven't written. I've been ill. It has not been an easy pregnancy. I think that was because I've been dreadfully unhappy. If this child lives, it will give me something to live for. If it dies, then I'll have nothing. And I don't know if I can go on. No, don't listen to me, it's that this business of having a baby is so trying. Did you feel so down when you were having your first? Tell me you did. It will cheer me to know that I'm not alone in this.

It was signed simply with an *M*.

"She appears to have been having a very difficult time. But I can't see that her death could be laid directly at the Captain's door. Nor does it explain these murders."

"No, perhaps not. But you're investigating the Captain's death. This shows you an entirely different view of the man from the effusive obituary that appeared in the Ely newspaper."

She went back to her desk and retrieved a card. "This is where my cousin lives in London. Perhaps you ought to speak to her. Alice Worth is her name."

He took the card and thanked her as he gave her back the letter and took his leave.

But as he was driving out of Burwell, Rutledge found himself thinking that Mrs. Sedley and Mrs. Harris had seen through the carefully cultivated facade that was the public Captain Hutchinson. Mrs. Sedley because she had watched him insinuate himself where he thought the greatest advantage lay. Mrs. Harris because she had wanted to find out whether her cousin had been right in her assessment of the man.

The question was, What did this have to do with Herbert Swift's death?

Or for that matter, the attempted murder of Mr. Burrows?

Chapter 13

Rutledge spent the rest of the day going through the list he'd made of ex-soldiers, this time in Wicken, but without any luck.

The constable there, a man called Lark, said, shaking his head, "I can't see that this is getting us anywhere, sir."

But somewhere, Rutledge thought, out here in the Fens or in a town close by, is the man who knows how to use a rifle and, more important, how to make himself invisible.

"Someone who came for the shooting?" Lark went on. "The autumn visitor. Or the winter. Miss Bartram over in Wriston knows who they were. Not many of them come now. But she must still have the names."

Rutledge said, "I can't see a connection to Swift and to Captain Hutchinson. Hutchinson hadn't come here until this summer."

"But he did come. And so the killing began."

It was an interesting way of looking at the murders.

"When did Swift come back from Scotland?" Rutledge asked. "Do you know?"

"Late 1918, as I remember. Constable McBride can tell you for certain."

"Close enough. Two years ago. And nothing happened to him. Then Hutchinson came to Cambridgeshire. The first time there was no time to plan. But when the Captain came again, he was killed. Then Swift, because he was already here, already available."

"But how does Burrows fit in?"

That was the problem.

Rutledge thanked Constable Lark, and turned back toward Wriston.

Where was the connection among these men?

Hamish said, "Swift would ha' left for London, if he'd won yon seat in Parliament."

"But his killer is here, not in London. And for some reason he can't go there."

"He couldna' carry the rifle with him."

That made sense. He could hide it here. He knew the land.

By the time Rutledge had arrived at The Dutchman Inn, he'd made up his mind.

The next morning, he left the Fen country for London, stopping in Cambridge for petrol.

It was late when he reached the city, and later still when he walked into his own flat.

On the long drive south, he'd decided where to begin. Captain Hutchinson's sister.

She had lived with her brother in a house in one of the elegant squares that had seen their heyday in the 1890s. Number 7 was, like its neighbors, large, well kept, still handsome. There was black silk on the knocker, a reminder that it was a house of mourning.

The middle-aged maid who answered the door told him that she would inquire if Miss Hutchinson was receiving visitors. When she returned, she reported that Miss Hutchinson was resting.

"Please tell her that Scotland Yard would like to ask her some questions about her brother's death."

It was several minutes before he was led to a sitting room where Miss Hutchinson was waiting.

She was tall and slim, a striking woman rather than a pretty one. She kept him standing as she said, "Inspector Rutledge? Have you found out who killed my brother?"

"Not yet, Miss Hutchinson. I wish I could tell you otherwise. Did your brother know someone named Swift?"

"Swift? I don't believe so. I didn't know most of his friends. He was, after all, a serving officer in the Guards."

"I understand he lost his wife in the early years of the war."

Her eyebrows rose. "That's true. What does that have to do with what happened in Cambridgeshire?"

"I don't know. But somewhere in your brother's past something occurred that may have brought about his death. Tell me a little about Mrs. Hutchinson."

She turned away. "Mary was from Warwickshire. She met Gordon at a ball. It was love at first sight, I've been told. She was about to become engaged to someone else, and broke it off to marry my brother."

"Did she come to regret the marriage?"

"No, of course not. That's a terrible thing to suggest."

"But there was some question about her death."

"I assure you, this had nothing to do with Gordon being shot in Ely. I wrote to Jason. I told him that this business must be some terrible mistake. That my brother had had no enemies."

"Was Captain Hutchinson in England when his wife died?"

"He was in France. The war was just becoming a stalemate, he couldn't leave. He wasn't even here for her funeral."

But an officer serving in France would have been given compassionate leave if his wife and their child had died. If he'd asked for it.

"How well did he know Major Clayton? I understand he attended the services for Clayton in Burwell."

"He'd met him in hospital, on a visit to the wounded that Gordon made with Colonel Fisher."

"Was it Colonel Fisher who traveled to Burwell with your brother?"

"I don't believe it was. I didn't know the Claytons, and so I didn't go with Gordon. You're grasping at straws, Inspector." She was impatient now, a little sharp.

"Did your brother know someone in the Fen country by the name of Burrows?"

"Was he in the Army?"

"No. He's an older man. A farmer."

"Well, then, I doubt it. Really, Mr. Rutledge, I can't see where these questions are leading. "

"Was this house yours, Miss Hutchinson? Or your sister-in-law's?"

She flushed slightly. "It belonged to Mary's family. It had been closed since her parents' deaths. My brother brought her to London and opened the house. She was pleased. She'd always liked it."

"And it's yours now?"

"Sadly, yes. As my brother's heir."

Hamish was reminding him of something. Mary Hutchinson's house . . . He said, "The staff here. Who hired them?"

"I suppose my brother did. It was fully staffed when he sent for me."

"There was no one who came to London with the new bride?"

"Yes, there was her maid."

"Where is she now?"

"Pensioned off, when Mary died. I already had a personal maid. There was no point in keeping her on."

"I'd like to speak to her. Can you tell me where to find her?"

She was exasperated with him. "Really, I don't know what Miss Newland could possibly tell you about something that happened in Ely."

"Nor do I. But I intend to find out. The address, if you please."

She went to the desk, found a small leather-covered book, looked up a name, and wrote the information on a sheet of stationery. Folding it, she turned and handed it to him. "I think you should leave now. There must be something you can do to find my brother's murderer. Searching out old servants doesn't seem to be very useful."

Rutledge smiled. "Scotland Yard prefers to be thorough," he answered and took his leave. She was frowning as he closed the door.

If Hutchinson had possessed great charm, most certainly his sister had none, he thought, driving toward Wiltshire. Perhaps with her brother providing for the two of them, she hadn't needed any.

When he arrived in Abbot's Green, he was surprised to find that the direction Miss Hutchinson had given him was a large, handsome brick house set back off the road on the far side of the small village.

He'd expected a pensioner's cottage, but it appeared that Miss Newland had found another position.

And this presented something of a problem. If Scotland Yard came calling, the mistress of the house would very likely insist that he interview Miss Newland in her presence. If he insisted on speaking to her privately, it would cast suspicion on the lady's maid. What had she to do with the police?

He drove up to the Georgian door, knocked, and asked for Miss Newland.

The maid who had come to the door said, "Who is calling?"

"My name is Rutledge. I'm here," he said blandly, "about a small legacy left to one of the staff at her former place of employment. I should like to trace that person, and Miss Newland might be able to tell me where to find her. A private matter, I'm afraid."

He was left to his own devices while the maid went to find Miss Newland. After perhaps five minutes, a woman in the severe black of her position came to the door.

"Mr. Rutledge?" she asked tentatively.

She was nearing forty, he thought, with fair hair that fought against the severity of the style that suited her dress, repressively impersonal. There was a small scar, round and rather unusual, on one cheek, near her mouth. It detracted from a pretty face.

"Yes." He looked up at the house. "Could we walk here in the drive for a few minutes? I'd rather not be overheard."

Mystified, she said, "You mentioned my former employer . . ."

"Mrs. Hutchinson. Yes. Will you walk with me?"

Reluctantly she came down the short flight of steps and followed him to the faun fountain that graced the circle created by the loop in the drive.

Certain now that he couldn't be overheard, he said quickly, "I'm from Scotland Yard, Miss Newland. I'm investigating the murder of Captain Hutchinson."

Shocked, she stared up at him. "Captain—but who—I didn't *know.*"

She wouldn't have seen the London newspapers. He explained what had happened. "And we have very little evidence to help us with our inquiries."

Her face hardened. "Good luck to him, whoever he is. I hope you never find him." She was about to turn away and go back to the house when he stopped her.

"Miss Newland. I need your help."

"I told you. I wish whoever it is well."

"Perhaps you do. But he's murdered another man, and shot a third. We need to find a killer."

"I haven't seen the Captain since I was let go. After Miss Mary's death. What can I possibly know that would be useful to you?" With one hand she shielded her eyes from the sun, searching his face.

"I have no idea," he said truthfully. "But a woman whose cousin Alice Worth knew your former mistress suggested that I look into her death. I called on Miss Hutchinson, and she was less than helpful."

"That doesn't surprise me. She didn't care for the woman her brother married, and he only married Mary for her money. He wanted that lovely house and the position the address gave him. Once he had what he wanted, he changed toward her. Mrs. Worth—the Alice you spoke of—was her only friend. He'd discouraged everyone she'd known growing up from visiting her. It wasn't convenient—she didn't feel well—they'd made other plans. After a while, they stopped asking to see Mrs. Hutchinson."

"Was he that cruel?"

"I don't think it was cruelty. He didn't care for them, you see. They could give him nothing he wanted. He brought his own friends round, and they entertained lavishly. Miss Mary enjoyed that. They were invited to teas and concerts and the theater, to dinner parties and weekends in the country, but these were people the Captain—he was a Lieutenant then—wished to impress. He expected Miss Mary to use them as he himself did. To cultivate them and curry favor, to do small things to put them in her debt, whatever he thought would serve him best. She wasn't comfortable using people in that fashion. The only times I saw him angry with her were over small things she'd failed to notice or do. He accused her of not caring, of letting him down. But she hadn't. It wasn't her way to look for opportunities to put herself or her husband forward. She hadn't grown up in that kind of life, she had a position, she didn't need to push so hard for recognition. It was just that he wanted even more fashionable connections."

"And when the war came?"

"He was in his glory then. He expected to end the war as a Major at the very least. But he never seemed to find the right opportunity to shine. He could be very brave when he had to, but he wasn't a good leader. Do you know what I mean? Miss Mary said to me once, 'He climbs on the backs of other people. He's never understood that.'"

"Were there other women?"

Frowning, she considered the question. "Oh, he charmed them, when they were useful or related to someone important. It never went beyond that. Well, there *was* one, perhaps, if you believed the rumors. The housekeeper wrote to me that he'd taken a fancy to one of the maids. This was after he'd come home from France. The spring of 1919. I never knew him to look twice at one of them, so I was quite surprised. And I told her so in my next letter. But Mrs. Cookson claimed he was besotted with the girl. And then one morning she was gone. Her things with her. Just like that. I expect she wouldn't stand for what he wanted. God forgive me, I remember thinking that it served him right, to be disappointed."

Some men considered the staff in their houses as natural prey. A pert maid, always underfoot, smiling . . . it could be tempting. But pretty or not, a servant girl was seldom related to a Colonel or someone in the Cabinet.

And then Miss Newland's next words changed his mind.

"Mrs. Cookson told me she was a Scottish girl, pretty as a picture, with the most charming accent. Even the tradesmen who came round wanted to hear her speak. But an excellent worker for all that."

"And that's all you know about this girl?"

"It's all that she wrote."

"Where can I find Mrs. Cookson?"

"I should think she's still at the London house."

"Do you recall someone by the name of Swift coming to the house? Or Burrows?"

Miss Newland shook her head. "I never met the guests."

"Tell me a little about Mrs. Hutchinson's life before she met the Captain."

"She was not the prettiest girl in Warwick, but she was well liked. And she had a way of putting people at their ease. I never knew her to be a wallflower. She always had partners at any balls or parties. I was over the moon when I was told I would be her maid. It was the best position anyone could ask for. We went to Newmarket for the races—her uncle was mad for the horses, and he'd spend a week before the flat racing calendar, going from trainer to trainer, looking over the field and deciding where to bet. He was good at it too. There was a man she met at one of the dinner parties. She pointed him out to me once. I was certain she was in love with him, and he with her. It would have been a fine match. She said they were well suited to each other. But her uncle felt she was too young, she should wait a year, and before that year was out, she'd met the Captain."

"What was her uncle's name?"

"Thaddeus Whiting. Sadly, he died soon after Mary's death. I think it broke his heart."

"And the other man?"

"He came to Warwickshire once to plead with her, to beg her to change her mind. But the Captain was exciting, charming. She thought that was what she wanted. A pity she was wrong."

Newmarket was only a matter of a few miles from the Fen country.

"What was his name? This man. Do you remember?"

"I should. Of course I should. But I can't bring it back. He took Miss Mary to a party at Warwick Castle, and I went along as chaperone. That was the only time I met him—"

The door had opened and one of the maids was standing there, beckoning to Miss Newland.

"I'm wanted, Mr. Rutledge. I must go. I'm so sorry I couldn't help you more. I'd have done anything for Miss Mary, and she knew that."

"How did she die?" he asked quickly, before she could turn away and go back to her duties.

"Miss Mary? She cut her wrists. In the bathtub. There was a picture in one of the books in her father's study. A man during the French Revolution did that, and he was painted lying in that tub full of bloody water. She'd had nightmares about it as a child. I expect she remembered."

And then she was hurrying back to the house.

Rutledge knew the rather dramatic painting. Marat lying in his bathtub. But he hadn't slashed his wrists. He'd been stabbed by a woman. Rutledge searched for the name. Corday. Charlotte Corday. But she hadn't been shown in the painting. Only the dying man. The child had remembered what she saw—but not what it meant.

When the door had shut behind Miss Newland, Rutledge went back to his motorcar and turned toward London.

He faced the same problem as before. Miss Hutchinson would either insist on sitting in on the interview—or would forbid it altogether.

Leaving the motorcar at the far end of the square, he walked back to Number 7, and this time went down the steps beside the iron railing to the tradesmen's entrance.

A scullery maid answered his knock and informed him that the housekeeper, Mrs. Cookson, was presently upstairs discussing the next day's menu with Miss Hutchinson.

"But you could wait in the housekeeper's parlor, if you like," she said with a cheeky smile.

He smiled in return and was led through the servants' dining room and down a short passage to the housekeeper's small parlor.

It was tastefully decorated with what must have been cast-off furniture from upstairs. There was a small table desk, a tea table with matching chairs, and a more comfortable chair next to a bookshelf holding cookery books, household hints, a volume on etiquette, and an older edition of *Debrett's Peerage*, well thumbed. He wondered if that had been a discard from upstairs.

He was still standing at the bookshelf when the door opened and Mrs. Cookson came in.

"May I help you?" she asked coolly. She was graying, her hair glossy and piled high on her head. There was a cleft in her chin, and her full lips were pursed in disapproval.

"My name is Rutledge. I'm from Scotland Yard. We're investigating the murder of Captain Hutchinson. I'd like to ask you several questions."

"The police were here the day after he—died."

"Yes, I'm sure you were very helpful." He smiled disarmingly. "But other matters have come to our attention since then."

"And they are?"

"How well did you know Mrs. Hutchinson?" he began.

Surprised, she said, "But she died during the early days of the war."

"I'm aware of that. Please answer the question."

"I was hired when the house was opened, while the Captain and Mrs. Hutchinson were on their wedding trip. I hadn't known her before that time. But she was quite lovely to work for, and I was as sad as anyone when she—she died."

"Why do you think she killed herself?"

"I—the inquest concluded she had cut herself in a fall. There was broken glass beside the tub."

"She brought her maid with her from Warwick. Did you know her well?"

"Miss Newland kept herself to herself. We were polite to each other, but not what you might call friendly."

And yet they had corresponded.

"Why did she leave?"

"After the funeral, she was given what was due her in Mrs. Hutchinson's will, and she chose to retire." Her voice was strained as she said the words.

He could hear Hamish telling him that she was hiding something.

"That's not what Miss Newland has told me." And Miss Hutchinson had said she had her own lady's maid . . .

"It was—there was some trouble about Mrs. Hutchinson's personal effects. I was told that Miss Newland claimed certain items as promised to her."

"What happened?"

"I wasn't there. Miss Hutchinson said afterward that Miss Newland was a thief and she'd told her to get out."

"And did she leave without a character?" Miss Newland had said nothing about the circumstances surrounding her departure. Was Mrs. Cookson given to exaggeration? Or had Miss Newland concealed the real reasons for being dismissed?

"She did. That very afternoon. I was sent to oversee her packing, as there had been the trouble over Mrs. Hutchinson's things. And she was blee—" She broke off, turning red.

"Bleeding?"

"I could only think that Miss Hutchinson had slapped her. One of her rings cut into Miss Newland's cheek." Without thinking, she touched her own face, where Rutledge had seen the deep scar on Miss Newland's.

The only way a ring could have cut that deep, he thought, was if Miss Hutchinson had struck her with the back of her hand.

"But she left, and that was the end of that."

"I did keep up with her. From time to time." Mrs. Cookson was walking the very narrow line between honesty and truth.

"In spite of the fact that she was accused of thieving."

Mrs. Cookson bit her lip. "She had known Mrs. Hutchinson since she was a small motherless child. Sometimes things are said. 'I'd like you to have this one day,' or 'It was my mother's. I'll leave it to you in my will, shall I?' Whether they are *meant* or not. I can see Miss Hutchinson's point as well. It was her brother's house, and he wasn't here to tell her his own wishes. There was no proof of promises on either side. Miss Newland must have been upset, close as she was to her mistress. She would have liked to take some small memento with her. In the heat of the moment, things are done and regretted later."

Mrs. Cookson was trying to be fair. Rutledge, reading her expression and listening to the tone of her voice, could see that she had had to side with her employer's sister, but she had been inclined to believe Miss Newland.

"I don't see why it should matter that Miss Newland left us when she did," she added, realizing that she might have said too much.

"It's not always possible to see the links. Tell me about the young woman who was taken on as maid at the end of the war. The one from Scotland."

"Catriona Beaton? You know about her as well? One of the maids left to be married, when the footman in Number 12 came back from the war. We advertised of course, and this young woman had excellent references. She was here some months. Nearly a year. She'd come down to London to make her fortune, and I wasn't convinced that service was the right choice for her, but I changed my mind in the end. A hard worker, never any trouble, knew her duties. And then one morning she was gone. Not a word, no request for a reference, not staying out her notice. Just—gone. I couldn't believe it."

"And you haven't heard from her since then?"

"I told you. Not a word."

"Why do you think she left?"

"She was young, eager to get on. I thought she'd found something better. That's why she didn't need a reference."

"There's more to it than that," he said quietly.

Mrs. Cookson took a deep breath. "I shouldn't be telling you this. It was the Captain. He'd been away, and he came home for a fortnight. She'd been here two weeks by that time. Even I could see where this was going. He'd never spared a glance for the staff before. I doubt he could recognize any of us on the street. Now he seemed to know which room she was working in, when she'd be coming to make up the fires or turn down the beds. I was worried, I can tell you that. He'd talk to her. About her afternoons off. About Scotland. About what she wanted to do with her life. I don't know what all. She asked me once what to do about him, and I told her, if he began to make her feel uncomfortable, I'd speak to Miss Hutchinson. One day she did come to me, saying that he'd asked if she'd have dinner with him one night. She didn't know how to refuse him. And so I went to Miss Hutchinson. She must have had a word with her brother, but it didn't do much good, I can tell you that. The night before she left, Catriona came to me, frightened and in tears. She wouldn't tell me what had happened. She just said she was afraid. The next morning, when she didn't come down, I sent one of the other maids up to wake her. And the room was empty. She'd gone."

"What did you think had happened?"

"That he'd offered to set her up in a house somewhere. As his mistress. I think she decided that the best way to cope with the situation was to leave."

"Had he set her up?"

"When he discovered she was gone, he went mad, accusing me of sending her packing, accusing his sister of the same thing, frantic to know if she'd left a forwarding address. And then one night he came in, and he was himself again. It was as if he'd never set eyes on her."

"He'd found her, then."

"No, I don't think he had. He'd just come to his senses. Or realized that he couldn't marry such a one. I don't know who it was spoke to him. Someone must have done."

Or he'd found her—and had it out with her.

What had become of the girl?

Hamish said, "He could ha' throttled her for leaving him."

The voice seemed to echo around the small room. Rutledge said quickly, "What do you feel became of her? She was here nearly a year. You got to know her well enough to judge her character."

"I was always afraid she'd done herself a harm. She was owed her wages, you see, and she never collected them. A girl like that? She wouldn't lose nearly a month's wages, if she could help it. And what about a reference?"

It was typical of the housekeeper to see the girl's death in such a light. She wouldn't want to consider that her late employer had driven a second woman to suicide.

Chapter 14

As Rutledge was opening the tradesmen's door, he glimpsed a motorcar just pulling up in front of the house.

He stopped where he was, waiting.

A man stepped out of the motorcar, walked to the door, and lifted the knocker. Rutledge could hear it clearly from where he was standing, the brass plate sounding sharply.

After a moment, the maid who had let him in greeted the caller and invited him inside, and the door closed behind him.

Rutledge stayed where he was, for the motor was still running.

Nearly five minutes passed, then the door above him opened again and Miss Hutchinson swept out, followed by the visitor. The chauffeur was standing by the rear door now, holding it open as the man helped Miss Hutchinson inside, then followed her.

The chauffeur shut the door smartly and went back to take his place behind the wheel.

And then they were gone.

Rutledge breathed a sigh of relief. It had been a near run thing. He didn't want Miss Hutchinson to see him again, not coming out of the downstairs servants' quarters. It was better for Mrs. Cookson if she didn't have to answer questions about his visit.

Leaving the area stairs, he walked back to where he'd left his own motorcar.

Hamish said, "It's a' verra' well to learn about the past, but it doesna' have a bearing on the murders."

It didn't. Rutledge had to admit it. But he'd discovered that there were at least two secrets in Captain Hutchinson's life. What were the others?

It was time to call on Mrs. Harris's cousin Alice Worth.

He found the card given him by Mrs. Harris, and discovered that Alice Worth lived in a tall, handsome house in one of the most fashionable squares in London. A dinner party was in progress when he knocked at the door—he could hear voices and laughter. What's more, the maid who answered his summons was uncertain what to do with the policeman on the doorstep.

She left him there, went to find her mistress, and in a few minutes he was whisked down a passage to a small morning room done up in pale peach and cream. Mrs. Worth swept in shortly afterward. A slender woman with fair hair and china blue eyes, she was wearing a very becoming evening gown of lilac and silver.

"I have guests, as you can see," she said abruptly. "I'm sure this could have waited until the morning."

"I'm afraid not," Rutledge replied pleasantly. "I'm inquiring into the death of Captain Hutchinson. Mrs. Harris, in Burwell, told me you could provide information about his late wife, Mary."

Her manner changed at once. Quietly shutting the door behind her, she said, "She was driven to her death. I'm convinced of it. If her husband wasn't guilty of killing her, he most certainly was morally responsible. I'm glad he's dead. I see no reason why I should help you find his killer. The man is to be congratulated on his good sense."

"Do you know who killed Hutchinson?" he asked, keeping his tone matter-of-fact.

"I am not required to answer your questions," she told him. "I'm not a suspect, and I have no proof. Therefore I will make no accusations."

"You do realize that whoever he is, he's killed another man, and a third is at this moment fighting for his life." It was only a slight exaggeration. But he could read her eyes, and she was unaware of what had happened to Swift and Burrows.

"Then I was mistaken," she said. "The person I suspected would not have done such a thing."

"Not even if he had been driven mad by Mary Hutchinson's death?"

"If he had been driven mad, as you put it, he would have found Captain Hutchinson and killed him a very long time ago. No, you're looking in the wrong direction."

"Revenge is best savored cold," Rutledge reminded her.

"Revenge or justice, I wouldn't know. I didn't kill him. Good evening, Mr. Rutledge."

With that she was gone, and the maid who had admitted him escorted him to the door and shut it firmly behind him.

Hamish said, "Ye canna' make her tell."

"She told me more than she realized. That whoever was in love with Mary Hutchinson is still alive and still has feelings for another man's wife. The question is, how well did she know this man? It's one thing to see Mary Hutchinson and whoever he is as star-crossed lovers, but Mrs. Hutchinson made her choice."

Still, it was frustrating to have come this far and be met with a stone wall. The letter sent to Mrs. Harris had given him the impression that Mrs. Worth was eager to see justice for her late friend. Instead she'd turned a policeman away.

Now the question was, should he make an appearance at Scotland Yard—or avoid it?

Looking at his watch, he realized that Acting Chief Superintendent Markham had long since left for the day. He found somewhere to have dinner, and then looked at his watch again.

The night staff would have taken over. Sergeant Gibson had most likely gone for the day as well.

But there were questions he needed to ask, and answers he needed to hear.

He drove on to the Yard, left his car some distance away, and walked in. His office was as he'd left it, several files still waiting for his attention. Nothing there from Gibson.

Dealing with the files quickly and efficiently, he carried them to Sergeant Gibson's desk and set them in the box for completed files. Then he swiftly searched the sergeant's desk.

He found what he was after and flipped through the pages, scanning the information they contained.

Gibson had found nothing new to report. And if Gibson couldn't, then very likely there was nothing more to be found.

Fallowfield, Lowell, Burrows, Swift, and his half brother Anson—they were all there along with Brenner and Montgomery, several with a mark by their names indicating the search for information had been conducted and the information conveyed to the Inspector who had requested it. In this case, himself.

Rutledge put the file back where he'd found it.

He was disappointed that nothing of interest had been discovered about Ben Montgomery, who had joined the Army and never returned to visit his family in Cambridgeshire, or about Jeremiah Brenner, he of the cold eyes and the need to drink to forget. They had been promising leads.

And then he left the Yard as quietly as he'd arrived.

Rutledge slept in his own bed that night and started for Cambridgeshire early the next morning. He stopped by the house that had belonged to his parents, where his sister Frances lived presently, and found her just having her first cup of tea in the small room overlooking the garden.

"Darling Ian, what a surprise. Sit down and I'll have Molly bring you some breakfast."

"I haven't time," he said. "Is there fresh tea in that pot?"

"Yes, help yourself. You know where to find the cups."

He did, and joined her at the table. "You've been away," he said.

"And so have you. I came round to call on Monday. Where have you been?"

"Cambridgeshire. The Fen country. And you?"

"I went to see Melinda in Kent. I wanted to tell her my news."

Rutledge smiled. She was engaged to be married now. Melinda Crawford was an old friend of the family, his parents' friend and now theirs. She would be one of the first people Frances would wish to tell.

That made it official. Real. He wanted nothing but happiness for his only sister. But when she had told him she was thinking of marriage, it had seemed that the bottom had unexpectedly fallen out of his world. It had taken all the will he possessed to smile and tell her he thought she'd made a good choice.

He had begun to come to terms with her engagement, but it had not been easy.

He drank his tea, listening to Frances's account of the visit to Melinda Crawford in Kent.

"She keeps asking me when you'll come to see her."

But he couldn't. Melinda had come from a military family, married into another, knew war and soldiers. He would betray himself, and she would know what haunted him. He cared too much for her good opinion to risk it.

Rutledge forced a smile. "The Yard takes most of my time."

"You could take leave, surely. You work too many hours as it is. A few days away from the Yard would be good for you."

"I'll try," he promised, and changed the subject.

Ten minutes later he was heading out of London, already considering where to look next.

Newmarket. Mary Hutchinson had fallen in love there. Who was the man? And how had he dealt with the breaking off of their engagement, after Mary had met Lieutenant Hutchinson?

Where was that man now? A loose end, and one that could matter. It was possible he'd not been free to pursue his revenge until now. If he'd returned to live in Newmarket, he could have killed Hutchinson in Ely and easily gone home without attracting attention.

Hamish was reminding him that a man who had loved Mary Hutchinson would have no reason to kill two other men, even if he'd shot her widower. Had Swift died only to distract the police from the real purpose of the crime?

That brought him back to why Captain Hutchinson had to be the first to die. The real target . . .

If that was true, then why shoot Mr. Burrows? An unnecessary risk, surely. And another dead end.

He spent the night in Cambridge again and arrived in Newmarket early in the morning. Horses were just coming in from their morning gallop, walking single file, their riders hunched in their saddles, thinking about breakfast.

The better part of the day, Rutledge and the local constable, an affable man called Henry, went searching for any evidence of Mary Hutchinson's presence here with her uncle before the war, any news of Herbert Swift, or proof that Captain Hutchinson had visited the town.

Swift, they learned, occasionally followed the horses, but he was generally the guest of an Ely solicitor, a man named Baron.

Captain Hutchinson had come once or twice in 1919, but always with a group of other young Army officers. No one could recall meeting him in 1914.

If the two men had crossed paths, there was no record of it.

As for Mary Hutchinson's uncle, Thaddeus Whiting, a few of the older trainers and jockeys remembered him and spoke warmly of him. Several recalled meeting his niece, but if she'd formed an attachment for anyone she'd met in Newmarket, they were unaware of it.

"Does anyone from Burwell or Wriston or Isleham frequent Newmarket?" Rutledge asked Michael Flannery, one of the trainers.

He smiled. "Of course they do. When they can. But they're not big punters, they come for the day, enjoy themselves walking around looking at the horses, and then go home. It's London and the shires that keep us afloat."

Rutledge thanked Constable Henry for his time and prepared to drive on to Burwell to look in on Burrows.

Constable Henry said, "I'll keep an ear to the ground, if you like, sir. You've given me the names. Where can I find you?"

"Wriston. Or Ely."

"That's fine, then, sir. Safe journey."

A safer one than his first visit to the Fen country, he thought as he drove into Burwell late on a windy afternoon.

Dr. Harris was pleased with the progress Burrows was making. "But it was a near-run thing. Infections like that can be very stubborn. Are you going his way? I'll release him if you are. He's to keep that face clean and dry. If he does, he'll be fine."

Rutledge waited while the bandages were changed and Burrows was given instructions about the care of the wound. And then the man came out. He looked better, his face less swollen and his eyes clear. He greeted Rutledge with a nod, turned to thank the doctor, and walked out to the motorcar. His daughter had already returned to Wriston to oversee the farm.

Waiting until Burrows was out of earshot, Rutledge said to Harris, "If you will, thank your wife for me, and tell her I did as she asked. But I'd like to know the name of the man Mary Hutchinson was engaged to before her marriage. If she can discover that, I'd be grateful. I'll be in Wriston until this inquiry is finished. Or in Ely."

"I'll pass the word. Thank you for listening to her worries. I don't know that it was helpful to you, but it will make my own life more comfortable."

Rutledge smiled. "I daresay."

Burrows was taciturn until they were well out of the village and on the road toward his farm. Even then his conversation turned to what he must do to make up for lost time and how well his daughter had managed in his place.

There were two questions Rutledge wanted to ask the man, and the first was the most innocuous.

"I see these fields," Rutledge said, gesturing to either side of the road. "You can't manage them with a handful of men."

"In the planting and the harvesting, I take on day labor. They know when to come. Some have been stringing the hops in Kent, or harvesting them. Others need work to put food on the table for winter. A few are Travelers—gypsies—who do whatever's to hand. I keep my eye on them. They're not to be trusted. But there's not much to steal. This year we've been lucky with the barley. The weather has held, save for the storm the other night. But it's time to bring it in." He touched his face. "Bloody man! He's cost me." It had been his own intransigence over keeping his wound clean that had sent him to Dr. Harris, but Burrows was having none of that.

"I assume you know many of the people who come to work. They're here year after year. Anyone among them who might have something against Herbert Swift?"

"I can't see why. They're in the fields all day, these workers. They don't go to the pubs, although sometimes they bring in beer without my knowledge. There's no time to waste in the villages. One or two of the young rascals, yes, but where would they come by a rifle, even if they'd wanted to shoot someone?"

"From their fathers in the war."

"Pshaw. That's as likely as my daughter shooting him. Except," he added hastily, "I don't have a rifle. But you have my shotgun."

"It's in the house now. You'll see it there. I'd put it away if I were you."

"All well and good." Burrows sat back. "I'll be getting myself one of these motorcars. One day. I've been saving for it. A good harvest this year will see me clear."

"Do you often go to Newmarket?"

He sighed. "Not as often as I'd like. There's the fields and the cows and never-ending work to repair the banks and keep up the buildings."

"Who else from the Fens goes there?"

"I've heard it said that Swift has been there a time or two since the war, with a friend from Ely. He's—he was no gambler. At a guess, he liked the excitement."

"Anyone else?"

Burrows named a dozen or so men, some of them ex-soldiers Rutledge had already interviewed. Among them was the man Thornton. "He's like so many of the others. The war changed him. He doesn't go to Newmarket or anywhere else there's a large gathering. I've noticed that."

"Know him well, do you?" Rutledge asked casually.

"Not very well, no. He's got more money than the rest of us put together. I hear he's thinking of buying steam tractors for his fields. I'd do it myself, but it's costly and so far I can find the workers when I need them."

"Ever see Captain Hutchinson in Newmarket?"

"If I did, I don't recall. He'd have been with a party of friends. We'd have nothing to say to each other except for hello and who do you favor in the next race, while waiting for a drink."

Burrows meant that as a generalization, unaware that he'd described Hutchinson well, a man who didn't waste his time with someone who couldn't advance his career or introduce him to someone even more important.

"What about Thaddeus Whiting from Warwick?" Rutledge asked as he pulled into the farm lane.

Burrows turned to him. "I haven't heard that name in—what is it?—five years or more. He's dead now. Why should Scotland Yard be interested in him?"

Because, Rutledge wanted to say, I spent five or six hours in Newmarket searching for information about the man and learned nothing.

"His name came up. Hutchinson's wife was his niece," he told Burrows.

"Well, I'll be damned. My daughter met her once. She wasn't married then, was she? It was the year before the war, 1913. Shy girl, but very pleasant."

"I'm told she was later engaged to someone she'd met at Newmarket before she was introduced to Hutchinson," Rutledge continued.

"Was she now? I can't think who that would be. My daughter might know."

But Miss Burrows, delighted and wary over her father's return, gave Mary Whiting Hutchinson scarcely a moment's thought.

"We didn't keep in touch," she said as her father carried on into the house, her gaze following him. "I liked her. But she wasn't engaged to anyone then. She'd have told me. There was someone she was seeing, I think, but I couldn't tell you whether he was at Newmarket or not that year." Miss Burrows smiled. "We spent an afternoon together. If he'd been there, she might not have had the afternoon free."

"If you remember anything else, send me word."

"I promise. But you're telling me that Mary was married to that man who was shot in front of Ely Cathedral?" He had her fall attention now. Shivering, she said, "But I didn't know. How awful."

"Mary Hutchinson died in the first months of the war. In childbirth. She and the child didn't survive." It was a kind lie.

"How very sad. There's something that Mr. Swift and that Captain had in common, then. Both lost their wives in the same way."

But not quite the same. One was a beloved wife deeply mourned. And the other was a neglected wife who was wretched enough to take her own life.

Rutledge thanked Miss Burrows and was about to leave when he remembered the barrister in Ely who enjoyed Newmarket.

Burrows scratched his chin. "I expect that would be Thomas Bacon. No, Thomas Baron. Ask anyone in Ely, they can tell you where to find him."

Miss Bartram was delighted to see him again. When he told her he'd been in London, she was eager to hear about his journey.

Mindful of what had kept this inn in business for so many years, he asked her, "Does the name Thaddeus Whiting mean anything to you? Did he ever come to Wriston for the shooting?"

"And who is he, when he's at home?"

"He's from Warwickshire. He came sometimes to Newmarket. It's possible he also knew about The Dutchman Inn."

She shook her head. "I'm sure I'd have remembered if he had. I'll look in my father's book, of course, but I don't expect I'll find him."

In Ely, Rutledge was greeted by a morose Inspector Warren.

"I hope you're bringing me good news. I've spent the past two days reviewing statements, and I'm damned if they're any more useful now than they were when they were written."

"We took Burrows to a Dr. Harris in Burwell. He'd neglected that graze on his cheek. And I went on to London, since London hasn't been very forthcoming with information. I'm beginning to see why. There's very little to be had. At the moment I'm interested in finding a barrister by the name of Baron."

"Baron? Good God, you don't think he's involved, do you?"

"He isn't, as far as I know. But he sometimes went to Newmarket with Swift."

"Now that's interesting." Warren got up from behind his desk. "I'll go with you."

They found Thomas Baron in his chambers, and after the client who had been consulting him had left, he ushered the two men into his office.

Warren made the introductions, and Baron asked how the inquiry was progressing. "I knew Swift. We weren't close friends, but we had consulted on several matters. Before the war we'd travel occasionally to Newmarket, enjoy an expensive lunch, and talk about anything but the law."

"Did you meet any of these people while you and Swift were there? Captain Hutchinson, Thaddeus Whiting, Whiting's niece, Mary, her fiancé, or a farmer named Burrows."

"Hutchinson? The man who was murdered? Never met him, but there were usually a number of Army officers up from London in the season. He could have been one of those. They kept to themselves as a rule. Thaddeus Whiting. The name's familiar. Before the war? If he brought his niece with him, I never heard of it. Burrows I know by sight, but I've seen him there only once or twice. I'll tell you who is mad about the horses—or was. Surprised me. The cooper over in Soham. Ruskin? I think that's his name. Thornton, in Isleham, used to be interested in racing, but the war put paid to that."

"How well do you know Thornton?"

"Not well. He's an interesting man to dine with. Very well read. Before the war, he and Swift sometimes got into heated arguments over obscure points of history. Mind you, neither man had been to Athens or Rome, but to listen to them you'd think they were regular visitors."

And yet Thornton had said he barely knew Swift.

"How heated?"

"No, no, nothing that would lead to murder. It was more the pleasure of proving the other man wrong." He smiled. "It was generally a chance meeting, a casual remark, and they were off. An entertaining evening for everyone."

Rutledge thanked him, and they left.

Inspector Warren said, "Who is this man Whiting?"

"Mary Hutchinson's uncle and guardian. He's dead, but the question is, since he knew Hutchinson, is it possible he also knew Swift? Is that our connection between the two victims?"

"They are all three dead," Warren pointed out. "You're not likely to find out."

"What happened to the windmill keeper in Wriston?"

"After the cottage beside it burned, he left. Drank himself to death, if you ask me. That's very likely how the fire started. Although there are some who said the cottage was haunted and the old man burned it down to rid it of its ghosts. God knows what he thought he'd seen. The way those wooden arms creak, you'd believe in anything."

Rutledge remembered their creaking, the night of the mist, and how unnatural it had seemed. Unnoticed perhaps in the daylight, when one could see them move. But in the mist or late at night, it would be very different.

He left Inspector Warren at the police station and drove to the Cathedral.

It was beautiful in the afternoon sun, and he wondered as he always had when looking at these Medieval masterpieces how they had been designed and built by masons and workmen who might not have lived to see their work finished. A leap of faith, leaving something to the future. A name scratched out of sight on a gargoyle's ear, or on a beam high above the nave, or wherever a man could leave his mark unseen. To show he had been there, and created something.

"What will ye leave behind?" Hamish asked into the silence.

"Nothing," Rutledge said, and turned to go to the motorcar.

And then he wheeled, realizing that the man standing nearer the Cathedral, staring up at it as he himself had been doing, looked familiar.

Sure now that he hadn't been mistaken, he strode forward just as the man began to walk away.

Lengthening his stride, he called, "Thornton."

The man looked over his shoulder to see who was addressing him. Startled to find that it was Rutledge, he hesitated for a moment, and then stopped to wait for him to catch him up.

"Inspector."

"Mr. Thornton. Admiring the Cathedral?"

"I always come here when I'm in Ely. It's an amazing building. I'd like to have a painting of the view I can see across the Fens. I'd think about that view when I was in the trenches. That was my escape."

For Rutledge, it had been the poems of O. A. Manning.

"I understand you sometimes went to Newmarket before the war."

"Another lifetime," he said wryly. "I didn't have the heart for it when I came home from France."

"Did you meet friends there, or go alone?"

"Does it matter? Sometimes with friends, sometimes alone. I was young, fancy free. It was something to do. Farming doesn't let you escape for very long. At least not as far as London. Newmarket was close enough to waste a few hours there."

"Did you ever meet someone named called Thaddeus Whiting?"

"I may have done. Is he a trainer? A rider?"

"What about Herbert Swift?"

"Ah. You're remembering what I'd said earlier. That I didn't know him well. It's true. I never visited his home or anything of the sort." Thornton smiled. "We were single, we'd come down from Cambridge, although he was ahead of me and I'd never met him there, and we made fools of ourselves a time or two, showing off our knowledge of the classical world." He turned to look up at the tower, sadness in his face now. "It was a very different time. Carefree and happy. Nothing could happen to us in that bright, sunny world. He was married shortly afterward, as I remember, and that put paid to visits to Newmarket and drinking ourselves silly of an evening. I didn't know him, what he feared or what he loved or what made him angry. Just that he had a very sharp mind and I could test my own against it."

"Did you marry, as he did?"

"I'd grown up in Isleham, I wanted to see a little more of life before I settled down. Then Germany attacked Belgium and suddenly I was at war. Marriage seemed to be a luxury I couldn't afford, given what was happening in France."

Rutledge thought he was telling the absolute truth—but not the whole truth.

He said, "And Captain Hutchinson? Lieutenant Hutchinson, as he was then. Did you meet him?"

"At Newmarket? No. I don't believe I ever saw him there. Or if I did, I had no way of knowing who he was." He looked up at the Cathedral again. "I was thinking before you spoke to me that it was shameful to use this beautiful edifice for murder. Whoever he is, I hope you find him."

And with a nod he walked away.

Hamish said, "Ye ken, he's a canny one."

Rutledge nearly answered the voice aloud. Why do you think that?

"I wouldna' care to play cards with him."

What had taught Thornton to conceal his feelings so well?

After a moment Rutledge walked back to his motorcar. If Alice Worth had given him a name, would it have been Thornton's?

He stopped again at the police station to ask if Thornton had had any encounters with the police. There was often inconclusive evidence or a warning given that never made it into official reports. Yet they formed a pattern.

But when he was asked about the man, Inspector Warren shook his head. "Impeccable record. Although I was told that once before the war, he was warned in Newmarket for public drunkenness. But he went home and slept it off. It was put down to high spirits, and that was that. He's not the sort of man you'd expect to see brought up before the magistrate. A gentleman. This is twice you've brought his name up. Any particular reason why?"

"Curiosity. He served during the war in the ranks." But Rutledge was wondering to himself if that one night of drunkenness had been the same night he learned Mary Whiting was marrying Lieutenant Hutchinson.

Inspector Warren looked at him straightly. "That doesn't make him a murderer."

"True enough."

"Did you ask him about arguing with Swift?"

"He told me it was before the war, a mere acquaintance, not a friendship. He claims it was nothing more than a kind of boasting. Certainly Swift stopped coming to Newmarket after his marriage."

"That was probably true enough. Swift and his wife were inseparable. Her death nearly broke the man. Some men take to drink or become reclusive after a wife has died. Swift wanted to turn his back on everything that could possibly remind him of her. To shut out the misery. It took him four years to work up the courage to come home again."

"Still—"

"I can't think Thornton harbored a grudge for six years, thirsting for revenge because Swift got a date in history wrong."

But it wasn't arguing with Swift that interested Rutledge. Still, he could see that when it came to choosing a second target—if Hutchinson had been the first and most important one—it might have appealed to Thornton to think of shooting Swift as having the last word. Rutledge remembered what he'd said to Alice Worth. That revenge was best savored cold.

"Is there any chance that Thornton was courting the woman Swift married?"

"I hardly think so. There have never been any rumors to that effect."

Rutledge shook his head. "Wherever I turn, there's no pattern to point the way."

"I don't like to say it, but so far you've done no better than I have in this search."

"Early days," Rutledge answered him grimly.

Rutledge left the motorcar by the Wriston inn and walked on to have a look at the ruins of the mill keeper's cottage.

Had the man who was charged with the upkeep of the mill tripped over a lantern in a drunken state—or set a fire to burn out the ghosts that haunted him?

Rutledge could understand how that might happen.

It wasn't his inquiry, it had nothing to do with this one. It was the mill that actually drew him here again, and the memory of Miss Trowbridge standing near it, looking up at the sky. There had been more than stargazing on her mind that evening. He wondered what it was.

Something twisted around his legs, and he looked down to see Clarissa winding herself back and forth, leaving a thick coat of white hairs on his trousers. When she lifted her head to beg for stroking, he could see that one eye was pale green, the other a pale blue. A striking combination. Mewing, she waited, and he reached down to touch her head, setting off a loud purring that made him smile.

"She likes you."

He turned to see Marcella Trowbridge standing at her gate, a shopping basket over her arm.

"I'm fond of animals," he replied.

"Sometimes they're kinder than people." As if she suddenly regretted the remark, she smiled and added, "They don't disagree with you or dislike you because you're grumpy in the morning or prefer your tea without milk."

Rutledge said, "Tell me about the man who used to live here."

"I liked him. He was kind to a lonely child. He'd sit with me on the steps and tell me stories or make things for me out of wood or string. My father had never had time to do that, and I never knew his father. My grandfather had died when he was still fairly young. My grandmother liked Angus too, and she was a very good judge of character. Mother would have been shocked if I'd told her I was entertained by the man who looked after the windmill. I sometimes wondered why Angus chose to live here when he could have lived in Scotland with his own people. But perhaps there had been a falling-out. I was far more romantically inclined, preferring to believe he'd lost the only woman he loved and had exiled himself forever. Too much Sir Walter Scott, I expect. But perhaps it was she who haunted him. Something did."

Her face colored suddenly, and she broke off. After a moment she asked, "Why do I tell you such things?"

He thought he knew the answer to that. She was very much alone in the world. And loneliness brought with it longing. Or emptiness.

Was that why Mary Hutchinson had taken her own life?

Chapter 15

Walking back from the windmill, Rutledge continued on to the police station, in search of McBride.

"Burrows is at home. A chastened man. I think he'll let his daughter attend to that wound now."

"Blood poisoning. He could have died." McBride stood up and stretched.

"Tell me what you know about this man Thornton. In Isleham."

"Not much, sir. Just that he's kept to himself since the war. People hardly ever see him out and about."

And yet he'd been in Ely today.

"He told me he barely knew Swift. And I've learned since then that they knew each other rather well, before the war."

"I doubt that makes him a murderer. People change in six years. And Swift wasn't in the Army, he never went to France. They wouldn't have much in common now, would they?"

"Probably not. Was Thornton ever engaged to be married?"

"I haven't heard anything about it. Not to a local girl, at any rate."

Alice Worth had the key to that question. And she refused to give up the answer.

"I'm driving back to Burwell. I want to speak to several people there. And then I'll speak to Swift's brother again. It may be late when I return."

"I'll pass the word to Miss Bartram."

Rutledge changed his mind and went first to call on Swift's brother, finding him just walking in from the fields.

The man grinned and said, "You came the right way round this time."

"I did," Rutledge said, answering the smile. "I need to ask a few more questions about your brother."

"Come in, then. I think there's lemonade on offer."

Rutledge accepted the invitation and sat with Swift in the kitchen, sipping the cool drink.

"Nothing like it on a warm day. But the lemons are hard to come by. And dear at any price. What is it you want to know?"

"Did your brother go often to Newmarket?"

"Newmarket? A few times with a friend from Ely."

"Did he see a man called Thornton there? From Isleham."

"God help me, I'd forgot about Thornton. They shared a love of ancient history, and my brother relished their arguments. I use the word loosely. Showing off was closer to the mark."

"Did they visit each other in Wriston or Isleham?"

"My guess is, they never did. And it was about that same time that Herbert met his wife-to-be. After that, he lost interest in horses and Greek history and everything else, spending most of his free time running up to Ely to call on her."

"What about someone called Thaddeus Whiting?"

"I don't think I've ever heard him mention that name."

"Mary Whiting?"

"There was a girl—Mary? Margaret? I can't be sure what she was called—who caught Thornton's eye. He met her in Newmarket, and that evening talked about nothing else, even refusing to take umbrage at something my brother brought up about Rome. Herbert came home gleeful, claiming that he'd found Thornton's Achilles' heel. That was before he'd met *his* wife, and he thought it amusing. Funny you should remind me of that." He stared off into the distance. "I do fairly well, as a rule. The farm keeps me busy, there's no time to mourn. And then something like this comes along and

I can see my brother's face as plainly as I see yours." He cleared his throat. "We were all young then. I'd been married a year myself. They called me the Old Man. I was all of twenty-eight. We didn't know what was to come, did we?"

Rutledge pressed, but that was all that Swift could remember. And then only because of his brother's reaction.

As he was leaving, he asked Swift if he was still worried about being a victim himself.

Shrugging, he said, "There's the farm. I don't have time to worry. But I keep a sharp eye out, all the same."

Driving on to Burwell, he sought out Mrs. Harris, telling her a little of what he'd learned in London.

"I can't think why Alice couldn't have helped the police. But she was Mary's only friend, and I expect she still feels strongly about what happened to her."

"And she said nothing to you about the man Mary had met, who he was, where he came from?"

"I don't think it mattered to her," Mrs. Harris said slowly. "He didn't come to Mary's rescue. No white horse, no shining armor. He left her to her fate."

"Perhaps he didn't know. Or perhaps she sent him away and asked him not to spoil her happiness."

"If he didn't know then, in the end I think he did. Alice wrote to him, I'm sure of it. She told me she was going to. I tried to talk her out of it, and she didn't mention it again. But I know her, you see. She wrote that letter and she sent it. She felt that strongly about what happened." She lifted her hand in a rueful gesture. "I always wondered what he made of her letter, if he was in France somewhere, fighting the Germans. Helpless to do anything. If he wanted to kill that man Hutchinson, why didn't he do it then? Men were dying every day."

"It's possible their paths never crossed."

"Well, there's that, I suppose."

"If you could persuade her to change her mind, I'd be grateful."

"That would be the same as sending him to the hangman. I'll have to think about that. I don't feel as fiercely about this matter as Alice does, but I'd hate to think my actions condemned anyone."

"It's possible he's killed two people."

"Yes, that's true. But why should he have shot Herbert Swift?"

And that was unanswerable. An opportunity to cast doubt on why Captain Hutchinson had to die? It always came back to that question.

Hamish said, "There could be two men. One who wanted Swift dead and the ither who wanted yon Captain dead."

That was possible. An unassailable alibi for one murder would tend to make the police think that that person was in the clear. But it was highly unlikely. How had the two men met and decided on murder? Why would they trust each other? And why should the owner of the Lee-Enfield need a partner when he could make his own kill so cleverly? It was the second victim that brought Scotland Yard into the picture—an unnecessary risk for Hutchinson's murderer, who had gone scot-free.

There had to be more than a love affair gone wrong to make someone kill twice and then wound a third victim. Unless the point was to confound the police. A cold-blooded decision.

He thanked Mrs. Harris and drove back to Wriston as quickly as possible, walking into the police station to ask Constable McBride for the key to Herbert Swift's house.

McBride said, "Everything was in order there. Inspector Warren was with me when I searched."

"I'm sure that's true. All the same, I'd like to look at some of his cases."

Reluctantly Constable McBride got to his feet, taking a key from the drawer of his desk. "It's beyond the second green. The Swift house."

They walked there in silence. McBride unlocked the door and stood aside.

The house smelled damp and musty, the faintest odor of cigarette smoke lingering in the air as well.

Swift had taken over a smaller house next to his, opened up a passage between them, and used that as his chambers. As they went down the passage, it creaked a little. And then they were in the cottage. The front room had become a waiting room, what would have been a bedroom had become an office, and the room in back was where his clerk must have worked.

"He had a clerk," Rutledge said. "What's become of him?"

"He went home to Norfolk," McBride said simply. "When we locked up here. These files will have to be turned over to someone to sort out."

Rutledge spent an hour going through past cases that Swift had handled. For the most part they were conveyances, wills, property settlements, and so on. Swift had been involved in three criminal cases. One was trespass, where two cousins had argued over an inheritance and the elder of the two had come looking for the younger, intending to teach him a lesson. Another was a drunken brawl ending in bodily harm, and the third was housebreaking, by what appeared to be a Traveler. They had been tried in Ely, and two of them had ended in guilty pleas. Only the two cousins had insisted on trial before they were satisfied. But there was nothing in any file to make Swift a target for revenge.

After a thorough search of the office, they went back to the main house.

If Swift had been guarding any secrets, they hadn't found them.

The sun was setting when they locked the door and walked down the green toward the police station. Once again the sky was radiant, ablaze with color from the softest lavender to a flaming red.

"I've never quite got used to the sunsets," McBride said into the silence. "I've only to step out of an evening, and there it is, surely different each time I look up. I was talking to a man who loved the mountains, and I asked him if he ever felt cut off, like. With no horizon, just more mountains shutting out the view. But it didn't appear to bother him."

Rutledge left him at the police station and walked on toward The Dutchman Inn.

A boy rolling a hoop came running down the street and nearly collided with Rutledge. Laughing, he ran on, the hoop bouncing and wobbling over the ruts in the road.

Hamish was asking, "Did ye no' think of leaving the farmer out of it?"

"Because he was wounded, when the man with the rifle could very easily have killed him?"

"Aye, it doesna' make sense."

"Unless his conscience troubled him."

"Aye, but would it? It's possible, ye ken, that he was intended to mislead."

"But the killer came back."

"Aye, someone did."

The presence of the dog had been a deterrent, because it meant that no one could steal up close enough to the house to see the man inside. And so there was nothing to show what the intentions of the intruder were. Still—he knew he'd missed . . .

Thornton had shown no signs of having been wounded by Burrows's shot. He didn't limp. There were no obvious bandages. Surely if he'd bled enough to leave traces on the ground, he'd have still been showing the effects of his injury.

"There's still Swift," Hamish was saying. "He claims he wasna' fashed with his brother o'er the inheriting of the farm. Ye have only his word."

"He was nervous when first I arrived at his door."

"Aye, he said he was afraid he might be next. But it's possible he was afraid of Scotland Yard."

"Why shoot Hutchinson first? If he'd been found out, Swift would still be alive."

"Aye."

He'd reached the inn, and for a moment considered walking on as far as the mill. There would be an even better view of the sunset from the little bridge.

On impulse, he did just that. He was watching the sun dip into the horizon when he was distracted by Hamish.

Frowning, he tried to see what was there in the middle distance. A man? Standing there for the same reason Rutledge had come to the bridge?

But the figure was in the middle of nowhere. What was he doing there? Where had he come from—where was he going?

Remembering the lights in the fields and the man he himself had encountered in the mist, Rutledge gauged the distance. Too far to run, but with his motorcar . . .

He turned quickly and ran in the opposite direction, toward the inn.

Turning the crank at speed, he nearly got caught by the backlash. Swearing under his breath, he got in and drove out of the village as far as the bridge.

The sun had gone down but the afterglow was dulling toward dark. He peered into the distance. The figure he'd seen was still there.

Turning in that direction, he headed straight for the figure.

And then it was gone. Rutledge blinked, peering out the windscreen. Whoever it was couldn't disappear into thin air.

Had the man seen the motorcar coming and chose to get off the road? But where to?

Down one of the embankments? Rutledge flicked on his headlamps.

If he was wearing dark clothing, he'd be the devil to find against the black soil.

Arriving where he thought the figure might have been standing, he pulled over and stopped. Reaching for his torch, he began to search the fields on either side of him.

Where the devil was he?

Rutledge walked some twenty paces forward, casting the torch beam to either side. Then he walked back to the motorcar and kept going for another twenty paces or more.

Nothing.

How had he vanished? Where had he gone?

He moved the motorcar forward twenty yards, and tried again.

His torch skimmed the black, peaty soil, the browning stalks of what must be barley, and then he crossed to the far side of the road.

Frustrated, Rutledge spent half an hour hunting for whoever it was. He came up empty-handed.

Finally returning to the motorcar and carefully reversing on the narrow road, he went back the way he'd come. And as he drove toward Wriston, he had the oddest feeling that somewhere in the darkness out there to either side of his headlamps, the man he'd seen was watching him go, and laughing.

Over dinner he asked Priscilla Bartram who might be out late, walking on the road.

"Hard to say. One of the farm tenants coming back from the fields? He'd know his way. Or a Traveler, up to no good. Even a tradesman, caught out after making a delivery."

But what tradesman walked? What goods could he carry, without so much as a barrow or bicycle?

He must have appeared to be skeptical, for Miss Bartram glanced at her kitchen windows, where the curtains had been drawn against the night.

"You don't think it could be the killer, do you?" She crossed to the door into the kitchen garden and tested the latch. "One can't be too careful. I've been thinking of getting a little dog. For company. I hear Mr. Taylor's bitch has had a litter."

And for protection?

How long had she lived alone in this house, without feeling the need for a dog?

A moth, drawn by the light, in spite of the curtains, threw itself at the glass, and she nearly dropped the spoon in her hand, turning toward the window. Then, feeling a little embarrassed, she said, "I shan't forgive whoever it is who did these murders. He's taken away my peace of mind."

"I don't think you have anything to fear."

"He walked into the ironmonger's house, didn't he? How did he know they weren't at home? What if Mrs. Ross had been lying down with a headache, and her husband had left her there while he went out to the rally? What then?"

It wasn't the first time Rutledge had wondered about such a possibility.

But he said, "He could have knocked at the door out to the kitchen garden. And when no one came, he walked in."

"I still say, what if Mrs. Ross was resting, a cool cloth over her forehead, and didn't hear the knock."

He had no answer for that.

The next morning brought news that Ruskin, the cooper in Soham, had gone on a rampage in the night, wielding a side ax. It was a blade that was razor sharp on one side and dull on the other, with the typical short handle that coopers used in the close-quarter work of their trade.

It could do serious damage, wielded as a weapon.

Because he'd been on the ex-soldier list, Rutledge went to Soham to interview him, and found him in the local police station with a heavy head.

Ruskin looked up as the cell door opened, and Rutledge stood there in front of him.

"What happened?" Rutledge asked. He'd asked the constable to stay in the tiny office and give him time alone with the man.

Ruskin buried his face in his hands. "I'd been to the pub, and I didn't want to go home. There's a cot in the loft of the shed, and I thought to sleep off most of what I'd drunk before my wife saw me. That's all I remember. Then I was back in Wriston, and the man in the window was shooting at *me*." He sighed, looking up at Rutledge. "Constable says I was running down the lane shouting and waving the side ax. I was looking for someone, and I was going to kill him. I'm told it was the hurdle maker I was chasing. I must have frightened him out of his wits. Then some men wrestled me down, took away the side ax, and held me until the constable came. One of them flung a pail of water over my head. By that time I was nearly sober. They clapped me up here for the night, all the same."

"Why were you searching for the hurdle maker?"

"God knows. I doubt I've exchanged a dozen words with him. Besides, it had more to do with the night

Swift was killed. The nightmares came back after that. A time or two I've tried to drink myself into forgetting."

That didn't work. Rutledge had tried it, found it made the nightmares harder to escape, and gave it up. But Ruskin would have to learn it for himself.

"Nothing happened at your shop after you got there last night? No one came to see you?"

"How do I know? I don't remember, I tell you. It's a blank, until I started dreaming."

"Then it was what you saw in Wriston."

"It must have been." He shivered. "I didn't want to kill anyone. I didn't want to be killed."

But what had triggered this particular nightmare?

Looking at Ruskin, he thought it was likely that the man himself would never know. It was locked in his mind with the war he wanted to forget.

Still, Rutledge tried. He kept his voice level, quiet.

"Was it a sniper, Ruskin? One of our sharpshooters?"

"No. No." Ruskin shook his head. "Don't ask me, don't make me remember."

"Then it was German. Am I right?"

Finally, Ruskin looked up, his eyes dark with pain. "It was outside Ypres. I saw him. Staring straight at me. I knew he was going to fire. And I threw myself to one side. But the man behind me didn't see him. Not in time. And he took the bullet meant for me. It was my *fault*."

Rutledge put a hand on the other man's shoulder. "You needn't think about it again," he said firmly. "You've done your duty."

Ruskin didn't answer, enveloped in a misery that nothing could stop. After a moment, unable to watch, Rutledge left.

He went to speak to the constable.

"Now he's sober, sir, we'll let him go with a warning. If it happens again, I'll have to charge him. That side ax could cleave a man's skull."

"He can't help responding the way he has."

"That may be, sir, but we can't let him endanger himself or others."

The constable was too young to have been in the war. He'd been sent to fill the shoes of an older man on the point of retiring, and he took his duties seriously.

"Lost your father in the war, did you?"

"Sir, yes. Early on."

Rutledge thanked him and took his leave.

Driving out of Soham, he said aloud, "I find it hard to believe Ruskin saw a German."

"Aye, that's true."

"Perhaps he saw what he feared to see."

"Aye, it's why ye never look into a mirror."

Trying to ignore that remark, Rutledge knew the answer must be there, in the depths of memory. He couldn't quite reach it . . .

Something he'd been told? Something he'd seen? A passing comment, a remark overheard. *What was it?*

Instead of driving on to Wriston, he decided to go to Isleham instead.

Rutledge found Thornton at home.

The man was surprised to see him. "I can't think why you've found it necessary to call on me again. But I'll help in any way I can," he said as Rutledge was ushered into the room with the globe and the maps and the books.

"I've been to see the cooper in Soham. The man called Ruskin. Do you know him?"

"I can't say that I've ever met him. Still, I'm sure we must own some of his wares. You can ask my housekeeper, if you like."

"He had a difficult war. Last night he ran amok, thinking he was being hunted by the man who'd killed Swift. He saw him, by the way. Just as Mrs. Percy had."

"Did he indeed," Thornton said, his eyes narrowing. "How did he describe this person?"

"He said he was a German sharpshooter."

Thornton stared at him. "Good God. He can't be serious."

"The hurdle maker didn't find it amusing."

"Are you saying Ruskin killed him?"

"Only that he was on a rampage and the hurdle maker got in the way. He wasn't hurt, as far as I am aware."

"But why did he think Swift's killer was German?"

"I'm not sure he did. But whatever he saw, it triggered that memory."

"They were devilishly clever at making themselves invisible. It was usually something in the landscape, something we'd never think twice about. That was early on, of course, before we knew what they were up to," Thornton said. "One of the worst we faced was in the stump of a dead tree. They'd reinforced it. We couldn't touch him. He was out of grenade range as well. Hardly the sort of thing you'd see in a dormer window."

Devilishly clever at making themselves invisible . . .

But *invisible* was the wrong word. *Invulnerable—*

There it was, the memory Rutledge had been looking for.

"They used a helmet sometimes," Rutledge said slowly. "Have you ever been to the Tower of London? I was taken there as a child, to see the ravens. The armor frightened my sister, I remember. Especially the casques, the helmets with the fanciful armorial figures. When the German snipers peered over the parapet of their trenches, they sometimes used a helmet, steel with slits for the eyes and mouth. Only much cruder, of course, than what's in the Tower. There was one man in particular. He was damned good. Something of a legend, I expect, on his own side, but someone we wanted badly. I never saw him, he wasn't in my sector. But when he was killed, in the next sortie someone found his helmet. That could explain what Mrs. Percy saw. Why Ruskin was so shaken." He paused. "Know anyone here in the Fen country who brought back such a souvenir?"

"No. I don't," Thornton said pensively. "Are you sure about this? I never saw it either."

Rutledge held out his hand. "Give me a pen and some paper. I'll draw it."

Thornton passed him what he asked for. And in that brief exchange, he could read the man's eyes, unguarded.

Speculation? Anger? Uncertainty? Or a succession of all three?

Sketching, Rutledge said, "A friend of mine described it." He finished and gave the drawing to Thornton.

It was more like half a cylinder than a helmet shaped to fit the head. Some of those for knights, he remembered, had even had ears. Here the eyes and nose had been crudely cut out, the mouth no more than a ragged slit. A face and yet more an ugly, terrifying rendering of it.

And Ruskin had seen it twice. In the trenches and in the upstairs window of the ironmonger's house.

Thornton leaned forward to examine it. "Nothing like that in our sector. Are you sure about this? Or is it apocryphal?"

"No, I think it actually existed. My friend knew what he was talking about."

He held out his hand for the drawing, and Thornton reluctantly passed it across the desk to him.

"I can see why this disturbed anyone who saw it. I'd hardly want that as a souvenir."

"But if you were—or had been—a sharpshooter yourself, you might find it interesting. Most particularly, if you were the one who'd killed him."

"Yes, I see. The question is, *who*?"

"I thought perhaps it might be you. You might have such a helmet."

"Me!"

"You lied to me about Swift. You knew him better than you were willing to admit."

"But why should I have shot the other man, Hutchinson?"

"If there's a reason, I shall find it," Rutledge said, rising. "I'll see myself out. Good day, Thornton."

Chapter 16

H e walked out of the room, leaving the man sitting there, a frown on his face.

As Rutledge turned the crank, Hamish said, "Ye canna' search every house in the Fens. And ye ken, the helmet and the rifle could be anywhere."

But Rutledge was trying to remember the rest of what he'd been told about the German sniper. It had been a chance meeting with Captain Graves in France, and they had had very little time to talk. *What else had he said about that particular sniper?*

A Scots company had killed the man. Was that it? Rutledge couldn't be sure.

The cat was out of the bag now. Thornton knew he was a suspect. But then he must have guessed in Ely that Rutledge was suspicious of the lie he'd told—and been caught in.

In Wriston, he left the motorcar outside the iron-monger's house and walked down the lane where Mrs. Percy lived.

She called, "Come," as she had before, and he found her sweeping her kitchen floor.

"You again," she said tartly. "I've told you it's use-less, I don't know anything."

He reached into his pocket, unfolded the sheet of paper with the drawing on it, and set it down on the table.

Curiosity got the better of her. She stood the broom against the doorframe, walked across the kitchen, and looked down.

He could hear her suck in a breath, the shock of what she was seeing hitting her like cold water in the face. She reached for the back of a chair to steady her-self, then turned to him.

Her eyes were wide, frightened. She cleared her throat, then had to do it a second time before she could find her voice. Even then it was more a croak. "Where did you come by this?"

"It's a drawing of a face guard—a protective cov-ering for the face—that the Germans sometimes used when they were shooting at us in the trenches. It's metal, smooth, dull metal. What you saw in that window above the ironmonger's shop was a soldier's disguise. Not a monster."

Her pale face flushed with rising anger. "You mean to say I was tricked?"

"Yes, in a way. If anyone was looking up when he took that shot, only that strange face could be seen. Its intent was to confuse and make people afraid." He waited. "Is this at all like what you remember?"

"It could be a twin," she said. "I haven't slept well since I saw it. I've been the butt of jokes. I've been questioned over and over again. I hope you find him and hang him, whoever it is."

"Will you give Constable McBride a new statement?"

"Of course I will." She wiped her hands on her apron. "I'll just fetch my hat."

Leaving him standing there, she walked away. Two minutes later, she was back, wearing a dark blue straw hat with pansies around the brim. It was the hat of a much younger woman, and he wondered if she had kept it all these years or had bought it at a jumble sale.

Rutledge accompanied her to the police station. McBride, staring at the sketch, said, "Well, I'll be—" He stopped in time. "But is this possible? How did he come by such a thing?"

"He was given it, he made his own from rumors he'd heard, or he stole it. We don't know. But there's your monster. Mrs. Percy has come to give you an amended statement. If you'll make a copy of it, I'll take it to Inspector Warren myself."

"Gladly. Thank you, sir. Now, Mrs. Percy, if you'll sit behind the desk here, I'll fetch paper and pen."

Rutledge left him to it.

He stopped at the market cross and looked again at the dormer window.

Given the torchlight and the smoke, the face peering down at the crowded square below, it would be easy to believe that a monster was up in that window. And because the killer had had to raise up to use the rifle, he'd needed a disguise.

And this reinforced Rutledge's belief that his man was an experienced sniper.

A master of disguises—no two the same. Keeping the police guessing, keeping witnesses too frightened to know precisely what it was they'd seen.

Who in Wriston—who in the Fens—had been a sniper and kept it hidden, a dark secret of the war?

Or had he learned the trade from someone else who knew it well? That too was a possibility.

Leaving his motorcar where it was for the time being, he walked back to The Dutchman Inn.

Priscilla Bartram, feather duster in hand, was putting the sitting room to rights. When she heard him come through the door, she hurried to meet him, duster still in hand.

"You were gone most of the morning," she said. "Is there any news?"

"I've been questioning a number of people," he said vaguely. "It's often the details that trip people up. Verifying this or that. Making sure that when someone says he was in such and such a place at such and such a time, he's telling the truth."

She would have preferred exciting information she could pass on to friends. Relenting, Rutledge smiled. "A dull morning on the whole, but I think we've discovered Mrs. Percy's monster. Just an ordinary man wearing a disguise."

He caught the apprehensive look she cast at the nearest window, as if expecting to see the face peering in. He didn't think she was the sort of woman whose nerves produced shadows where there were none. And yet the killing of Swift had given her cause to worry. After all, she had seen him die.

She led him back to the kitchen, where there was cool water waiting for him, and with it she offered a plate of biscuits.

He ate them to please her, and then was about to leave for Ely when she stopped him at the kitchen door.

"I was thinking," she said hesitantly, as if reluctant to be considered a meddler. "You asked me, didn't you, if I recognized anyone from Wriston at the funeral of Major Clayton."

"Yes. Have you remembered someone else?"

"Not precisely. There were several other people I recognized, from other villages. Is that important? If not, I won't bother you with it."

"Make a list for me. That would be very useful."

Happy to have been helpful, she nodded. "I'll have it ready when you come back."

Retrieving the motorcar, he set out for Ely.

But Inspector Warren wasn't as pleased as Rutledge had expected him to be.

"All well and good," he said. "But the Chief Constable was here late yesterday, a musical evening at the Cathedral. He stopped to see me and told me again how anxious he is to see this matter brought to a successful conclusion."

"We aren't dealing with an ordinary murderer. This man is clever, and winkling him out of wherever he's been hiding will be difficult."

"I understand. The point I'm making is that the Chief Constable doesn't. He was expecting the Yard to make swifter progress."

"And so we are," Rutledge said, smiling. But when he left the police station, his face was grim.

He shut himself in the hotel telephone closet, and gave what he was about to do some thought.

First the call to Gibson.

The sergeant answered in his usual taciturn manner.

"Anything for me?" Rutledge asked. He weighed the silence before Gibson spoke. Then he could hear the opening of a drawer, the rustle of papers.

"The servant girl. Catriona Beaton. Seems she left the house in the middle of the night, and wasn't seen again. But a body that might have been hers was found near the railway tracks in Hampshire some weeks later. There was enough clothing left to make a tentative identification. She'd been buried in a shallow grave in a stand of trees above the tracks, and her remains were washed out by that heavy rain. Schoolboys, playing the truant, found her. According to the inquest, she was murdered by person or persons unknown. Girls without references face a heavy go of it."

Rutledge asked, "Was she pregnant, do you know?"

"That couldn't be determined."

"Did Hutchinson own a motorcar? Did he have a chauffeur?"

"He did own a motorcar, but he chose to drive himself."

"What did Miss Hutchinson have to say about the girl's death?"

"That she'd been a good, hardworking young woman, and that it was a tragedy for the entire household.

What's more, she paid for the girl to be buried decently. Apparently Miss Beaton had no family."

It was often those women without a family, without a protector, who suffered most from the attentions of their employers.

Neither Miss Newland nor Mrs. Cookson had told him anything about the girl's body being recovered.

"Did the police speak to the staff?"

"Miss Hutchinson told them it would be too upsetting—she'd break the news herself."

And she hadn't. The question was, why? Had she told her brother?

Or had she feared he'd killed the girl himself? Love scorned could lead to murder as quickly as love satisfied. It was very likely that Miss Hutchinson wouldn't wish the household to speculate and gossip—and reach unwelcome conclusions.

And Mary Hutchinson? He put the thought into words.

"And Mary Hutchinson?"

"Orphaned young, brought up by her uncle, married, and died of overwhelming grief after losing her child."

The attending doctor had been kind. They often were in cases of suicide.

"Any information on Anson Swift?"

"That's the lot. Except to add that the Whiting you inquired about died of natural causes."

Necessary information, although it left much unanswered.

Rutledge thanked him and put up the receiver.

His next call was to a friend at the War Office.

When he explained what he needed, the voice at the other end of the line said, "You do realize that this desk isn't an adjunct to Scotland Yard."

Rutledge laughed. "Where else will I find such an excellent source of information?" Then he added in a very different tone, "This man has killed twice. If he's reverting to what he did in the war, I need to hear about it. If he's using his training in France to rid himself of enemies in England, I want to know."

"How many names have you got?"

Rutledge told him, and heard the groan at the other end.

"It would be simpler to search Regimental records than hunt for a single man, regiment unknown, service unknown. If they used sharpshooters, it's usually found there. All right, give me the first ten."

When that was finished, Rutledge said, "And then there is Captain Gordon Hutchinson. Did he have anyone up on charges? Were any of his men taken up for cowardice and shot? What was his record?"

"I'll do my best."

Rutledge gave him the number at the hotel, and thanked him. "The hotel will forward any messages to Inspector Warren."

"You owe me a bottle of the finest whisky money can buy," the voice said, and rang off.

All I need is one good bit of evidence, Rutledge thought, not moving out of the telephone closet. But everywhere I turn, it's not there.

Hamish said, "Go to Warwick."

That was where Mary Hutchinson had grown up.

There was a tap at the door. He looked up to see a man standing there impatiently waiting his turn in the telephone closet.

Rutledge left him to it, and turned toward Wriston.

Whoever this killer was, he knew how to stay out of the public eye. Whether he was the old man, the owner of the barrow, someone from the Fen villages, or one of the wedding guests, he'd successfully evaded being seen by anyone. And while he had been visible in Wriston, he had given away nothing.

The one person Rutledge had spoken to in all the Fen country who'd impressed him as the most likely suspect was Thornton. The man was intelligent, clever, well read, and probably could outwit all of them put together. Brenner was more of a hothead, and while hotheads could be dangerous, these murders had taken meticulous planning.

Had Thornton been a sniper in the war? Or the spotter for one? Given his propensity for living as a recluse, it was possible. And there had also been men who were natural shots, who could hit targets with ease, once they were accustomed to their weapon.

And if the Chief Constable was pressing Warren, the Acting Chief Superintendent would soon be recalling him.

When he came down to dinner later that evening, Priscilla Bartram had gone to great lengths to make up for dining in the kitchen. The large round table with its eight chairs was covered with a pretty cloth embroidered with—not unexpectedly, given the glass cases in the sitting room—pheasants. He was glad to see there were none of the stuffed birds in this room, brought in to complement the cloth.

As he ate his dinner and carried on a conversation with Miss Bartram, he wondered what she would do if the wildfowlers didn't return to Wriston. Her chances of marrying were small, given the loss of a generation of men. Her chances of keeping the inn were even less. Marcella Trowbridge had said Priscilla Bartram could use the money, and he'd been generous when she'd set her terms for meals and lodging.

When they had finished, Miss Bartram carried their dishes out to the kitchen, then turned to Rutledge.

"That list I promised you. It's in the sitting room. Shall I bring in a fresh pot of tea and a little of that cake you enjoyed last night?"

"Yes, thank you." He got up and walked to the sitting room. There, feeling the gaze of the glass eyes all around him, he picked up the list.

There were only a handful of names on the sheet, but her handwriting was an ornate copperplate and not easy to read.

Three men had come from Soham, and he didn't recognize the names, which meant he hadn't interviewed them. Ex-soldiers?

A third, from Wicken, he had already spoken to.

Miss Bartram came in with the tray, setting it on the tea table at his elbow.

"The first two names from Soham and the one from Wicken are fathers of men who'd served with the Major but hadn't come home," she said. "It was rather sad, really. Almost as if, since they couldn't bury their own, they could at least bury their sons' commanding officer. Adam Lindsay didn't stay for the luncheon. I wouldn't have known who he was, but one of the Soham men spoke with him. And that last name, the one in Isleham, was odd. He was there at St. Mary's but he never went inside for the service. He was still standing in the same spot when we came out. The only reason I know *his* name is that just before the war he came here with some others from Isleham for a Maundy Thursday service. That was when the roof of St. Andrew's in Isleham sprang a leak and the church had to be closed for the weekend." She smiled. "He certainly set the village girls in a twitter."

But Rutledge hadn't been listening. The final name, the one in Isleham, was Kimber Thornton.

He stared at it, then asked Priscilla Bartram to repeat what she'd just said.

She did, adding, "Is this useful at all?"

"Very much so. You say Thornton just stood outside St. Mary's? He didn't go in for the service? Did he speak to anyone?"

"He was never near enough to speak to anyone. And he didn't come to the committal service, either. By the time we walked back to the church again, he'd left."

"You are certain he didn't come to the luncheon."

"I'm positive."

"This is very helpful, and I'd appreciate it if you didn't say anything to anyone else."

"I understand." She was a little flushed with pleasure, but as his words sank in, she said quickly, "You're not thinking that *Mr. Thornton* is the murderer?"

"Every new bit of information fits into the puzzle," he said. "I shall have to ask him what he saw while he was standing there."

Mollified, she nodded. "I see." But he didn't think she did, and he was glad.

He excused himself soon after, and went out to the motorcar. It was a fair night, and there were no clouds on the horizon. It was later than he liked, but this couldn't wait.

Setting out for Isleham, he thought, A second lie on Thornton's part. He didn't attend Major Clayton's funeral—and he didn't know Swift very well. What else has he lied about?

Hamish said, "It wouldha' been better to wait until ye hear from London."

"It will take too long to sift through regimental records, and Gibson has already told me that he couldn't find very much about Thornton. I asked that he try again, but he's not likely to learn more than he already has."

"Still . . ." Hamish said.

Thornton, as it happened, hadn't gone to bed. But he had taken a walk, according to the housekeeper whose prim mouth indicated that Rutledge was out of order for calling so late.

"Where is he walking?"

"I don't know, sir. Sometimes he doesn't sleep well. And then he walks for a few minutes or for hours. I never know which it will be. I just leave the door off the latch, and he locks up when he comes in."

He could see that it was useless to ask to wait, at this hour.

Thanking her, he drove around to the far side of the church and left his motorcar there. And he walked the narrow streets of Isleham, looking for Thornton. He was nowhere to be found. Rutledge even stepped into the pub in the event he'd stopped in for a last drink.

If Thornton was in Isleham, he was invisible.

The only other possibility was that he'd called on someone. At this time of night?

Rutledge waited for a full hour, and still Thornton hadn't returned.

Where the hell had the man got to?

Finally giving up, Rutledge drove back to Wriston. Priscilla Bartram had already gone upstairs and he was glad not to be asked where he'd been.

On the spur of the moment, he walked as far as the police station, but it was dark as well. London would still be lively at this hour, in many parts of the city, but in the Fens it seemed that people had little use for late-night revelry.

He went down Mrs. Percy's lane and stood for a time staring out at the fields.

Here was where someone going home from The Wake had seen lights bobbing in the fields. But there was nothing out there tonight. Everyone had assumed that the sighting had something to do with the murders. But perhaps they hadn't. Perhaps it had only been two boys making mischief or even oblivious to the stir they'd created, then were unwilling to step forward—

He heard something at the head of the lane and whirled.

Someone was pedaling down the High Street on a bicycle, hunched over the handlebars, as if tired and still a long way from home. The cyclist was heading toward the windmill. But where was he going from there? Burwell? Isleham?

His first thought was that this could be Thornton.

Racing up the lane toward the High Street, he skidded to a stop and looked both ways.

But the cyclist was nowhere in sight.

Had he heard Rutledge's footsteps on the hard clay of the lane and speeded up? Or was he approaching the windmill, said to be haunted, and hurrying to put it behind him?

One ghost avoiding another . . .

The thought passed through his mind, and Hamish said derisively, "Yon rider wasna' a ghost. Go after him."

Rutledge ran on to the motorcar, turned the crank, and leapt behind the wheel. But by the time he'd reached Miss Trowbridge's house and driven up and over the bridge beyond the windmill, he couldn't see the cyclist—or anyone else—along either of the straight lines of roads.

It wasn't until he had driven back to The Dutchman Inn that he realized that he hadn't looked behind the mill. A man could conceal himself and his bicycle there and outwait the motorcar at his heels.

Cursing himself for a fool, he went back to the windmill, on foot this time, carrying his torch with him. Flicking the torch on, he shone it into the high grass at the mill's broad base. Stems and blades had been bent and flattened. Very recently, because a few were already beginning to right themselves.

"Who's there?" A voice came out of the darkness.

He turned.

Miss Trowbridge was standing in the road, a shawl around her shoulders against the night's chill.

"Rutledge," he said, coming round the mill so that she could see him.

"What on earth are you doing behind the mill? What are you looking for?"

"Curiosity," he said, not wanting to frighten her. "I couldn't sleep."

"But I thought I heard your motorcar just now, passing by and returning."

"So you did. Did you hear anything else?"

"No. I told you. I'm used to the sound the bridge makes when something heavy, like a motorcar, crosses it. You probably haven't noticed the slight noise. But I know it well."

She must, living here on the outskirts of the village.

He walked through the high grass to where she was standing on the road. "Can you hear people on foot, say, or on a bicycle?"

"No, of course not." She hesitated. "Are you telling me that you believe this is the way whoever shot Mr. Swift left Wriston without being seen?"

"It's more likely," he responded, "that he left by running along the embankment that separates the village from the fields on that side."

"Yes," she said slowly, thinking about it, "but he would have to know what he was about. We played there as children. The Loon River, although it's presumptuous to call it that, once flowed on that side of the village. It's hardly more than a ditch with standing water now." And then she turned to him, her eyes large in the pale oval of her face, all he could see in the dark. "You're telling me that he—whoever he is—must be a local man. That someone from Ely, or Cambridge, or even Peterborough wouldn't have known he could escape that way."

"Unless of course he'd studied the land. He must have done in Ely to know where the best concealment was. He didn't intend to get caught."

"That's horrible to think about. That someone plotted to kill two men."

Rutledge said, "I don't want to frighten you. Still, since I've been here, I've seen Wriston so empty of an evening that you'd be hard-pressed to find anyone in the High or on the lanes. And yet someone has been abroad. On foot, on bicycles. Who do you think they are?"

She hesitated. "People do walk from place to place at night. I've wondered sometimes if they're Travelers, using the roads when no one else does. The windmill often seems to fascinate them for some reason. Clarissa pricks up her ears and stares in that direction, then after a bit relaxes and goes back to sleep. She must hear something, not just a mouse in the wainscoting."

"Does anyone come to your door?"

"No, never. Well, sometimes a London policeman lost in the fog." She said it with a wry smile.

But he himself wouldn't have found her door if there hadn't been someone else in the mist that night. Someone who knew there was a cottage here, and where to find the gate.

Someone who had searched his motorcar and his valise.

"I'm not afraid," she said, as much for her own benefit as for his, he thought. "I don't know why, but I've always felt very safe here in this cottage. As if my grandmother's love still surrounds me."

He said, "You shouldn't have come out to see who was here. Remember that. And I'd still lock my door at night."

"I do. And there's Clarissa."

Thinking about the ferocious dog that Burrows had borrowed to help him keep watch, Rutledge smiled.

They turned and walked back to the cottage.

"How much longer will you be here in Wriston?" she asked, looking up at him.

"Until I find a killer. Do you know a man called Thornton in Isleham?"

"I've met him a time or two. Very quiet, but nice enough."

"Someone named Adam Lindsay in Soham?"

"Sorry, no. I don't go to Soham very often. If I have marketing to do, I'll go to Burwell. Or Ely."

"Ruskin, the cooper there?"

"I know his work. People complained during the war—he was in France but he was needed here, they said. Is there any reason you're asking me about these men?"

"Just filling out my knowledge of the Fen country. It helps to have different perspectives on the local people. Know anyone who was a sniper during the war?"

"Snipers? No." Her tone of voice was enough. No one she might know could stoop so low.

He stood by the gate until she had gone in her door and closed it behind her. He waited and heard the latch turn, then went on his way.

I shouldn't have stopped and talked to her, he thought. I should have driven on to Isleham, to see if Thornton came home on a bicycle. It would be a long ride, tiring for him. A man could sleep after that, if he tried.

Chapter 17

The next morning after his breakfast, Rutledge asked Priscilla Bartram if she would accompany him to Burwell and show him precisely where she had seen Mr. Thornton standing.

"Is it necessary?" she asked reluctantly. "I can't be sure of the exact spot, I wasn't really there to watch Mr. Thornton."

"It doesn't have to be precise," he said easily. "Just the general idea." He glanced at the window. "It's a lovely day for an outing."

"Yes, of course. Well, I'll get my shawl, shall I? And my hat."

It was nearly a quarter of an hour before she came back down the stairs wearing an attractive hat, carrying her gloves and a shawl. She was anxious as he followed her out to the motorcar and helped her into the seat. But once settled and on her way, she was a little more at her ease.

She said as they went over the bridge by the mill, "The butcher's boy, when he delivered the sausages this morning, told me that Mr. Banner—the butcher—told *him* that his knee was throbbing at dawn. It means a change in the weather. Mr. Banner's knee is as good as a barometer."

Looking up at the sky, Rutledge said, "It appears to be clear enough now."

"We're due a little cooler weather soon."

And that could mean fog.

When they reached Burwell, he left the car below St. Mary's and they walked around to the west door.

"Were people gathering here before the service?"

"A few, greeting each other."

"The door was open?" "Oh, yes, the church was half full by the time I arrived."

"And you went directly inside?"

"No, there were several people before me, standing just beyond the doorway, where their voices didn't carry. But they had made it difficult for me to pass by. And so I stopped and looked around. That's when I saw him. There." She pointed to her left.

"Not under the trees by the churchyard."

"No. That tree, the large one, just below that house. He was standing in its shadow."

"And yet you recognized him." There was doubt in his voice.

"Would you remember a pretty girl you'd seen one Sunday going into your church and sitting just ahead of you?" she asked tartly.

Rutledge laughed. "Very likely."

"He'd changed, of course. After all, it's been six years. But I knew him."

"Was Captain Hutchinson standing outside the church at that time?"

"You know, I do believe he was. Yes, that's right. He was one of the group of men waiting for the coffin. I'd forgot that. I didn't know who he was, at that time, you see. Not until the luncheon."

"This is why I wanted to bring you here. To help you remember. What did you do then?"

"The knot of people ahead of me turned and went inside, and I followed. It was getting on to time for the service. I didn't wish to be late."

"Did you expect Thornton to come in and sit down?"

"Yes, of course. There was a vacant place beside me. I'd moved over a little to make room."

"But he didn't come in?"

"No, at the first hymn I looked to see if he'd taken a place behind me. And then the service was beginning, and I didn't think about him again."

Rutledge felt that part not quite true, but he said, "And when the service ended?"

"The coffin was taken out, and Miss Clayton followed, with Captain Hutchinson supporting her, and the Colonel on her other side. I was not that far behind, the coffin was just being carried into the churchyard over there. The path. And I looked up. He was still there. Mr. Thornton. As far as I could tell, he'd been there all along."

"Could you see what he was looking at?"

"Not really. I expect he was watching the coffin being carried out, and Miss Clayton with the Colonel on one side, the Captain on the other. You couldn't have missed their uniforms, could you?"

"And then?"

"We went into the churchyard to the family's grave-side. I couldn't see Mr. Thornton then. And when the committal was over we spoke to Miss Clayton. She was very cut up, losing her brother. After that we went in twos and threes to the luncheon. Mr. Thornton was gone. I didn't know which direction he'd taken, and I thought perhaps the service was too—emotional, and he would join the mourners for lunch. But he didn't. I didn't see him again."

Rutledge said, "Stay here, if you will. I'll walk over to the tree where Thornton was standing. It will help me to see what he must have seen."

He moved toward the tree, taking his time, and when he got there, just under the overhang of branches heavy with dark green leaves, he turned.

Lifting his voice a little, he said, "Is this about right?"

She could hear him, but barely. He thought that with the organ still playing as people left the church, Thornton could see but not hear what was happening. Even during the funeral service, he probably heard only the music and perhaps the responses.

"Yes, that's it," she answered.

Rutledge stood there, looking toward the church and the leafy, shaded churchyard. Could he pick out a face? Certainly he could recognize Priscilla Bartram. But someone else? Someone he hadn't expected to see? A sniper was chosen for his superb eyesight.

Surely if Thornton had come this far, into Burwell, he would have joined the others in the church. And yet he hadn't.

Why?

At that moment the door of the church, just behind Miss Bartram, opened and the Rector stepped out. Even at this distance, Rutledge recognized him at once. The

Rector paused to speak to Miss Bartram, and Rutledge could just hear the murmur of voices. But reading her reaction to the Rector finding her there, he could see that Miss Bartram was at a loss for what to say.

Then, in desperation, she turned and gestured in his direction. The Rector, following her pointing hand, seemed surprised. He collected Miss Bartram with a casual hand on her elbow, and the pair walked toward Rutledge.

He left his vantage point, having seen what he needed to see, and went to meet them.

"Good morning," the Rector said. "A bit early for police work."

"Miss Bartram was helping me understand what was happening during the funeral for Major Clayton," Rutledge said easily.

"Yes, I see. But surely you aren't suggesting that you now have evidence that involves St. Mary's?"

"Not at all," he responded. "But I did wonder at what vantage point someone might have been standing when Captain Hutchinson arrived. I'm not satisfied that the killing in Ely was the first that someone had seen of the victim. Perhaps it was here that the idea for killing him began."

"Oh, I think not," the Rector said. "That would mean someone in Burwell was the guilty man."

"If not this village, then another one," Rutledge reminded him. "Our killer must come from somewhere."

"Well, I shan't keep you," the Rector said. "I have a betrothed couple to counsel. Good day, Inspector. Good day, Miss Bartram. I shall pray for our killer as you call him. And for you as well, as you close the circle on this man."

With a nod he was gone.

Miss Bartram said, "I couldn't think what to say when he asked what brought me to Burwell. It was such a shock to meet him again."

"It doesn't matter," Rutledge said. "You've been quite splendid," he added with a smile. "It couldn't have been easy for you."

"No. Not when I realized that the Captain was there, not a foot from me. What if someone had decided to shoot him then?"

"I should think there wasn't time to plan his death. But later, when he came to Ely, it was the best chance anyone could have asked for."

He led her back to the motorcar, and as they walked, she said, "I shouldn't like to be a policeman, always suspicious of everything and everyone."

"It's not as bad as it sounds. Not everyone has a secret to hide."

At that she looked quickly up at him. Then she changed her mind, in the end saying nothing until they were in the motorcar, driving out of the village toward the road to Wriston. "Why are you so interested in Mr. Thornton? You're thinking he must be this murderer. But why? I don't see that he could be that sort of man."

"He was there on the one day Captain Hutchinson came north to the Fens. How many people do you think knew he was coming then? And Thornton, of all the mourners, stayed outside. It's a question that must be answered."

"Well, I hope you're wrong. I must tell you that."

He didn't reply. A murder inquiry was inexorable, and there was nothing to be done if the killer was a neighbor or a cousin or a father. When the facts fell into place, nothing could change them. Not even pity.

When he had taken her back to the inn, leaving the motor running as he helped her down, she said, "You're going to ask him about Burwell, aren't you?"

"I have to do that."

"Don't tell him I was the one who gave him away. Will you promise? I don't think I could bear it if you did."

"I shan't tell him. But if he's taken into custody, you'll have to testify that you saw him that day in Burwell. There's nothing I can do about that."

"But only if you're sure," she pleaded. "Only if he's taken into custody. When that happens, it won't matter, will it?"

"I promise." But he thought he had very little hope of living up to that promise.

When Rutledge reached Isleham, he found that Thornton was in.

There were circles beneath his eyes, as if he'd spent a restless night.

Rutledge's first question was "Do you own a bicycle?"

Thornton regarded him warily. "Why are you asking about bicycles?"

"It's a quiet and simple means of travel. The roads are flat, if long, and the distances are not too great." He smiled. "No hedgerows with blind corners."

"Yes. I do, as a matter of fact," Thornton said. "I prefer the motorcar these days, but I used to enjoy riding."

"Were you riding it last evening?"

Thornton was alert now. "No. I was not."

"Yet your housekeeper told me you'd gone for a walk. I also walked around this village. And if you were here, where were you?"

"We probably just missed each other."

"How long was your walk?"

Thornton shrugged. "I wasn't concerned about time. I was trying to rid myself of cobwebs. You don't do that by looking at your watch every few minutes."

"You lied to me again, you know," Rutledge said pleasantly.

"Lied? I assure you I did not."

"I remember asking if you'd attended the funeral services in Burwell for Major Clayton. You told me you hadn't. That you avoid funerals and memorial services."

"That was the truth."

"Was it? Then how do you explain the fact that someone saw you there, at St. Mary's Church, and recognized you?"

That was a shock. Thornton couldn't quite conceal it. "I told you the truth. I did not attend the funeral. Nor did I go to the luncheon afterward."

"What you didn't tell me was that you were in Burwell at the time. And standing within sight of St. Mary's. Where you could watch mourners enter and leave the church."

"I've told you I don't do well with funerals. I paid my respects in my own fashion. And that as far as I know is not a crime."

"You also saw Captain Hutchinson there."

"What of it? Do you think if I'd wanted to kill him, I'd have waited until he happened to come to the Fen country? It doesn't say much for the depth of my desire for revenge. Still, it does rather point a finger in my direction. Do you think I'd be so foolish?"

Rutledge judged he was lying again. "But you didn't have to wait very long. He came to Ely for the wedding."

"How could I have known that? I wasn't invited to the wedding, if you remember."

"You didn't need an invitation. The wedding guests were mentioned in the Ely paper."

"I'm sure they were. But I don't take the Ely newspaper. The *Times* is delivered to me. A day late, of course, but it's my choice in newspapers."

Pinning this man down was nearly impossible. Rutledge was annoyed with him.

He said, "There are several things recommending you as a candidate for villain. You've lied to me several times. You served under Major Clayton. You were in Burwell on the day he was buried, and you knew Swift far better than you'd led me to believe. If this is coincidence, then it's leaning heavily in the favor of suspicion."

"All right. Answer me this. Why should I kill Captain Hutchinson, a man I didn't know and had no reason to hate."

Rutledge took the gamble.

"Because," he said slowly, "you were the man Mary Whiting was engaged to when she met Hutchinson and was swept off her feet."

Thornton's face flamed, anger almost a visible thing in the room.

"Who the hell has filled your head with such nonsense?" he said finally, getting himself back in hand.

"Is it nonsense? I think not. I haven't been able to learn that man's name, but Alice Worth knows it. It's only a matter of time before I'll have it from her. She was Mary's friend, you know. In fact, she would prefer to see Hutchinson's killer go free, because she knows why he wanted to kill the Captain."

"Alice who? Did you say Worth? I don't know anyone by that name. Are you quite sure she'll point to me?"

"She lives in London. She knew all about Mary's visit to Newmarket with her uncle Thaddeus. And that Mary fell in love there. She knows too that Mary changed her mind about marrying the man she met there. Mary lived to regret it. That's why she slit her wrists, she had nothing to live for and much to regret. Not even the child she'd been carrying lived to comfort her."

When Thornton said nothing, his face like stone, Rutledge asked, "Have you no defense to offer?"

Instead Thornton walked to the door of the room. "You can leave now. I have nothing more to say to you."

"Was the child yours, not Hutchinson's?"

Thornton wheeled. "*Damn you, she wasn't that sort of woman.*"

"Then you knew her."

"*Yes,* I knew her. I was in France when she died. She wrote to me. A farewell letter. She said she had no reason to live. She told me how much she regretted leaving me. She told me she'd made the wrong choice and had suffered for what she'd done. She thought the child's death was her punishment. I could tell—I knew her that well—that she was going to do something silly. I went to my sergeant and begged for leave. He knew I wasn't married and so I told him my mother was dying. But things were going badly, we were being pushed back, pushed hard in those early days of the fighting. He refused permission, and so did the Lieutenant. I was frantic, I wrote to her and told her that life was worth living, that we would find a way to be happy. But she was dead before the letter reached her."

"How do you know?"

"The letter was returned with DECEASED printed across the address. I wanted to kill Hutchinson. Our paths never crossed. He spent more time at HQ than in the trenches, or so I was told. I looked for him in

London when I came back. He was still in France, something to do with the treaty. And then he came to Burwell, and I could have killed him with my bare hands. But it was Major Clayton's funeral. I couldn't do it."

"Then Ely was your next chance."

"I thought it was. Instead someone else killed him before I could."

"You expect me to believe that?"

"I don't care if you do or you don't. I didn't kill the man."

"What I don't understand is why you killed Swift."

"I didn't. Why should I? He had nothing to do with Mary's death."

"To confound the police? Unfortunately, instead it brought in Scotland Yard."

"I can't think of anyone else who hated Hutchinson as much as I did. As much as I still do. But someone must have had a reason. Whoever he is, he's cheated me of the satisfaction. And you must ask *him* why Swift died."

"Nevertheless."

"I'm not a solicitor, but I'm sure you can't charge me with one death when there's no evidence of my involvement in the other one. And if I protest my innocence of Hutchinson's killing, then I must protest my innocence in Swift's. I shall hire the best attorney in Ely or even Cambridge if it comes to that. And when it's finished, you'll look a fool." He was still very angry.

"I very much doubt that. The Chief Constable is pressing Inspector Warren in Ely for a swift closure of this case. He'll be very pleased that we've finally done just that."

The two men considered each other.

"I expect we've reached an impasse," Thornton said after a moment.

"Hardly an impasse," Rutledge said. "I have the authority to take you into custody and let the courts sort out the question of guilt."

"Yes, that's true." Thornton was standing by the globe. He twirled it with his fingertips, watching it spin, and then turned to Rutledge. "Are you a betting man?"

"I'm not. I haven't been lucky."

"In life? In love? Very well, don't answer that. But I'll make you a sporting proposition. One that I think will appeal to you."

Rutledge smiled. "Indeed? What do you have to barter with?"

"For starters, my life," Thornton said, quite serious. "And my own need for answers. Someone killed Hutchinson for me, but I don't find that acceptable.

And so I don't owe his killer anything. I didn't have the pleasure of watching the man die at my hands."

"Only through the sights of a rifle."

"You were in France. Did killing men with your rifle or your revolver give you any satisfaction?"

"No. They had to die or my men would."

"Precisely."

"We can search this house and the outbuildings. Is the rifle here?"

Thornton took a deep breath. "You *are* a determined man. Let me finish. I will help you with this search for Hutchinson's murderer—and Swift's. In return you'll leave me free to do just that. Rest assured, I won't kill the bastard when I find him. The hangman can do it for me."

"I don't consider that much of a bargain, when I can stop this nonsense now and be on my way to London tomorrow."

"Is it nonsense? I know these Fens. Far more intimately than you ever will. Did you find your valise intact after my rather cursory search?"

It was Rutledge's turn to stare. He hadn't expected Thornton to confess to that.

"Yes, I was there in the mist. Searching. When I stumbled on you, I did wonder if you were the person I was after. I could have let you wander about until you'd broken your neck falling into a ditch or off the bridge. Instead, I made sure you weren't stalking a new victim and then I got you to safety. I've walked these villages, ridden my bicycle through them, driven along every mile of road. He's out there, I tell you. Elusive, a shadow. But together we just might find him."

It was a persuasive argument. Yet Hamish was urging Rutledge to decline the bargain.

But Rutledge was an experienced policeman. And he wanted proof. Not promises.

"I could claim the same thing. That you were walking into Wriston to search out a fresh target. Which of course you did. Burrows."

"Burrows was surely a decoy. I can't think of any reason for wanting him dead, short of madness. And this killer isn't mad. He knows what he wants, and I have a very strong feeling he's finished his work here. We can still lose him, you know. Both of us."

"An interesting theory. But you can't prove it. It won't be proven until we have our man. At the moment, you're the one I want. You're too clever by half. And I have no reason to trust you."

"Then I'll give you what I know. He uses a bicycle to get around the Fens. He moves at night."

"But you were on a bicycle. Last night."

"Where?" he asked sharply.

"On the High Street in Wriston. Pedaling in the direction of the windmill."

"But I wasn't in Wriston. I was in Wicken. Don't you see, that was *him*."

"Prove it."

"Actually I can. Tom Hendricks's little dog got out and was barking at me. Tom came out to see what the fuss was all about, and he called off his dog when he recognized me. I told him I'd been visiting friends and was on my way home. He thought at first it must be the murderer. Everyone is worried he might be a neighbor or the ironmonger or the man who keeps bees."

"When was this?"

"Close on ten, I should think."

If it was true, then Thornton couldn't have been in Wriston.

"I'll find this Hendricks and ask him."

"Even better, I'll accompany you, shall I? It will save time." Thornton walked to the door. "After you, Inspector."

When they had arrived in Wicken, Rutledge said, "It will do no good if you are standing there, coaching the man to give the right answers. I'll interview him alone." Thornton was about to argue, but Rutledge said, "If you prefer, I can take you to Ely and leave it to Inspector Warren to speak to Hendricks."

"Yes, all right," Thornton retorted impatiently.

He pointed out the Wicken village store, which Hendricks owned, and Rutledge left the motorcar down the lane just beyond where it stood on the main street. He walked around the corner to the door just as Hendricks himself stepped out to watch workmen repairing a roof across the way. Rutledge quickly discovered that it wasn't going to be as simple to question him as Thornton had promised.

Scratching his ear, the man said, "Yes, Mr. Thornton was in Wicken. My dog took out after him something fierce. Teddy doesn't care for bicycles."

"Can you tell me what time it was when you saw him?" Rutledge asked.

"As to that, now, I'm not sure. I didn't take any notice. Late, I'd say."

"Closer to nine o'clock? Or after eleven," Rutledge asked.

"I'd fallen asleep in my chair, you see. Teddy's barking woke me up. Given all that trouble in Wriston and Ely, I got up to find out what the matter was. But I never looked at the time. I went back inside and went to bed."

"It's rather important, Mr. Hendricks."

"I'm sorry. I've no idea. My guess is closer to ten, but it could have been as early as nine. Why does it matter?"

"We're trying to sort out a problem. Thank you, Mr. Hendricks. I'm staying in Wriston just now. If you remember anything that would be helpful, you can send word to the constable there."

"That will be McBride, would it?" He moved aside so that two women, their market baskets over their arms, could enter the shop. "I must go. They'll be wanting help," he said, and turned away, stepping back inside.

He'd verified that Thornton had indeed been in the village. But it was the time that was critical, and that the shopkeeper had failed to supply.

Rutledge walked back to the motorcar, debating with himself whether this had been a wild-goose chase or if Hendricks would conveniently remember the time when the local constable took down his statement.

The motorcar was where he'd left it, just past the corner.

And it was empty.

Swearing, Rutledge looked up and down the lane in both directions, but there was no sign of Thornton.

Chapter 18

I should have kept my eye on him, he thought. *Damn the man!*

He got into the motorcar and quartered the village, following first one lane to its end and then the next. He was just coming up the last one when he saw Thornton leaving a house.

He hailed Rutledge and said, "The Petersons live here. Next door to Hendricks. But he swears he never heard the little dog."

Rutledge didn't answer. He was too angry with Thornton.

After a moment's hesitation, the man got into the motorcar and said, "For its size the blasted little dog made enough racket to wake the dead. But neither Peterson nor the man on the other side of the Hendricks admit to hearing anything."

"So much for proof."

"Look, I was *here*."

Rutledge said nothing. He drove out of Wicken and toward Wriston, intending to continue on to Ely while Thornton was in the motorcar.

They were not far from Wriston when Thornton said, "Have you considered? I'm talking about the way Hutchinson treated Mary. Was there another woman? I could never understand why he treated her so shabbily."

"It was very likely her money he was after. His sister is still living in the house in London that had belonged to Mary."

"Then why hadn't he remarried? There must be other wealthy women he could charm."

Rutledge remembered what he'd been told about Hutchinson's attentions to Major Clayton's sister. And then he'd gone back to London with the Colonel because she was staying on in Burwell for a few days. Because he discovered she was already engaged?

"There's a missing servant girl," he suggested, testing the waters.

Thornton shook his head. "He wouldn't be such a fool. She'd be poor as a church mouse. And Hutchinson falling in love boggles the mind. What did you learn in Ely? There must have been something useful—there must have been what? Half a hundred people there, if not more."

"They saw nothing."

"Ah. That explains why you moved on to Wriston. I'd wondered."

"I thought Swift's murder would be easier to solve. As it has turned out, I was right from the beginning. Hutchinson's death was the one that mattered."

"You won't know that until you've found out who killed Swift." Thornton put a hand to his forehead, massaging it as if it ached. "Did Swift and Hutchinson ever cross paths?"

"If they did, we haven't found the link."

"It's there. Have you talked to the police in Glasgow or wherever it was Swift spent his war?"

"Not yet."

"Well, then, how can you tell me that you've concluded I'm the killer? I've never been to Scotland. The question is, had Hutchinson?"

"There's Susan," Rutledge said, remembering. "She used to keep house for Swift before his wife died."

"Did she go to Scotland with him?"

"She didn't. In fact she became the Rector's housekeeper after Swift left. Still, he wrote to her once or twice after he was settled in Glasgow." She had read them over and over again, until she committed them to memory. Or to be precise, those sections that meant the most to her, those referring to her relationship with her employer. He'd had no reason until now to wonder what else had been in the letters that hadn't been important enough to her to remember.

It was unlikely that Swift would have mentioned a casual acquaintance with a young officer or anything that had come of that meeting. Not to his late wife's former lady's maid. But it had to be looked into.

Rutledge was relieved to find that the Rector wasn't in when he knocked at the Rectory door and Susan herself answered.

He'd brought Thornton with him. Susan seemed to be taken aback to find the man from Scotland Yard with a stranger in tow, asking to speak to her.

"I've the Rector's tea to make. He'll be home again in a few minutes."

"It won't take long. If it does, I'll explain to the Rector myself."

Still uncertain she asked them in, took them to the sitting room, and stood there before them, awaiting their questions.

Rutledge said, "When I spoke to you earlier, you told me about letters from Swift while he was in Scotland. Do you still have them?"

"Yes, sir. I saw no harm in keeping them."

"And there is none. I'd like to read them, if I could. There might be something in them that seemed unimportant to you, but in hindsight might lead us to Mr. Swift's killer."

"I'm sure there isn't anything, sir. It was just a kindness to let me know all was well with the poor man."

With an apology, she left them to go up to her room. A few minutes later she had returned and handed the letters to Rutledge.

They were worn almost to the point of illegibility, folded and refolded countless times. He gently removed the first letter from its envelope and spread the pages across his knee.

They seemed immediately familiar, and he realized that she had memorized the opening, thanking her once more for her care of his late wife and asking if she was comfortable in her new position.

Rutledge read on.

I have begun to settle in. It's so unlike the Fens that I'm at a loss to know what to think. A large river, a different pattern of farming, terrain that rolls, so that when I look to the horizon, there are trees and rising land in the way. The weather is cooler, but then it's moving toward late fall. And the accents of the people I meet are almost impenetrable sometimes. It will be some weeks before I am comfortable with it. The people here are different as well. There are tenements in Glasgow as well as handsome streets of handsome houses. The Cathedral is large but not so fine as Ely. I try to tell myself that I am here to look forward and not backward, but my heart is in the churchyard in Wriston. Still. I have made some changes. I have moved from the hotel where I stayed after my arrival. It was very dear, as rooms are difficult to find, given the influx of people. The house is tall, three stories, but quite narrow. The furnishings are not the best, but comfortable enough. I tell myself that I know ancient Rome better than I know my own country. I could find my way to the Forum with the ease of someone born there. Finding my way through the twisting streets here is a lesson in humility. But I am satisfied, and much of that satisfaction is due to the maid I have hired to keep me in order.

There was no mention of friends or acquaintances. Or those Swift must have met during his day. It appeared that he was more homesick than he chose to admit.

Turning to the second letter, he found only two references to Swift's work for the Navy.

It's time-consuming and that shortens my day, no leisure in which to look back.

And again, *I like those I work with well enough.
They come from all over the country, uprooted as I
have been, missing families and friends as I have done.
But we have high hopes that the war will end soon.
While I am in agreement with them, when it does end,
I shall have to find another exile.*

It was on the last page that Rutledge stopped
skimming.

A name seemed to leap off the page.

*Catriona has kept my house in order, as you once
did. She came well recommended, although she is
hardly more than a child and had not been in service before this. She tells me she too is an exile, a
long way from her home in the Highlands. She
wants a very different life from that of her friends
growing up in the small glen where she was born.
Her grandfather didn't approve, but she is a determined young woman and won his permission to
spend six months in Glasgow. But I expect she will
have something to say about returning to a nar-
rower life. Her grandfather had lived in England,
and it's possible that she had heard his tales of his
time there. She was very disappointed to learn that
I'd never been to London. She seems to think that
we must all have been there often, drawn by its*

wonders. That and the fact that Ely isn't a large and bustling city has diminished me in her eyes. But she's a good worker, cheerful and pleasant, and I am growing fond of her lighthearted presence in the house.

Was this the elusive connection he'd searched for and not found? Was this the same Catriona who had worked in the London house that belonged to Mary Hutchinson?

If it was, how had she gone from Glasgow and Swift's house, to London and the home of Captain Hutchinson? Catriona was not an uncommon name.

There was nothing more about her until Rutledge reached the last of the letters, this one written after the war, a month before Swift was scheduled to return to England.

I am no longer the man I was when first I came here. I have had to learn to put the past away, and it was a hard lesson. Returning to the house in Wriston where we lived so happily, my wife and I, will be difficult at best. But I must try for my own sake as well as for hers. If there was another choice open to me, I think I would leap at the chance to take it. But there is not. Perhaps God wishes me to find

*that courage, before He shows me His grace again
as He did when I was offered this post in Glasgow.*

Hamish said, "Ye ken, it's why he stood for yon seat
in Parliament. London was a long way fra' here."

And it was the explanation—perhaps not what he
told the men who approached him about serving, but
what led to his personal decision to stand.

The final lines returned to Catriona.

*She's grown into a young woman, our Catriona. If I
had had a daughter, I couldn't have been more
proud of her. She reminds me of someone I once
knew, that same thirst for life. I cannot bring her
with me to Wriston—she will not come. And so you
will not meet her. She has been searching for a position in London, and there is one that she likes very
much. Her cousins, who have the care of her, are
not best pleased, nor is her grandfather. They blame
me for opening her eyes to this other world, but
she's too intelligent and too well read to go back to
the glen. It would be a tragic waste. And they must
see that. Still, I am writing to the woman in London
to find out for myself if this is a suitable household.*

*Tomorrow I begin to pack up this new life and
say good-bye. . . .*

Thornton was standing by the window, restless and still angry.

Rutledge ignored him.

Instead he returned the letters to Susan, saying, "I'm glad you kept these. They do more to explain Swift to me than all the statements Constable McBride collected. Thank you for allowing me to see them."

Susan flushed a little with pride. "I do treasure them, sir. Rector has been good to me, but I miss my mistress as much as *he* did. Mr. Swift. It was a comfort, his writing to me. And I understood why he couldn't have me back when he came home again. It would have been hard for both of us without Mrs. Swift there."

Rutledge thought that Swift had been more than a little selfish in his grief. But he said, "Thornton, we must go. I don't think we need to wait for the Rector."

Thornton followed him out to the motorcar, saying, "What was that all about? Those letters from Swift? What did they tell you?"

"I must go to London. The question is, what am I to do with you?"

"You *were* taking me to Ely," Thornton said dryly. "If you've forgot why, I'll be happy to find my own way home."

But Rutledge stood there, his hand on the crank, thinking.

If he took Thornton to Ely, Inspector Warren would hold him until the man's solicitor and a local barrister came to post bail. That could happen long before Rutledge got back from London.

He said, "Fancy a drive south? It won't be comfortable, but it's the best I can offer."

"Why?" Thornton demanded suspiciously. "Are you taking me to the Yard rather than to Ely?"

"Not precisely. I believe I've found a connection between Swift and Hutchinson. The question is, does that connection in any way change the likelihood that you killed both men? I think not. Still, it's a distraction. And I don't care for distractions."

"Are you accustomed to traveling around the countryside with an alleged murderer in your motorcar?"

"Not as a rule," Rutledge answered, turning the crank and ushering Thornton into the nearside door. "The thing is, if you escape, it will only serve to prove your guilt. And that will please the Chief Constable here in Cambridgeshire, as well as the Acting Chief Superintendent at the Yard. They are looking for a scapegoat, you see. And you'll do as well as the next man. The courts will sort it out, and I won't have to face my superior with the news that I haven't a clue who killed Hutchinson and Swift."

Thornton stared at him. "Are you quite serious?"

"That's for you to decide. Shall I take you to Ely, or would you prefer a few more days of freedom? Such, of course, as it is?"

"Put that way, how can I refuse?"

Rutledge reversed and turned the bonnet toward the London road. As he passed the police station on the far side of the pond, he saw McBride staring at him. But he was not ready to talk to the constable about Thornton. At the turn, Miss Trowbridge was just walking up to her door with her hands full of freshly cut flowers, Clarissa winding sinuously around her ankles, looking for an invitation to go in.

She turned as she heard the motorcar coming toward her, and she too saw Thornton in the seat next to Rutledge.

Frowning, she watched them out of sight.

Thornton said pensively, "She's a very attractive woman. I would give much for a proper introduction. We've met only a few times in very public circumstances. Not the sort of thing one can pursue."

"I thought your heart belonged to Mary Hutchinson."

"It does. I was hoping that by killing Hutchinson I could lay her soul to rest finally. It has been a long road. But I wasn't the one to send him to hell, where he belonged."

Rutledge was reminded of the letter Swift had written. The contrast of his devotion to his wife and Hutchinson's callous treatment of his.

"Are you sure that's what Mary would have wanted?"

Thornton turned to stare at him. "I—never considered that."

"She thought she loved him enough to marry him. Perhaps she forgave him even as she died."

"Dear God. *No, don't even suggest that.*"

He turned away, and Rutledge let a silence fall between them. It was not until they stopped for petrol and a late dinner that Thornton said, "Did you mean what you said as we were leaving Wriston? Or were you hoping to make me angry enough to force a confession?"

Rutledge waited until they had given their order to the man who was serving them, and then he answered.

"Perhaps I can be more objective. You have Mary Hutchinson's letter. Still, you don't know what was in her mind at the end, when she was dying. It's also possible that the last thing she expected of you was to waste your own life in avenging her death."

Thornton pressed his hands against his face, then dropped them. His eyes were haunted. "Is that why I never acted until Hutchinson came north? Because I was afraid it wasn't what she wanted?"

"Only you can answer that."

But Thornton said no more. He changed the subject by asking about Rutledge's war, and they spoke of other things until the outskirts of London.

Dawn was rising in the east when they turned into the street where Rutledge lived.

"You'll need a shave and a fresh shirt," he said. "I can offer both."

Thornton's hand rasped as it brushed across his chin. "My God, aren't you tired?"

"I can't afford to be tired." He pulled up in front of the flat and got out.

Thornton followed him, and twenty minutes later, they were leaving again, this time for the house where Hutchinson had lived.

Thornton stared up at it with interest. "This was Mary's. This house. I never came here, although she spoke of it often. She liked London. Her uncle preferred the country, but he brought her out in London. I didn't know her then. I'd have lived anywhere that made her happy."

"I'd rather not let the occupants know that you had anything to do with Mary Hutchinson. Can you keep your head—and your temper—or must I handcuff you to the motorcar?"

"I'd like to go inside."

It was early to make a call. The household was awake and already about its duties, but Miss Hutchinson, they were told, had not yet come down for breakfast.

They cooled their heels for half an hour in the drawing room. And still Miss Hutchinson hadn't come down to speak with them.

Angry, Rutledge went out to the stairs. Short of bearding her in her bedchamber, the next possibility was to find the Hutchinson housekeeper on his own.

He and Thornton walked unhindered to the door to the kitchen and made their way down the twisting steps.

A scullery maid looked up from cleaning carrots for the midday meal. Startled to find two strange men coming toward her, she dropped her knife and fled to find the cook, or failing the cook, anyone else of sufficient authority to deal with the interlopers.

The housekeeper, frowning in disapproval, came hurrying down the passage toward them.

It was on the tip of her tongue, Rutledge could see, to tell them the tradesmen's entrance was outside. Then, realizing that Rutledge had been here before, asking questions, she wiped the frown from her face and asked coolly, "How may I help you?"

Rutledge said pleasantly, "I see you remember me, Mrs. Cookson. Could we speak to you in your parlor, please?"

His expression, belying his voice, brooked no objections. She said, "This way, if you please," and led them to the small room where he'd interviewed her before.

"Is this about the late Mrs. Hutchinson?" she asked, offering them chairs.

"In a way. I've come to ask about the young woman Catriona Beaton. Can you tell me what her references were, when she came to you?"

"I don't know that Miss Hutchinson would ap—" she began, but Rutledge cut her short.

"I'm sure she would approve of your helping Scotland Yard. To be sure, I can ask for a search warrant, but she might not care for that added unpleasantness."

Mrs. Cookson, still standing, said, "I have the box just there."

She indicated a large flat box on a shelf behind him, and he passed it to her. Inside were packets of envelopes, each packet tied with a ribbon and each one including a small card indicating the name of the servant in question. She thumbed through them quickly, finding the one he'd asked for. Taking it out, she untied the ribbon and began to look at each of the envelopes.

"Here is the recommendation."

Rutledge took it from her and withdrew the sheets of paper inside.

He scanned them quickly, then went back to read the pertinent parts.

I cannot recommend her highly enough. She's intelligent, quick, willing, and eager to serve in a larger household than mine. I believe you'll find her a very fine addition to your staff.

The second page of the letter was more to the point.

She has grown up in my house, and I feel responsible for finding her a suitable position. You will understand that I should like reassurances that she will be cared for with diligence and that the distance from her home to London will not be viewed as relinquishing our duty. Her family will expect no less.

It was most certainly to the point. And the signature was what Rutledge had expected to find there.

Herbert G. R. Swift

Swift had written the recommendation and the Hutchinsons had accepted Catriona Beaton into their household on the burden of that recommendation.

But who the devil had set out to avenge Catriona Beaton?

Chapter 19

T urning to Thornton, Rutledge said, "What do you know about a Catriona Beaton?"

"Catriona Beaton?" he repeated, frowning. "I don't think I know anyone by that name."

Rutledge was returning the sheets to their envelope and handing it back to Mrs. Cookson, but his eyes were on Thornton's face.

"There's another letter here. From her grandfather," the housekeeper said. "It came after she had left us." Taking it out of the packet, she handed it to Rutledge.

He opened it and found a very brief message inside.

We have heard nothing from you for the past two months. Whatever is wrong, we will help you, you must know that. Just write. For the love of God, write.

It was signed, *Your loving grandfather.*

"Did no one answer this man, when the letter came?"

"She'd left of her own accord," the housekeeper protested. "We didn't like to write and tell him so."

"Did he ever come to the house?"

"If he did, he never identified himself as a relative of hers."

Then had the grandfather found his missing granddaughter?

If he had, there was surely no reason to hate either Herbert Swift or Captain Hutchinson.

Or was there?

He looked at the envelope in his hand. The return address was MacLaren, Trahir House, followed by an address that Rutledge thought must be north of Stirling, in Scotland. A man of substance, this grandfather, not a simple clansman.

Thanking Mrs. Cookson, he left, and Thornton said, as they went out the door and down the steps to the motorcar, "What the hell was that all about?"

"I don't know," Rutledge said. "But I intend to find out."

He sat for several minutes in the motorcar, staring across the road at the grassy expanses and tall trees of the square, enclosed by its iron fencing. That reminded him of Marcella Trowbridge's cottage. Setting the memory aside, he considered his position.

No doubt Sergeant Gibson could find the information, given time. But that would mean going to the Yard. And explaining Thornton. It had perhaps been a mistake to bring him, but by the same token, keeping an eye on him was paramount until a proper search of the man's house could be made. So far there had been no time for Thornton to dispose of anything incriminating. Including a rifle . . .

Who else, then?

Mr. Belford came to mind.

But did he, Rutledge, wish to be beholden to the man?

They had worked together—in a manner of speaking—on another case. And neither man had quite trusted the other. Rutledge had looked into Belford's past while Belford had explored Rutledge's. An uneasy truce had been declared.

But there was the fact that Belford had probably worked for Military Intelligence, even though his curriculum vitae showed he'd spent the war in the Military Foot Police. It was as good a cover as any. His contacts went beyond any information that Gibson had access to, and time at the moment was important. Something had to be done with Thornton, and soon.

Hamish said, "It's haste driving ye. And you'll find yoursel' owing the Devil his due."

It was a risk. He knew that. But what choice did he have?

Taking a deep breath, Rutledge turned the motorcar toward Chelsea.

It was very likely, he thought, that Belford wouldn't be at home. But as luck would have it, when he knocked at the door, a footman told Rutledge that he was in.

A few minutes later, Rutledge and Thornton walked into Belford's study.

Nothing on the desk would indicate what the man had been working on before Rutledge came to the door. It had been cleared away with swift precision, and somewhere in this room, he thought, would be a drawer designed to hold whatever had been there.

"Mr. Rutledge," Belford said, rising from his desk. A tall, trim man, he seemed to be a gentleman of leisure, not a master of information. "What brings you here? And who, may I ask, is your guest?"

"This is Mr. Thornton, a suspect in a double murder. If you don't mind, I should very much like to lock him in a room while we talk."

Thornton said, "Here—!" and stepped back as if expecting to be taken away.

Belford said, "If we are circumspect, no harm done. Let him stay."

Rutledge smiled. Did nothing catch this man off his guard? Taking one of the chairs pointed out by their host, he said, "There were two deaths recently, one in Ely and another in the nearby village of Wriston. A Captain Hutchinson and a Mr. Herbert Swift were shot by someone using a rifle. Suspects had a good reason to kill one or the other, but not both. Unless of course the second man was a—er—distraction from the real target. Until yesterday I could find no connection between these two men. Now it appears that one of them, Swift, employed a young girl, Catriona Beaton, as housekeeper while he was working for the Admiralty in Glasgow. When the war ended, the young woman, as she was then, decided she preferred to seek employment in London. In due course, she went to work in the house of Captain Hutchinson. And in due course, she went missing from this house, and no one seems to know where she went. Or indeed if she is still alive. A body was found later, the identification uncertain. The only connection we have with her past is her grandfather, a man by the name of MacLaren, who lived at Trahir House in Scotland, somewhere north of Stirling, if I remember my geography. He could well be dead. If he isn't, he could possibly tell me what became of his granddaughter. And whether the police ever told him about locating her remains. And whether or not she could have been the reason these two men were killed."

"You think someone in her family could have been out for revenge."

"It's a long way from Scotland to Ely."

"And Mr. Thornton here?"

Thornton spoke before Rutledge could answer. "I knew Hutchinson's wife. I was to marry her. She chose Hutchinson instead. It was not a successful match, and she killed herself." It was bald, emotionless, and yet there were brackets of pain—or anger?—around his mouth. "I would have enjoyed being the one to kill Hutchinson."

"In short, you're the first string to Rutledge's bow?"

"I believe I am."

Belford turned back to Rutledge. "Is there a good reason why Mr. Thornton is here and not in gaol in Ely?"

"There hasn't been time to search his house for the murder weapon."

"And so he's here, meanwhile? Rather unorthodox, but effective." Belford toyed with the inkwell on his desk. It was surmounted by a rather handsome eagle, and Rutledge wouldn't have been surprised to hear that it had once belonged to the Kaiser. "I do happen to know of a MacLaren. I expect he isn't your man. He was in the Lovat Scouts—the Boer War. One of their finest shots. My uncle delighted in telling us tales of his prowess. But he resigned when the war was over. And was never heard of again. It was generally thought he'd gone back to Scotland."

Thornton said, "His children would have been MacLarens. But his grandchildren could have borne any name."

"I don't believe he ever married," Belford responded. "That was said to be the reason why he took on the most dangerous assignments."

"Nevertheless," Rutledge returned.

"I'll look into this matter. He shouldn't be difficult to find." Belford glanced at Rutledge. "Are the resources of the Yard no longer available?"

"They are—if one wishes to be found out by a superior who is anxious to see this inquiry closed," Rutledge retorted.

"Ah. Markham, is it? He had something of a reputation in Yorkshire. But then he knew his turf, and he was seldom wrong. London is a very different matter, I should think."

They rose, and as Rutledge moved toward the door, Belford added, "Where can I reach you?"

"My flat. I'm sure you know where that is."

"Quite."

As the door was closed behind them, Thornton said, "Remind me never to cross that man."

Rutledge grinned sardonically. "One sups with the Devil when one turns to him."

"I shouldn't think the Yard would approve."

Rutledge didn't answer him.

They spent the rest of the morning and half the afternoon in Rutledge's flat. Thornton paced the floor like a caged lion, back and forth, back and forth, while Rutledge sat by the door and waited, fighting sleep, which kept threatening to overwhelm him.

It was nearly three o'clock in the afternoon when a messenger arrived with an envelope.

"Rutledge?"

"Yes."

The man handed him the envelope, turned back to his motorcycle, and was gone in a roar.

Rutledge sat down again, hesitating before he broke the seal.

I was right. MacLaren was in the Lovat Scouts. And quite a dangerous man with a rifle. He acted as a sharpshooter in several matters where it was deemed necessary to—er—take certain measures. He never married.

However, it is reported that he had one child out of wedlock, and she in turn had one daughter. The mother of that child was killed in an accident when the girl was five. Her father died in France during the war. Her name was Catriona Beaton. MacLaren has not been seen at Trahir House for some years. It's thought that he is dead. The house is now occupied by his brother's family. I did not speak to them, leaving that to you.

I shall collect my fee for this information at some future date.

It was signed with a *B*.

Hamish said, "Aye, you've made your bargain. It willna' sit well at the Yard."

Making an effort to ignore the voice, Rutledge considered the problem of this man MacLaren. He could worry about Belford later. Where, he asked himself, was this Lovat Scout? And how much did he love his granddaughter? He was alive when she vanished. But a Scot in Cambridgeshire would draw attention the instant he opened his mouth. And someone would remember . . .

And what was he to do with Thornton while finding out?

As if he'd heard Rutledge's thoughts, Thornton said, "Don't mind me. I'm enjoying this quest of yours. It's likely to clear me."

Rutledge turned to him. "Were you a sniper in the war?"

The question came out of nowhere, and Thornton wasn't prepared. His face betrayed him before he could school it to show no reaction.

He didn't need the War Office now to tell him the truth. But verification would serve the K.C. to prepare his case.

"A battlefield promotion. You must have done something extraordinary to deserve that. What was it?"

"That's none of your damned business."

"But it is. Anything to do with you is my business. Did you bring your rifle home with you? Against all orders?"

Thornton was prepared this time. He said blandly, "What use would I have for a rifle in waterfowl country?"

"It was your closest companion—no one else except your commanding officer accepted what you did as brave. Shooting from cover? And there was Hutchinson. Did you think it might be useful one day to kill him? It was your weapon of choice. Not the Gurkha knife. Nor the thuggee garrote."

"I wasn't ashamed of what I did. It saved lives, my skill."

As it had done. Rutledge took a deep breath. "All right. Let it go. But if I find you've armed that old man and sent him out to do your dirty work for you, I'll have you up as an accessory, to hang beside him."

"Did you know that the windmill keeper was a Scot?"

"The windmill—the one in Wriston?" And he remembered. Discussing Hogmanay with Marcella Trowbridge, who knew the man as a child. Who had told him that Angus was likely to be dead. McBride had suggested he'd drunk himself to death after the fire in the windmill cottage. But had he? And if he had, where was he buried? More urgently, was he a MacLaren?

Rutledge sprang to his feet, weariness forgotten. "We're going back to Cambridgeshire. Now."

He was on the road before he thought of something. He'd been mulling over all the evidence as he threaded his way through the London traffic, and he turned around, heading back into the city.

It was Miss Hutchinson who knew the answer, and he would see her this time if he had to break down her bedroom door.

Thornton, alarmed, said, "What the hell? I thought we were going to Wriston."

"Not yet. I want to speak to Miss Hutchinson again."

This time he found her at a late lunch, sitting at the head of the long table in the splendidly proportioned dining room. The table, he thought as he was ushered in by the housekeeper, would easily seat twenty-four.

She looked up in annoyance at the interruption, recognized Rutledge, and said, "I thought you'd left."

"I had. Another question occurred to me. Where was your brother when Catriona Beaton left this house?"

"Where he always was. He'd just returned from France, where the ministries were meeting to discuss the treaty. Where power was, there my brother could be found." There was pride mixed with bitterness in her voice. "That week, he'd gone to Gloucester with some Colonel or other. I think that's why Beaton chose to leave then."

"Because she knew he would follow her and possibly find her?"

"Don't be ridiculous. I daresay she found this household too restrictive for her—er—tastes. London had changed her. Once she had left, she was no longer our responsibility."

"Who did she know in London? Where could she have turned until she had found a new position?"

"Without a reference, she wouldn't have found a new place. No, she was most likely on her way to Scotland, where she came from. If she'd saved her wages, she could have taken the train. There was no certainty that the body the police found was Beaton's.

We made the assumption, of course, but there you are."

The housekeeper had said she hadn't collected her last month's wages.

"Yet two months later her family had had no word of her. Or from her."

"I'm not aware of any correspondence from her family. Or that she had any family living."

"Mrs. Cookson received such a letter."

"Did she? She's responsible for the staff, of course. I leave such matters to her."

"Which tells me that her family was left to wonder what had become of Catriona."

"I remind you again that *she* chose to leave. Ending our duty to her as a member of this household."

"She was young, Miss Hutchinson. Surely you felt a personal responsibility."

"I was young once, Inspector, with only my brother to take care of me. Our parents left us very little. I'm well aware of the pitfalls and dangers of being a woman without protection. We lived in lodgings, we were dependent on his officer's pay. We were shunned by people who now respect us. I wore gowns I'd refurbished myself because I couldn't afford new ones. If I survived, I believe she was clever enough and determined enough to survive as well. If she didn't, if the body was hers after all, you must look elsewhere for her murderer."

And yet Fallowfield, in Ely, had believed Hutchinson had been left comfortably fixed by his parents. A claim to wealth and position to conceal his struggle to keep up appearances? Judging by the bitterness in Miss Hutchinson's voice, he thought her version of their past was very likely the truth.

"Now," she was saying, "I should like to finish my lunch in peace. Good day, Mr. Rutledge. Good day, sir."

She turned back to her plate, ignoring them. But Rutledge had got what he wanted.

Leaving her with a curt nod, he walked out of the dining room and said to Thornton, "All right, now we can go north."

"I don't see what you learned here."

Outside, cranking the motorcar, Rutledge said, "The Hutchinsons were rather cavalier about the disappearance of Miss Beaton. Her grandfather would have considered that unconscionable. But would it have driven him to kill Hutchinson? Quite possibly. On the other hand, Swift did everything that was in his power to see that this position was safe and responsible."

"Did MacLaren know that?"

It was a very good question. The young girl he had allowed to live in Glasgow had matured and decided to test her mettle in London. And something had gone wrong. Had she turned to Swift? Or tried to reach Scotland? Or had she died, an anonymous death in a city where life was cheaper than she knew? The London police had closed that case.

And where did Thornton fit in? He'd asked that before, and was still undecided. It was time to take him to Ely and arrange for a search warrant before the man could destroy any evidence. Inspector Warren could see to that.

Again Thornton seemed to know what he was thinking.

"You won't cut me out of this inquiry. Good God, it's my life that's on the line. I'm your only suspect. And I'll be damned if I won't see this through to the finish."

Rutledge remembered what Belford had said about Thornton's presence: *Unorthodox—but effective.*

Tired as he was, Rutledge knew he dared not sleep in this man's company. To sleep would mean to dream, and to dream would mean betrayal. Of himself, of Hamish.

The sooner he reached Ely, the sooner he could rest.

They were on the outskirts of Cambridge when Rutledge heard, as if from a great distance, Thornton swearing and grabbing his arm, then the wheel.

Rutledge came awake with a start to find the motor-car running down the low embankment that led to a shallow farm pond. He pulled on the brake almost reflexively, and the motorcar juddered to a stop on the brink of the water's edge, sending ducks and drakes scattering in a loud cacophony of angry quacks.

Thornton said, "If you have a death wish, I don't. Let me drive. I slept for three hours out of London, remember?"

But the shock was enough to wipe away that leaden need for sleep. Rutledge backed up with great care until the tires were on the high road once more. What had he been dreaming? Something about ambulances—avoiding ambulances as he and his men marched along the rutted stretch of muddy track toward the front lines.

They drove on, Thornton finally asleep again at his side. But it was impossible to reach Ely. They ran into a heavy storm just beyond Newmarket, black clouds pushing toward the coast. He could hear the steam pumps clattering away, straining to keep up with the incessant downpour, and ditches were running strong with rainwater, threatening to overflow.

He pulled into Wriston, still well short of Ely, noticed that there had been hail here as well as rain, and drove on to the police station. McBride wasn't there, but he took Thornton, arguing angrily, back to the single little cell, leaving him there. By the time he'd reached

The Dutchman Inn, he was wet to the skin. Priscilla Bartram opened the door to him, and with apologies, he barely made it up to the room set aside for him. Stripping off his wet clothes, he fell across the bed and slept for nine hours.

When he woke, he knew what it was he had to do. Dressing, he went down to find tea and breakfast waiting for him, although it was nearly six o'clock in the evening. He ate it to please Miss Bartram, who was eager to learn why that nice Mr. Thornton was in custody. Gossips were already busy.

He avoided the question and ten minutes later was walking up to Miss Trowbridge's cottage.

The rain had stopped, a watery sun was out, and there were standing pools in the ruts of the High Street. Most of her garden was beaten down by the force of the wind, and there were petals scattered along the walk, bruised and wet.

She came to the door, acknowledged him with a nod, and then as an afterthought, invited him inside.

Clarissa stood up in her bed by the hearth, stretched, and came to inspect his shoes and trousers.

"You've been away," Marcella Trowbridge said, gesturing to a chair.

"To London. I find that you can help me with something that has been puzzling me."

"I can?" she asked, surprised and then wary. She'd been about to sit down, then thought better of it.

"You told me once about the windmill keeper. That he was a Scot."

"Angus?"

"What was his surname?"

"Do you know, I never heard it. He was always— Angus."

"Where was he from? What part of Scotland?"

"I don't know. Does it matter? I told you, he must be dead by now."

"Let me tell you a story. When Herbert Swift was in Glasgow, he took on a young girl to keep house for him. When the war ended and he was returning to Wriston, she chose not to come to Cambridgeshire with him. She was old enough then to know her own mind, you see, and she wished to go to London. The only training she had was in service. And so Swift found her a position that he believed to be safe. But it wasn't. Months later, she left one night late, bag and baggage, without the wages due her. And she disappeared. Her grandfather tried to find her. But there was no trace. It's likely that she's dead. The police concluded she was. Still, she's the only connection I've found between Swift and Captain Hutchinson. For it was his house she left that night."

"Dear God. You don't believe Angus—but he had no granddaughter. No daughter. He never married."

"Was he in the Boer War?"

"I—yes, I believe so. Does it matter?"

"When he left here, did he return to Scotland?"

"I have no idea. I'd known him all my life. But he didn't tell me where he was going. That's odd, isn't it? I just never thought of it in that way until now."

"Your grandmother lived here before leaving the cottage to you in her will. Did she know anything about his past?"

"I can't think she would. She liked him, of course. As did I. He was an interesting man. But except to speak to him, I doubt she knew him any better than I did."

But a child couldn't have judged what an older woman knew and felt unsuitable for young ears. All the same, it couldn't have been shameful, or she would never have let the child meet the man, much less become friends with him.

Where to go from here?

"And you've heard nothing from him since he left here?"

"Nothing. Except once, when I'd just come home from visiting friends in Bury. I found Clarissa in a basket on my doorstep. She was tiny, with a blue ribbon around her neck. There was no card, no message. I asked Priscilla and the constable and everyone I could think of, but no one seemed to know anything about her. It wasn't long after Angus had left. And I wondered if perhaps he'd brought her to me. She's been such great company."

Rutledge thanked her, rising to leave. She asked, "Will you be looking for Angus? Because you think he's got something to do with these murders?"

"I have to be thorough, Miss Trowbridge."

"I refuse to believe any such thing. Still—if you should find Angus, will you ask him? About Clarissa?"

"Yes, I promise."

When he reached the police station the next morning, Rutledge found Thornton fuming and pacing his cell.

"Let me out of here before I go mad. I'd confess to killing Caesar if I thought it would buy my freedom."

Rutledge had once been shut into a cell. He remembered the claustrophobia it had brought on.

Rutledge smiled grimly. "I'm going to look at Swift's house. There was nothing of interest there earlier, but we know rather more now than we did then."

"Let me go with you. He was a classical scholar. As I am. There might be something you've overlooked."

"Or something you can destroy."

"Damn it, man, I kept my word. All the way to London and back."

"So you did. All right, I'll take you with me."

Rutledge had got the key from McBride, who had all but insisted that he come as well. But Rutledge was not ready to tell the constable or anyone else what he was searching for.

The rooms were still, musty. Thornton searched through the bookcase, an occasional comment escaping him as he found a particular volume. Rutledge concentrated on the desk. But there was no correspondence from the grandfather of Catriona Beaton. Frustrated, he went through the drawers a second time, then went to search the bedside table. Swift must have read before he went to sleep, for there were several books perched precariously between the lamp and a small carriage clock.

Rutledge had thumbed through them before and found nothing. In the drawer of that table was a well-worn Bible, and Rutledge took it out, leafing through the pages a second time. He was about to put it back where he'd found it when he spotted a small handbill in the back of the drawer.

It advertised the shoemaker in Soham. He was about to put it in the drawer once more when he saw that something had been scrawled in pencil on a blank space on the back, and he held it up to the light to read it. The words had faded, almost to the point that they were illegible.

You're no better than he is. So be it.

For some reason, Swift had shoved it out of sight rather than toss it into the dustbin or the fire.

Rutledge called, "Thornton. Do you know of a shoe-maker in Soham? Someone by the name of Morton?"

"Only that he's no longer in business. He must be all of seventy."

"Who has taken over his shop?"

"I don't think anyone has."

"Then let's have a look."

They had reached the motorcar after returning the key to McBride when a motorcycle came roaring down the street, stopping in front of the police station. He handed McBride a message as they watched, and McBride hailed them.

"For you, Inspector. From Inspector Warren."

"It can wait. I'm driving to Soham."

"Sir." McBride stood watching as they drove away.

"You could have asked him, you know. About the shoemaker."

"I'd rather see for myself."

When they arrived in Soham, Thornton directed Rutledge to the shoemaker's shop. It was on the outskirts, not far from the cooper, Ruskin. The sign above the door was faded, and peering in the single dusty window, Rutledge could see bundles of reeds stacked in a corner or lying spread across the floor to dry. Certainly not the tools of a shoemaker.

"He's the hurdle maker," Thornton said in surprise. "Try in the back of the shop."

They walked around to the rear of the shop, where they could see stacks of hurdles in the open shed. Wooden frames where reeds or withies had been woven to form a barrier for a gate or a garden or a pen for animals. Rutledge remembered hearing Priscilla Bartram describing such a one in the prow of the flat fowling boat her father and grandfather had used.

No one was there. A bicycle stood propped against the back wall of the shop. That was the only sign of life.

"He cuts the osiers and the reeds and the withies in the spring, prepares them, and then makes the hurdles as needed. People come and buy what they want."

"Then where is he today?"

Thornton said with some surprise, "It's Sunday. The shop would be closed."

"So it is. Where does he live, this hurdle maker?" He remembered something McBride had said about the hurdle maker. What was it?

He couldn't bring it back.

"I have no idea. I leave such matters to the man who keeps my gardens."

"Ruskin's shop is just up the street. The cooper. He may know." He'd hardly said the words when he remembered. It hadn't been McBride, it had been Ruskin, giving an account of the night he'd been drunk enough to run riot with the side ax. It had been the hurdle maker he'd been chasing, unaware of what he was doing.

But Ruskin's shop was closed as well. He lived with his wife somewhere else. That too Rutledge remembered. They walked on, leaving the motorcar, looking for someone to question. This was a street of craftsmen. The cooper, the hurdle maker on this side, there the brick maker, and then just beyond, the wheelwright. A cabinetmaker had his shop where the lane met the street, and Rutledge could smell aged wood as he passed. It wasn't until they had reached the street that they met a young couple walking out together.

"Hallo," Rutledge said, smiling. "I'm trying to locate the hurdle maker. Or failing that, Mr. Ruskin. Can you tell me where to find them?"

They directed him to the cottage where Ruskin lived with his wife, and there Ruskin told them how to find the hurdle maker.

"Do you know his name?" Rutledge asked.

"He's generally called Lovat. He came here about the time the shoemaker died. The family let him have the shop for less than what it was worth. It 'ud been closed for several years as it was. No one else wanted it. The carriage trade seldom comes as far as the lane these days."

"Where can I find him?"

"There's a stream on the far side of Soham, where he finds his materials. Sometimes he makes baskets with the reeds. The greengrocer sells them for him."

Rutledge finally found the place Ruskin had described. The hut as he'd called it was actually a small house set by the water's edge, half hidden by a stand of reeds and other tall grasses. It was sturdier than it first appeared.

Turning to Thornton, he said, "Wait here."

Thornton was about to argue, but Rutledge said, "I want to speak to him alone."

He walked around the house to find the man he was after sitting cross-legged on a square of canvas, weaving the circle that would become the bottom of a basket. He looked up, greeted Rutledge, and returned to his work.

Rutledge studied him. Tall, slender, but very strong, his short cropped hair an iron gray. His hands, long-fingered and deft, worked with the reeds with the skill of long practice.

"Mr. Lovat?"

The man nodded.

"My name is Rutledge. Scotland Yard. I've come to ask you about your granddaughter."

Lovat looked up, his gaze alert and focused on Rutledge's face. His eyes were a startling blue.

"My granddaughter?"

His voice was as strong as his body, and Rutledge could hear only the very slightest trace of the Highlands there. Was he being careful, or had time lessened his accent?

"She went missing some time ago. Nearly a year, in fact. While she was a maid in a house in London."

"I was never married," the man said. He set the work aside, letting his hands dangle as his wrists rested on his knees.

"Perhaps not. But you had a child, nevertheless. A daughter. And she in turn had a daughter. *Her* name was Catriona Beaton."

"If you've come to tell me you've found this girl, I'll be glad to hear of it. But my name is Lovat."

"I think not. You were in the Lovat Scouts at one time. But your name is MacLaren. Angus MacLaren. If I found you, I was to tell you that Marcella Trowbridge is grateful for the cat you left at her door."

The man smiled. "I won't take credit for what someone else has done."

"I have only to take you in custody and we will soon discover whether you are a Lovat or a MacLaren. It might be more satisfactory to answer my questions now."

"I've nothing to say to you."

"Where do you keep the rifle? And the mask? And the straw disguise you used to shoot a farmer by the name of Burrows?"

Lovat gestured to his house. "You may search, if you like. I'm a poor man. It won't take you long."

"I'm sure that's true." He studied the man's face. It had aged well, the features still firm, the jawline taut. He'd been handsome in his youth. He was handsome still.

Hamish said, "Ye've been verra' blind."

"You say you've never married?"

"That's true."

"But a man can have a child out of wedlock. Who was the mother?"

He saw the flick of anger touch Lovat's eyes. Instantly it was gone.

Priscilla Bartram and Marcella Trowbridge were too young. Swift's housekeeper, Susan, wasn't old enough. Who else, then? Burrows's daughter? The wrong age again. Mrs. Percy might know. But there wasn't time to consult her. Leave this man here and he could vanish before the police arrived to arrest him. He had nothing to hold him here.

But *was* he MacLaren? And was Catriona Beaton his granddaughter? There could be other secrets he didn't want the world to know.

Where did the truth lie? If this man had continued to live in Cambridgeshire, something must have held him here.

Rutledge pictured the windmill in his mind, the house that had burned to the foundations. The Trowbridge cottage close by. The Bower House.

A bower.

A retreat. A hideaway.

From what?

And then he had it. The sophisticated woman who had preferred that lonely cottage near the windmill when she might have lived a very different life in Bury. The woman who had willed it to her granddaughter, not her son.

Had she had a lover—and another child?

He remembered something Miss Trowbridge had said. About her father being the village doctor who bought this cottage for her grandmother when she was a young widow. But had he? Was it her own money? Her grandmother had very likely married well, possibly even an arranged marriage in her day, rather than a love match. Her husband had died, and for some reason she'd not wanted to go on living in Bury. Had she already met Angus MacLaren? Or was that after she came to Wriston to live? She had let her grand-daughter make friends with the man . . . Marcella had liked him. Unaware that he must have been her grand-mother's lover for many years.

How had she concealed a pregnancy? She could have gone away for a time, and then left the child to grow up in Scotland with MacLaren's family. She might even have visited in the summer. No one would question her wish to travel.

And after her death, Angus had stayed by Marcella as long as he could. Beside the cottage he'd known well. Until his grief for her grandmother became more than he could bear, when he'd burned down the windmill cottage and its secrets and gone away. To Scotland? But he'd been drawn back. And he'd left Clarissa to keep Marcella company. It could be checked later, all these details.

Rutledge said aloud, "Marcella couldn't be your child. There was another one, one that Mrs. Trowbridge couldn't claim. One who must have been raised in Scotland with cousins. Catriona was that child's daugh-ter. And you killed two men for not taking proper care of her."

The man who called himself Lovat lunged to his feet.

"I'll see you dead if you drag *her* name into this business."

"You'll have to stand trial. There's blood on your hands, MacLaren. The truth will have to come out. Whether you like it or not."

"I learned to kill in the Scouts. You don't forget how to do that."

"No. You were very clever. If I hadn't discovered something you'd written, hidden in a drawer in Herbert Swift's house, I'd never have found you."

"They never found *her.* Catriona. I don't think they really looked, although they claimed they had, claimed they'd found her body in a wood. One more serving girl. But she shouldn't have been a servant. She was educated, she had prospects. Still, she was mad to go to London. After all, she had an English heritage. And that was the simplest way."

"Why did she leave the Hutchinson household? Was it Hutchinson who drove her away?"

"He drove his own wife to suicide. A servant girl would be easier."

"I can see killing Hutchinson. But Swift?"

"He did nothing. When Catriona went missing, he did *nothing.* I wrote to ask what had become of her.

I asked him to act for me. As a solicitor. He told me I should find someone in London."

"What did you do?"

"I went to the police. But everything pointed to her leaving of her own accord. I knew better, and still they wouldn't listen. They told me the case was closed. I investigated on my own, but there was no trace of her. No cabbie who had helped her with her valises. No porter at the railway station who had helped her on a train. I knew then she was dead. That he must have lured her away and killed her."

But Hutchinson hadn't been in London when Catriona had left the house. And he hadn't been home when his wife killed herself.

A scrap of conversation came back to him.

What had Miss Hutchinson said?

I'm well aware of the pitfalls and dangers of being a woman without protection. We lived in lodgings, we were dependent on his officer's pay. We were shunned by people who now respect us. I wore gowns I'd refurbished myself because I couldn't afford new ones. If I survived, I believe she was clever enough and determined enough to survive as well.

What if Hutchinson hadn't tried to seduce Catriona? What if he'd fallen in love with her? And she with him? Even a man out for the main chance might fall in love with a poor girl. Only he hadn't known, had he, that she came from very different stock.

His wife had died while he was in France. Catriona had disappeared while he was away in Gloucestershire.

Miss Hutchinson hadn't come north when her brother was murdered . . .

That handsome house on a handsome square.

Rutledge said, "Dear God. I'm not sure that he did."

"Did what? What are you talking about, man?"

"I don't know that Hutchinson had anything to do with your granddaughter's death. It was his sister. And that house. It had belonged to Mary Hutchinson. She was pregnant. The child had died, but there was every likelihood she would have another. An heir. The question is, was she driven to kill herself, or was she murdered?"

"What are you saying?"

"I'm not sure. But I think both of us got it wrong. It wasn't Hutchinson who was responsible for her death, although he was self-absorbed enough not to realize his role in it. It was his sister. Any woman Hutchinson married would be mistress of that house. And now Miss Hutchinson is. Because everyone else is dead. Her brother's wife. Catriona. And the Captain."

He was still trying to work it out, his mind rapidly sorting through what he knew. But MacLaren was there before him. He picked up one of the lengths of wood that framed the hurdles and swung it with all the strength of his lean body.

Rutledge dropped like a stone, in spite of Hamish's warning. His guard down, it had taken precious seconds to realize what was happening.

Dazed, his wits scattered, he lay there, fighting to hold on to consciousness. And then Thornton was bending over him.

Even as he did so, he straightened, whirled around, and said, "*He's taken the motorcar.*"

Rutledge struggled to his feet. "It's MacLaren. He's on the way to London."

"There's my motorcar. But it's in Isleham."

Shaking his head, desperate to clear it, Rutledge said, "We don't have time. Find someone with a motorcar. Quickly." He put up a hand and touched the wetness on the side of his head. His fingers came away dark with blood.

"You're in no condition to drive. You need a doctor. Let Warren deal with it. They'll find him soon enough."

"Damn it, I'm ordering you. Find a motorcar. You can drive it, can't you? We can't let him reach London or there will be another murder. I'll explain on the road."

Thornton turned on his heel and ran out toward the street. It was nearly a quarter of an hour later when he came back, driving a well-polished Rolls with a dark green body. Rutledge was standing by the road, waiting.

"I had to twist some arms. Get in."

Rutledge did. It was a chauffeur-driven car, and they sat up front. Rutledge could smell something but dared not look over his shoulder. Later he discovered a bouquet of wilting heliotrope in the crystal vase on the lady's side of the passenger compartment. For hours its heavy sweetness made him feel slightly ill.

Gingerly leaning his head back, he closed his eyes and let Thornton drive. After they had passed Newmarket, Thornton said, "Are you going to tell me what happened?"

"All right." He told the story slowly, putting it together in his own mind as he did.

Thornton swore. "It wasn't Hutchinson who killed Mary?"

"I've no doubt he neglected her. He was a selfish man, looking out for himself. Still, I wouldn't be surprised if the sister had done all she could to make her sister-in-law wretched enough to believe he didn't care for her, only for the house and the money."

"I was there at your last meeting with her. A cold woman. She was sitting at the head of the table, did you notice? Her brother's chair. Not at what must have been her usual place. What do you think MacLaren will do?"

"I don't think he has a weapon." But what about that sharp knife used to cut the osiers and withies, the stiff stalks of reeds and young trees? Easier to carry inside a London house than a rifle.

Thornton was making good time, but they were still nearly half an hour behind MacLaren, and Rutledge's touring car was probably faster. As it was, they were thundering down the long straight roads. It would be different once they had left the Fens behind. Their speed would have to drop considerably. And so would MacLaren's.

It was some time after Cambridge that Thornton said, "He killed two people. MacLaren. The wrong two people, as it transpired. He'll kill her as well. I don't know that I wouldn't much prefer arriving too late to stop him. I loved Mary, you know. Very deeply. And there was nothing I could do."

"Just as well. You'd hang instead of MacLaren. Pull over, I'll drive now."

"You've a lump the size of a goose egg on the side of your head. I don't want to find myself in a ditch."

On the outskirts of London, late into the night, Rutledge said, "I'll drop you at Scotland Yard. Ask for

Sergeant Gibson. If he isn't there, tell someone where to find us."

"I told you," Thornton said grimly, "I'll see this through."

"And if he's there? If he hasn't killed her by the time we reach the house? Will you stop him—or stop me?"

Thornton considered the question. "I'd rather not hang. That's the only reason I'd act. But if God is good, she'll be dead when we get there."

There was no time to argue, although Hamish was warning Rutledge that he was taking a grave risk. But Miss Hutchinson's life hung in the balance, and he would have to take his chances with Thornton.

The late traffic was heavy, laden wagons and lorries and vans bringing foodstuffs and flowers and everything else London lacked to stock the markets and the shops for the coming day. They followed a butcher's van, the back open, great carcasses of beef and pork swaying as it made its way over the uneven cobbles. And then they were in the clear, only a mile or less from the square where Miss Hutchinson lived. As they turned into the street, even in the gray light of a cloudy dawn, they could see Rutledge's motorcar standing before the house door.

"He's here."

Thornton sped down the street, braking sharply as they reached the house. The front door stood open, and they could see a lamp lit on a table by the stairs.

Thornton didn't waste time pulling in behind Rutledge's motorcar. He left the borrowed vehicle in the middle of the street and was close on Rutledge's heels as they raced to the door and up the stairs. Rutledge had no way of knowing which room belonged to Miss Hutchinson. He stopped at the top of the steps, and Thornton nearly plowed into him.

Somewhere they could hear a woman crying, soft mewing cries.

"This way, I think." Rutledge moved swiftly down the passage, found an open door, and stepped into the room.

It appeared to be the master bedroom, very masculine, with dark woods and heavy drapes over the windows. There were no lamps lit. Rutledge stepped forward and flung open the drapes. In the pale light coming through the glass, he could see Miss Hutchinson lying across her bed. A pool of dark blood had soaked the sheets and the coverlet, and her hair was black with it.

Cowering by the washstand, he saw Mrs. Cookson, the housekeeper. Looking up with tears running down her cheeks, she said, "I tried to stop him. I thought he would kill me too, when he was done."

"Where is he?"

"There." Thornton pointed to the shadows beside the bed. The hurdle maker was lying there, blood blackening the front of his shirt, his head bowed. Rutledge went across to him and knelt by his side while Thornton bent over Miss Hutchinson.

MacLaren was still alive. Just.

He glanced up at Rutledge, his eyes a fierce blue. "It's better this way. She told me. She took Catriona to the country and stabbed her. In a wood. Hers was the body the police had found, after all. My darling girl buried in a pauper's grave. She feared her brother was going to marry Catriona. He loved her, she said. And it wouldn't be like before, when he was away in France. I killed that woman in spite of her confession. She had no room for mercy. Nor did I." The Highland accent was more pronounced now, as if he were too tired to care.

Thornton said, from where he was standing by the bed, "Too late. She's gone."

The blue eyes were dulling, his breathing more difficult. "Don't tell Marcella it was the windmill keeper. He died long ago, anyway. He had nothing to live for."

"But you continued to live as Lovat."

MacLaren smiled faintly. "The Boers always said I couldn't be killed. I tried drink. It didn't dull the pain of losing Ellen Trowbridge. I tried to starve myself, and my body refused to quit. In the end, I came back to the Fens and simply existed. To tell truth, I'm glad it's finally over. There will be no trial. No need to sully *her* name."

He meant the woman he'd loved.

His body shuddered and the knife slipped out of his hand, falling down beside his hip. He paid it no heed. "I'm sorry for nothing. Except perhaps for the farmer, Burrows. He was merely a diversion. Still. It was his own stubbornness that nearly killed him. The wound was slight enough. I made sure of that."

And then he reached out, his fingers fastening over Rutledge's wrist. "Please. Tell them I killed for Catriona. A servant girl. But don't tell them who Catriona really was. Don't shame the memory . . ." His voice caught. Then it strengthened again. "I was always a killer. It was my skill, and they'd taught me well. *She* taught me love."

The grip tightened, almost as a death grip, and then MacLaren's hand fell away. The blue eyes were empty, the strong face now slack.

After a moment Rutledge reached out and touched the man's throat. Rising to his feet, he said, "He's dead."

"I'm glad he won't hang." Thornton walked away to the window. After a moment, he added in a very different voice, "How do you cope with this sort of thing? God, it brings back the war!"

But Rutledge was bending over Mrs. Cookson, helping her to her feet and drawing her out the door. "Go down to the servants' hall and send someone for the constable. Tell him to go for Sergeant Gibson at Scotland Yard. At once."

She clung to his arm, still weeping. "I couldn't stop him. He was too strong."

"You did your best," he told her. "Now you must go for the police."

"But you *are* the police."

He had to help her down the stairs, but when she saw the door standing wide, she seemed to come to her senses. She hurried to close it, and then turned toward the servants' hall. He watched until she had shut that door behind her, then went back up the stairs.

Thornton was still by the window. "Am I a suspect?"

"Until this is settled. So far we have no rifle. And until we do, you're under suspicion."

He cleared his throat. "Are you going to keep Miss Trowbridge's grandmother out of this?"

"Yes. And I'd advise you to do the same. All that matters right now is the hurdle maker Lovat whose granddaughter went missing in London."

Turning, Thornton nodded, then added, "I feel like a fifth thumb. How will you explain my presence to the Yard?"

Rutledge looked toward MacLaren's body, half hidden in the shadows by the bed. "I'll think of something," he said. "You're a witness, after all."

"I wish I hadn't been," Thornton said under his breath. Then aloud he said, "It's different from the war, isn't it? Murder."

Listening to Hamish in the back of his mind, Rutledge said curtly, "Very."

"Mary is avenged. Why don't I feel happier about that?"

But it was a rhetorical question, and Rutledge let it go. He went to another room and found two chairs, setting them out in the passage for himself and Thornton.

And there he waited for Sergeant Gibson and the machinery of the Yard.

Chapter 20

When the bodies had been removed and the master bedroom shut off, when Rutledge and Thornton and Mrs. Cookson had given their statements, it was finished.

Acting Chief Superintendent Markham made an appearance, striding into the house with the air of a man who was pleased to see an inquiry closed.

But Rutledge told him quite frankly that it was necessary to return to Wriston and Ely. "We don't have the rifle, you see. Or the helmet. We need them to connect the dead man with the shootings there. Otherwise, that inquiry is still open."

"See that you're quick about it, then." Markham rubbed his hands together in a gesture of satisfaction. "Took you long enough, Rutledge. But well done. Well done, I say." He seemed to notice Thornton. "Who is this?"

"His name is Thornton. He's been helping us with our inquiries."

Markham looked the other man up and down. "He has the look of a soldier." There was speculation in his gaze. "Certain he's no more than that?"

"Not unless the rifle turns up in his house."

Thornton threw Rutledge an angry look, but Markham said, "See it doesn't." And then he was gone, followed by one of his people.

"Who the hell was that?" Thornton asked. "I can't say I like him."

"He's my superior," Rutledge said mildly.

"More's the pity," Thornton retorted and walked out to the motorcar to wait.

Rutledge took two rooms in a hotel in Cambridge where they slept most of what was left of the day and started early the next morning for Soham. They had brought both motorcars in tandem, Rutledge's and the one Thornton had commandeered.

Rutledge had remembered the message from Inspector Warren that he'd neglected to answer, but it could wait another day. In Soham, after restoring the motorcar to its still irate owner, they searched both the small house where the man who called himself Lovat had lived and the shop where he dried the reeds and made his hurdles.

All they found were the belongings of a man who lived quietly and frugally. Rutledge even emptied the dustbins, and there he found several bloody bandages. Had MacLaren been wounded by Burrows's shotgun? It hadn't been visible. And it hadn't slowed the man. But here was proof.

Where then was the rifle?

Standing where Lovat was sitting when he first saw him, Rutledge looked down at the bottom of the unfinished basket the man had been making. A rain had fallen, and the reeds had begun to curl.

MacLaren had been a tormented man, and Rutledge knew a little about torment. But it was Thornton who said, "I think he was glad of a reason to die. Finally. Better than the hangman."

The tone of his voice conveyed what he'd left unsaid, that he also knew what torment was.

After a moment Thornton added, looking up and down the stream that flowed quietly just beyond where they were standing, "He must have known all these waterways. He went out to find his materials for the hurdles. He could have stowed anything anywhere. It would take weeks to search." Turning back to Rutledge, he went on. "Are you going to keep me here until you find the rifle?"

"If I must." He walked back into the house. "He was a tidy man. I don't think he would leave the rifle to be caught in a storm and ruined." Stepping outside again, he said, "But there is one place he could be sure to leave something. Back to the motorcar, Thornton."

They drove on to Wriston but didn't stop until they'd reached the windmill and the ruins of the keeper's house.

"Why here?"

"Because no one would connect anything found here with the hurdle maker in Soham."

He got out of the motorcar and moved carefully into the foundations. Anything salvageable had been taken away long since. The rough stones of the foundation itself were still in place. The ground here was too low to dig a proper cellar, but there were steps leading up to what once had been the main door, and opposite them on the far side, a second pair of steps going to the small back garden and the path to the windmill.

Was this the reason why the ruins were said to be haunted? Because MacLaren had come here, like a shadow in the night, to retrieve what he needed?

Rutledge searched carefully, testing every crack and crevice, to see if it yielded anything that might be a hiding place. It would make sense, if Rutledge found what he was looking for here.

But there was nothing, not so much as a hollow behind those steps, no receptacle large enough for a rifle and the other things the man would wish to hide. Still—it couldn't have been left where someone might stumble over it—a curious child or a scavenging Traveler.

Rutledge refused to give up, probing every inch of the ruins.

Nothing.

Where, then?

Thornton swore as he tripped on rubble. "He'd have broken his neck, coming here in the dark. He must have been more clever than that."

"What are you looking for?"

The two men turned in unison. Marcella Trowbridge was standing in the road, watching them.

Rutledge said, "There has been a suggestion that the shooter might have left his rifle here."

"But that's impossible. Who would do such a thing?"

Rutledge's gaze met Thornton, then he said, "Someone from Soham."

"Oh. No one I know. That's all right, then."

He went on searching, to no avail, and then walked to the windmill. But that was now managed by the ironmonger, he remembered as he looked up at the weather-stained sails. It would not serve MacLaren to have the ironmonger pawing through his things, out of simple curiosity.

Miss Trowbridge was still there on the road watching. Rutledge said to Thornton, "For the love of God, go and distract her."

Reluctantly Thornton did as he was told.

Rutledge moved on to the humpback bridge, scrambling down the embankment to look under the arch for a hiding place.

But there was nothing here either. And in a storm the high water would brush against anything hidden here and possibly dislodge it.

He clambered back up to the road again and stood there, wiping his muddy hands on his handkerchief.

Had MacLaren lied to him?

Or had he hidden his proof where no one would ever expect to find it?

Think, he ordered himself. If it wasn't the windmill house, if it wasn't the bridge or the mill, where then? Miss Trowbridge's house?

Hamish said, "He wouldna' put the lass at risk."

That was true. What's more, she believed MacLaren to be dead.

What do I know about the man?

Rutledge stood there, searching through every fact he'd learned about the hurdle maker, and still he came up with nothing.

Was Thornton his killer after all? At the very least, of the two men, Thornton had easier access to the new army rifles than MacLaren did. After all, MacLaren had used a knife, not a rifle, to kill Miss Hutchinson.

He refused to believe it. It was Catriona who connected the two dead men. Not Mary Hutchinson.

Then where was the proof he needed?

A memory came back to him. The Green Man. The church and the feel of those cold, worn steps leading up into the pulpit, pressing hard into his back. The Rector, Mr. March, finding him there.

No, before that. *What had he seen in the churchyard?*

And then he remembered.

The mausoleum. But Miss Trowbridge's parents had not liked Wriston. They would surely have been interred in Bury.

He hurried back to where Miss Trowbridge was standing with Thornton. "Where was your grandmother buried, do you know?"

"She had a horror of being in the ground. There's a mausoleum in the churchyard here in the village."

"It must be locked. Most such tombs are. Do you have the key?"

"Do I—I never thought about it. I expect it's in my grandmother's things. My father was not happy about her choice. He wanted her to be laid to rest in Bury, beside her husband. But she insisted, and it was her money, after all. So she built it. I wondered if she hadn't loved my grandfather very much. She'd married him to please her own father. He died quite young. She went away for a time, to mourn properly, she said. And when she came back, she wanted to live here. In this cottage bought for her. She told me several times that her heart was here, not in Bury."

Rutledge said earnestly, "If there is a key, I must open the mausoleum. No," he added as she started to interrupt him. "Only the outer door. It's unlikely, of course. But someone could have found a way in."

"That's horrible."

She turned, was leading the way toward her cottage, and inside, she left them standing in the small parlor while she went on into her bedroom. In a few minutes she came back with a lovely carved box in her hands.

"It's from Africa, this box. She never told me how she'd come by it, but it held her most treasured things. I never felt like opening it. I still don't. It's—very personal."

She held the box out to Rutledge, and he took it over to one of the chairs by the cold hearth. Clarissa stirred from her bed on the far side, then subsided into sleep once more.

"It's locked," Rutledge said, looking up from his examination of the top.

Miss Trowbridge, frowning, said, "I believe the key is there. On the side."

And she was right. He found the key set into a small opening in the side of the box, invisible if you didn't know where to look for it. Carefully removing it, he inserted it into the lock and turned it. Lifting the lid, he looked inside. Thornton came to stand beside him. Miss Trowbridge made a movement to stop him, and then stayed where she was.

There were papers inside. One of them caught Rutledge's eye. In an elegant copperplate it said:

My Last Wishes. To be opened by my granddaughter after my death.

Rutledge glanced up at Miss Trowbridge. It was not his place to look at these papers. But Marcella Trowbridge had told him she had not wished to pry.

And so he broke the seal and took a sheet of paper out of the envelope.

Miss Trowbridge cried, "Stop. You were looking for a *key!*"

He had already seen a name. He said, "You must read this, I think."

"No, I told you. She was a very private person, my grandmother. I won't pry into her secrets now. It would be wrong."

"You have no choice. Look." He passed the sheet to her.

She gazed at him for a moment, then against her will, unfolded the sheet.

"Oh!" she gasped, reading it once, then going back to the beginning. "She wants—she wanted Angus MacLaren to be buried beside her. *Angus?* The windmill keeper? But why?"

"I believe it must be the same man," he said carefully. "Perhaps he was a friend when she needed one."

"But I thought he was long since dead. I don't know what to do."

Thornton spoke then. "He died in London this past week. I—happened to come across the obituary. Would you like for me to see to it for you?"

She stared at him. "In the normal course of events, I'd have asked Mr. Swift."

"I owe Mr. MacLaren a debt," Thornton answered her. "This will be my opportunity to repay it."

Unconvinced, she turned to Rutledge. "I don't know what to think."

He said gently, "It would appear that she cared for him. You must do as she asked."

"She liked him—she—I was so young, you see." Frowning, she added, "I liked him too. I've told you that. But to bury him beside her? I don't think that would be right."

Rutledge handed her the envelope. "It's what she wanted. You can see for yourself. She expected you to do as she asked."

"But what will people *think*?"

"Does it really matter?"

"No," she said slowly. "Not really."

He went back to the box, and in it he found a record of the marriage of Ellen Trowbridge and Angus MacLaren. Next to it, he found the record of a child's birth. Catriona's mother, who had married a Beaton.

She hadn't been able to keep the child. But she had kept this piece of paper, if any question had ever come up about its heritage.

Society wouldn't have approved of what she had done. Not her family nor her friends in Wriston or Bury. It would appear that there was too vast a difference between the man and the woman in station and in everything else, in spite of his standing in his own glen. What's more, according to the marriage record, he'd been two years younger. But they had found a way. And no one had ever guessed.

He felt a great sadness for Ellen Trowbridge and Angus MacLaren.

The Bower House . . .

Rutledge set these back into the box. He didn't think Marcella Trowbridge was ready to learn the truth about the grandmother she'd adored.

At the bottom of the box, under the papers, lay the photograph of a small child sitting on the back of a pony. The background wasn't the landscape of the Fens. A baronial hall and mountains instead. Catriona's mother as a little girl? And beneath that lay the heavy iron key to the mausoleum. Someone had put it there. Had Angus been given another?

Closing the box, Rutledge gave it to Thornton, who handed it to Miss Trowbridge.

"What do you want with the mausoleum key?" she asked again, worried. "I don't understand. Why would someone desecrate a tomb?"

"I'm only being thorough," he said with a smile. "We were looking for something and thought perhaps it had been left here. By the ruins—er—where no one would think to look for it. Or in a mausoleum where no one would think to search. I shan't disturb your grand-mother. It will be all right."

"I'll come with you," she said resolutely.

He glanced at Thornton. "I think it would be best if both of you stayed here. This is police business, after all. I'll bring the key back shortly."

Still she protested, and it was several minutes before Rutledge could persuade her that it would attract unwanted attention if all three went to the churchyard.

"It won't be in her coffin, what I'm looking for. Just inside the door." He hoped he was telling the truth. It was what he believed MacLaren had done. Which meant that there was another key to the mausoleum and MacLaren must have kept it on his person. He hadn't searched the dead man's pockets, he'd left that to Sergeant Gibson. The list of items would be on file at the Yard . . .

"Is it something—awful?"

"Nothing so important. That's why I haven't asked for a search warrant."

Finally she agreed to allow him to take the key. He could see that Thornton was eager to accompany him, but he didn't want the man there, any more than he wanted Miss Trowbridge to come.

Walking out to his motorcar, the key heavy in the palm of his hand, he wondered if he was right. If he would find what he wanted.

It took no more than five minutes to drive down to the church. He left the motorcar behind some trees, out of sight, and then crossed the grassy churchyard to the mausoleum.

It was built more like a Greek temple than the usual edifice of this kind, he thought, and perhaps that was what Ellen Trowbridge had wished to have. He stood for a moment, looking up at the inscription above the door. She had been buried under the name of the husband who had died. Had that rankled?

And then he set the key into the lock.

He expected the key to turn with some difficulty. Instead it clicked open without a sound, and he swung the gate wide. It moved smoothly on its hinges. The second lock yielded just as easily. And he knew then what he would find inside.

There was an opaque glass window in the back of the mausoleum. It gave a little light, enough to see the coffin of Mrs. Trowbridge to the right, and an empty ledge to the left.

And against the back wall in the space between the ledges was a small altar with a photograph and a candle and, of all things, a Celtic cross, not an Anglican one.

On the floor just inside the door was a large canvas sack.

So it was here after all. Almost a sacrilege, to leave evidence of murder in the tomb of the woman MacLaren had loved so deeply.

Or perhaps it was not. Catriona was her granddaughter too. And if she loved Angus MacLaren, then she knew the depths he was capable of. It was possible that she herself would have wanted to see Catriona's persecutor dead.

Only MacLaren's revenge had gone wrong. Was that why he'd killed himself? Or had it been to spare Marcella Trowbridge the truth about her grandmother's other life? Or for Ellen MacLaren?

There was no way of knowing now.

Rutledge knelt on the smooth cool stone, his hands on the length of rope that tied the top of the sack. Then, remembering that he was in the churchyard where anyone might pass by, he decided against opening the sack here. Instead he picked it up to carry back to his motorcar. It didn't clank or rattle, he noticed. Giving nothing away.

There was no one about when he locked the door and the gate again. He shouldered the heavy sack, pocketed the key, and started for the motorcar.

Halfway there, a voice called to him.

Rutledge turned to see Andrew March striding across the churchyard toward him.

Tensing in every muscle, he stopped.

"What have you got there?" March asked, coming up to him.

"Evidence, I'm afraid," he said. "It's a police matter."

March looked around. "Did you collect it *here,* in the churchyard?"

"It was hidden here. It belongs—belonged to someone in Soham."

"Ah. Not a Wriston man, then. Well. I'll pray for his soul all the same. And how are you? Have you considered my offer of a little talk?"

"I—don't believe I'm ready. But I'm grateful, all the same."

March nodded. "I understand. But I will tell you that the longer you keep your fears trapped in your head, the harder it will be to free yourself from them. Remember that. And if you don't come to me, find someone else to trust."

Rutledge said, before he could stop himself, before Hamish could warn him to beware, "It was a letter, Rector. I received it just before I came north. It was from someone I cared for. Rather deeply." He stopped, and then added, "It closed a door."

It was offered as an explanation for Hamish's presence, vigorously pursuing him from the time he left London. He wasn't certain the Rector would understand. But it was the best he could do.

The letter had come from Meredith Channing. It had told him she wouldn't be returning to England, that she was staying in Belgium with the man she believed was her missing husband.

I must do this, she had written. *For my sake as well as yours. We would have nothing if we tried to build on a broken past. But I have given my heart in your keeping. And if you find someone else to love, then you must promise to send it back, so that I will know.*

And enclosed in the letter was a gold locket on a chain. The initials engraved on the front were those of her maiden name, not Channing. He'd thought it must have belonged to her as a young girl, for it was small and delicate, the sort of thing a child might have been given on her birthday. His parents had given his sister Frances a similar gift when she was twelve. Not a heart but a book that opened to show the photographs of her parents.

He hadn't opened Meredith Channing's locket. He didn't want to see what was inside.

March, watching him, said, "And so the nightmares have been worse. Yes, it explains so much. Well, I'm here. You can always find me here."

And he turned to walk away, not looking back.

Rutledge carried the canvas sack the rest of the way to his motorcar, and there he opened it.

Inside, well wrapped in wool, he found the steel helmet that a German sniper had worn, a Lee-Enfield rifle, with the name H. R. I. BEATON roughly carved into the stock, a medal with the same name on the back. Catriona's father, who had died in the war? Brought home on leave, a gift from a present-day sniper to a man who had served in the Lovat Scouts? There was also a German sniper scope. Under them lay a smaller holdall with what appeared to be the tools of a scissors sharpener, a long-haired wig made of silk threads, and a gray cloth.

Rutledge stared at the last item and then reached into his pocket for the handkerchief he'd kept there, folded over a gray thread. He gently put the two together.

The thread and the cloth matched perfectly.

Rutledge stowed the items in the boot of his motorcar, all except the medal. He saw no reason why that should become the property of the police. It belonged in the African box.

Driving back to the Bower House cottage, he found Miss Trowbridge and Thornton waiting for him in the parlor.

She rose at once as he came in the door, saying, "What did you find?"

He handed her the medal. "I was mistaken. There was nothing to find. Except this, caught in the doorway. Someone must have wanted your grandmother to have it."

She looked at it, then turned it over. "Beaton? But I don't know anyone by that name."

"Perhaps your grandmother did. I shouldn't worry about it, if I were you. I'd put it in her box. After all, she'd have explained if she'd wanted you to know."

Nodding, she said, "Yes, of course," and then took the key from him as well.

Rutledge turned to leave. Thornton hesitated. "I'll be in touch," he said finally to Marcella before they walked to the door.

Miss Trowbridge, smiling, thanked him for offering to see to the windmill keeper's remains, and then she stood in her doorway, watching as the two men went out to the motorcar.

After they were well away, Thornton said, "What did you discover? Surely it wasn't just that medal?"

Rutledge pulled to the side of the road. It was empty in both directions, the day quiet, the land basking in the sun. He went to the boot, retrieved the sack, and showed Thornton the contents.

He whistled. "Good God. Is that what he was wearing when he shot Swift?"

"Very likely."

"Where's the straw suit he wore when he shot Burrows?"

"If he was as clever as I think he was, he's burned it long since."

Rutledge showed him the thread and how it matched the gray cloth, explaining the connection with Ely Cathedral.

Thornton shook his head. "Remarkable. His planning—I couldn't have—I'd have been caught straightaway."

Rutledge put everything back in the boot, got back behind the wheel, then turned to stare at Thornton.

"If I had obtained a search warrant, what would I have found in your house?"

Thornton blinked. Then he said, "Only a few unimportant souvenirs."

Rutledge nodded. "I thought as much," he replied
dryly.

Inspector Warren was not happy to have missed the
conclusion of the inquiry. He looked at the items that
Rutledge had spread across his desk, and said, "You're
sure of your information? You're satisfied with it?"
His glance strayed to Thornton, standing in the doorway. "It will all be in your report?"

Rutledge said, "Everything you will need to know
will be in my report. I'll finish it tonight." It was not
quite what Warren had asked for.

But the Inspector was moving on to what had happened in London. "And you say this man Lovat is
dead?"

"Ruskin and others in Soham can show you his
place of business and where he lived. They should be
searched."

"Then why were these items found in Wriston?"

"Would you keep evidence that would send you to
the hangman in your house?"

"No, I expect I wouldn't."

They went over the details a second and a third time
before Warren was satisfied. And then he remembered.

"That washerwoman. The one you questioned. She sent me an urgent message. I passed it on to you. What did she want?"

Rutledge had all but forgot about the messenger and his urgent summons.

"I haven't spoken to her yet."

"Then I'll go with you."

Hamish was in the rear of the motorcar as Inspector Warren stepped in. Rutledge tried to shut the thought out of his mind as Thornton turned the crank and they went to find Mrs. Boggs.

They were forced to wait for more than an hour until she came home from her work in the households of the well-to-do.

Her face was flushed, her eyes tired, but she smiled when she saw the three men on her doorstep.

"Well, then," she said, "I thought perhaps it wasn't important. What I've got to say. No one came to ask."

"I was in London," Rutledge told her. "Mr. Thornton here has also been helping us with our inquiries, and you know Inspector Warren, I think."

"Indeed," she said, nodding to him. She insisted that they come inside and have a cup of tea, and Warren, trying to quell his impatience, reminded her that he was expected back at the police station sooner rather than later.

Disappointed, she offered them the chairs in her tiny front room and sat on the end of her own as she faced them.

"You'd said, Mr. Rutledge, that if I remembered anything I thought might be important I ought to speak to Mr. Warren, here. And I did. I don't quite know what brought it back to mind. I was doing some mending at the time, so I expect it was looking for my scissors."

"What did you see?"

"I did tell you that I came quickly to see what the fuss was about. There were all these ladies and gentlemen come rushing out of the church, staring up where that poor man, Captain Hutchinson, was lying. It was then I saw him. The scissors grinder. He came out of the Cathedral behind them and walked away down the street there, toward the school or perhaps the shops. He had his canvas holdall, and I wondered what he was doing in the wedding, if someone putting up the ribbons and the flowers had sent for him. And then the police came, and he went clear out of my head."

"Did you know him?"

"I'd seen him there and about. But he seemed a little taller than I remembered. I expect that was just because he was standing a little straighter in that company. I mean to say, he was the *scissors grinder*. The old man. As ordinary as can be. Still, I thought perhaps he might have seen something, and you'd want to question him if you hadn't already."

"Yes, that's very true, Mrs. Boggs. We appreciate your help," Rutledge said. "No one else reported seeing this man." But he was thinking that even if he'd known about the scissors grinder, it wouldn't have led to Lovat. Now, however, it reinforced what he knew.

They rose to leave, and Mrs. Boggs, basking in their gratitude, thanked them for coming, as if they had been valued guests.

In the motorcar, Rutledge said to Inspector Warren, "This scissors grinder. Who is he?"

"Old as he is, he gets about on his bicycle, going door to door, or wherever anyone stops him and asks for his services. He was at our kitchen door only last week. My wife was complaining that her scissors and some of the knives needed a new edge. My God, it never occurred to me to ask if he'd been in the Cathedral that day."

"I doubt he was. But someone had a bicycle and tools. And he went unnoticed because everyone was accustomed to seeing him—or someone like him—around the countryside."

"He's a religious man," Warren said. "He's often coming in or out of a church."

And MacLaren had somehow discovered that. It had been useful.

Thornton, listening, said, "Dear God."

Rutledge knew what he was thinking. That whatever he himself had considered doing to Captain Hutchinson, it was MacLaren's clever plan that had made it possible to kill the man.

They left Inspector Warren at the police station, still fingering the items from the canvas sack, as if still only half convinced that Rutledge was right.

From there, Rutledge drove to Isleham and set Thornton down at his house.

"It was a near-run thing," Thornton said. "I could be facing trial right now."

"Is that why you were searching for the killer on your own?"

"I wanted to know who held a grudge stronger than mine. I wanted to know who had killed the man I hated so much. I didn't know what hate was."

"Do something about your own rifle," Rutledge warned him. "Don't leave it for someone else to find."

"I told you, I have nothing more than a few souvenirs."

Rutledge said nothing, his gaze never leaving Thornton's face.

"Damn it, you're as sharp as that man Belford," Thornton said finally. Then, "You must have kept your service revolver."

Rutledge had. It lay in his trunk beneath the bed. Waiting until Hamish became unbearable. Cleaned, oiled, and ready to use.

Thornton must have read something in his face, in spite of his effort to school his expression.

"Most of us need a way out," he said with a nod, and walked to his front door. Opening it, he went inside, without looking back.

Rutledge, trying to ignore Hamish's voice from the empty rear seat, turned the motorcar toward Wriston.

There was Constable McBride to see, and then one last night at Miss Bartram's while he wrote his report for Inspector Warren and another for Acting Chief Superintendent Markham. A cleverly expurgated version, both of them. The MacLaren laid to rest in the mausoleum would have no connection with the man Lovat in Soham. It was not necessary to ruin more lives. Justice had been served.

He was nearly to Wriston when he noticed a bicycle approaching. As it got closer, he saw the lined face and long white hair of the scissors grinder, his satchel over his handlebars, his eyes tired.

Rutledge stopped and offered him a lift to wherever he was going.

HARPER LUXE

THE NEW LUXURY IN READING

We hope you enjoyed reading
our new, comfortable print size and found it
an experience you would like to repeat.

Well – you're in luck!

HarperLuxe offers the finest in fiction and
nonfiction books in this same larger print size and
paperback format. Light and easy to read, HarperLuxe
paperbacks are for book lovers who want to see
what they are reading without the strain.

For a full listing of titles and
new releases to come, please visit our website:

www.HarperLuxe.com

SEEING IS BELIEVING!